ASHES

BOOK 1
IN THE *ASHES* SERIES

A NOVEL BY KELLY COZY

ISBN: 978-0-9851234-5-1

ACKNOWLEDGMENTS

A thousand thank-yous to those who've given their support along the way: Mom and Dad, Loa Allebach, Meg Gerzevske, Richard and Aljean Harmetz, Billie Martin, Faith Martin, John McKiernan, Speer Morgan, Bret and Colleen Nelson, Linda Palkovic, Jim Reilly, Pete and Debbie Stefansky, Mark Sweet, and Stanley and Janice Thompson.

Very special thanks to the Constant Reader Brigade: Erik Hoard, Gerry Hoard, Alyca Tanner, Albert Muller, and Karen Girard. I couldn't do it without your encouragement and feedback.

Much love to Scott and Alex, for cheerfully shepherding the burden of living with a writer and for their unflagging enthusiasm.

A nod of appreciation to the Womenread book club of Pasadena, California for their enthusiasm; to the Southern California Writers' Conference for advice and encouragement at a crucial juncture; and to the fine folks at BookBalloon for (virtual) tea and sympathy.

For providing a fine writer's refuge, my thanks go to the city of Solvang, California and especially to the Royal Copenhagen Inn, The Book Loft, The Bulldog Café, and Paula's Pancake House.

Book cover design by GoOnWrite.com

Smite Publications logo by alanNdesign

"He who has injured thee was either stronger or weaker. If weaker, spare him; if stronger, spare thyself." - Seneca

Chapter One

Downtown Los Angeles glittered in the sun, seemed to preen. The city knew its best light — a spring morning, the sky cleansed of smog by the past weekend's rain — and its best angle — from a distance.

Driving south out of the scrubby Glendale foothills, Jennifer Thomson took a moment to appreciate the city. In the clear March air, the skyline had a glamour it lost the closer she came. She took the moment but did not cherish it, for she did not know that before noon the sky would be sullied by a column of smoke and dust, that the skyline would be forever altered, that the sound of police and news helicopters would be audible for miles.

Jennifer drove as quickly as she dared without catching the attention of the California Highway Patrol. She was not anxious to get to work. Rather, she was trying not to be late. She had no one to blame but herself, having hit the snooze button once — or was it twice? — more often than usual.

But judging from the lighter-than-usual traffic, Jennifer thought she wasn't the only one who would be tardy today. She wouldn't have cared about being five (or fifteen) minutes late, but her boss did care, and Jennifer had no desire to hear Maggie Stone remark on her tardiness again.

Luck was with her. In the underground garage she found a parking spot close to the elevator. The maintenance man even took a break from hauling trash cans and held the elevator door open for her. Jennifer smiled and thanked him, then punched the button to floor eighteen. Now, if only her luck was in.

It was. Maggie Stone was nowhere to be seen, and the other employees were too busy getting their morning caffeine fix to notice her late arrival. Jennifer took advantage of the reprieve and paused to give her outfit a once-over. The gray skirt and pink sweater hadn't needed ironing, but she wished — not for the last time that day — that she'd worn more sensible shoes. She ran a brush through her hair, picked up her travel mug, and went in search of coffee. A pot of French roast had just been brewed. Jennifer smiled, hoping that her luck would hold.

It would. Just enough to keep her alive.

She worked in a twenty-story federal building where the gears of government bureaucracy turned, slowly and inexorably — keeping records, allocating funds, processing forms, renewing licenses.

Her office was a branch of the grants department, and as undistinguished a cubicle farm as any she'd ever worked in. Pale gray partitions and mauve accents on the walls left over from the early 1990s. Inspirational prints with images of sunsets and mountain climbers, symbols of success and teamwork, bought frames-and-all from the discount office supplier. Modular desks, a PC resting on each. Plants on the desks and dotted around the room, nourished by fluorescent lights; the African violets thrived but did not bloom.

A small sign, *Jennifer Thomson, Receptionist,* marked a corner desk as hers. The desktop was more or less tidy — Friday had been a slow day, time for her to clean up. The bulletin board behind her held a calendar, a few Dilbert cartoons, a postcard her sister Cindy had sent her from Niagara Falls. Jennifer set her mug down and turned on the computer. She settled into her chair, with neither resignation nor enthusiasm. How had she described the job to Cindy? *The career path of least resistance.* Still, it paid fairly well and the benefits were good. What else could she ask for?

"Hi, Jen-Jen!"

10:17 a.m., and Jennifer was on her way to the photocopier when she heard Carrie's voice. Jennifer smiled; she could take or leave most of her coworkers, but she liked Carrie, always had. "Hi, Carrie. How was your weekend?"

Carrie shrugged. "Got stood up. Again."

"Oh, I'm sorry."

Carrie grinned. She was a buxom type in her late forties, determined to live life as a blonde, and always ready to share her dating stories. "Don't worry about it. I smelled this guy would be trouble the moment I met him. Literally. He bathed, I kid you not, *bathed* in Canoe aftershave."

"At least it wasn't Aqua Velva."

"Thank God for small favors. Speaking of getting stood up, the copier guy didn't come by Friday."

"You're kidding. The machine's still down?"

Carrie nodded. "Only one still working is all the way over in HR."

Jennifer rolled her eyes. "One of those days. Guess I'm off to HR."

"Have fun. Be sure to leave a trail of breadcrumbs."

Jennifer started down the hall, then turned back to Carrie. "Do you want to go out for lunch today? I didn't have time to pack anything. There's that new sushi place."

"Sure. 11:30 do you? Beat the rush?"

"OK. See you then." Jennifer gave Carrie a little wave, and walked down the hall to HR. She never saw Carrie again.

There was no line for the copier, and the papers didn't jam once. Her luck *was* holding, Jennifer mused as she started back down the hall, though it would have been better if the damn copier repair guy had shown up. Still, she couldn't —

The floor trembled and she stopped, had just enough time to think *Earthquake?* and wonder where the nearest doorway was when the entire building shook madly, whipsawed back and forth. She was on the floor, papers scattered around her, as the building shuddered and rattled. There was a roar, a giant's bellow. She heard screams from the halls and offices, knew that she herself must be screaming but she could not hear it, could only feel her throat burn with the force of the cry. Overhead the fluorescent lights popped and broke, glass and plastic rained down, and now chunks of plaster and acoustic ceiling tiles joined the deluge. Jennifer curled up into a ball, hands covering her head, arms covering her face, feeling her breath on her forearms but still not hearing herself scream.

The building gave one last shudder and silence fell. No doubt there was more sound, plenty of it, but so deafened was Jennifer that she heard nothing. She felt cool air on her forearms and head. She pulled her arms away from her face but dared not open her eyes yet. There was light on the other side of her closed lids, more light than there should have been. She told her eyes to open but they would not obey at first. Finally she jerked her head and her eyes opened.

For twenty feet in front of her the hallway continued on. Full of plaster and ceiling tiles and bad art, but it was there. Beyond that, open air, the sky, an eighteen-story view of Los Angeles. Half the building had been torn away. Bits and pieces still fell past the gaping hole she looked out of. A live electric cable twisted in the wind, an angry snake spitting sparks. Office paper drifted down like oversize confetti, incongruously festive.

Jennifer's eyes saw it but her brain was numb, unable to take it in. What had happened? It was unreal. Buildings simply did not split in two, leave you staring out a hole at eighteen stories of sky and the city below. It simply could not be —

She heard a scream and a man plunged past the hole in the building and kept going. Even through the ringing in her ears she could hear his scream, diminishing as he fell to whatever wreckage lay below. Another cry, this one words instead of a scream, a man's shout of, "Jesus God!" and he was falling, like the first man, from the nineteenth or twentieth floor. He was flailing instinctively, somehow caught hold of something, and dangled there in front of Jennifer.

She wanted to help him but could not move; he did not ask for help, only stared fixedly. He began to shake, then jitter wildly, and Jennifer saw that he had caught hold of the electrical cable, his hands frozen in a death grip as the voltage coursed through him. She was transfixed, unable to look away as he jittered and shook; she hoped he was dead already, that he was not alive to feel his hair and clothes burst into flame.

Only when the smell of him burning reached her did she break her paralysis. She scrambled to her feet and fled from the burning man, from that dreadful hole in the building, looking for something or someone that would explain what was going on. She ran around the corner and right into Mr. Danvers, the department vice president. There was a cut across his head and blood in his hair but he was calm. He grabbed her by the shoulders, shook her. "Jennifer!" he yelled. "Come on, Jennifer! Are you OK?"

For a moment she could not find her voice. At last she croaked, "I think so there's this man there he burnt up and what's going on?"

He shook her again. "It's a bomb or something. We've got to get out of here. I'm going to go see if I can find anybody else, you go on. Get out of the building, fast as you can."

Automatically she started toward the elevator. He grabbed her by the arm and pulled her back. "No, the stairs, take the stairs. Just run, keep going."

Jennifer watched him run down the hall and soon he was gone, disappearing into a cloud of dust. She stood for a moment, unsure of what to do, and now she could hear things. Screams and moans. Crumbling

12

plaster and breaking glass. And a deep groaning — the sound of a building that had taken more damage than it could stand, was ready to come down.

Soon.

Get out. Fast. She could do that. Could she?

Jennifer ran for the stairs. Just before she reached the stairwell she passed by a conference room and for a moment stopped, looked in. The walls of the conference room had been glass, and the people inside had been cut to ribbons. They lay bloody and silent amid their coffee cups and meeting notes. She recognized a few of them. Some their own mothers would not have recognized. She stood and stared. It couldn't be real, couldn't. They were filming a movie or something, she must have missed the memo. Soon the director would yell *Cut!* and all these people would get up and wash off the fake blood and everyone would have some donuts and she could get Bruce Willis' autograph.

Jennifer felt someone — she never knew who — shove her and she joined the people running for the stairwell. Not many of them heading for the stairwell, not many at all, and she wondered how many were trapped or dead or dying in the wreckage.

She didn't know. All she knew was that she did not want to be one of them.

Jennifer started down the stairs. Under normal circumstances eighteen floors would have been nothing more than a good workout. But now the stairwell was full of people, more of them every minute, some of them hurt and all of them frantic to get out before the building collapsed. Now the air was thick with panic and dust. Every time the building let out a groan or shudder they all froze, waiting, and when nothing happened they kept going. Halfway down someone panicked, started screaming that they had to go faster, damn it, faster. But for the most part they made the journey down in grim silence, perhaps afraid that any sound they made would hasten the building's collapse.

At the third floor, the heel broke off one of Jennifer's shoes and there was a dull flare of pain as she twisted her ankle. She stopped to take off her shoes and rest her foot for a moment. "Jennifer? You need a hand?" She looked up at the familiar voice. It was Carlos, one of the account managers. "Come on, we need to keep moving."

"Thanks," she said. He put one of her arms across his shoulders, and they began to make their way down the stairs. Now that they were so close, some of the panic left her. They were going to make it.

At the second-floor landing she said, "I think—"

She never finished the sentence. There was a grinding roar from above them and something crashed through the wall. The stairway buckled and they fell. Jennifer felt something hit her on the head with a heavy but painless blow, and then felt nothing.

Jennifer woke lying on her left side, arm pinned under her. The stairwell was lit only by a flickering fluorescent bulb; the air was heavy with dust that she could taste on her lips and tongue. Her body ached dully. She sat up slowly and pain shot through her shoulder and her head. Her left arm wouldn't move. With her right hand she touched her head, felt wetness. When she looked at her fingers, they were red.

At least she could see. "Carlos? Carlos are..."

She could see Carlos, lying at the bottom of the stairs, his head cocked at what even to her unlearned eyes was a very wrong angle, eyes open and unseeing. "Oh no," she whispered.

The building did not just groan; it screamed. So did she. "No!" Jennifer hauled herself to her feet with her good arm, her twisted ankle and lost shoes forgotten, and began limping down the buckled steps.

The door to the lobby was ajar a little bit. She tried to open it wider; it wouldn't budge. Jennifer sucked in her breath and forced herself through. For a moment she was trapped, thought she would die stuck in this doorway, and if she had been able to breathe she would have screamed. Another burst of effort, the buckled metal tearing her sweater and scraping her back; she was through. The lobby was full of debris, twisted steel and broken glass that she dodged as best she could. Once a huge chunk of metal fell and she felt the wind of its passage as it missed her by inches. Out of the corner of her eye she saw a gaping hole in the lobby floor, dared not look closer. She squeezed through one more doorway and was outside.

Out. But not safe. She saw people waving at her, making frantic *Hurry!* gestures and understood that the last scream of the building had been its death cry. It was coming down.

Jennifer ran. She heard the sound of impact behind her and was lost in a cloud of dust, feeling debris fly around her.

She wanted to run, but couldn't see where to run to. She tried to scream, but could not even breathe.

Chapter Two

The house was like the others on the block: small, undistinguished. The lawn was a vibrant green well-nurtured by the Florida rain. Jade plants and bird-of-paradise, low-maintenance and pleasant enough to look at, flanked the doorway. The mailbox was bright white, the numbers 606 and the name Anderson neatly lettered in black. The red flag on the mailbox was down; no letters to go out today. A dwelling unremarkable in every way.

The man who walked out of the house was equally unremarkable in appearance. He wore running shorts and a T-shirt that suggested people visit Reno, Nevada; he himself had never been there. He stood in his driveway and stretched, warming up for his morning run. If someone had looked closely they would have noticed a wiry strength that set him apart from an ordinary runner; would have seen watchfulness in his eyes as he gave the street a quick up-and-down glance, a careful assessment of details.

But no one looked closely. In this central Florida town, few people paid attention to much of anything. Not that he cared. After all, it was the reason he was here.

He jogged in place a moment, then began his run. Up and down the suburban streets with names like Sunflower and Cypress and Sycamore. He had seven different routes for his run, one for each day of the week. It kept the routine from getting stale, kept his observation of the surroundings sharp. There was no need for it in this place, after all this time, but old habits died hard.

Old fears died hard as well.

He ran until his lungs burned and ran some more, as he always did. He came back, as he always did, with his shirt and shorts plastered to him with sweat; with the nagging feeling that he had not run enough; with the unwelcome awareness that he was not as fast as he used to be. As he walked up the drive to his house he saw his next-door neighbor, out tending her roses. He went quickly through his bag of disguises and came up with the placid suburban smile. "Hello, Gladys."

"Oh, hello Mr. Anderson," she called out. "You know, you shouldn't run like that when it gets so hot. You'll have a stroke."

"I'll be careful. I promise," he said.

She waved goodbye to him and watched him go inside. Such a nice young man (Gladys was pushing ninety and any person under sixty qualified as young to her). She felt sorry for him, here on his own. An early retiree, he said. He'd taken a big pension and lived here. Alone. No wife, no children. But so nice and polite.

She went about tending her roses, unaware that her next-door neighbor had not been a telecommunications professional, and that he was not a retiree — at least, not the usual kind of retiree. And that his name was not Anderson.

His name was Sean Kincaid, and like everyone else in America he watched the day's events unfold on television. It was the time-honored ritual. They'd done it when Kennedy was shot and they'd done it for the space shuttle explosion, for Waco and Oklahoma City, for 9/11. And, he thought with a sardonic grin quite unlike the smile he'd bestowed on Gladys, they'd likely do it for the Four Horsemen.

Why not? What could be more truly American than to watch disaster from the comfort of an easy chair, the remote ready to skip from network to network, snacks just a few steps away in the kitchen? The audiences at the gladiatorial matches in Rome never had it half so good.

It was strange to be on the observer's side of the television screen. But this was the first catastrophic event to rock the U.S. since they'd put Sean out to pasture, and it was apt that he sit here in his bungalow with its tasteful Navajo White exterior, and watch the horror unfold on the idiot box like the rest of his neighbors.

It made him one of them. After all, blending in had always been his best talent. The Chameleon, Fredericks had called him. Not that Sean had liked the nickname, or Fredericks, either. Fredericks had clever nicknames for all the agents, and for himself as well; thin and fast and wiry, he'd called himself the Snake. Behind Fredericks' back they'd called him the Ferret, hyperactive and sticking his nose where it was likely to get him in trouble. Though, when Sean thought about it, maybe the Snake had been appropriate; when Fredericks had come back from the mission in Chechnya it had been in pieces. *Don't tread on me.*

Sean blended in, more than he wanted to. What he saw on the TV should have made him angry. It should have roused the quiet, cold anger that made everyone — even his superiors — walk carefully around him. The Chameleon could bite. He should have said, *How could you not see this was going to happen? When a wasp stings you, don't shoo it away. Kill the son of a bitch before he brings his whole nest down on you.*

But he was out now, had been for four years — long enough to let cheerful cynicism take over. It was what all the "retirees" did. That, or eat a bullet one night, and despite everything he still liked to live.

Even in Florida.

Sean wondered if any of the old crowd — those who were left — were watching. Wondered what Robert, especially, thought of it all. Wondered if Halsey was regretting all those walking papers he'd issued.

He hoped Monique was nowhere near L.A., but did not worry too much. Her business travels seldom took her to the Left Coast, as she called it, and no doubt she was safe from this trouble. He might call, though. Just to be sure.

The volume of the TV was low; his experienced eyes saw more than any newscaster could tell him. A federal building in Los Angeles, half of it torn away by a bomb blast, the other half ready to collapse at any moment. Soon, it would be very soon. Pieces were coming down already, the whole thing was beginning to shiver like a man in a dying tremor. Anyone who wasn't out by now was most likely —

Hold on.

The camera whipped from the newscaster to the building. They'd all seen it.

There. Coming out of the building. A young woman, mid-twenties, in a gray skirt and pink sweater. She knew what was happening; Sean could not read her expression but saw her fear in the way she ran.

He had been sitting back in his chair, watching disaster unfold. Now he leaned forward. His hand crept to the TV's remote and he turned up the volume.

"A person just got out of the building," the newscaster was saying in a surprisingly composed voice. "This is the first we've seen come out in almost a half hour and...Oh God."

The building was coming down.

"Holy fucking shit!" yelled a voice from somewhere off camera, the live feed uncensored. America had bigger problems than profanity today.

Down. It was down, and a huge cloud of dust and debris billowed out, swallowing up the woman in the gray skirt.

Babble of voices from the TV.

"—collapse—"

"—chances of survival are—"

A firefighter ran into the dust cloud.

Sean waited. They all did, millions across the nation forced into an unwilling communion, all waiting to see if the woman was going to make it.

Seconds passed. He wanted to look at his watch to see how long, but dared not take his eyes off the screen.

Something coming through the dust cloud. Blurred, indistinct. Then, a firefighter, carrying something in his arms. The woman. For a moment, mere silhouettes in the dust, they might have been lovers, he carrying her away to some romantic destination. Then they were out of the dust cloud, into the clear.

Sean leaned forward, closer to his television. For the first time, something flickered behind his eyes.

Both firefighter and woman were covered with dust. Dove-gray with it, they reminded Sean of the human statues in Pompeii caught by the volcano's ashes. Her left arm dangled limply, broken. Her scalp was lacerated and blood trickled down the side of her head, making dark trails through the dust. Her shoes were gone, her feet scored and bloody. Her right hand clutched at the firefighter's coat, and he cradled her in his arms as if she was a weary child who needed to be carried to bed.

Sean, quite unaware of what he was doing, rose from his chair. He knelt in front of the television and placed a hand on the screen, as if he could reach across the miles to the two people there. He watched as the woman let her head fall against the firefighter's shoulder and she began to cry, tears mingling with her blood. Sean's eyes, which had looked on countless sights of destruction and death with nothing but businesslike detachment, brimmed with tears.

Chapter Three

Cradled in the safety of an ocean to the west, three thousand miles of country to the east, Los Angeles was late in falling prey to a terrorist attack. Until now, the City of Angels' demons had come from within.

Nevertheless, its citizens had been well-schooled by countless hours of television news. The stage was set, and all the actors knew their roles.

First came the firefighters and the rescue workers, sifting through wreckage. They searched for survivors, and found fifteen. After that, bodies were all they found, and as time went on and hope waned, bodies were all they looked for.

The lawmen were present as well. They fenced off the site, and soon the chain-link border was garlanded with yellow police tape that looked strangely cheery, like party streamers. The city's men and women in blue came to stand guard and keep order. Representatives of a larger law came in as well, black-jacketed FBI agents searching for evidence, and shadowy men in suits whose purposes were less clear.

The citizens came as well. Those who worked in the area came, beholden by job demands and paychecks to walk past the wrecked building every day. Some stopped and stared. Some wept, some were stony-faced. Some walked past, head down, refusing to look, only to be lured to their office windows during coffee breaks, where they gazed silently at the site.

The curious also came, driven by many things: a desire to help, a need to see and therefore believe the unbelievable, a dark wish to look upon death and feel themselves more alive, a simple offering of support. Some stood and watched, others joined in the rescue and cleanup efforts. Nearly all left some mark of their pilgrimage and soon the chain link was hung not just with police tape but cards and poems, pictures of the Virgin of

Guadalupe, messages of sympathy in all the languages of the polyglot city. Flowers real and artificial, teddy bears, American flags, and other tokens were laid there in a pledge of condolence, vengeance, and unity.

Those who had lost husbands, wives, children, lovers, or friends in the blast came, easily recognizable by their manner — equal parts desperation and dignity — and by the tokens they carried — recent photographs, happy scenes at odds with the demeanor of those who held them. The days went on and the chances of anyone surviving burned low, guttered, and finally died out. Still the bereaved came, hoping their dedication would bring about a miracle.

The survivors came, those who could. Some were in the hospitals still. Others stayed away, unable to face the scene again. No one blamed them for this. Whether they blamed themselves was another matter.

Cindy's knock at the bathroom door was gentle, less a knock than a faint tap. "Jennifer? Coffee's about ready."

"Be there in a minute," Jennifer replied. The bathroom was dim with the light off, and dimmer still with the shower curtain pulled all the way around the tub. She lay in the warm water, submerged save for her head, and for her left arm, which hung outside the tub so the cast would not get wet. The air was heavy with steam, the mirrors opaqued. Tiny beads of water clung to Jennifer's hair.

Despite the room's humid warmth she shivered. Chilly somehow even now, and she could not explain why. She'd been cold ever since she'd come home from the hospital. She could not bring herself to ask a doctor about it, for to do so she would have had to talk about the bombing; instead, late at night when Cindy slept and Jennifer could not, she consulted some websites and found no definitive reason for her chill other than "stress."

The cold followed her everywhere. No matter how many blankets she piled on at night or how high the thermostat was set she felt it. No matter that the Santa Ana winds had come, bringing their dry northeast heat. It followed her every place but here, the bathtub, and consequently that was her haven, here in the steamy dimness. She ran her right hand over her face, relishing the warmth of the water on her skin. Jennifer took a breath and slid down, under the water's surface, eyes closed, wishing she had gills and could stay here forever, be safe and warm and untouchable.

Jennifer in her jeans and a loose-fitting t-shirt that was easy to manage with her cast, her hair wet but combed out neatly, sat at the little dining room table she had bought on sale at Ikea with her Christmas money. She sipped her coffee and looked curiously at the table's surface. She had never noticed the little patterns in the wood grain before. Had they been there when she bought the table? Was this the table she had bought? She couldn't remember.

"Want some cereal? Toast maybe?" Cindy was in the kitchen, slathering butter and boysenberry jam on her English muffin. Dear Cindy, Jennifer's kid sister. She'd left her twins in the care of her husband and mother-in-law, braved the fears of further attacks, had come out from New Jersey on a three-quarters empty plane. She made herself at home on Jennifer's lumpy couch for the first night. Until the memories of the bombing got into Jennifer's dreams and made her wake moaning and crying, and then Cindy slept in the bed with Jennifer, as they had during childhood summers when they visited their grandmother's house and shared a bed. Cindy cooked comfort-food meals like roast chicken and mashed potatoes, tomato soup made with milk and a little dollop of butter. Cindy rented movies for them to watch, fluffy romantic comedies. Cindy fielded the phone calls that came in from well-wishers, reporters, and lawyers; she took Jennifer to the doctor to make sure her injuries were healing. She was good as gold, Jennifer thought, better even, and if none of it really helped it was not Cindy's fault.

"Jen?"

"Sorry. Toast, if it's no problem."

"Sure. Medium-burnt?"

This was an old family joke. All the Thomsons liked their toast well-done, the only question was just how burnt they liked it. "That's fine," Jennifer said. "No jam, just butter."

"Coming right up." After a few minutes the smell of charring bread filled the kitchen, and Cindy placed three slices of toast in front of Jennifer. She sat down and watched as Jennifer nibbled at the toast. After a moment she said, "Jen, are you sure this is a good idea?"

"The doc says I'm doing fine."

"It's not that. I mean, it's only been a week."

"Nine days," Jennifer said before she could stop herself. She hadn't wanted Cindy to know she'd been counting.

"Nine days," amended Cindy. "Are you...I don't know. Up to it?"

"I think so. I mean, I just feel it's the right thing to do."

"OK," said Cindy. "I'm going to go have a shower and get dressed. Then we'll go. All right? And we'll stay only as long as you want to."

"Thanks."

Cindy left the table and Jennifer sat, drinking coffee and eating toast without tasting either. She could not tell Cindy the truth, that despite the constant news coverage and the nightmares and the dust that still hung over downtown Los Angeles, she could not believe that it had happened. It was too much to take in. She needed to know it was real.

Perhaps seeing the site would help. She did not dare to think that it might not.

For something to do, she looked over the list of phone messages Cindy had written down. Reporters, so many of them. People from the government. One name appeared over and over again: Amber LaSalle, from Ellis and Associates Representation. Jennifer shrugged, pushed the list aside. She had no plans to call any of these people.

Halfway through her second piece of toast, her throat locked up. These days, she could hardly eat. Her body let her eat only enough to maintain and then, abruptly, took all the desire for food from her. There was no nausea or revulsion, merely a complete disinterest in food. If it happened while she was chewing, she had to spit out that mouthful; she had tried to swallow when this happened and could not. If she had looked at herself in the mirror, she would have seen that she was already losing weight. But she could no more stand to look in a mirror than she could force down any more of this toast.

She dumped the last of the toast into the sink, fed it into the garbage disposal, and sat down, waiting for Cindy.

Though they were only half-siblings, Jennifer the child of their mother's first marriage and Cindy the child of the second, Cindy was a true sister. Trying to do right by Jennifer, Cindy had kept some things from her.

She had not told Jennifer that, according to the news reports, there had been no claims of responsibility for the bombing, and no immediate suspects other than the usual Middle Eastern extremists. She had not told Jennifer of the death toll, 361 as of this morning, nor that Jennifer was the only survivor of the grants department.

She had not told Jennifer that she was famous.

Televisions across the world had been capturing the events, and nearly every major news media outlet in the U.S. had been there when the firefighter carried Jennifer out of the dust cloud. The image of Jennifer crying in her rescuer's arms had made it to every newspaper; had been the cover image for *Time, U.S. News and World Report,* and *People*; was replayed endlessly on TV; had been duplicated and downloaded all over the internet.

Jennifer and Cindy made their way to the fence surrounding the site. There were nudges and whispers from onlookers, but Jennifer noticed nothing. She was focused on the building beyond the chain-link fence.

A thin haze of dust still hung over the site. Most had been blown away by the Santa Anas. A section of wall, with a window miraculously intact, was all that remained of the building. The rest was a heap of rubble — concrete and steel and plaster and office furniture and glass all in one great heap. Nothing recognizable any more.

Real. All real. Jennifer hooked her fingers through the fence and stared, watching the crews tear apart the wreckage. The caution of the first week had disappeared. After nine days, there was no hope left.

Real. She waited for relief, and felt nothing. It was still too hard to believe that this building was gone. That so many people with their lives and families, loves and hates, endearing habits and annoying tics, were gone. Forever.

She had nearly been one of them.

Jennifer turned away from the fence; breathing hard, not wanting to because of the smell of destruction that still hung in the air but unable to stop. She walked to where the relatives stood, with pictures in their hands, hoping. As she walked, Cindy beside her, she began to hear the murmurs of the strangers nearby.

"Her. That's her."

"Oh my God, the girl from the —"

"—last one out, one more minute and —"

She wondered who they were talking about, why the crowds miraculously parted for her and Cindy. Wondered why the cops and firemen gave her grave, respectful nods. She only had eyes for the people standing with their pictures, because she recognized one.

The woman stood, wearing a dark blue dress, one hand clasped over her pregnant belly, the other holding a picture. A picture of Carlos: the account manager who had helped Jennifer down the stairs, the pregnant woman's husband. Jennifer swallowed hard, remembering how happy Carlos had been at the department Christmas party when he'd announced that Nancy was expecting. Remembering that she and Carrie had been taking up collections for a gift basket full of necessities for the baby and little luxuries for Nancy.

Remembering Carlos at the bottom of the stairwell, his neck broken.

Nancy stood, eyes dark and wide, always with one hand over her stomach and one holding the picture. "I'm going to talk to her," Jennifer said to Cindy.

"Do you want me there?"

"Just stay nearby."

"OK."

She walked up to Nancy, unsure of what to say. But Nancy spoke first. "Jennifer. How are you doing?"

What could she say? *Hanging in there? Doing fine?* Instead she asked, "How are you?"

Nancy bowed her head, her long black hair falling forward, and she was perversely lovely, a grieving Madonna. "I've come here every day. I know that it's too late. I know that Carlos isn't..." She sighed harshly, looked up at Jennifer. "I know, and I can't help it, I keep coming here." The hand clasped over her stomach was not empty; Jennifer saw a rosary entwined in Nancy's fingers.

Nancy bowed her head again, eyes closed. Her fingers moved to the next bead on the rosary but her lips did not move. Jennifer swallowed hard. "Nancy." She could not go on.

"You know, don't you?" Nancy asked without looking up.

"He helped me down the stairs. I hurt my ankle, and he was helping me down the stairs. And, I don't know, maybe there was another explosion and we fell..." She trailed off, unsure of what to say.

"You don't have to tell me the rest," Nancy said. She clenched the rosary beads. "He's dead?"

"Yes." Jennifer had never found it so hard to say one simple word.

Nancy's head was still bowed. "He didn't...suffer?"

"No." She somehow forced the word out through the vise of pain around her throat.

"I knew he was gone. I knew," Nancy said, and then she had her arms around Jennifer, and Jennifer was hugging her back with an awkward one-armed embrace. Nancy cried and Jennifer could not somehow, much as she wanted to.

After a few minutes Nancy pulled away. "Thank you for telling me."

"Do you need a ride home?" Jennifer asked.

"No. I'll stay here for a little while." Nancy returned to the stance Jennifer had found her in, her fingers moving over the rosary beads. "Thank you," she said again, and then began murmuring soft Spanish prayers. "*Dios te salve, Maria, llena eres de gracia.*"

Not wanting to intrude further on Nancy's grief, Jennifer turned away. She was exhausted, numb inside, chilly on the outside. She wanted to find Cindy and go home, wanted to crawl into a nice hot bath. As she walked, searching for Cindy, she became aware of the click and whir of a camera. Who or what were they taking pictures of? Simultaneous with the realization they were photographing *her*, a well-coiffed reporter accompanied by a cameraman appeared in front of her.

"Miss Thomson, could we have a word with you?" he asked. She vaguely recognized him from the local news.

"How do you know my name?" she asked.

He and the cameraman exchanged glances. He did not answer her but instead asked, "How do you feel, coming back to this scene?"

"What?" she asked, still wondering how he knew her name. Her eye caught a nearby newsstand. There. Her picture on the magazine covers. Now it all fell into place, and she had to...

"Find my sister. I'm sorry." She pushed her way past the reporter, head down but still trying to look for Cindy, and then Cindy caught hold of her good arm.

"Come on, Jen, let's go home."

"Yes, please."

The reporter persisted. "Miss Thomson, if I could just—"

"Take a hike," Cindy snapped.

They got into the car and drove back in silence, for Jennifer could not bring herself to tell Cindy about Nancy. Nor did she know what to think of her picture and the way everyone seemed to know her.

At home, Jennifer took a long bath and tried to think only about Nancy. For the first time, she felt a little better about things. At least she had been able to give Nancy some comfort.

She went back two days later. Cindy was gone, shooed out the door by Jennifer. "You need a day when you're not taking care of me."

"You'll be OK?" Cindy asked.

"Yeah. I'll probably just be here today, watch a movie or something."

Instead, she took a cab to downtown Los Angeles. She stood by the fence, and things were much the same as they had been two days ago. Nancy was not there, but that was the only difference as far as Jennifer could tell. She stood, watching, not talking to anyone, just looking on as the crews continued their grim work.

From time to time reporters hovered near, tried to ask questions, but she ignored them. She heard the steady clicking of cameras, and tried to ignore that as well.

"How does it feel?" said a voice.

Jennifer looked up at the speaker, a blonde woman in her early forties. Even without the photo she held, Jennifer recognized her.

"Mrs. Danvers." The wife of the man who'd told her to run, stopped her from taking the elevator instead of the stairs. If she was here, she was not just his wife, but his widow.

"Mrs. Danvers," she began. "I'm Jen—"

"Oh, I know who you are." Madeline Danvers said. She had lost weight since Jennifer had seen her last, her nose and chin were sharp. "Everyone knows. The last one out. The only one from grants to make it out."

The only one? Surely that couldn't be right. "I didn't..."

"How does it feel?" she asked again. "What's it like knowing you made it when everyone else didn't? You just love posing for those cameras, don't you? You've got that noble-and-tragic pose down. Thought about who'll play you in the movie?"

"Your husband helped me, he told me to get out and then he went back to help."

"Why didn't you go with him?"

Jennifer had no answer. She opened her mouth but nothing came out.

Madeline Danvers leaned close to her. Her voice was low, almost a whisper, but the words stung. "I know why. You saved your own hide. My husband stayed to help, and he's dead. That man who helped you down the stairs, he's dead too. What makes you better than them? How come you're here and they're not?"

Jennifer turned and ran, not caring where. She ran until she found herself on a downtown street blocks away from the bombing site. She leaned against a phone pole, lungs burning, a stitch jabbing into her side. For a moment she feared she would throw up, then the feeling passed. A cab drew near and she hailed it, got in.

"Jen?" Cindy's voice at the bathroom door. "You have an OK day?"

Jennifer took her face out of the towel she had been crying into. It was wet with tears and mucus. "Yeah," she replied, praying that her voice sounded normal. "Not bad."

"It's my last night, you know? Want to go get some dinner?"

"Sure."

"You sure you're all right? Did something happen today?"

"No, no. Everything's fine. I'll be out in a minute."

In the bathroom, shower curtain pulled around the tub, blinds pulled against the light. Jennifer dropped the towel to the floor, turned over, immersed her face in the water and screamed, the sound rushing past her ears in muted bubbles. She raised her head, took a breath, and howled into the water again. And again.

It was not what Madeline Danvers said that made her scream.

She screamed because she had been saying the same things to herself ever since the bombing.

Chapter Four

Thursday mornings were slow at the Gulf Coast Gun Range. The owner, last name of Peake, was playing solitaire when the first customer came in. Peake swept the cards into a pile — he was losing, anyway — and sighed inwardly. The customer was no doubt some accountant on his day off, deep in the throes of mid-life crisis. Peake's least favorite type. They never knew the rules and regulations, never knew how to properly store their guns, usually had to be shown how to load, and couldn't hit the broad side of a barn. They always walked out arrogantly, as though a half hour on the range had given them a fresh jolt of manhood; Peake thought that you didn't have to be Freud to figure that one out.

Worst of all, they were rude.

He was surprised when the accountant type gave him a quiet but perfectly sincere, "Good morning. Have any lanes open?"

"Take your pick. You're the first one in today."

Without Peake asking, the customer laid the case containing his weapon on the table for Peake's inspection. Inside the case was a nine-millimeter Sig Sauer P210, and Peake felt both admiration and mild dread. It was an excellent gun, but not cheap, and Peake had seen more than his share of people who owned the P210 just because it was expensive and hadn't realized that it was a European design, one you couldn't learn how to load and take down from watching the movies. But maybe this fellow was different; he had four magazines, so he was primed to do some serious shooting.

"Looks in good shape," said Peake. "Need anything?"

"Three boxes of rounds and some targets."

"Getting serious this morning?"

"You could say so." The accountant type smiled. It was a mild smile, nothing unusual about it, but Peake felt something strange. A vibe, he would have said back in his college days, that this man was not getting serious. He *was* serious, through and through.

Peake watched while the customer, who was most certainly not an accountant, walked to a nearby lane and began preparations. He worked swiftly, smoothly, without any hesitation or need to get his bearings. He had all four magazines loaded and the gun ready to go in half the time it would have taken Peake to do it himself, stood with safety glasses and hearing protectors on, the target at twenty yards.

He began firing.

Peake thought that if any of his usual Thursday morning customers could see this, they might well flee the range.

Eight rounds fired, eight holes punched in the black of the target. Empty magazine out, full one in, another eight rounds fired in rapid succession. Unload, reload. When all four magazines were empty he replaced the target with a fresh one, this one at twenty-five yards. The ritual — Peake could think of nothing else to call it — was repeated, and repeated again at thirty yards.

When it was done, silence fell on the range, eerie in the wake of gunfire's roar. Peake saw that only once — at thirty yards — had the shooter hit anywhere but the black center of the target.

"I knew I was looking at a professional," Peake told his wife that night.

"You mean a cop?" she asked.

"No. A professional."

What Peake thought, as he watched the man pack up his gear: *God help whoever ends up on the other side of this guy's gun, because nothing else will.*

And yet the shooter gave Peake a nice smile, wished him good day, and was out the door. Peake watched as the shooter got into his car, a generic sedan. There was a curious expression on the shooter's face; resolute, anticipatory, strangely gentle.

Sean turned on the television when he arrived back at the house, put it on the 24-hour news channel. He lowered the volume to a dull murmur, trusting selective perception to call his attention to the television at the right moment.

It was most unlike him. Under normal circumstances his television was little more than a glorified monitor for his DVD player; he had watched a lot of movies over the last four years, and his home theater system was the one luxury in an otherwise spartan house. Under normal circumstances he paid little attention to TV or print news; he knew too much about the way things really worked to trust the media's account of world events.

But these were not normal circumstances, had not been since that day now nearly three weeks ago when he'd watched the firefighter carry the girl away from the bombed building. Sean had sat in front of his television, touching the screen as if he could reach through time and space and offer something — a word of comfort, a soothing touch. Anything. The cameras followed the girl and the firefighter as he carried her to the rescue area, followed her as she was put on a stretcher and carried to one of the vans taking the less seriously injured to the hospitals. That was the last the world saw of her, for a while.

He'd forsworn his movies, and kept the TV tuned to the cable news channel in hope of learning more about her. Instead of merely subscribing to the paper to preserve the illusion that he was an ordinary suburbanite, he actually read it, or at least skimmed through it. Eventually, buried like rough jewels in the mass of wild speculations and human interest drivel, Sean found the details he needed. Jennifer Thomson, twenty-eight, a receptionist in the grants department, the only survivor of that department.

There had been one glimpse of her since then. Nine days after the incident, a TV camera caught her as she stood talking with a pregnant Hispanic woman. Caught Jennifer as she and the pregnant woman embraced, and he burned her image into his mind. Hair that dishwater shade between brown and blonde, eyes blue. Thinner now, if she didn't start eating something soon she'd be a scarecrow. Stunned, still, by everything.

She had no idea that the whole world had been watching; that was clear when the reporter walked up to her and spoke her name. There was no mistaking the confusion in her eyes, the realization that she was no longer a person but a symbol.

Sean wondered how much Jennifer knew, not just about the photo of herself but the number of people who'd died. When he saw the other woman — they had the same eyes, perhaps they were sisters — gently guide her away he knew that Jennifer had, rightly or wrongly, been shielded from the worst of the knowledge. But that shield could not last forever. He had some knowledge of what it was like to be a survivor, to be Ishmael, alone to tell you all. He knew that when she finally understood and felt everything it was going to hurt her like a bandage ripped from a fresh wound.

But maybe he could ease the pain for her.

Monday morning. Three weeks after the incident in Los Angeles. Sean could not wait any longer, had to do something. Anything.

The train to Washington, D.C., slowed, came to a stop, disgorged its load of passengers. Businessmen mostly, a few tourists, a school group up to observe democracy in inaction. He was carried along in their flow, appearing to all eyes a businessman here for a conference or merger meeting. Gray suit, tie a year or two out of date, shoes with a bit of scuff to them. The gun lay concealed under his jacket.

Sean hailed a cab and took it to a hotel where he had never stayed before, nor would ever stay again. He checked in, respectfully declined the amenities of morning newspaper and nightly turndown. For a moment he stood, gazing out the window, wondering if he should call Monique. They could get together, if only for lunch. No, better to wait, he decided, and left the hotel, making his way to a strip mall four blocks away.

The pay phone was at the end of the strip mall. Last time he had used this phone, it had been outside a convenience market. The market had been replaced by a video game store that did not seem long for this world; the posters in the window were sun-faded, the store bereft of customers. Sean picked up the phone, deposited his change, and dialed a number.

He hadn't made the call in four years, but the number still worked. The code he gave worked too, and a smooth female voice asked him to please hold. He waited, outwardly calm but inside him doubt gnawed. Because while there were few rules in his line of work, there was one that always stood, unchangeable.

You did not go to them. They came to you. You waited for the call. They gave you the task you were to perform. You did not ask for an assignment.

But it had been three weeks with no call. It surprised him, that he could be so worried. After all, he'd known that the chances of them calling him again were slim. Halsey had made that clear. Sean had not realized just how badly he wanted back in, to go after these bastards. To help Jennifer Thomson. He had thought himself past such feelings. Past caring.

Apparently not.

The female voice was back on the line. She gave him an address and a time. Tomorrow morning.

It felt very good to be getting back to work.

The meeting was at a coffee shop near the airport. He didn't know if that was good or bad, that it was here instead of HQ. But Halsey was already there when he arrived, and perhaps that was a good sign, that Halsey had come rather than send some flunky.

Halsey sat in a booth near the back, an untouched glass of grapefruit juice in front of him. His eyes were paler than usual in the restaurant's fluorescent light, but otherwise Halsey appeared much the same as he had four years ago. He'd been across a mahogany desk then, making an offer of early retirement.

Except it hadn't an offer. There were no offers, only orders.

"Halsey. Been a while," Sean said as he sat.

Halsey nodded, flagged down the waitress.

Sean ordered coffee and waited for Halsey's words of welcome. There were none yet, just the frosty gaze and the face, tight-mouthed and unmoving. That wasn't surprising — Halsey had never been known for his charm. Finally Halsey said, "How is Florida?"

Sean felt his disquiet ratchet up a notch at Halsey's use of the present tense. He let none of it show, only replied, "Florida's fine."

"Good. Glad to hear it." Halsey picked up the juice glass, set it down without drinking any, said nothing more.

The bastard was going to make him say it. Fine. "You probably know why I'm here."

Silence his only reply.

"The recent unpleasantness in Los Angeles. I want to help on this one. I want back in."

The waitress walked past. Halsey waited until she was gone, then said, "You remember our procedure, don't you?"

He kept his face calm, even as he felt his disquiet turn sour, turn to something else. "Yes."

"Did you get a call from us?"

"No."

"And this means…"

Damn schoolteacher act. Sean hadn't liked it then and he liked it less now. "You do not need my services."

"Good. Next time try to remember that and save us both some trouble." Halsey glanced at his watch.

Sean wouldn't beg — not out of pride but because begging didn't work with Halsey, only favors and money did. Forget that. He'd try reason. "I want back in. Just for this mission. I can go deep and get to the people who did this. And not just the ones who set it. The top ones, the big guys. You know I can do this."

"No."

Before he could ask why, Halsey sighed, settled back a bit in his seat. "I have places to be, so I'll be brief. Your methods are not what we need now."

He did not bother to keep the anger out of his voice. "Really? And why is that?"

Halsey thrust his head forward, going into speech-making mode. "Your way takes too long. We need results, and we need them fast. The people want satellite pictures showing them where things are happening. The press has to feel like they're in on it. Things need to be quick. Which means the administration can't afford to wait. And there's the budget to consider, of course."

"I see." He did. And Sean could no longer be bothered to check his tongue. "So you'd rather let the bastards get away with it than risk making some low-level bureaucrat mad. You'll spend a hundred times what you would have paid me or Robert or Beatty on space junk that won't work when there's sunspots just so the voters can get off on the technology and some company the president's in bed with can sponge off the funding. And you're forgetting—"

"That's enough."

"—that it's people who do these things. People. All the technology in the world can't help you if you don't have someone who knows what makes these guys tick. Satellites can't get inside, only people can. And I mean people who know the territory and can blend in, not some glorified pencil pushers like you."

"I said that's enough!"

"I was out there in the field while you were riding Daddy's coat-tails into business school. You're a bean-counter, Halsey. Nothing but a fucking bean-counter."

Halsey's ears got red, his nostrils flared. "You can't talk to me that way. You know what you are? A dinosaur. Your day's over, and you know it. Almost over," he amended. "You may come in handy one day, who knows? Now go back to Florida. Don't come back unless we call."

The dull heat of anger had faded, and Sean felt calm. "Call all you like. It's done. I'm out."

The red spread from Halsey's ears, down his neck. "You are out when I say you are out, and in when I say you are in. Do you hear me?"

"Oh, I hear you." Sean got to his feet. "But I'm out for good. I owe you nothing anymore." He fished out some bills, enough for his coffee and a generous tip for the waitress. "I won't even let you pay for my coffee."

Sean turned and left. His heart was pounding with the enormity of what he had done, but he felt the mad happiness a skydiver must feel when he throws himself into the air and trusts in only luck and a flimsy billow of silk to keep him from death.

For the first time in four years, he felt alive.

Chapter Five

The speaker was a tall, well-groomed woman who had a habit of pausing, looking down at the podium, and then looking up demurely at her audience when she wanted to make a point. "And most of all, we're here to help you find your way toward." Pause. Down, up. "Closure and healing."

Jennifer sat in the next-to-last row. Gathered in the hotel meeting room was a group of twenty-five survivors from the bombing. Like all the rest, she'd gotten a call from a government representative inviting her to come. Counselors would be there. So would refreshments. They would even pay for cab fare.

So she went. Why not? It wasn't as if she had anything else to do.

It was over a month now, but Jennifer thought sometimes that time was playing tricks on her. A month should have been ample time for her to start putting it all behind her. To start feeling some of that closure they kept talking about.

She had not been able to work. *Go on, Jennifer, if you fall off the horse, you have to get back on again soon,* her mother had said, trying to be helpful. She had tried, had even arranged two interviews through a temp agency. But the moment she stepped into the lobby of the first business, though she had never worked there it was too familiar, the cubicles and the office chatter and the fluorescent lights. With every step she expected to feel the floor shake under her feet and the building rip apart. She fled the lobby, called to apologize and plead illness. The same thing happened with the second interview, and after that she could not bring herself to try again. She rarely went out, and when she did she kept to the suburbs. She could not pass by tall office buildings without looking to see if they were swaying, crumbling, ready to fall.

No matter where she went, someone recognized her. Every time she convinced herself the whispers and looks had nothing to do with her, someone removed all doubt by coming right up to her, offering sympathy, telling her how brave she was. One even asked if he could sign the cast on her arm.

Jennifer never knew what to say or how to accept their sympathy when there were others far more deserving of it. Others who were widowed or orphaned, blinded or maimed. All she had lost was her car, her job, and the use of her arm for a few weeks.

She had even less to say when they told her how brave she was. Brave? Was a rat fleeing a sinking ship brave? Was a man who threw others out of the lifeboat to drown showing courage? If she had shown any valor, it was on those levels, a medal of tinfoil instead of gold.

The woman at the podium droned on and on about finding inner strength and the courage to heal, about facing the fear. What next? Would they pass out free copies of *Chicken Soup for the Soul* and ask everyone to think about their power animal?

"And now," the woman said, "I think we should all take a break for a few minutes, and then we'll split up into groups, so you can talk, and share your experiences."

They all rose, and so did Jennifer. She walked with them toward the back of the room but she did not stop at the refreshment table. She kept walking, down the hotel hallway and out a set of glass doors. There was a patio there, and a fountain that had been turned off, and blessed night silence. She went to the edge of the patio, stared down at the glittering lights of Los Angeles. So lovely, a bright shiny lie. One would never know carnage had happened there recently.

Soon the refreshment break would be over and people would be gathering in their groups. Perhaps healing and closure would be found there, but not for her. She could not go back in that room, could not sit with people and tell them that she'd run like a rat. She could not tell someone who had lost a loved one that she was afraid to go back to work. She could not tell them that she felt so dead inside when she should have been happy to be alive.

Alive. When would she feel that way again? Would there ever be a week, a day, or an hour even that she didn't think about the bombing? When did it stop?

Perhaps it would not stop, ever.

I'm afraid. Two simple words and yet they summed up everything. The distant city lights blurred in her vision and she wept, leaning on the patio rail and swiping a sleeve across her eyes and nose.

When her weeping had tapered off a bit she heard a voice say, "Here."

Jennifer looked and saw a man. Her father's age perhaps, tall, his dark hair and beard going gray. He held out a handkerchief.

"I'll mess it up," Jennifer said. She had never used a cloth handkerchief before.

"That's the idea," the man said and smiled gently. The sticker on his blazer said he was Dr. Duncan Levinson.

"Thank you." Jennifer took the proffered handkerchief, attended to her nose and eyes. She didn't know whether to return the handkerchief. What was handkerchief etiquette?

But the man did not seem interested in the handkerchief. He stood beside Jennifer, leaned on the railing. "I don't come up here to L.A. often, but when I do I always like to look out at the lights. Man-made things usually aren't so pretty."

Jennifer had seen the man inside, knew he was one of the counselors. It was such a surprise to hear him talk about something besides the bombing; it seemed to Jennifer that she'd heard talk about nothing else this last month. Before she knew what she was saying, she blurted out, "When I was little we went up to the Planetarium, at Griffith Park, you know? And I thought the lights looked like the biggest Christmas tree in the world. And now..." She stopped.

"Now what do you see?" asked Dr. Levinson.

"I don't know. Nothing. It's like I see it but it doesn't mean anything. It's like a word in a language I don't understand. And it's not just the city, everything's that way now." She caught herself starting to cry again and bit her lip hard to keep the tears back. Crying solved nothing.

She could see through the glass doors that everyone had gone back in the meeting room. "The break's over. Do you want to go back inside?" she asked.

"Do you want to?"

"No!" She said it louder than she'd intended. "No, but go ahead, I'm fine."

"I'll stay."

"Are you sure? Don't they need you in there?"

"I think I'm needed here," he said.

Jennifer opened her mouth to protest that there were others far more deserving of Dr. Levinson's help than she would ever be, twenty-four of them in that room, then turned away. She sat down on the edge of the fountain, and caught a glimpse of her reflection in the water.

Over the last month she'd mastered the art of drying her hair and dressing without seeing more than the general outline of herself. It could have been the ripples of the water, but there was no face she recognized as her own in that reflection. She reached out to touch the reflection, and it broke apart as her fingertips touched the water's surface.

All the fear that had been building up inside her this last month could no longer be contained. "I'm so scared," she whispered.

"Of what?" Dr. Levinson knelt beside her.

"I don't know anything anymore. I don't know who I am or why or anything." Jennifer started to cry again because she wasn't making any sense, the doctor would think she was nuts. But she felt a comforting hand on her shoulder, and Dr. Levinson didn't seem to mind that she was making no sense. She cried for a while and when it seemed the flow of tears had eased, at least for a while, she blew her nose in the handkerchief. "I keep messing up your hankie," she whispered. "I'm sorry."

"It's a hankie, mess it up all you want. If you use my sleeve, then say you're sorry," he said with a smile. "Come on. Let's go to the coffee shop down in the lobby. It's too cold to stay out here much longer."

You don't have to stay, Jennifer started to say, then stopped. She couldn't do this on her own any more. "Sure. Let's go."

They sat in the leatherette booth, off in the back where they would not be disturbed. "I'm buying," said Dr. Levinson. "Get whatever you want."

"I'm not hungry."

"At least order something. You're a rag and a bone and a hank of hair."

"OK." She had never felt less like eating, but she was afraid Dr. Levinson would leave if she didn't. "I'm sorry, I just haven't been much on eating lately."

"Why so?"

"I don't know, I just can't. It's like my body says, OK that's enough to stay alive, no more for you."

"Do you have any idea why that is?"

"I'm not sure. I mean, there's nothing wrong with me. Physically, you know. I'm fine, except for the arm. But I feel cold all the time and I don't want to eat. I feel..." Jennifer swallowed hard, felt a click in her dry throat. She wanted to say it but could not. If she said it, it might become real.

The waitress brought them drinks, an iced tea for Jennifer, decaf for Dr. Levinson. Jennifer dumped a packet of sugar into her tea, stirred it longer than necessary. She took a sip, and later wondered if he had somehow slipped one of those truth serums they used in the spy movies into her tea, for she began talking and could not stop.

"It's so many things, all at once. Maybe if it was just the bombing. Or if it was something like a car wreck, where it was just me. It's just so big, all those people hurt and killed. And everywhere you go it's on the news and I think, won't I ever have one day when I'm not thinking about it? All I want is one day when something won't remind me of it, and it's stupid things that do, you know? I can't go back to work because the office buildings remind me of it. I couldn't go outside the other day because it was the winds, the Santa Anas, they were kicking up all this dust and it was like the dust in the air when the building went down. That was the worst part. I couldn't see. I couldn't breathe. Everything was spinning and getting dark and..." Jennifer took a breath. "And ever since then I haven't been able to get rid of it. The feeling that..." She stopped.

"What is it?" asked Dr. Levinson, so softly that Jennifer thought it was her own voice, in her mind.

"I feel like I've died. Maybe that's why I feel so cold and I can't eat, maybe I'm dead and I don't know it, a ghost or something. And I know that's not true. But it is in a weird way. It's like my whole life up to that day is gone. It's so far away from me and I don't know if I'll ever get to be that person again. I'm not Jennifer any more. I don't know who I am. And I don't know why."

"Why the bombing happened?"

"No, why I made it. Why me and not them? There's nothing that makes me special. I'm nobody. A monkey could do my job. All those people and they all had better reasons to make it than I did. And that picture, that damn picture, total strangers come up to me and tell me how sorry for me they are, how brave I am. I'm not brave. I didn't help anyone. I could have gone to help Mr. Danvers and I didn't, I just ran away."

Jennifer stopped. She had not meant to say so much, but there it was, all out in the open.

"You ran. You got out," the doctor said.

"I feel like you're charging me with a crime."

"I'm stating the facts. Did Mr. Danvers ask you to help?"

"No. He just told me to get out. He told me to take the stairs, not the elevator."

"Did you shove people out of the way to get to the stairs? Trample old ladies?"

"Stop it. I know what you're trying to do."

"What's that?"

"Make me feel better about it."

He shook his head. "No, Jennifer, only you can make yourself feel better about it. If you want to." He reached out and took Jennifer's hand in his. "The past is not where you find answers. The reason things happened is because they happened, and the reason why is simply because."

"So it's all for nothing?"

"I didn't say that. What I mean is that you had no control over events. You made your choices, and they were good choices. Perhaps there could have been better choices. Or maybe they would have only been different. Maybe you are what you say you are, nothing. But that's not what matters. What matters is what you do now. What you become. How you earn the life you've been given."

"But people deserve it more than I do."

"Look around you, Jennifer. Who has exactly what they deserve? Life's not a movie where the bad guy gets his just desserts in the last reel. It simply is. The past is past. The question you need to be asking yourself is not what you've done, or even what you didn't do. But what you *will* do."

Jennifer was silent for a moment, then said, "Do I have to go save the world or something? Find the cure for cancer?"

"What did Mr. Danvers say to you again, there in the building?"

She thought hard. For some reason it seemed important to repeat exactly what he'd said. "He asked if I was OK. He said he was going to see if he could find anyone else from our department. He said ... he said, 'You go on. Get out of the building as fast as you can.' And then I went for the elevators, I wasn't thinking, and he said, 'No, take the stairs, keep going.'"

"A dozen words, thirty? Just some words, but those words probably saved your life, didn't they?"

Jennifer nodded.

"A few words can make all the difference sometimes. We're so fixed on the grand gesture that we forget it's the small things that matter most. And sometimes you don't even know how much they matter until later. Your old life may be over, but your new one is starting." Dr. Levinson closed his eyes, said softly, "'What falls away is always. And is near. I wake to sleep, and take my waking slow. I learn by going where I have to go.'"

What falls away is always. And is near. "That's lovely."

"It's from a poem by Theodore Roethke. A colleague of mine says that poetry is the only antidepressant that works for everyone, and no side effects to worry about." He fell silent for a moment. "Would you do something for me, Jennifer?"

"Yes." She was too confused to know what was going to happen next, exactly, but knew that Dr. Levinson had given her the key.

"Call me if you ever need me. Promise me that."

"I will."

He smiled. "Would you at least let me see you eat?"

"What?" Jennifer looked down at the table. She hadn't seen the waitress arrive with the food. Nor could she remember what she'd ordered. Apparently it had been pancakes, with bacon and eggs sunny-side up. She began eating — the food was a bit cold but quite tasty — and waited for her body to reject the food. It did not.

"One last thing," Dr. Levinson said as he signaled the waitress to bring the check. "Do this for me. Learn by going where you have to go. And tell me what you find when you get there. Please?"

"Yes. I'll do that."

It was late, past midnight when Jennifer arrived back at her apartment. There was a message on her answering machine. She pushed *Play* and recognized the throaty voice of Amber LaSalle. The reporters had given up, but Amber LaSalle of Ellis and Associates Representation was still persistent. Not a hint of impatience in her voice as she asked Jennifer to call at her earliest convenience.

Jennifer did not go to sleep or retreat to the bathtub, but instead pulled the duvet off the bed, wrapped it around her shoulders like a shawl, and stepped out onto her apartment's tiny balcony. She gazed out over the quiet suburbs, thinking.

What falls away is always. And is near.

No, she wasn't Jennifer any more. Not that Jennifer. That life was over, done with. She had to find another life.

I learn by going where I have to go. "I can't stay here anymore."

The city was no longer hers. The lights that had so entranced her with their magic when she was a child were now just bits of electricity, nothing more. This apartment, the furniture, the books and movies, the stuffed animals, everything. Not hers, any more. Someone else's. Some other Jennifer. That girl in the picture, the crying girl, that was not her. Once, in a high school science class, she had seen a snake shed its skin, and what had been so lovely and glossy black on the snake's flesh was a crumpled bit of nothing, fragile as candy floss. An old life sloughed away. Nothing there that she wanted. Or needed.

She watched the sun come up, and thought about what she needed. To leave. To go where she had to go. Where that might be, she wasn't sure, yet. And how to get there? The break had to be clean. All at once, like a snake shedding its skin. She needed help. As the sun began to warm the boxy apartment buildings and people began to stir, she knew who could help her.

She went inside, tossed the duvet on the bed, and made coffee. As it brewed she unearthed the list of messages Cindy had written down. Jennifer found Amber LaSalle's number with no trouble at all.

She waited until 9 a.m., and then picked up the phone, dialed. After three rings a receptionist's voice welcomed her to Ellis and Associates Representation.

Chapter Six

It had been easy for Sean to be flippant to Halsey, to act as if it was no great matter to leave it all behind. Easy, because he neither liked nor respected Halsey. But Sean could not pretend to himself that it had not been a heavy blow. For more than half his life he had been in their service. He had forsworn the life of an ordinary working man and all its attendant miseries and joys, and the contempt he often professed for those who led such simple lives could not hide the sense of loss he sometimes felt for having missed the commonplace pleasures of wife and children and home. He had given them the full benefit of his mind and skills, and they had thrown him aside like a broken tool.

No. The tool was still useful, but they no longer wanted it.

The euphoria he'd felt when he walked out on Halsey faded by the time he reached his hotel. He packed quickly, meaning to be on his way almost immediately. But as he closed the duffel bag he stood for a moment, fingertips running idly over the worn canvas, and the full weight of it fell on him. He was out. Finished. It was over. He had spied and betrayed trust and killed and served his country well, and it was all for nothing.

The weight of it pressed down on his shoulders. If he let it, the weight would crush him and he would crawl back to Florida. Emptiness would eat at him until he drowned himself in a bottle or in the Gulf of Mexico. Then it truly would have been for nothing.

Sean slammed his fist into the wall. Once, twice, three times, so fast an observer would have been hard pressed to see it. The walls were cheap, his hands hard and his strength considerable; he stood gazing calmly at a dent in the wall and a dust of white powder on his hand. He flexed the fingers; they were not broken. Beyond that the pain was irrelevant. Indeed, he hardly felt it. Both pain and despair had been replaced by a calm — almost cold — feeling of purpose.

He was never one to linger on the past. Not on its triumphs and not on its mistakes. He had closed the door, and there was no opening it again, not even if he had wanted to. What mattered now was bringing those who had hurt Jennifer Thomson to justice. What Sean needed was counsel, and he knew where he could find it.

A quick consultation with a phone book, a taxi ride. He signed forms, paid cash, and minutes later was driving in a rented car. Heading north. As he left Washington behind, it began to rain.

Robert lived in a medium-size town on Maine's rocky coast. Somewhere around New Hampshire, the rain had turned to snow, not much more than a flurry, and Sean thought of Christmas. That was when he'd last heard from Robert, who had sent him a card. Unusual, that, and even more so was the message inscribed below the card's generic happy holidays message, in Robert's elegant yet very readable writing. *I've been thinking about the old days a great deal recently. If you have the time, why not tear yourself free from the sunshine state and visit? We'll eat lobster and talk.*

Guilt was not an emotion he felt often — they broke you of that one early on — but he felt it now for not coming up here, for just sending Robert a note that said yes, they'd do that, some time. Because Robert had taken Sean under his wing when Sean was still young and green, had taught Sean a thousand things. Robert knew so much, yet he never passed on his knowledge in a patronizing manner. He knew about far more than weapons and intelligence and how to extract information from uncooperative sources. There had been countless times when they played the waiting game that was so much of their work, and Robert talked. His voice had lost its Czech accent save for a certain cadence to his sentences. His talk: a running discourse on everything from a rain of frogs he'd seen in the Australian outback to a bar he'd once visited where a caged parrot spoke in Ernest Hemingway's voice. There was money in Robert's background and education as well, but none of those things had made Robert soft. On the contrary, Robert was the best shot he knew, and had once, down in Central America when their transport broke down and they had to slog through the jungles on foot to escape guerrillas, executed three prisoners, one of them a woman, so the prisoners would not slow them down.

And though Robert had been retired longer than Sean, Robert had more connections to agents active and retired, and might have an idea of where Sean could start.

He arrived late in the morning, the day after his meeting with Halsey. Robert's house, surrounded by a wrought-iron fence, was on a secluded street near the coast. Ivy, winter-brown and skeletal, lightly dusted with snow, covered the fence and the entry gate, blocking Sean's view of the house. He stepped out of the car, feeling the cold breeze cut through his clothes; if he was going to stay, he would need a warmer jacket. The ocean's tang carried on the breeze, a deeper, colder smell than the Gulf of Mexico. To the right of the gate was a small intercom box. He pressed the button. No answer. He pressed again. No reply but the distant sound of the sea, the snow ticking softly against the brown ivy.

He could stay and wait, but he did not want this to feel like a stakeout. So he drove into town and stopped at a bookstore to while away a few hours.

The store was one of the chains, large and bright with a coffee bar over by the periodicals. He sat down with a cappuccino and watched the shoppers with deceptive idleness. His instincts hummed into life a second before his eyes registered what they saw. There. Heading over to the reference books. He could always spot someone who had been in his line of work; they had an air of alertness that they never lost.

He finished his cappuccino, then got up and walked casually to the reference section. Robert stood with his back turned to Sean, holding a book and turning the pages slowly; it was a dictionary of Shakespeare quotations. So strange to see Robert here in this suburban stronghold. He was several yards away, about to speak, when Robert, without looking round, chuckled. "I thought I'd be hearing from you."

"Tell me, what did you do on your summer vacation?"

"Watched a lot of movies. You?"

"Caught up on my reading."

They were at Robert's house, sitting by the living room hearth where a fire blazed cheerfully. The wood burning in the hearth was cedar and its sweet smell perfumed the room. Sean glanced around the room; it was everything he would have expected. Bookshelves lined the walls, filled with handsome leather-bound editions and battered, read-to-death paperbacks. The hardwood floor shone. Odd knickknacks that Robert had picked up in his many travels were scattered about the room. He thought that he was looking at Robert's fortress, his kingdom of one.

Only one thing would have appeared strange to a casual observer. There were no photographs of friends or family. That did not surprise Sean. He did not have any in his house either.

"How did you know it was me?" he asked.

"You have a slight limp that becomes worse in cold weather," Robert replied. "The right knee. It was the unpleasantness in Afghanistan, yes?"

"Right on the money. As always."

Robert smiled, settled into his chair. "I also heard about your little *tête-à-tête* with Halsey."

"News travels fast."

"I keep my ear to the ground. You didn't think what you said to him would stay quiet, did you? Not what I would have advised."

Sean felt his ears burn. He hadn't expected Robert to take him to task for that. "You know as well as I do that Halsey's nothing but a numbers man. All he knows are dollars and cents, not what it's like out in the field."

"Did I say I disagreed? On the contrary, you nailed him precisely. *Zatraceny' blbec.* Him, not you. All I said was that it wasn't what I would have suggested. They're very jumpy right now and not taking kindly to criticism from any quarter. Still," Robert shrugged, sipped his coffee. "what's done is done. And I have to say that burning your bridges must agree with you. You haven't aged a day."

"You're looking well yourself." But he didn't mean it, because while he might not have aged, Robert certainly had. His hair and beard were almost entirely gray and his broad shoulders slumped a bit. There was an extra caution when he walked, as if he were favoring some part of his body, but what was wrong was not immediately clear.

"Thank you." Sean could tell that Robert knew he was lying. He waited for Robert to say more, but nothing on that subject was forthcoming.

They talked the afternoon away, about the old days mostly. They kept the conversation on lighthearted things, for pleasant times were few in their line of work, and those moments were all the more cherished. The time in Minnesota, Sean and Hamilton going after a neo-Nazi group. The group's sniper missed he and Hamilton, hit a six-point buck instead. They'd taken out the sniper and had a fine venison dinner that night. Or the time he and Robert and Beatty were taking some R&R in Bangkok. Beatty had decided to celebrate the end of the mission by going on a bender and had disappeared for two days; Sean and Robert had finally found Beatty in a dive, passed out cold. They dragged him out while on the tables stark naked women did innovative things with ping-pong balls and bananas, and had only an hour to sober him up before a debriefing with the top brass. Or when Robert had "persuaded" the security guard at the Louvre to let him stay after closing, and had wandered the galleries until morning.

Robert made dinner, the long-promised lobster, and they ate and talked some more, but even so he could not help noticing that Robert ate sparingly. Sean did justice to his share; it was no obligation. Robert was an excellent cook, and his own cooking was adequate at best.

After dinner, with fresh wood on the fire and a glass of brandy for each of them, Robert finally said, "The reason you came here wasn't simply my Christmas invitation."

Because it was a statement and not a question, he could answer freely. "No. I need your help." He paused, trying to think of how to say it right when he had not fully articulated his feelings even to himself. "The reason I wanted back in is because of what happened in Los Angeles a few weeks ago. To be honest, not what happened, but..." He took out his wallet. The picture was tucked away, folded to the size of a credit card. He unfolded the picture, cut from an issue of *Time* magazine. He smoothed it out, sat looking at the image for a moment. He knew it by heart now. The not-blonde not-brown hair covered with dust and matted with drying blood. The unnatural bend in the left arm. What looked like a high school class ring on the third finger of her right hand. And most of all the look on her face; fear and disbelief that she was alive and anger and sorrow all mingled. Pain, inside and out. He thought, as he always did when he looked at the picture: *I'll help you. I'll make the pain stop.*

He handed the picture to Robert, who nodded. Sean said, "When I was watching all this happen on TV, it wasn't shocking to me. We don't believe that it can't happen here. But when I saw that poor girl come out of the building and knew she just had seconds if she was going to make it at all ... I can't explain it even now. I wanted to know that she was all right. I wanted to help her. I cared. When was the last time I cared?

"These last few years, I think I stopped caring about anything. If I let myself feel it would just be missing the work, and people like you and Beatty and Hamilton. But now I care, and it's driving me crazy. I want to help this girl. I find myself wondering how she's doing. Is she all right? Is she getting over this? I want to do something for her."

"You sound like a man in love."

Sean suppressed a laugh. "No, it's nothing like that. It's like someone did this to my sister or my best friend's wife. That's all."

"And that's why you wanted back in. To get the people who did this, yes?" Robert said, swirling his brandy in its snifter gently.

"Yes. And being out doesn't change it. I want this, and I will have it."

"You do know it will be much more difficult."

"I can deal with that. All I need is where to start. I'll take it from there."

"How do you propose to make an arrest if you work from the outside?"

"I don't plan on making an arrest."

"Assassination?"

"No." Sean thought for a moment and the idea that had been forming in his mind during his drive north crystallized fully. He smiled. "I'll bring him to her," he said, gesturing to the picture of Jennifer Thomson. "I'll let her do the honors."

Robert looked startled, eyes wide over the brandy snifter. Sean could not recall the last time he had seen Robert taken by surprise. "I don't know whether to praise your sense of honor or doubt your sanity." Robert shook his head, sat in thought for a moment.

Sean waited. It was a crazy idea, he knew. But he also knew that he could pull it off. He thought of bringing the creep who had done this to Jennifer, thought of putting the gun in her hand, and a surprisingly sweet smile graced his face.

Robert watched him, and smiled back. "It's utter lunacy. It's foolhardy and romantic and the last thing I would have expected from you. It's also completely against the law, and disloyal to our former employers. Therefore," he sighed, took a large sip of brandy. "I have no choice but to help you. It won't be much, but it should be enough. One thing I should tell you first. You'll have to watch your back."

"You think they'd send someone to take me out?" Sean hadn't considered that.

"If you go back to Florida, most likely not. They'll think they can get you back if they wave a tasty enough prize in front of you. But if you strike out on your own, no matter what your intentions are, they'll see you as a rogue. If they can't control you, how can they trust you?"

"I see." He felt he was standing at the midway point on a rickety bridge, danger ahead and behind. Was he putting Robert in danger, simply by being here? "Don't tell me any more. Please. I probably should go now, I don't want you to get in any trouble."

Robert shook his head. "I wouldn't help you if I didn't think it was worth a little risk. Besides." He stared fixedly at his brandy for a moment, downed it quickly in a most uncharacteristic way. "I'm on borrowed time as it is."

He knew, then. All he needed were the specifics. "What is it?"

"Liver cancer," Robert replied, calmly.

He felt as he had in his hotel room, that a weight was pushing down on him. "How long?"

"To be honest, I don't know. They start chemotherapy next week."

"I'm sorry." There was nothing else to say. He had been a witness to and bringer of death for longer than he cared to admit, but that had been part of his job. He had accepted that the moment he accepted their invitation. Why did Robert's news fall on him so heavily? Had he lived with unnatural death so long that a natural end seemed wrong? "Is there anything I can do?"

"No. Thank you, but no. I'm glad you came here. I've been thinking about the old days a lot."

"You said that in your card."

Robert nodded. "Time brings perspective to things. Tell me, do you see what you're doing for this young lady," he gestured to the picture of Jennifer Thomson, "as redemption?"

Sean frowned. "I don't understand."

"Making up for the sins of the past."

"No, I understand what you're asking. But redemption for what? We did our work. We did a damn good job of it. We were the good guys."

"Were we?" Robert sighed, poured himself another brandy. "I wish I could be as certain as you are. I can't help wondering if what we did was of any real consequence. Alliances change and power shifts. The game is the same. Even the players are the same. They've just shifted their positions around the board. Now I lie awake at night and think of all the things I've done and seen, and I cannot shake the feeling that we were used. You, I, all of us. We were used and thrown away when our usefulness was done, and it made no difference in the end.

"I don't know if I'll see next winter, and that frightens me. But what makes me even more afraid is the feeling that it was all for nothing. I've bloodied my hands and I don't know what I could do that's enough to wash the blood away. Nothing, probably."

Sean watched as Robert turned and stared into the fire. For a moment he felt dreadfully certain that Robert was right, that they had sold their souls for nothing, had been puppets used in a bloody and meaningless show. He could feel the knowledge roll across his mind like a thunderstorm rolling in across the ocean. Then he shoved it away. If he let it in he would never be strong enough to do what he had to.

"Robert," he said, "you don't mean that. You're going through a bad time. You can't start thinking this way. It'll drag you down if you do. Please." He changed his tone, made his voice lighter, jocular. "Come on, let's talk about the good times. Did I ever tell you about when I was in El Salvador? Nearly got myself killed trying to jury-rig a TV antenna because I didn't want to miss *Twin Peaks* if you can believe that."

To his relief, Robert turned his gaze away from the fire, and smiled. "Go on, tell me."

Sean was nowhere near the cook Robert was, but his one specialty was a good corned beef hash. Robert's dark mood of the night before was gone, and after they finished eating, Robert pushed the plates aside and addressed the problem with his usual aplomb.

"So," Robert said. "Tell me what you know, I'll tell you what I know, and we'll see what we get. Agreed?"

"Agreed." Sean paused, collected his thoughts for a moment. "I'm going off what I've read in the papers, so I wouldn't bet my life on it, but all the sources say the same thing, so I don't think we're too far from the real story. It looks like our friends put plastic explosive around structural support pillars in the parking garage." He set a candlestick on the table. "And then they directed the charge by arranging some heavy things — probably trashcans filled with water or something easy like that — around the pillars." He reached over to the cabinet, grabbed a handful of napkin rings, and arranged them around the candlestick in a circle. "That way they have enough weight to direct the charge and your average employee won't notice or think anything of it if he does. They did enough to take down one half of the building. Whether they knew the other half would come down, I don't know."

"Why do you suppose they didn't take down the entire building?"

"Too much time, too many materials to get. Too much risk of getting caught." They both gazed at the candlestick and napkin rings, then Sean swept it all aside into a meaningless jumble. "The official line is that it's the Middle East. I don't buy it for a minute. They're more of a smash-and-grab type. Fly a plane into the building, use a truck bomb, something like that," he said. "This took time. They needed to get materials in and get everything set up without making people suspicious."

"Perhaps it was a mole?"

"Someone got on the maintenance staff, I'm thinking. Set up a false identity, get inside. Who would notice? The people who work there wouldn't pay attention. Security's too busy with the front door. The mole pulls a disappearing act, sets the charge off remotely, and if he's never found they'll just say that nice Mr. Janitor was in the wrong part of the building at the wrong time and got vaporized." He picked up a napkin ring, spun it on one finger like an oversize wedding band. "So that, as far as I can tell, is how. Now the only question is who."

"Who indeed," Robert said. He poured himself more coffee. "And you're right. It's not the Mid-East. This one's home-grown."

"Are you sure? Most of those groups are too mom-and-pop for something like this. Shooting abortion doctors or burning a synagogue is the worst they get. Plus, even if they do pull something off, like McVeigh, they get caught in what was it? Hours?"

"In the past, yes. But there's been no chatter from overseas, not a bit. And there's been new stateside groups coming together since we retired. Most, as you say, strictly amateur. But one or two are smart and stealthy. A bad combination."

"So why aren't the Bureau or an ops team going after them?"

"Because the only ones in greater denial than the ordinary citizens are the people at the top. It doesn't reflect well on Homeland Security if it's found to be fellow Americans who did this. It's safer politically to blame the Arabs. Even if they didn't do it."

"Bombing Afghanistan into the Stone Age won't hurt anyone's re-election chances."

"Precisely."

Sean sighed, stared down into the black coffee as though it were a scrying mirror. Politics. That was all it was. He wondered if it had always been that way. He hadn't thought so, back in the early days. Had the world changed or had he? "Well," he said, "At least I don't have to worry about a passport. Can you tell me more?"

"I'll tell you what I know," Robert replied.

Robert had said he was welcome to stay another night, but he declined. For all Robert's assurances, Sean did not want to put him at risk for any trouble. But he mentioned none of this, and instead lightheartedly said, "I should hit the road. Miles to go before I sleep and all that. Thank you," he said, shaking Robert's hand. "And good luck."

"Good luck to you as well. And thank you for coming by."

He turned and was halfway down the walk when Robert said, "Sean, wait." They stood in the late-winter early-spring gloom, a few errant snowflakes landing on their hair and shoulders.

"I have to ask, much as I don't want to," Robert said. "Are you sure your girl, this Jennifer ... Are you sure she wants this?"

Sean was nonplused. Barring a saint or two — and he seriously doubted saints existed, God knew he had never met one — who *wouldn't* want such an opportunity for vengeance? "Yes, as sure as I can be."

Robert looked him over, a careful scrutiny that Sean had not felt in years. "I hope so. Because all day I've been feeling uneasy about this."

"What's wrong with the plan? I can change things, it's not carved in stone."

Robert shook his head. "No, the plan itself is good. It's the whole idea. Something does not feel right about it." Robert hesitated, then said, "I'm afraid for you."

For the first time since he'd left Washington Sean felt the sting of doubt. Because Robert had always gotten hunches about things. Many had come to naught, and Robert was the first to admit this. But enough of Robert's hunches had borne fruit to give him pause. He remembered the mission in Tel Aviv, when Robert, acting on one of his hunches, had refused to go back to the safe house. He and Robert had gone to ground elsewhere; Hauser and O'Brien had gone to the safe house. They found Hauser two days later with three bullets in his head. O'Brien they never found at all.

He waited for Robert to say, *It's probably nothing.*

Robert did not.

But not even for Robert could he let himself be dissuaded. "I'll be careful," he said. "I promise."

Robert nodded. "Fair enough."

"And I promise that when it's over, I'll come back here. We'll take a trip to the Riviera and play baccarat. Like in the movies." Thinking: *I don't know if I'll see you again. If this is the last time we meet, let's end it all on a good note.*

"Only if you buy the tickets. And I insist on first class," Robert said with a smile. "Be seeing you."

"Be seeing you," he replied, turned and left. As he drove away he looked back once at the house behind its ivy-shrouded gate. Though the heat was on in the car he felt cold, for it seemed he was no longer looking at a fortress. He was looking at a prison.

Chapter Seven

When Katie Granville arrived at the Sunshine Coast Realty office, the client was already there waiting for her. It was the first time Katie had seen the client; until now she had been just a voice on the telephone. Katie put little trust in the first impressions of a voice, and even less when that voice came through so much distance. Katie never felt like she had a true connection with a client until they met face-to-face.

She rummaged on the passenger seat for her glasses, papers, and purse, all the while keeping a covert eye on the client. Mid-twenties. Hair that shade Katie's mother had always called dishwater blonde. The client would have been pretty had she put on a few pounds, but it seemed to Katie that all the Americans she'd met were either too thin or too fat.

It was strange, Katie thought as she got out of her car and walked toward the client. There had been more and more Americans moving to what they considered the fifty-first state over the last few years, but most of them stayed close to the big cities like Vancouver, as if they were afraid to stray too far into foreign territory. As if they could not feel safe without knowing that their home country was only a quick hop over the border. Not that Katie's territory was that far from the States. But it was unusual that this client had specifically asked not to live in a big city, but for some place "small, but not too small. Do you know what I mean?"

Katie thought she did.

"Hi," Katie said. "I'm Katie Granville."

The client smiled and extended her right hand. "Jennifer Thomson."

Learn by going where you have to go. And where might that be? Possibilities were suggested, examined, rejected. How these decisions are made no one really knows, any more than the gambler knows which card to draw. But finally a name came to her, nothing so specific as a town; a place she had only been to once before, years ago. And yet the name had come to mind, bringing with it images that were partly memories, mostly distant recollections of travel magazines and TV programs. British Columbia, Canada.

As good a place to find refuge as any.

Jennifer bit back an apology; Katie had shushed her after the first one. "Don't worry about it," Katie said breezily, and despite everything Jennifer had to smile. *Aboot.* "No one ever finds the right house first thing." *Hoose.*

Jennifer tried not to think about all the people she'd known who had found the house of their dreams on the very first outing, or on a casual drive-by. She knew she shouldn't be nervous, but it was difficult. She was not sure she was doing the right thing, and neither was anyone else.

"Canada?" Amber LaSalle had asked, incredulity in her voice.

"Oh Jennifer, it's so far away." That was from her mother, who then suggested Jennifer move to Fresno for a while, until she got back on her feet. Even now, Jennifer shuddered at the thought. Things were bad enough in Glendale. How much worse would it be in Fresno, with none of a small town's fabled charm and all of its prying and provincialism? Especially now.

Even Cindy, the one person she thought would support her, hadn't come through. "It seems like a real big step, Jen. You sure you're ready?"

No, I'm not sure I'm ready. Not sure at all. But if I wait until I'm sure, that could be weeks. Months, maybe. And I can't wait that long.

No, she couldn't wait. Because any fragile peace she might have found in Los Angeles had been smashed when she had hired Amber LaSalle to represent her. Just as it had taken only minutes for the bombing to wreck her life, in the course of a morning's news report she'd gone from the haloed icon of that March day to a scavenger hungry for whatever spoils she could get. She got the first phone call minutes after the news hit the Web. A woman's voice snarling, "Hey, bitch. I hope you enjoy your blood money." After a few more calls like it she let the machine answer the phone. Each night she sat, drank too much Chardonnay, and listened to the messages, every single one. Listened with a taste in her mouth not of wine but something like ashes, the bitterness of shame and the sharp tang of resentment. She never answered but sometimes she wanted to say *I'm sorry,* and sometimes *Leave me alone,* and sometimes *All I wanted was to have a nice day at work and not die. What is wrong with that?*

When she pushed the *Delete* button for the last time each evening, her resolve to escape Los Angeles and start anew only became stronger.

Escape. Somewhere pretty, somewhere quiet. Somewhere safe. "Sanctuary," she said aloud.

"Pardon?" asked Katie Granville. There were in a restaurant, having coffee and pie. On the table between them was a list of possible homes, half a dozen crossed off the list already and Jennifer no closer to a decision than when she'd gotten off the plane in Vancouver.

Nothing, Jennifer started to say. Oh, what the hell. Maybe it would help. "Sanctuary. Someplace safe. That's what I'm looking for."

Katie nodded. She took a quick glance at her list, then she smiled. Pure pleasure in that smile, none of a salesperson's calculation. "I think I have just what you're looking for."

In Katie Granville's blue sedan again, heading north. "It's a bit further away from the city," Katie said, but Jennifer was unconcerned. The drive to Vancouver might daunt a Canadian, but it was nothing to a veteran of Los Angeles' freeways. It was mid-afternoon, and as the sun descended it burnished the trees with a golden glow, like the warmth left by a lover's kiss. They drove north, then west, the sea ahead of them and the mountains behind them, the evergreens thinning as they neared the coast. The cool tang of the ocean filled the car. At the side of the road, a sign read *Welcome to Haven Cove.*

Past a few isolated houses, and then they were in the town. "This is the main commercial row," Katie said, gesturing around her. Jennifer rolled down her window and leaned out into the sunshine and salty breeze, looking at the businesses. Restaurants. Boating and fishing supplies. Bed-and-breakfast hotels. St. Anastasia Catholic church. Salto Family Mining Supply. The Starlight Theater, showing the latest Johnny Depp film.

Katie turned onto a road leading away from the coast, up a gentle grade, and pointed to the left and down. "That's the marina," she said. "Still quite a few fishermen in Haven Cove, thought not as many as in my parents' day. It's the safest marina on the Sunshine Coast. A south-facing beach, you see. Keeps the boats sheltered from storms. The old-timers call it Port Hidey-Hole."

Jennifer smiled. Haven Cove was well-named indeed. The peninsula curved protectively around the marina, seeming to hold the boats tenderly, the way someone would hold a tiny kitten. She was a bit sorry when they made another turn and the marina was lost to her sight. But not sorry for long.

"Ah, here we are," Katie said.

She did not know who had owned 314 Douglas before her. But they had loved it, and well. That was clear the moment Jennifer set foot on the walkway, red brick in a herringbone pattern. The house was cream-colored, with shutters and trim and door in dark green. Window boxes, although empty, nonetheless brightened the house with their cedar hue. The lawn was slightly overgrown but this only enhanced the appeal, gave the grass the look of a plush carpet. Rosebushes, stems hanging heavy with seashell-pink and lipstick-red blooms, flanked the doorway like sentries.

Katie unlocked the door and the two of them stepped inside. She followed discreetly, letting Jennifer discover the house for herself, only offering comments when she saw a questioning look in Jennifer's eyes.

Jennifer was never able to describe, exactly, what she felt when she entered the house. It was not *deja vu* — she had no sensation that she had been here before. The feeling was not familiarity but comfort. The living room: a wine-colored carpet and the walls done in a marble pattern, creamy white with gentle threads of rose and gray, the fireplace in gray riverstone. The dining room: country blue accents and a plate rail that simply begged for knickknacks and bric-a-brac. The kitchen: more country blue except for the stove, a gleaming, stainless-steel beast that Jennifer had seen on cooking shows. A bathroom: not much counter space but a large clawfoot bathtub, snowy porcelain on the inside and deep cobalt blue on the outside, the walls painted blue with bright tropical fish stenciled in. A bedroom at the back: its windows looking out to the west, where the sun glittered on the ocean and slanted in the window, giving the room its golden light. Another room: too small for a bedroom but big enough to be a study or a sewing room or whatever she wanted it to be. A tiny backyard, big enough for a hammock.

Not a big house. A cottage. The sort of place that was called "charming" in the real estate listings. But size did not matter. Jennifer wandered the rooms, walked through them in a loop. She was not searching. She was drinking in the feel of the house, its comfort, the feel of an embrace from an old friend. Or a new one.

A little more than a month later and Jennifer, wearing sweatpants and a T-shirt, sat on the floor, a cup of coffee in one hand and a half-eaten banana in the other, trying to summon the will to unpack. In spite of her resolve to start afresh it seemed she'd brought quite a bit from Los Angeles. And what had never seemed completely real through all the days of packing and signing papers was now very real indeed. She was an expatriate. An innocent abroad. It certainly sounded romantic, but in reality she was surrounded by boxes and furniture placed helter-skelter, there was nothing in the refrigerator but a six-pack of Coke and a jar of applesauce, and she couldn't go get more food because she wasn't entirely certain where the grocery store was. She supposed she could knock on one of the neighbors' doors and ask. She peered out the windows. The house on the left looked as if the owners had gone to work for the day. The house on the right seemed occupied — she could see a light in the kitchen and make out the faint sounds of the TV, Elmer Fudd declaring that he would kill the wabbit with his spear and magic helmet. Jennifer smiled in spite of herself, almost lured by the sound of beloved cartoons and the desire for companionship, but stopped. That feeling of being a stranger was on her, as was the sensation of being on-stage, caught in the spotlight, that had dogged her since the bombing. She didn't want to be introduced as the survivor from the Los Angeles bombing last March. She wanted to make friends the way normal people did it. Commiserate over the quality of the tomatoes at the produce section. Say hello when bringing the garbage cans out to the front. That sort of thing. Knock on the door and ask where the grocery store was.

The doorbell's ring took matters out of her hands. She put down her banana and coffee, opened the door.

"Hi neighbor!" sang out a voice. The woman standing on the doorstep was maybe a few years older than Jennifer. Her reddish-brown hair was frizzy in the damp coastal breeze. She had a baby balanced on her left hip, a plate with an angel food cake on it in her right hand, and another child standing by her side, hanging onto the skirt of her denim jumper.

Jennifer wondered how she'd managed to ring the doorbell with her hands so full. "Hi," she said, feeling at a loss for what else to say. "Here, you've got your hands full," she said and took the cake. "Thank you."

"Just a little welcoming treat," the woman said. "When I moved in, I had so much unpacking I couldn't find my way to the stove for a week. I'm Suzanne." She held out her hand and Jennifer shook it.

"I'm Jennifer." She realized there was nowhere to ask people to sit, nor was she sure where all the dishes had gotten to. Great, she couldn't even offer her new neighbor some coffee. Off to a wonderful start. "I'm sorry about the mess."

Suzanne waved dismissively, adjusted the baby. "You should see my place. These two look sweet but leave them alone for five minutes and boy! It'd be even worse if I had them 24 hours."

Jennifer was puzzled. Was this some strange custody arrangement? But Suzanne must have seen her look; she smiled. "Oh, they're not mine. Bill — that's my husband — and I don't have any. Yet." Suzanne paused for a moment, as if thinking of something. "This one," she patted the older child's head, "Is Hannah. Say hello, Hannah."

Hannah, who had not stopped staring around Jennifer's house and its disarray with her huge dark eyes, made a noise that sounded vaguely like a greeting. Jennifer smiled and Suzanne was unfazed. "Shy girl. And this is David," she said, jiggling the baby on her hip as he spouted an infant's doggerel. "David's not up to hello yet."

"I'll take ba-ba-goo as a hello," Jennifer said.

"They're Mrs. Reisman's, from three doors down. She went down to Vancouver to see her mother and left these two with me. Have you met the Reismans yet?"

"I haven't met much of anyone. I just got here a couple days ago. Which reminds me, can you tell me where the grocery store is? I've been living off what I get at the little quick mart."

"Oh, don't do that. You get anything that's perishable at that place and you're asking for trouble. Look, why don't you come over for dinner tonight? Bill and I can tell you what you need to know. How's that sound?"

For a moment Jennifer could not reply. No doubt Suzanne thought it shyness, but it was need, and loneliness, and the desire for companionship uncomplicated by the past. For a friend to whom she could just be Jennifer, the next-door neighbor. Who never had to know about that other woman, the one that had been left behind in Los Angeles. "I'd love it."

"Great!" Suzanne said with a grin, and after a few more pleasantries she was gone in a swirl of denim skirt and cluckings to David and Hannah. Jennifer caught glimpses of Suzanne throughout the day, pushing Hannah on a swing set in her small backyard, handing the children over to a woman in a silver minivan later that afternoon.

That night she joined Suzanne and Bill for dinner. Bill was a big man with a deep voice and a rumbling laugh, Santa Claus' great-great-great-grandson, and between his wry comments and Suzanne's chatter, Jennifer felt she had a pretty good handle on life in Haven Cove, or at least on her new neighbors. And now she knew where the grocery store was.

Spaghetti and garlic bread and a decent red wine, and Jennifer felt herself relax for the first time in months. Over chocolate-chip ice cream, Bill asked her what brought her to Haven Cove.

"A change of scene," she replied with a smile. It sounded so simple, and it was. Who knew that it could be this easy to fashion a new life out of the wreckage of the old? She smiled and said her thanks for dinner. Her sleep that night was dreamless, and she slumbered not knowing that she had brought far more burdens with her than the boxes scattered through her house, and not realizing that it would take more to start a new life than a change of scene.

Chapter Eight

Wait, Robert had counseled. *Make time work for you.*

Sean knew how to wait. It was not something he enjoyed, but one of the first things he'd learned was that waiting could make all the difference between success and failure. Or between life and death. He returned to Florida and resumed his old routine. Ran, watched movies, read the occasional book. Did nothing to arouse suspicion, for he knew they were watching him. The signs were all there. The gray sedan he saw sometimes while on his morning runs, which slowed ever so slightly as it passed him. The soft click he heard when he picked up the phone. A faint thumbprint on the envelope of his credit card bill.

In a way, he did not mind. Welcomed it, in fact. It brought his instincts back into sharper focus. Anxious as he was to start on the mission, there was no hurry. He and Robert had talked about it, and they both knew that a cold trail suited his purposes better than a warm one. "They'll still be watching their backs," Robert said. "There's nothing official linking them, but they know better than to let down their guard. You'd do better to wait a while. You stand a better chance of working your way in."

So he waited. It was hard, because there was nothing concrete to tell him when it was time. No dossier from his superiors, no phone call. He could not even risk a letter or phone call to Robert, though if the penalty would have fallen on his head alone he might have tried it. But he could not put Robert at any more risk, especially now.

He did not wait for things to become safe. There was no such thing as safety. There was only an acceptable level of danger. His prey would never let down their guard completely, and his former employers would never stop watching him. All he could hope for was that he would have enough

---

74

time and wiliness to throw pursuit off his trail and lose himself in the world of his prey.

Sean bided his time, kept up appearances, and made arrangements quietly. Erased the hard drive of his computer and destroyed all correspondence, no matter how old, taking special precautions to leave no trace of communications with Robert or Monique. Bought timers for his lights and television. Set up a bank account and arranged for his utilities to be paid directly out of it. Went shopping, paid cash, slipped the supplies he needed for the job in with ordinary household items. Got the money and papers he needed from his hiding places.

There came a morning in early September, when the Florida air hung thick with humidity. Robert had once told him about a rainstorm down in Brazil, when the water came down so heavily that people actually suffocated. Sean hadn't believed it, but on some Florida mornings he conceded such a thing might happen.

He woke, not drifting up from sleep but all at once, as he always did. It was time. There was nothing to tell him this. He simply knew. *Go. Now.* It didn't take him long to get ready; his preparations were well-made. He showered, dressed, called a cab, gathered up his two travel bags. He looked like a man headed for the airport, on business or perhaps to visit his aged mother. Stopped at a diner on the edge of town, perused a newspaper's classified ads, made a few calls from the pay phone. Sean found a man who wanted to sell a van, wanted cash fast, no questions asked and as little paperwork as possible. An unsavory type, no doubt, but he would be dealing with a lot of unsavory types from now on.

Once in the van, Sean drove north. He did not look back once, not when he left the county that had been his home for four years, not when he crossed the border into Georgia. He knew that no matter how things ended, he would never see the house in Florida again. He would miss the DVD collection in the months ahead, but beyond that he had no regrets whatsoever.

Because he was doing the right thing. He was sure of it. Though he was not superstitious, he felt he'd been given a sign. At the diner he'd found the latest issue of *People* magazine. On the cover, a photo of the bombed building in Los Angeles. *Six Months Later...* the headline read. On page 32, a *Where are they now?* feature. Two photos of Jennifer Thomson. The first was *the* photo, the icon. The second a blurred, grainy picture, obviously taken by an amateur with a cell phone, Jennifer walking with her head down and holding a cardboard moving box. The caption read, *Jennifer Thomson's narrow escape from the building captured the attention of the entire nation. She received considerable criticism for selling the rights to her story, which is currently being optioned for a book and a movie for television. Ms. Thomson did not return phone calls for this article. Her agent, Amber LaSalle of Ellis and Associates Representation, said that Ms. Thomson has moved to British Columbia, Canada.*

He took the magazine from the diner, and now it lay on the passenger seat of the van. British Columbia. It would make bringing the perpetrator to her a bit more difficult, but he could not blame her. He'd been to British Columbia twice, both times for pleasure rather than business. Once for R&R after a particularly dangerous mission; once for a weekend with Monique, when they'd both happened to be in Vancouver. He'd always wanted to go back there. So cool and green, so quiet. Peaceful. A good place to start over. For that was what she'd done, taken what she could and started over.

Go on, Jennifer, Sean thought as the road north unrolled before him. *Lick your wounds, and don't worry. I'll make sure you get justice.*

Chapter Nine

Mining was a business of rock and dirt, Jennifer mused, but you wouldn't have known it from the offices of Salto Family Mining Supply. The lobby was glass bricks and brushed chrome, pale gray cubicles, and a steel-blue carpet that had recently been steam-cleaned; a faint smell of cleaning solvent still hung in the air. Other than the name on the door, the only hints at the company's nature were the catalogs and brochures, arranged in an attractive fan shape on the lobby table, and a few trade publications. While she waited, she picked up one of the trades. *Ornamental and Miscellaneous Metal Fabricator.* Now that was some light reading.

Jennifer hadn't expected the owner, Alex Salto, to look the way he did. A whiff of cologne preceded him, and he stood in the lobby, smiling, running a hand casually through his thick black hair. "You must be Jennifer. How nice to see you." His dark eyes had a dancing light in them; he seemed to be contemplating some secret but pleasing prospect. His teeth were a little too white, a movie star's smile, but perhaps that was just the contrast between his smile and his black mustache.

She stood, held out her hand. "Yes, I'm Jennifer. It's good to meet you." They shook hands; his hand was not soft but smooth, uncallused; she let go before he did.

"Care for some coffee?" he asked as they sat down in his office. His leather upholstered chair creaked as he settled into it.

"No, thanks."

"Tea? Water?"

"No, thank you very much."

Alex shrugged, gave her a grin. When he spoke, his voice was as smooth as his hands. "Well then, let me tell you about our little enterprise. I say little, but actually we're the second largest mining supply company on the Sunshine Coast. We provide supplies for copper mining mostly. Do you have any copper jewelry? No, I can tell it's not your color. Anyway, as you can see." He gestured around the room with a casual wave, and she noticed that his nails were manicured. "This is just the business end of things. You won't be getting dirty here. The job's mostly files, phones, setting up client meetings, that sort of thing. Can you do all that?"

"Yes, I can. It's all down there in the resumé."

"Ah." He picked up the resumé from his desk and glanced at it. She had the feeling this was the first time he'd given it a serious look. "What's your typing speed?"

"Seventy-five words per minute."

"Fast fingers. I like that."

She didn't quite know what to make of that, so she said nothing, gave an uncertain smile. He smiled back, offered her his hand again. "Well, Jennifer, welcome to Salto Family. You can start Monday. Sound good to you?"

"Sure," she said.

Technically, she didn't have to take the job. She supposed she didn't have to work at all, at least not for a while. Amber LaSalle had done her work well, and there had been enough money for the move, to lease the house at 314 Douglas, to get some new furniture and odds and ends. There had been enough for a car, one of the new VW beetles. Her brother Jim, an accountant, had helped her invest the rest.

But once the unpacking was done and the new furniture and dishes purchased she found herself sitting in her house with an entire day and evening ahead of her and nothing to fill the time.

She felt like kicking herself. She had, at least for a while, what most people would kill for — the time and money to pursue whatever she wanted. Except there was nothing she could think of to want. She knew what she *should* do. Write a novel. Learn to paint. Take up needlework. Read the great works of literature, for real this time instead of the Cliffs Notes. Sign up for guitar lessons. Start puttering around in the kitchen, see if she couldn't whip up something on that big stove besides TV dinners. Go to the craft store and buy things like dried flowers and ribbons and glitter, make cute decorations for her new lodgings. Anything.

But she knew how to do none of these things. It didn't occur to her that she could learn. Set adrift, surrounded by flotsam, she grabbed at the buoy that was most familiar and the one that seemed most likely to keep her afloat, and climbed aboard as an admin for Salto Family Mining Supply.

"Salto Mining? Oh, they've been around since my grandma's time," said Suzanne, as she took the foil off a plate of brownies and put the plate on the dining room table. She was watching Hannah and David Reisman again, as well as the Joplin twins from two blocks over. "Around for donkey's years, as Bill would say. I'm sure Alex will give you the whole song and dance if he hasn't already."

"What song and dance is that?" asked Jennifer as Suzanne poured milk for the children and coffee for herself and Jennifer.

"Oh, the usual. Grandfather immigrated to Canada and built the business out of nothing." Suzanne shrugged, raised her voice slightly over the children's clamoring for brownies and polite *Thank you Mrs.*

Delacroixs. "You're lucky. Jobs are kind of tight up here now. When do you start?"

Monday, she went in and Alex introduced her to the rest of the staff. Brandy, who handled billing, Tracy in accounting, Cammie and Betty who handled the orders, Darren and Phil the sales reps. Alex took her to lunch that first day and as Suzanne had predicted, gave her the song and dance. Told her all about his grandfather, Renaldo, who emigrated from Portugal with nothing much beyond the clothes on his back and became a self-made millionaire. Told her about his second home, up in the woods, he held a New Year's Eve party there every year and she should be sure to come, it would be a blast. Noticed that she was from the States, told her about his last trip to Seattle, how bad the traffic was getting. Later, she realized he hadn't asked her a single thing about herself.

Adrift, she sought the cold comfort of routine. Each morning she woke, showered, drank coffee, drove to work. She filed, made coffee, ordered supplies, and mailed out letters. She typed up press releases, interpreting Alex's illegible scrawl as best she could, smiling at the compliments he paid her, politely refusing his suggestion that they go out for a drink some time. She brought her lunch three days a week and ate out with the office girls the other two days. They ate pasta or Chinese or salads, and all they knew about her was what she told them. After work she drove home, made her simple dinner, soup or a sandwich or a microwave entrée. She drank wine and watched TV. Not the news, never that; not the U.S. news with its wars and rumors of war, not the Canadian news which still seemed to her a broadcast from a foreign country. She watched sitcoms and *Jeopardy*. Sometimes she rented movies, romantic comedies the details of which she could not recall later beyond boy-wins-girl-back and happily-ever-after. Sometimes in spite of three or four glasses of wine she lay awake for an hour or more before dozing off, but when she did sleep it was deeply and without dreams.

On weekends she slept late. Mowed her tiny lawn, swept the walk, pulled weeds. Asked Suzanne's advice about the coming winter, and what clothes she would need. She shopped for those clothes, boots and scarves and wool pants, did it feeling like she was buying presents for someone else. She could not truly believe that she would have cold and snow this winter, for her time in Haven Cove still felt unreal, like a vacation. It did not feel like home. She had not made it her home yet.

Sometimes she woke, lay staring at the ceiling. Her bedroom was the one room her predecessors had not worked their decorative will on. Nor had she, for she could not think of what she wanted the room to become. So it remained a white box, and some mornings, as she looked up at the ceiling, its tiny cracks and textures already familiar, she felt unable to move, as if she lay under something far heavier than a duvet. There was no fear, no sensation of being crushed or trapped. Just immobility, a strangely free sensation, for if she could not move, that also meant she didn't have to.

She'd been at work for a month, was reviewing the morning's schedule when Amber LaSalle called. "Jennifer. How are you?"

"Fine, Amber."

"Keeping busy? Not too busy, I hope?"

"No, not too bad."

"Oh, that's good to hear. Listen, I was wondering if you would be coming back to California for the holidays. Have a nice, warm Christmas."

Though Amber was always polite and did her work well, Jennifer couldn't quite make up her mind how she felt about Amber. Jennifer was never comfortable with the deal she had made and consequently never comfortable with Amber either. "I could make it down there for a few days. Let me put in the vacation request."

"Let me know the details as soon as you can. I've got a ghostwriter lined up for the book we discussed. He's terrific."

"Thanks, Amber. I have to go, I'll call you in a few days to set things up. Bye." Jennifer hung up quickly. She never could talk to Amber for very long, and it wasn't Amber's fault. Amber's voice always brought Jennifer back to her visit to the bombed building, when the air was still heavy with the scent of destruction, to the billboard with its pictures of the dead, and Madeline Danvers asking her how she liked being famous.

There was no point in thinking about any of it now. It was the past. She busied herself with the schedule, and when Alex sauntered in she asked him about having a few days off around Christmas.

"No problem. Business is always slow around here at that time anyway. Talk it over with Brandy or Tracy. Just make sure you're back here for New Year's. Don't want to miss the big party, eh?"

"I'll be back for it."

"Great." He grinned at her. "Come on, Jenny. Smile. It gives your face something to do."

She rang Suzanne's doorbell after dinner, the travel iron she'd borrowed in hand. Suzanne greeted her, took the iron, invited her in. Jennifer declined, said she had to get back to her house, needed to make a phone call.

Suzanne looked Jennifer up and down for a moment. "Jen? Are you OK? I mean, you just look kind of..." She didn't finish.

Kind of...what? Jennifer didn't know. How could she? There was nothing wrong. Nothing at all. "Must be a little tired," she replied with a smile. "Everything's fine." She even believed it.

Chapter Ten

The geography of America might be, as the song said, amber waves of grain and purple mountain majesties, but Sean thought of American life as the surface of the ocean. Static yet always in motion. Sometimes peaceful and glittering in the sunlight; sometimes tempestuous and roiled by storms. But even on its calmest days, deceptive — for he knew about the undertide, the current of discontent and anger below the surface. It was always there, sometimes weak, sometimes strong. The current slackened, went deeper after Oklahoma City. In the wake of the attacks on the World Trade Center and the Pentagon, of the flag-waving and newfound patriotism, that undercurrent was all but forgotten. But it was always lying beneath the surface, biding its time, keeping its danger hidden.

He had the sensation, as he drove north, that he was diving into deep water, that as the weather grew cooler he was actually going deeper, searching for the undercurrent. Seeking out the darkness.

North. Georgia, Tennessee, West Virginia, Ohio, Pennsylvania.

Sean attended gun shows, perusing the wares and taking the handouts. Sat in the middle rows at church hall meetings about avoiding federal taxes. Stood in the crowds at auctions of bankrupt farms, listening not to the auctioneer's gabble but to the disconsolate mutterings of those around him. He eased his way into conversations, a remarkably simple task, for so many of the discontented simply wanted to talk and he gave them that chance, offered an easy smile and a receptive ear. He joined men outside to smoke (he hated having to take up the habit again, but it was a necessary evil) and make conversation. He commiserated about lost jobs, easily spinning lies about his own disenfranchisement at the hands of the government. Countless hours he spent in diners, over bad coffee and good chicken dinners, nodding and making proper noises of sympathy as they told him of family farms lost forever, the garbage kids were being taught in the schools, the tax audit, the gun laws, the thousand grievances real and imagined, trivial and true. He offered a light for cigarettes, paid his fair share of the diner meals, plugged quarters into jukeboxes.

They talked, and most of the time talk was all they had to offer. Some few made noise about teaching those in the government a lesson. But he had learned years ago to distinguish between mere venting and a dangerous level of discontent. He listened, as he had to, for he had no strong leads. All he knew was what Robert had been able to tell him: The group responsible for the Los Angeles bombing was probably based in the north Midwest, most likely Michigan or Minnesota. The members — or at least the leadership — were men of intelligence, able to not only pull off something like Los Angeles, but to keep from getting caught.

More than that Robert did not know. The intelligence team assigned to domestic terrorism had its funding cut drastically several years back, its forces routed to foreign assignments. What was left of the domestic force had been sawed off at the knees, discredited by a lack of results and a botched assignment in Arizona. They were now little more than a token force; even if he had still been inside, Sean doubted they could have offered him much help.

So he navigated the currents on his own, frequenting the places the discontented were likely to gather. He went to libraries and Internet cafés, searching out the gun nuts and the hate groups, lurking in chat rooms and reading online newsletters. Time passed, and he did not find anyone willing to claim responsibility for Los Angeles, or even to hint at approval. This was annoying but not discouraging; he had enough faith in Robert's intel and his own instincts to know he was on the right track. It was going to take time, that was all. He had funds and time in abundance, and he had dedication. His loyalty to his superiors was forsworn, given instead to a woman he had never met, whose picture and plight still had power to touch him. Every morning he looked at the pictures, the one of Jennifer in the arms of the firefighter and the one of her with her head down and moving boxes in hand, preparing to flee. Looked at the pictures and felt resolve strong within him. Time, and watchfulness, and casting the net out. They would bring him results, eventually. Given enough time, they always did.

Indiana.

Strange that he should find a promising lead there. Indiana, the place of Sean's birth, a place he had fled thirty years ago, had never thought to return to. He had felt no omen crossing the border from Illinois. It was merely another state on his itinerary. It was where he found Henry Connolly.

Henry Connolly, then. Henry to his mother, "that no-good slacker" to his stepfather, Hank to his friends and colleagues, Boomer to his drinking buddies. Henry "Boomer" Connolly, red hair and freckles, Tom Sawyer crossed with Alfred E. Newman and Charles Starkweather, "what, me worry" grin and cold green eyes. Eyes that, if you were to look into them, could give you the owner's history entire. First five years of his life spent on the family farm in Iowa, until his father was killed when his tractor rolled over on him, and the farm was repossessed. Until his mother, the light in her eyes dimmed by her husband's death and extinguished forever by the loss of the farm that had been in her family for four generations, went to Michigan to live with relatives, taking Henry and Henry's two sisters with her. A year of a cousin's charity, the cousin's resentment of the Connollys growing with every mouthful of food the family consumed and every noise the children made in the formerly quiet house. Another year, this one of happiness, when Alice Connolly wed Warren Smith and there was a house of their own and good times again. A happiness that ended more or less forever when the tides of commerce shifted and Warren Smith lost his job at the plant, watched his bosses sell the company overseas, drifted along with the jobs that he could and took his anger out on his stepchildren.

Henry had the seed of bitterness and resentment well-planted, nurtured by his stepfather's rage. He drifted through school, performing adequately at best in his studies but more than making up for this — in his view, at least — on the gun range he visited after school and on the weekends. There he was a stellar student. After high school he went into construction, the flexibility of his schedule allowing him to join shooters' clubs and frequent the region's many gun shows, join a local militia. For a time he considered joining the military, but his lackluster grades would not give him anything more than a grunt's position. He wanted more. Deserved more, he was a white American, God damn it, and don't anyone forget it. Two years ago, Henry had cast aside his thoughts of the military as a career, becoming a soldier in a very different kind of war.

It was the day after a big military surplus show. Henry was in good spirits, having had a fine time at the show. He'd enjoyed the wares and demonstrations, bought the goods he'd been sent for, and found some new toys for himself. He'd even made a few friends. One of them was here in a booth at the Bang Bang Bar, sitting across from Henry. Sam was a nice guy, around the age of Henry's stepfather but not a bastard like Warren Smith. Seemed happy to have someone to talk to. Was suitably impressed by Henry's knowledge of firearms. Eyes lit up like a Christmas tree when Henry suggested Sam accompany him to the range sometime if he was up in Wisconsin, shoot off this bad-ass Spas 12 Henry'd gotten on the black market some years back.

"A Spas 12," Sam said. "That's a nice one." He finished his beer. "You want another one?"

"I can't let you keep buyin', man."

Sam shrugged. "Don't worry about it. This show's the first fun I've had in ages. Come on, another round."

"OK, if you're buyin'." It would be Henry's fifth beer. He failed to notice that Sam had only just now finished his first.

As they started in on the next round, Sam sighed and said, "It's bad enough you can't get stuff like the Spas 12 any more. I'm down to a .38 and an old shotgun. My Daddy, God rest his soul, left me a lot of stuff but I've had to sell most of it. Sold his broom-handled Mauser last year and that near broke my heart."

"A broom-handled Mauser? Holy God, I hope you got good money for it."

Sam shook his head, sadly. "I did but...you know, it's almost not worth it. I felt like I was giving up a part of my Daddy's memory, know what I'm saying? No man should have to do that."

Henry nodded.

"But still, you have to do what you have to do. Especially nowadays. I've been out of work ever since I got banged up on the job. Fucking government says I'm not bad off enough for disability and I'm out of medical insurance so I can't get a doctor to tell them I *am* bad off without it costing me an arm and a leg. And then last year, tax time... Oh, I'm sorry Hank, I shouldn't be putting all this on you."

Henry spread his palms out in commiseration. "Hey, we're in this together." He downed the beer, started in on another one. He was getting pretty buzzed, but what the hell. It had been a good weekend, he was feeling pretty righteous. And he felt sorry for Sam. He'd heard plenty of stories like Sam's and they never failed to burn him up. He took another deep swallow of beer. *Seriously* buzzed now! He'd have to sleep it off a bit before he drove back up north with his haul from the show. "In it together man, and we can show the G where to stick it, like we did in —"

Henry stopped, conscious even through his alcohol haze that he'd said too much. He glanced at Sam quickly, to see his reaction. It was not that he suspected Sam of anything. Hell, he liked him, liked him a lot. Still...

But Sam was not even looking his way. He had a palmful of change in his hand and was poking through it. "You have a quarter, Hank? I'm fresh out and I wanted one for the jukebox."

Henry sighed inwardly, relieved. "Sure thing. Listen, you got the beers, I'll get the tunes."

Sam smiled. "Thanks, Hank. Thanks a lot."

An hour later. Henry Connolly walked out of the bar. He was still weaving from the beer but that didn't bother him. He'd driven further when he was drunker than this. As Henry left the bar, he did not notice that Sam was no longer in the booth. He did not hear the back door of the bar open and close quietly, did not see Sam slip around to the side parking lot. He did not see Sam's shoulders straighten or his gait change to a predator's stealthy tread; did not see Sam take a small bottle and a cloth handkerchief from his pocket. In fact, Henry had nothing more on his mind than wondering if the convenience store was still open so he could buy some cigarettes. He was reaching into his pocket for his keys when an arm locked around his throat, a hand clamped a wad of cloth over his mouth and nose. He instinctively drew in breath to yell, inhaled an acrid chemical stink, and everything went dark.

A plastic tarp covered the van's floor. Three feet in front of Sean, Connolly sat in a wooden chair, completely bound to the chair by duct tape that shone a dull silver in the light of the camping lantern. Only Connolly's head was free to move, and his fingers, which dangled off the ends of the chair's armrests. He waited for Connolly to come out of his ether doze, and when Connolly began to make feeble motions toward consciousness, Sean took his gun out of its holster, and checked his back pocket to make sure the cable cutters were at the ready.

Nothing in his world was exact, nothing was totally predictable. He'd seen men live through gunshots to the head, seen explosives go off long before they should, long after they should, and everywhere in between. That was just the technology. People were even less predictable. He had seen people sacrifice their lives for persons they didn't even know, seen people endure torture and death for a lost cause. Not all the unpredictability was noble. Once he had seen a woman blow up herself — and the infant in her arms — with a grenade rather than submit to capture. No, after all these years, people still had the capacity to surprise him.

One thing was predictable, though. Everyone had a breaking point.

He wondered idly when Connolly's point would come.

Even as Sean thought this, Connolly's eyes fluttered open; he stared for a moment, tried to move. Connolly's mouth was taped shut, but Sean understood Connolly's grunts as clearly as if they had been words. First, confusion. *Where am I? What the hell is this?* Then a sort of querulous protest. *Let me go! This isn't funny, man!* A brief flare of anger — *Son of a bitch, let me go!* — and then, what Sean was waiting for. Fear. Connolly sitting there silent, sweating, eyes wide. Not showing whites all the way around the irises, but wide enough for now.

"Hello, Henry."

A questioning grunt that might have been *Sam?* was the reply.

"You have something I want, Henry. Any idea what that could be? No? I think you're lying. You've got a pretty good idea of what I want. You knew when you made that little slip of the tongue back in the bar."

Anyone, Sean thought, could just pummel the information out of Connolly. No, the key to a truly professional interrogation, he'd always believed, was in making it last. And not just the physical part. You could wear down plenty by words alone. By making them wait for when you would stop talking and start in on other things.

"It's a well-known fact that alcohol, consumed in sufficient quantities, makes people careless. It takes away that bit of your mind that tells you to keep your mouth shut. What I'm saying in a roundabout way is that you fucked up, Henry. Big time.

"Now, you can choose Plan A or Plan B. Plan A is, I ask questions, and you tell me what I want to know. Plan B, I ask questions, you don't answer, and I *make* you tell me what I want to know." He pointed the gun at Connolly, watched Connolly turn white and shake his head. "You make the call. It's up to you, though I must say, if it's Plan B," Sean smiled. "That's fine by me."

He stood. "I'm going to take the tape off. And if you scream, or if you make me think you're going to scream..." He placed the gun's muzzle against the center of Connolly's forehead. "Understand?"

Connolly's nod was faint — as if he feared his movement might set the gun off — but it was there.

He took the tape off Connolly's mouth. Connolly took in a shuddering breath. "Please, Sam, whoever you are. I don't know anything, I really don't."

He said nothing, let Connolly dig himself in a little deeper.

Connolly must have sensed that protestations of ignorance weren't going to help. "Please let me go. I have a wife and a, uh, little girl."

"What are their names? Where's your ring?" Sean held up Connolly's wallet. The plastic insert contained two photos, both of Connolly and his farmboy buddies looking thoroughly shitfaced. "Where's the picture of the family?" He tossed the wallet to the floor. "I don't like bullshit. Not at all. You'd do better to spare me your lies and we can get this unpleasantness over with."

Connolly lost it a bit. "Who are you, anyway? What are you, some kind of Fed? You can't keep me here like this! I know my rights! You got nothing on me. I want a lawyer and —"

Sean felt a wave of disgust ripple along his skin. Connolly was still yammering about lawyers and constitutional rights and suing somebody. Cold fire flared up in Sean's brain; he switched the gun to his left hand and slammed his right fist into Connolly's stomach.

Connolly's words cut off as if he'd been shot. All the color drained out of his face, his eyes rolled back and his mouth turned into a tragedy-mask grimace as he fought to get his breath back. He finally managed to drag in a deep breath, and as he expelled it he also vomited up those beers that had gotten him in trouble.

Sean waited for Connolly to get some control back, watching calmly as some of the moldy-cheese color left Connolly's face. When he judged that Connolly was able to listen, Sean grabbed him by the hair and turned Connolly's face up toward his own. "You disgust me. Spear carrier for your little groups. Making your plots and bitching about the G. Playing the big man, so proud of what you helped happen in Los Angeles, and when you're caught, what do you do? Beg for your constitutional rights. If you stood up for what you believed in, I could respect that. But you're just a nothing.

"And now listen to me, *nothing*. I'm not John Law. You have no rights with me. You can't cut any deals. All you can do is tell me what I want to know."

Connolly jerked his head away, defiance glaring in his eyes. Was that bravery or stupidity, or some combination? Likely the latter. "And what if I don't talk? If you kill me, you'll never find out what you want to know."

Sean laughed. Connolly, who clearly considered this his trump card, looked ill and dismayed. Sean grinned at Connolly, who started trying to squirm back in his chair. "Oh, look, it's trying to think! Here, Henry, let me put things in perspective for you."

He sealed Connolly's mouth with the tape again and holstered the gun. He stepped behind Connolly, out of his prisoner's field of vision. Almost before Connolly knew it, Sean took the cable cutters from his back pocket, slipped the blades around Connolly's right pinkie finger at the joint. There was a brittle snap, like shears through a thick rose cane, and Connolly's finger fell to the tarp.

Connolly howled behind the tape, twisted in his bonds. His remaining fingers wiggled frantically. Blood from the severed digit pattered onto the tarp.

Sean stepped into Connolly's view once more. "Now," he said with a smile that promised many things, none of them good. "Let's talk."

Forty-five minutes and three fingers later, Sean had what he wanted.

"Any more to add on that subject? Or should I go for a thumb next?"

"That's all I know, I swear." Connolly groaned. "Believe me."

He turned Connolly's face back up towards his again, looked into his eyes. "I believe you," he said quietly.

92

Connolly's head sagged down onto his chest, which hitched with the beginning of sobs. "Can't you give me something for my hands? It really hurts."

"Do you expect me to feel sorry for you? You helped kill 361 people, and for what?"

"I didn't blow the place up! All I did was —"

"Help with the plans and the coordination. Do your bit. You're a good soldier, Henry." He walked behind Connolly, took the gun from his holster and the suppresser from his bag, began screwing the suppresser onto the barrel. "But you've been cooperative. I thank you. Jennifer thanks you, too."

"Who?"

"Never mind." He didn't want to discuss Jennifer with Connolly.

"Just let me go. I won't tell anyone about you. I won't talk, I swear."

"I know," Sean said, and shot Connolly in the back of the head. Connolly's fingers — the ones that were left — twitched a bit, then the body sagged lifelessly in its bonds.

He gazed pensively at Connolly's corpse for a moment or two. An observer might have thought he was regretting his actions of the past hour. He was thinking that the worst part about being outside was that he could not simply make a phone call and have someone take care of the mess. He'd have to clean it up himself.

But that was no problem. After all, he'd done it before.

Chapter Eleven

Jennifer did not realize how much she had been dreading Christmas until her plane touched down in Fresno. It had been raining in Vancouver; in Fresno it was sunny and mild, but the sunlight seemed unreal. After the rich ocean and pine scent of Haven Cove the air in Fresno felt stale, used up. Her nerve endings seemed to stretch out beyond her skin; she caught herself flinching when people moved close to her.

Out of the sunlight and into the relative dimness of the airport terminal. When she got to baggage claim she craned her neck, searching through the crowds, and then saw her mother waving at her frantically. "Hey Mom," she said and put her arms around her mother, relieved that she felt genuine gladness to see her again.

"Jen, Jen." Her mother broke the embrace, held Jennifer at arm's length, looking her over. "It's good to see you, honey. God, I've missed you."

"Same here," Jennifer said, and meant it.

She stayed in the spare room of her mother and stepfather's house. Once Cindy and Jim had left home, the folks had sold the old place and moved to a smaller, two-bedroom house. Which meant the spare room held no memories for her. Neutral carpet, off-white walls, a framed print of a Monet painting on the wall. A twin bed, the mattress stiff, the nap on the chenille bedspread still fresh. Only the guest towels stacked at the foot of the bed were familiar. Pink and green, bought for the bathroom back at the old house, their texture rough now, the hem at the ends partly unraveled. The towels were the only thing that made this room different from a hotel.

The first night was good. Jim and his family were in town, staying at a hotel nearby, and that night all of them went to dinner at a steakhouse. Jennifer told them about Canada, peppering her talk with amusing anecdotes from work and waxing enthusiastic about the local scenery. At times it seemed that her chatter was feverish, that she was using it to keep from talking about something else. But after all, they did want to know about Haven Cove and her new life there. Why not tell them?

She soon wished that she had rationed her talk more carefully. The next day she had little to say. But plenty to hear. From her mother. *Oh Jen, I do wish you hadn't moved so far away. I worry about you. Oh Jen, I do wish you'd call and write more often. Oh Jen, I do wish you'd eat more, you're still so thin. Oh Jen, when do you think you're going to meet some nice young man and have a family? I'm not getting any younger, you know, and I'd just love another grandchild.*

Plenty to hear from brother Jim the CPA as well. *So Jen, how much did you end up getting? That include royalties? So Jen, how you managing the taxes up there in Canada? I hear the taxes are really a nightmare, or is that different with you being an American and all? You are still an American? Hey, just kidding.*

They meant well, they loved her, they wanted only the best for her, and God, they drove her *insane.*

Heedless of the gas bill, she cranked up the heat on the outdoor pool and swam tirelessly. When she lay on the inflatable chaise lounge with her sunglasses on she could pretend to be asleep and avoid her mother's chatter. Even better was swimming, diving underwater so she didn't have to hear anything from the outside world, could disappear into a world of smooth concrete walls and crystal blue water.

She told her mother not to worry, everything was fine. And above all, smiled. Smiled through the days leading up to Christmas, smiled through the church service at First Episcopalian, smiled through the gift-giving and the holiday dinner: ham and mashed potatoes and gingerbread. Smiled. It was something she was getting very good at.

Christmas evening, and Cindy called. "Jen, it's your sister," her mother said and handed Jennifer the phone.

She took the cordless into the spare bedroom, where the suitcase was already mostly packed. Tomorrow she was bound for Los Angeles for two days, to see Amber LaSalle, and then back up to Haven Cove. Not soon enough.

"Hey, Cindy Lou Who. Merry Christmas, little sister," Jennifer said.

"The fleas on my dog," Cindy said and they both laughed. When Cindy was little, she'd misheard the song "Feliz Navidad" as "the fleas on my dog" and it still amused them. "I wish I could be there."

Jennifer was a moment replying. The smile she'd worn since she'd arrived in Fresno vanished, and she nearly sighed with relief as the muscles of her face relaxed. "I wish you could be here too." Her voice was quieter than it had been the last few days.

"How's Mom? Hovering?"

"Practically forcing food down my throat."

"At least you had her good ham. Remember how my turkey was underdone last year? This year I burnt it."

"The Thomson sisters aren't known for their cooking. At least the turkeys balance out. Maybe next year."

"Maybe."

They talked about gifts. What clothes their mother had given them, and what they would exchange those clothes for. Cindy's twins liked the boxes more than the toys this year. Cindy's mother-in-law had done the Christmas dinner dishes and now Cindy probably wouldn't find most of her utensils for another month.

Jennifer said again: "I wish you could be here, Cin."

She meant it. Because only Cindy really understood. Only Cindy knew how it had been, at least those first few days. Jennifer had told her mother and Jim and all the others that she didn't want to talk about it, but even if she had wanted to, what could she say? Where would she even start? *I walked down the hall to make some copies and on my way back, ka-boom! Half the building was gone, just like that! Oh, and I saw this one guy get electrocuted, and a bunch of other people all got turned into hamburger by broken glass. This nice guy who helped me down the stairs? Got his neck broken. And when I did get out, the whole building was toppling down. A real frying-pan-into-the-fire situation, don't you think? So this nice fireman saves me. And here's the kicker — everyone's acting like I'm some kind of hero when I didn't do shit. One minute I'm on this pedestal, my picture on every magazine cover,* on fucking T-shirts, *and the next minute I'm like a leper or something. I sell my story so I can get some money and go somewhere I can get some peace and quiet and I get phone calls from people calling me a fame whore. No, wait, here's the real kicker. I'm in this pretty town that I like a lot and I've got a sweet neighbor but none of it's real to me. Most of the time nothing's real to me and when it is, like this Christmas, it drives me nuts. And God I don't know why. I really don't.*

"Jen, you there?" Cindy must have asked her something.

"Sorry, I spaced there for a moment."

"I asked if you were OK."

She said the first thing she could think of. "I'm fine, Cin. I'm fine."

Saying *I'm fine* was like the smiling. She was getting very good at it.

Four days later, back in Haven Cove. Sitting at her desk at Salto Family, playing solitaire on the computer. 10:30 a.m. and the phones hadn't rung once. Tomorrow night was New Year's Eve, and it seemed the entire mining industry, at least in British Columbia, had closed up shop and said *See you next year!*

New Year's Eve. It rang a chord in her memory, but she was so distracted by Christmas she couldn't think of what it meant. She still felt fidgety, a hangover not from last night's wine but from those days in Los Angeles, telling her story several times over to the ghostwriter. Felt on edge because the peace she had expected to find on her return had not materialized. In sunny California she had longed for the coolness of British Columbia. In the crowded cities she had thought of the quaint homes and the pines. Now that she was back it all seemed fake, like Main Street at Disneyland. She walked down the street and half expected Mickey and Donald to show up.

"Oh there's no place like home for the holidays," sang out a voice, and Alex Salto was there. His tie had a picture of the Grinch on it. "Glad you're back."

"Glad to be back."

"You haven't forgotten about the party tomorrow night? Up at my mountain place? I think the girls are getting a limo, why don't you catch a ride with them?"

A party. That's what she'd forgotten. She was prepared to beg off, then thought, no, she wouldn't. If it was fun, well it had been a hell of a long time since she'd had any fun. She was entitled to it. And if it wasn't fun, that's why God invented cabs.

"So, Jenny, you in?" Alex asked.

"I'm all over it," she replied with a smile. Yes, getting very good at it.

Chapter Twelve

The old-timers were saying it was going to be a cold winter, and Tess Perkins believed them. Indian summer had decided to give Wisconsin a miss this year; the days were gray, uncomfortably chilly and damp, yet not quite cold enough for snow. People walked with heads down, leaning into the wind, ducking their faces away from the drizzle. Already Tess was weary of gray skies and brown mud. She lugged a space heater into the manager's office of the Lakeview Terrace apartments and filled the room with ferns and African violets that flourished in the near-tropical heat. Her enormous gray tabby, Godzilla, would not leave this warm room except to eat or use the litter box, and she could not blame him.

Tess sat at the desk, looking over the books, wondering when the cable TV man would grace her with his presence. The cable had gone out yesterday, and Tess wanted to get it back up and running as soon as possible. She had inherited the Lakeview Terrace apartments from her father. In his day, it had been home to teachers and young couples on their way up. Now that the business center of Du Lac had shifted and the economy had gone sluggish, her renters were older people, divorced men, or people drifting from job to job and town to town in search of something they could not find. But while other managers would have yielded to this downturn and let the apartments slide into disrepair, Tess refused. To not fight the good fight was an insult to her father's memory. So she worked tirelessly to keep the walkways swept, flowerbeds full, repairs attended to, and complaints addressed. Her dedication paid off, for while her tenants were often transient, and many did not stay for more than a year, they left their apartments clean and kept themselves well-behaved. The police were seldom called to the Lakeview Terrace.

Outside, a gray van pulled up, and a few minutes later a man entered the office. "Ah," he said, his pleasure in the office's warmth evident. "I haven't felt this cozy in ages."

"Are you here for the cable TV?" she asked.

He smiled, shook his head. "No, I wanted to rent an apartment. I saw the sign, do you have places available?"

"Oh, I'm sorry. I saw your van and thought ... My mistake. I'm Tess Perkins."

"Sam Lewis. No problem with the mistaken identity."

Godzilla, lolling on the desk, raised his head and regarded the new arrival with sullen yellow eyes. While Tess gathered her papers, Sam reached out and scratched the cat behind the ears. Godzilla, usually a standoffish cat, closed his eyes and purred.

Tess laughed. "Well, never mind references, Godzilla seems to like you well enough. Any preferences on which floor? You can choose from one, two, or three."

"Floor doesn't matter." He cast his eyes down, as if shy or embarrassed to be making this request. "A corner place would be nice, if you have it. I have trouble sleeping sometimes and a corner place is usually less noisy."

"Well, the neighbors here are pretty quiet, but we do have a corner unit on the second floor. Like to see it?"

Sam gave her such a nice, sweet smile that Tess caught herself wondering if her friend Allison would like to meet him. She filed that thought away in her mind for later, and took him on a brief tour of the apartments. Not that there was a whole lot to see, but it was the thought that counted. He was recently divorced, he said. He and his wife had split after he was laid off, and now he was picking up work where he could. A cousin had word of jobs in a nearby town, "and here I am," he said with a shrug. It was a familiar enough story for Tess; the same thing had happened too often in her own family for her to be judgmental.

She showed him the corner unit. One bedroom with a Murphy bed that folded down out of the wall. One bathroom, tile on the floors instead of linoleum. A kitchen, a front room. Very clean. The windows faced out the back of the apartments, overlooking a cow pasture. Tess herself preferred to see lights and people outside her window; she was at times a lonely person, and seeing signs of human life soothed her. But cows seemed to suit the new tenant just fine. Within half an hour the papers were signed, money changed hands, and he drove his gray van around to the parking slot for 233. Didn't have much, he said. She gave him the name of a local place where he could find decent furniture at low prices. He thanked her for her thoughtfulness.

Tess went back to her office, where Godzilla, no fool, still slumbered in the warmth. She went back to her bookkeeping, not even minding that she still had to wait for the cable TV man. Getting a good new tenant always put her in a cheerful mood.

It was true, what Sean had told Tess Perkins. He had a few things — essentials for the mission, for he was going to be here a while. Dishes, a few pots and pans, bedding. A decent TV and DVD player (he couldn't resist, he could always say that he'd gotten those and his ex had gotten everything else). But there were a few boxes, labeled "kitchen" or "misc." that contained supplies of a different sort. Hidden under concealing layers of excelsior and crumpled newspaper were the things he'd taken from Henry Connolly's truck.

In fact, Henry's truck and what it contained had proven as informative in their own way as Henry himself. Hidden under army blankets and camping gear he'd found three Mini-14 semiautomatic rifles, four nine-millimeter Glock pistols, and several shotguns, along with a large amount of ammunition for all the weapons. Also a couple of knives — good quality and practical, not sword-and-sorcery shit — and two Kevlar vests.

There was also nearly $2,000 in cash. Last but certainly not least, a Ziploc bag full of reefer, which was no doubt for Henry's personal consumption. "Naughty boy, Henry," he'd said when he made that last find. Most of the goods he'd left in Connolly's truck, along with Connolly himself, but he'd kept a few things: one of the Minis, the vests, the knives, and all the ammo. Sean had been a Boy Scout once, and knew that it was good to be prepared.

He lay awake on his bed, eyes open. The room was in darkness but that suited him perfectly, for his focus was inward. Gathering and sorting information. He did not need to write anything down, it was all organized in his brain, ready when he needed it.

Most of the militias and antigovernment groups favored the leaderless resistance approach. Tiny cells or individuals striking out against the government without plan or leadership. The idea was that if captured, there was no leader for a member to betray, and that the law would be busy swatting at many wasps rather than aiming for the hive and its queen.

It was a good theory, but someone had realized that it wasn't working. Instead of stinging, the wasps buzzed about ineffectually, talked about attacking but never put stinger to flesh. Someone understood that the wasps need a reason to sting, need to be fed a potent brew of anger and inspiration. And someone knew that it was best to let the weak and the stupid strike out on their own. Let a person with both brains and authority gather the capable and the clever — but not too clever, not anyone who would want to seize power — and there was something to be reckoned with.

Thanks to Henry Connolly, he had a name for that someone. Richard Blaine, who owned, of all things, a Christmas tree farm outside of Du Lac, Wisconsin. Blaine sometimes spoke at local meetings, more often spread his message by way of emissaries. They kept their eyes open and their ears to the ground, approaching those they thought would be good candidates and inviting them to join the group.

Sean's assessment of Connolly as a mere spear-carrier was on target. He had been an errand boy, sent for supplies and coordinating transportation; he didn't know who actually had set off the bomb. Surely it had not been Blaine, who clearly was smart enough to delegate the dirty work. But, Sean thought now, staring up at the ceiling, that didn't matter. If he had been in search of a legitimate arrest, it would be important. But really, all he needed was a name, which he had, and a location, which he also had. Now it was a matter of insinuating himself into the outer circle, and then getting them to offer him an invitation.

It would take time, for he would need to play his hand carefully. The group was, in a strange way, like his former employers. You did not go to them. They came to you. He could not wheedle an invitation. He needed to come across as competent and dedicated, not too eager, content to be a reliable follower rather than a leader. To be...what?

A good soldier, Sean thought with a faint, cynical smile. Yes, a good soldier. Well then, that should be easy. It was the role he'd played for nearly all his life.

With that thought he fell asleep. His sleep was, as always, without dreams. The last image to flicker across his brain before he descended into sleep's oblivion was Jennifer Thomson crying in her rescuer's arms.

The invitation came a few days before Christmas.

It was at a weekly meeting, one held in the hall of Du Lac's Grace Methodist Church. A town hall meeting, they called it, but though some of the local government occasionally attended it, they did not sponsor it. It was a meeting like so many others he had attended, one where tales of economic woe were shared, where the moral decline of the country was decried, where webs of dark theories and conjecture were spun. He sat in the middle of the hall, in the middle of the row, not too eager, not too reticent, asking good questions and volunteering comments that were neither too cautious nor too outlandish. During the last few meetings, with the sixth sense innate to those who are both hunter and hunted, he'd known he was being assessed.

After the meeting, punch and coffee and cookies in the back of the hall. Sean was pouring himself a cup of coffee when there was a tap on his shoulder. *Now it begins.*

"Yes?" He turned and saw a man, in his mid-forties. Scandinavian ancestry, with sandy blond hair and a slightly upturned nose, receding chin.

"Mr. Lewis, I presume?"

"Call me Sam."

"Sam." The man nodded. "I'm Doug MacReady. I liked what you had to say in the meeting tonight."

He shrugged. "Just my thoughts on things, that's all."

MacReady gave a slight tilt of his head toward the end of the hall, away from the madding crowd, and they began to casually stroll that way. "Well, I've seen you at a few of these meetings. You say they're just your thoughts on things, but you know, it's a shame to let good thoughts and good people go to waste."

Sean kept silent, kept his face attentive, inquiring. Waited for the invitation.

"A shame," MacReady repeated. "But it doesn't have to be. There's a meeting we think you'd be interested in attending."

"We?"

MacReady smiled. "Some people who share your thoughts on things. Good people. Give you a chance to talk about things and..." MacReady shrugged enigmatically.

"That could be interesting," he replied, his tone noncommittal.

"I think it will be."

"When and where?"

"New Year's Day, at the Deer's Head Lodge. We'll watch the bowl games." And more, of course, that was clear in MacReady's eyes.

It was the chance he'd been waiting for and he had only to take it. He wanted to, but an interior voice — the one you learned to listen to unless you wanted to end up dead — urged him to wait. Too much eagerness was a betrayal greater than any slip of the tongue.

But he wanted it badly, so it was with real regret that he said, "I can't. New Year's I'm over to St. Paul."

"Time with the family?"

"Yes. My mother, mostly. It's her lungs, all those years of working in the mills." He sighed. "I think this is her last Christmas with us."

MacReady shook his head in commiseration. And why not? Even members of antigovernment groups loved their mothers. "I understand. Well, I hate for you to miss it. But I'll keep a weather eye out for you after the new year. Sound good?"

"It does. And thank you."

They shook hands. MacReady nodded, turned, and disappeared into the crowd. Sean lingered, making small talk, having another cup of coffee. His mask did not slip away until he was in his apartment, in the safety of darkness and a warm bath. Only then did he smile, like a hunter hearing the deer approach.

Chapter Thirteen

It was snowing lightly when they left Haven Cove. The limo rolled on, untroubled by the weather; its dark, sleek bulk gave it the appearance of a lambent-eyed whale cruising through the sea. Inside the limo there were laughter and giggles, and the scent of five different perfumes intermingled.

"I am *so* glad we got this limo instead of driving," Brandy said, pausing to adjust her stockings. "Let some poor sap be designated driver." She playfully thumped the partition between passengers and driver. The limo driver paid her no heed.

"Well, it certainly makes sense, what with Alex hosting the party," said Cammie.

"What do you mean?" Jennifer asked.

"Oh, didn't you know? Before his dad retired Alex was a bartender. Went to bartending school and everything." Brandy smiled. "Ask him to make you a Blue Floyd, you won't regret it."

"Speaking of hooch, I say we break out the champagne," said Tracy, producing a bottle of Bollinger from her handbag.

Jennifer, who had only seen Bollinger in James Bond movies, asked, "Tracy, where did you get that?"

Tracy shrugged. "New Year's Eve present from Alex."

"The soul of generosity," sighed Betty.

After a good deal of fussing with the wires and foil and complaining about chipped nail polish, they got the bottle open. "Don't spill that in here," the driver said in a bored tone.

"We won't," five voices sang out.

Soon plastic glasses were found and a substantial amount of Bollinger poured into each. "Ladies," said Cammie, holding her glass high. The words *Happy New Year* on the glass in bright pink letters. "To a new year."

The words clanged in Jennifer's mind. A new year. What about forgetting the old one? Well, perhaps she could do something about that. "Bottoms up," she said, and drank down her champagne in one draught. It was the best champagne she'd ever had, not at all like the cheap stuff she remembered from college parties. This was honey-sweet on her tongue and went to her brain almost instantly. The knot of tension in her back and shoulders eased a bit, and though small, the relief was at the same time very great, and she longed for more. "Hey, Cammie," Jennifer said. "I need a refill."

Alex Salto's second home was on an enviable spread covering two acres. The driver skillfully negotiated his way up the mountain roads and along the circular driveway, past the cars already parked there. "We're here," he said.

The doors were flung open and the women tumbled out, gathering purses and coats. Cammie, Betty, Tracy, and Brandy all headed to the door. Jennifer stopped to tap on the driver's window. He rolled it down, gave her his look of bored professionalism. "Yes, ma'am?"

Jennifer had three champagnes in her and a silly grin on her face. She couldn't help it. She had the giddiness of an injured man whose morphine shot has kicked in, the goodwill of a paycheck-to-paycheck woman who has won the lottery. "I just wanted to thank you for the ride," she said. "Happy New Year."

"Happy New Year to you too," he replied. It was the first time in three years of New Years' Eve driving duties that anyone had bothered to thank him.

Jennifer gave him a wave and ran to catch up with the other women, sliding a little on the icy pavement. The driver put the limo in gear so he could park, smoke, and listen to the radio until it was time for the return trip.

Jennifer was no architectural expert but even she recognized the style of Alex's house as she walked inside and put away her coat and purse. It was Frank Lloyd Wright ripoff, post-and-beam with lots of open space and a rain forest's worth of teak. A fire roared cheerfully on the hearth, and on tables by the bar she spotted tables laden with food. Smoked salmon pinwheels, sushi artistically prepared by some Japanese expatriate, chicken satay on skewers. Behind the bar was Alex himself, sleek and dark and smiling. "Hi ladies," he called out. "I'm taking requests tonight. And I'm making my specialty. It's a little number I invented, called 'I Left My Heart In Wango Tango'."

"You invent drinks?" Jennifer said as she sat on one of the bar stools. Her tongue was loosened by champagne. "Alex Salto, multitalented. Who knew?"

"Hah!" Alex grinned at her, the dancing light she'd seen in his eyes when they first met now back full force. "I knew there was a funny party girl hiding inside you, Jenny."

"There's lots about me you don't know." Jennifer took the cocktail he offered her, some fruity concoction with dark rum and maraschino cherries in Christmas red and green. Smiled at Alex, and why not? Fog had fallen over her mind, and it was such a relief to not think of anything beyond the pleasure of the moment. To not worry about when she would start to think or remember, and what she would do when that happened. It was a new year and she was newly born, blank slate, nothing had happened before the ride in the limo and its liberating champagne, and as for what happened tomorrow, well, she would worry about that tomorrow.

Somehow the Wango Tango was gone already and she pushed her glass toward Alex. "Cammie — no, Betty. Oh hell. Anyway. One of the girls said I need to ask you for the Blue Floyd."

"Done and done," Alex said, after a few minutes produced a drink the color of window cleaner and topped with a plastic sword impaling pineapple chunks and more maraschinos. "Anyhooo, Jenny, what's your New Year's resolution?"

She took a deep drink of candy-tasting Windex blue. "I haven't thought that far ahead."

It was the truth, but Alex thought it was wit. "I like it. 'Haven't thought that far ahead.' That's a good one. Well, if you're interested," he said, his dark eyes never leaving her face, "my New Year's resolution is to have as much fun as possible as often as possible. After all, here today, gone tomorrow. Know what I mean? Now what if your old buddies down in the States figure they want to start World War Three? You want your last night to be spent doing something boring? Or having a good time? Hmmm, Jenny?"

She wondered, later, if he knew who she was. She had told no one. Not the realtor, not Suzanne, not any of the office girls, and not Alex. But perhaps he knew, for his talk of *here today gone tomorrow* slipped its way into her fogged brain like a hand slipping under a skirt. Because she knew how true it was.

Maybe it was just chance that he'd said the right thing. Or the wrong one. However you wanted to look at it.

"Having a good time. I'll drink to that," she said, and their glasses rang together in a toast.

She did have a good time, she could never deny that. The house filled with people and she laughed and made jokes and talked about

110

inconsequential things, and none of the partygoers knew anything about her except that she was Jenny Thomson from the States, just moved up here a few months back and how did she like it here anyway? Oh, fine, really enjoying it. So nice to have snow for the holidays.

She mingled and had another drink, ate smoked salmon and sushi and those cute little mini-pizzas, danced with Darren from the office, and was Alex's guinea pig for a "new drink I've been working on, something special, I call it the 'King of Bongo'." When the magic hour came round she stood with all of them, raising glasses high, yelling out "Happy New Year" and was too far gone to even feel happy that it was a new year, and she was here to greet it when so many others were not.

The party resumed but Jennifer remembered very little of it beyond a blur of dancing and food and drinks. She was sitting at the bar, nodding over another Blue Floyd, when Alex's voice came through to her, asking something she didn't quite hear.

"I'm sorry?" she asked.

"I asked if you wanted to dance."

"Sure." She slid off the barstool gracelessly, her velvet skirt slippery on the leather upholstery. As she walked to the space that had been cleared for dancing, the room seemed strangely quiet, and she realized as if from a distance that she and Alex were alone. She had the vague idea this was important but couldn't think of why.

The song was one she liked. It seemed very natural to dance close to Alex, her left hand in his right, his arm around her waist, her hand on his back. Every time she looked up at him his eyes were locked on her face, and he was smiling as if he knew some marvelous secret. "I missed you in the crowd when midnight came," he whispered. "Don't I get a New Year's kiss?"

"Just one."

"I'll make it count." Then his mouth was on hers and oh God, it had been so long, almost a year since anyone had kissed her, she'd nearly forgotten. One kiss became several and then the number of kisses didn't matter because there was no pause between them. The music had ended but they weren't dancing any more, just stood with hands running over each other, mouths locked together. Somewhere in her brain a voice of sobriety asked her if she really wanted this, wanted where it was most certainly going to be heading in the next few minutes if she didn't call it off, and then he got his hand under her skirt, between her legs, and that was it, she wanted this as she'd wanted the evening's liquor and mindless chatter. It was sweet oblivion, losing herself and all her thoughts of past and future. Nothing mattered anymore, not the bombing, not herself, not the fact that Alex was a conceited jerk. And it was such a relief to not have anything matter.

She wasn't sure how they got to the bedroom. All that mattered was that she was on her back in bed. What mattered was not Alex but what she felt as she lay under him, which was animal pleasure. Nothing more. Nothing less. It was like going up a spiral, up and up, until she was seized by the climax, shaken by it, and then she tumbled back down the spiral into sleep.

Jennifer woke slowly, had plenty of time to puzzle out each anomaly as her hazy mind registered it. Why was the light so strange? Because these windows faced east, not west. Why did the bed feel so strange and squashy? Because it was not her bed, and it was a waterbed to boot. Why was she naked instead of in her nightshirt? Because she'd slept with Alex Salto. And now for the final round, who was that person snoring next to her? Take one wild guess.

So it was without surprise that she opened her eyes and saw not the familiar plaster of her own ceiling but the post-and-beam architecture of Alex's. She peeped cautiously over at Alex; he was buried so deeply under sheets and blankets that all she could see was a tousle of black hair. Jennifer sat up, slowly, carefully, her head still swimming with liquor and too little sleep in an unfamiliar bed. She tried not to slosh the waterbed, made sure her body was shielded with sheets should he wake. But she needn't have worried. Alex, hungover and satiated, didn't so much as twitch as she slipped out of the bed. She stood, unsteady on her feet, her head reeling in one direction and her stomach in another, and started looking for her clothes. They were scattered in a Hansel-and-Gretel trail through the bedroom, down the hall, down the stairs. Underwear, skirt, tights, blouse, shoes. She dressed as she collected them and ended up fully clothed, more or less, in the living room. The room was strewn with glasses and their fruity-drink dregs, plastic plates, crumpled napkins, cigarette butts, and — oh, *there* was her bra.

She knelt to pick up the bra, felt the dizziness ease up, felt the beginnings of a monster headache coming on. Stood, put the bra in her skirt pocket. Tried to think. Coffee. In the fog of her brain she felt a brief flicker of interest. Yes, coffee. That would do the trick.

Jennifer shuffled into Alex's kitchen, and was starting the not-inconsiderable job of finding the coffee and deciphering the workings of the coffee grinder and espresso maker when she caught a glimpse of the world outside. All thoughts of coffee left her as she stared out the window.

Christmas.

That was her first thought. Because it was how the world should look at holiday time, even a native Californian like her knew it. She walked, more quickly than before, to the living room and got her coat. After some fumbling with the locks she stepped outside.

She found herself in a world of silence and white. The sky gray overhead, a few errant flakes still fluttering down. No breeze, no sound of wind in the pines. No sounds of town or harbor, no TV from a nearby house, no dogs barking, no hum of wheels on asphalt. Sometime in the night, a white blanket had been nestled around the world, hushed it into gentle sleep.

Oh, she thought, did not say it, reluctant to disturb the silence. She had been holding her breath without realizing it, and as she exhaled her breath smoked. Everywhere a carpet of white, untouched save for a few bird tracks. The branches of the pines were heavy with snow. As she watched, one branch surrendered its burden, sent snow to the ground in a soft shower. The branch waved as though saying farewell.

Jennifer stood hesitant, afraid to sully the peaceful scene but longing to be part of it, to feel the silence all around her. She breathed deep — the air's coldness made it feel cleaner somehow, made her feel refreshed. Her hangover headache and nausea faded. Jennifer walked along the deck toward the back field. She had never walked in snow before and felt a child's delight in the way her booted feet sank into the snow so effortlessly. She giggled, kicked one foot high in the air to send the snow high and feel it rain down on her.

She swung her foot down. It went through the snow and found not the deck but empty air and Jennifer pitched forward, arms flailing, and fell to the ground, rolling down the slope several yards. She came to a rest, spitting out snow, flat on her back, the wind knocked out of her, looking up at the gray bowl of the sky. She fought to get her air back and was back in Los Angeles. Back at the federal building. Back in the dust cloud, the roar of the collapsing building still ringing in her ears. Her mouth full not of snow but dust, coating her tongue and filling her nostrils. The silence of the Canadian woods was full of sound now, rending steel and peoples' screams, police helicopters and a man's voice calling out *Lady, lady, can you hear me? Move toward the sound of my voice.* She tried to answer but the dust was choking her, she tried to get to the voice but her legs failed her. She was falling to the ground, the world going dark. *Please, I really don't want to die.* Then strong arms were around her and an oxygen mask was on her face, giving her air.

She took a deep breath, finally, and the winter air seared her throat but that was all right, just fine because she was back now, back in Canada. Back here, back home, but it wasn't fine because she lay sprawled in the snow in Alex Salto's back field, hungover, skirt tangled around her legs, suede boots slowly getting ruined, hair knotted and full of snow. Was lying here with no one who knew where she was, and if she had hurt herself badly in the fall she could stay here for hours, until the snow covered her from sight and become not a blanket but a shroud.

With a hoarse cry she sat up, gingerly moved her legs, wiggled her fingers and toes. Nothing but some bruises, but what did that really change? Nothing.

I am alone. She sat in the snow, face almost as white as her surroundings. Because who was there to know or care anything about her? Alex? Don't make her laugh. The office girls? They had left her behind, left her in a severely intoxicated state with a man whose intentions were written in letters a foot tall, and Jennifer knew with a chill deeper than that of the winter air that if mood and circumstance had been different, last night could have ended in a rape. And no one would have cared.

Why should they care? She had done nothing to earn anyone's friendship. Her days were proceeded through as methodically as marking dates off a calendar. There was Suzanne, but when had her talk with Suzanne gone beyond the weather or the kids Suzanne watched? Even Suzanne knew nothing about her, had no reason to care. She had used

Suzanne and Bill to feel like she was a part of life. Just as she'd used Amber LaSalle. And Alex.

She heard Dr. Levinson's voice from the survivor's meeting. *I wake to sleep, and take my waking slow. I learn by going where I have to go.* Pretty words, but she hadn't woken, was still sleeping, drifting through her days. She had gone where she had to go, but had learned nothing, done nothing. Nine months since the bombing and what had she done with the life she had pulled from the ashes? Nothing.

Above her the sky rotated, in her stomach acid burned. She rolled onto hands and knees and threw up, all those sugary drinks from last night gone sour and burning up her throat. She retched and heaved until there was no more left and crawled away from the steaming hole in the snow, feeling dirty. Nine months of life squandered, and how many of those lost 361 people would have done something worthwhile with that time? Nine months and she had not done a single thing that she could point to with pride or happiness. She prostituted herself and her story, lived in her leased house like a tenant, lived in her new town without becoming part of it, took a job that offered her no enjoyment or challenge, rang in the new year by fucking a man she didn't even like. She felt...

Unworthy.

Jennifer Thomson sat in the snow and, for the first time since she'd left Los Angeles, cried. Cried noisily, unprettily, until her eyes and nose were red and puffed, her face stiff with frozen tears. And some time later, stood up on feet that felt half-frozen and legs that were shaky. Tottering like a baby learning to walk. *No more hiding. No more running away.* She would start earning the life that had been awarded to her. She would start today.

She walked back up to the deck, shivering, tears frozen on her face. But with her head held high.

She was sitting outside on the deck drinking coffee when Alex finally showed up. He ambled onto the deck, clad in a robe and slippers though it was nearly noon. "What a night! How's *your* head this morning?"

She shrugged, finished off her coffee.

"Been up a while?" he asked.

"A bit."

He put one hand on her cheek. "A bit? Jeez, you're half frozen."

She jerked her head away, but he didn't seem to notice or care. "You should come inside," he purred, putting his hands on her shoulders. "Get warm." He laughed and slid his hands down her blouse. "Baby it's *cold* outside!"

"Knock it off!" She twisted away from him.

"What's your problem?" he asked, and put his hands on her shoulders again.

"I don't want this, any of it. You hear me? I don't want this," she said, pushing his hands off her. She turned to look at him. "I don't want you."

He stared at her, shoved his hands into the pockets of his robe. "That's not what you said last night."

"Don't flatter yourself. As drunk as I was, Bozo the Clown could have shown me a good time."

His face went red, a dull brick color, the black eyes were no longer dancing but flashing, like lightning. "So. That's how you want it. Well then. You're fired."

Jennifer shrugged again. It was pretty much what she had expected. She started to walk into the house to call a cab, then stopped and turned to Alex. "Is it OK if I come in Monday, get my stuff?"

He thought it over for a second or two. "Sure," he replied. "I'm a reasonable guy."

Chapter Fourteen

Deer's Head Lake was frozen over, a sheet of ice that, seen from high above, would indeed have been in the shape of a deer's head. Sean was on the peninsula that formed the space between the deer's muzzle and neck. Across from him, a little less than two kilometers away, was the Deer's Head Lodge. A two-story building of heavy logs, the perfect place for a fishing trip, a weekend getaway. The perfect place for the sort of meeting happening there today. One road in, easily watched. Woods on two sides, the lake on the other.

He lay behind a log; on the other side of the log a slope of about ten feet, and then the lake. Cattails, brown and stunted with the winter's cold, poked up through the ice here and there. Sean raised his head over the log and brought binoculars to his eyes. They would be arriving for the meeting soon, and he wanted to observe from a distance. Assess the quarry.

Overhead the sky was gunmetal gray. He lowered the binoculars, looked up at the gloomy sky. Sighed, for he felt some of that gloom inside him. It was the day, of course. He should have expected it. New Year's Eve was his favorite holiday, had been for many years. Most holidays he could take or leave, but he loved New Year's Eve, and had tried to spend it in the States, on R&R, as often as he could. Because whether he was in the heart of the crowd in Times Square or alone on the Pacific coast, whether he was talking with one of the old crowd, Robert or Beatty or Hamilton, or enjoying the pleasure of Monique's company, he could hear the clock chime midnight and think: *Another year has arrived and I'm still here to greet it.*

He was still here. But last night there had been no one to share that moment. That would have been all right, if he had been able to make a phone call. To Robert, to find out how he was doing, if he had beaten the cancer. To Monique, even if she was married now, just long enough to say Happy New Year and wish her well, hear her voice. Someone that he didn't have to lie to. Or didn't have to lie to very much.

But Sean would not risk a call to anyone he cared about, not Robert who was his friend or Monique who had been his lover. He had not forgotten Robert's warning to watch his back, and knew that his former employers were not above using those he cared for to get at him. So he had spent last night with a bottle of champagne and done a great deal of channel-surfing.

Sean allowed himself only one longing thought of past New Year's Eves: Monique standing on the bed in their hotel room, drinking Dom Perignon from the bottle, wearing a party hat and not much else, singing, "Mack The Knife." She'd bungled every verse, but he hadn't complained one bit. Asked for an encore, even. One moment to savor the memory, then he closed the door on it. Time to attend to the task at hand.

He turned his gaze toward the lodge across the lake. Trained his eyes to focus on the long distance. He'd noticed that refocusing his vision had gotten a bit more difficult the last couple years. Still, at least he didn't need glasses. Yet.

He kept his mind from wandering as best he could. Soon, thankfully, the cars began to arrive, and he raised the binoculars to his eyes. Pickup trucks mostly, with ladder racks and tow hitches, the tailpipes rusted and salt-corroded. Five vehicles in all. The men clad in jeans and boots, shirts plaid or denim beneath their coats. Talking, jokes. An easy familiarity about most of them. Of course. Not just anyone would be let into the circle. And he needed more than that. To not just enter the circle, but to get close to the leader. To Richard Blaine.

He wondered which of the men gathered there outside the lodge was Blaine. He scanned faces, postures, looking for that aura of leadership. Because kings did not need crowns or ermine robes to demonstrate authority. Knowing that you were king was often enough. All the trappings were secondary.

Sean saw no kings across the lake, and relaxed a bit. Blaine might have inspired loyalty in Henry Connolly and others, but he was no king, only a little tin god, and tin was flimsy, easily crushed. No, not a —

Wait. One last person arriving. Sean was too far away for sounds to carry across the lake; he sensed the arrival in the way the other men turned to look, the expressions of respect on their faces. He followed their gaze to the man who now arrived, not in a pickup truck but on horseback. Bringing the focus of the binoculars in as close as he could he saw a horse, and on its back a man with dark hair and a close-cropped beard. He was broad-shouldered and tall, and when he dismounted it was with grace. He was mingling with the men now, and though the words could not be made out, the sentiments could. Greetings, asking after the family. Authority without arrogance, commiseration without condescension. Here, undoubtedly was Richard Blaine.

Here, Sean noted with both interest and dismay, was a king.

The king now arrived, they all went inside. To warmth and companionship, talk and plans. Sean had no particular interest in these things, at least not with this group of men. But he was interested in Richard Blaine. He decided to forgo his original plan of returning to his apartment to plan, decided to wait. Partly to see how long the meeting was and add that information to his growing store, partly to get another glimpse of Blaine and see what he could see.

He waited. Time passed: an hour, two. Would it be possible, he wondered, to slip around closer to the lodge, get a better view, possibly even catch some conversation? Abruptly he lowered himself to the ground, began reaching in his back pocket for his map of the lake area.

Sean heard the bullet hit the log first, and then a second later the report of the rifle. Instinctively he pressed himself to the ground, realized that the shot had come from the woods behind him, and hurled himself up and over the log, feeling the gun slip from its holster and fall to the ground. As he rolled over the top of the log there was a sharp burn as a bullet grazed his leg; he did not hear the shot. He came to rest on the other side of the log. The ground sloped away sharply on this side and he was able to crouch instead of lie flat, breathing hard, listening. He wanted to reach over the log to retrieve the gun but dared not. Could he dig under the log and get it that way? No. A quick glance told him the earth was too full of stones to make the digging quick.

It had been a long time since he was in this kind of danger, and he felt the old sensation of alertness fill him. It was not the panic acid bath of adrenaline, more like an electrical current, running from his brain to his nerve endings. He took a deep breath, not hyperventilating, just a deep breath, the oxygen adding to his alertness. Coldly he assessed the situation. One sniper, possibly more. In the woods, cutting off his escape that way. The only other way out was across the ice, a slow, slippery passage and him an easy target on it. No, not that way. Even the pistol would not help much; his assailant had a rifle, standard hunting gear from the sound of it, had the advantage in range and most likely a scope. All he had on him was the knife in its leg sheath. Without taking his eyes off the woods he patted his leg. Yes, he still had the knife.

Who was it? One of the group? Had his refusal of the invitation brought suspicion on him? Possibly. But it felt wrong to him. Listening hard, he heard a faint rustling. Someone walking. Changing their position.

Most likely not peering down the scope, assuming of course that there was only one sniper. He had to know.

He took a quick peek around the side of the log. An instant's glance, but it gave him everything he needed to know.

You'll have to watch your back, Robert had said. Sean hadn't wanted to believe it would happen. He didn't want to believe that it would be someone he knew. But it was true. He'd caught a glimpse of the shooter, and though he hadn't seen him in five years, recognized him instantly. Pale blonde hair, rugged good looks. Beatty.

Sean felt a twinge of some unnamable emotion. Beatty had been in the ops team as long as he had. Beatty with his knack for languages and his talent for fast driving and his weakness for skinny blonde women. Beatty with his bottomless reservoir of bad jokes. *Hey, Irish, I got another one for you. Don't look at me like that. This one's funny, I promise.* They'd run missions together, mostly in Europe. Russia, Bosnia, East Germany. Beatty had saved his life once.

And now had been sent to take it.

Sean wondered if this assignment had been the cost of Beatty's entry back into the fold. He could imagine it clearly: *You'll have your old job back, all your privileges, rank, and salary. Just tie up this loose end for us.* Halsey pushed his picture, probably some surveillance photo taken in Florida, across the table to Beatty. Beatty gave it a cursory glance, no more. Beatty knew what he looked like. Halsey asked, *Will this be a problem?* And what did Beatty say?

What would Sean have said, had he been given the choice? He hoped he would have rejected the offer, not stooped so low as to kill an old comrade. But hoping was not the same as knowing. Sean didn't blame Beatty, much. Who could say what his own choice would have been?

He knew who his assassin was. Now he needed to make that knowledge work in his favor. Beatty, then. What did he know about Beatty? Dog-loyal and committed to their employers. Had been retired a year before Sean. Had never been the greatest shot, especially with a rifle. Was certainly out of practice if he had not only missed twice but was changing his position already instead of waiting it out. Still, Beatty had considerable advantage.

Silence from the woods.

Cautious. Beatty was cautious. Liked to have a situation sized up. Liked to know the job was done. Liked completion. Would make his first shot the chest, for greatest stopping power and easiest aim. Would follow it up with a head shot, at closer range.

Make the enemy's weakness work for you. One of the first lessons learned.

Make Beatty come to him, to within range of the knife, or his hands. If he could get the rifle away from Beatty or get rid of it altogether Sean stood a chance. He was shorter than Beatty but faster, more agile.

But how to make Beatty come to him?

It had to be a tactic that Beatty would never think of using himself. Sean remembered Robert saying, "Beatty's good, of course. Dedicated. But he's not like us. He's somewhat lacking in imagination."

A plan came to him. It was risky, perhaps complete folly. Yet what else was there to do?

He ran a hand down the Kevlar vest that was under his clothes, one of the vests he had taken from the supplies in Henry Connolly's truck. He slipped the leg knife out of its sheath, gripped it tightly. On his hands and knees, he took a deep breath and crawled out from behind the shelter of his log. He turned toward the woods, pretending to reach for a backup weapon, and the bullet hit him a glancing blow in the ribs on the right side. It was years since he had taken a bullet and even with the vest, the feeling was every bit as unpleasant as he remembered it, like being hit with a sledgehammer. Sean fell backward, lay supine with his head pointing down the slope toward the lake. So far so good — he'd held on to the knife, he could see up the slope and into the woods without moving his head. He was lucky it had not been direct impact: after a moment he was able to breathe again. A sharp pain in his ribs; he'd most likely cracked one. No matter. If he got away with nothing more than some cracked ribs he'd be well ahead of the game.

Sprawled on his back, the knife in hand, ready to throw. A deceptive vacancy in his eyes, the image of a man in shock. The crunch of boots on snow and winter-dead foliage, and Beatty standing by the log.

Even with so much at stake, Sean could not help noticing that Beatty had put on a lot of weight.

Beatty stood, the rifle raised at the ready. Then, abruptly, lowered it. Beatty sighed. "I'm sorry, Irish."

Before Beatty could raise the rifle again, Sean threw the knife. His aim was off; the knife struck Beatty in the shoulder. Beatty staggered back, the rifle's shot going wild into the trees, and Sean was up and the two of them grappled for the rifle. They fell, tumbling down the slope, each trying to prise the rifle from the other's grip, rolled down the slope and landed with a heavy thump on the ice. The struggle for the rifle renewed, push and pull on the slippery ice, edging away from shore, further out onto the lake. No words from either of them, only harsh breathing.

Then Beatty threw all his weight into a shove. Sean lost his grip on the rifle and tumbled to the ice, tried to get up, slipped, got to his hands and knees. He looked up and saw Beatty on his feet, the rifle aimed and ready for a head shot this time. Sean saw the rifle's muzzle like the opening of a dark tunnel into eternity, saw Beatty's eyes above the rifle, blue ice eyes with something like regret in them.

He raised one hand, in appeal to that regret. "Don't do this."

"I have to," Beatty replied.

He had time to think, *Jennifer, I failed you, I'm sorry,* and then Beatty pulled the trigger.

Nothing happened. The rifle was jammed.

For a moment they were both frozen, astonished, and as Beatty moved to drop the rifle and reach for his sidearm Sean slid across the ice, hitting Beatty in the shins with his body and knocking Beatty's feet out from under him. Beatty landed hard on the ice, his breath wheezing out of him, a .38 in his right hand, arm outstretched. Sean grabbed the jammed rifle by the barrel, raised it high over head and brought the stock down on Beatty's right arm, hearing bone crack as Beatty howled and let go of the .38. Beatty lashed out at him with legs and his left arm, and in the struggle the .38 was knocked skittering over the ice out of their reach.

Now Beatty on his back, Sean straddling Beatty, aiming the rifle's stock at Beatty's head. Brought it down, Beatty jerked to the left, and he missed. Again, and Beatty jerked to the right. Through it all, Sean could hear a sound. A soft, creaking groan. Something distantly familiar, an old fear resurrected.

It was a sound from his boyhood Indiana winters. The sound of ice weakening.

Beatty threw him off, and in a few seconds they were both on their feet, circling each other warily. Sean held the jammed rifle, his eyes on Beatty, his ears straining for the sound of the weakening ice. Did Beatty know that sound? Probably not, Beatty was from Arizona. They circled, each waiting for the other to make a move. He had to end it soon. That creaking groan was getting louder, and sooner or later Richard Blaine and his cronies would come out of the meeting and see the two of them tangoing out on the ice.

Finish it. One way or another.

Sean eased his feet along the ice, searching for something to brace himself against. He found it, a protruding piece of driftwood. It was all he needed.

He began trying to clear the rifle, his face lowered to the weapon but eyes covertly watching Beatty. He saw Beatty take his chance, come toward Sean with all the speed he could muster.

Perfect.

When Beatty got close Sean dropped the rifle, caught hold of Beatty's wrists, twisted so his hip caught the force of Beatty's charge. It was a throw-hold, an old judo technique he'd learned years ago, and it worked as well as it ever had. Beatty was thrown over his hip and went flying, landing with all the force of his weight and the momentum of his charge, flat on his back. The ice broke beneath Beatty and he plunged into the black water.

Sean threw himself backward and away from the hole, trying to distribute his weight as evenly as he could. He watched, waiting with held breath for Beatty to surface, but there was only white ice and black water.

He let out a deep sigh, a plume of steam from his breath rising into the air. It was over, he had only to get off the ice and gather the weapons. Everything was going to be —

Thud.

From the ice underneath him. Two more *thuds* in quick succession. Like someone pounding on a wooden door.

Don't look. Don't. But of course he did, and saw Beatty, his image opaqued by the ice but clear enough for Sean to see not just Beatty's face but the terror in his eyes.

No, he didn't want to see this, didn't want to watch Beatty drown. But when Sean tried to look away, he could not. He could not even close his eyes. He could only watch while Beatty hammered uselessly at the ice, listen to the thumps of his fists. It went on for much longer than Sean would have thought possible, thrashing and hammering and eyes wide in a mute plea for mercy. Beatty's struggles became frenzied, convulsive; he screamed. His cry, though muffled by ice and distorted by water, was not just a scream but a name. Sean's name.

Beatty gasped like a landed fish, choking, breathing in the wrong element. His struggles slowed and then all but ceased; his terrified expression gave way to a vague look of dread and resignation. Three more blows against the ice, the last one scarcely more than a tap, and then Beatty was sinking down to the bottom of the lake, where he would not be found until spring. The only mercy of it was that the ice obscured the look in Beatty's dying eyes as he sank. Sean's last glimpse of Beatty was of his hands in their tan leather gloves, stretched out toward the surface.

Beatty vanished from his sight, and Sean could move again. He half crawled, half staggered to the shore, up the slope. There was a tall pine there and he sank to the earth by it, propping himself against its trunk, panting, keeping his back to the lake. He was slimed with sweat, felt it soaking into his clothes, yet inside he felt cold. He was afraid, but it was not a kind of fear he had felt before. It went deeper, to the core of his soul, and he remembered Robert telling him that something did not feel right about this mission. Was this it?

It was not just that he had killed Beatty. He had killed before, many times. But he had always prided himself on making his kills quickly and without unnecessary suffering. He saw it as business, the way a veterinarian puts down a rabid dog. A gunshot to the head, the snap of a broken neck, the stiletto in the heart. Even with Henry Connolly, once he had gotten the information he wanted he'd ended it quickly. Professionally. Mercifully. Those people hadn't died in slow suffocating pain. They hadn't screamed Sean's name with their dying breath.

Beatty had been his compatriot. Had been a friend, or as close as any of them got to having friends in their profession. Had saved his life once, and now he had repaid the favor by consigning Beatty to a death worse than any he had dealt before. Sean shut his eyes, still breathing harshly, afraid for the first time of something other than failure or death. He'd thought those were the only things to be afraid of, and was now terribly certain that he'd been wrong. Robert knew, had tried to warn him, but Sean hadn't listened.

He pushed the thoughts away, forced his breathing to slow. It was done, and that was all. There was no taking it back. It was over and he'd had to do it. Beatty had been sent to kill him, after all.

He had to get out of here. He was in no shape to continue the stakeout, and he had to get rid of the weapons and anything else he and Beatty had left. Getting to his feet, he had to rest leaning against the tree until his knees stopped shaking. When he felt steady he walked to the fallen log, picked up his gun and holstered it. He found the knife, sheathed it. At the lake's edge he found Beatty's .38, slipped it into his pocket.

The rifle was still out on the ice.

Sean hesitated. Then eased his way out onto the ice, trying not to look down for fear that he would see Beatty again, blue with cold and drowning, wearing the grin of the vengeful dead. But of course there was nothing. He picked up the rifle, and for a moment was tempted to throw it into the hole in the ice, whether as a gesture of respect or superstition he did not know. In the end practicality won out, and he kept it.

Once on land again, he breathed a deep sigh of relief, and began the walk back to his van. For a moment he stopped, was tempted to look back, but did not want to see what was behind him. As he walked, it began to snow. Before too much time had passed his footprints were filled, and only the hole in the ice showed that anything had happened here today.

Chapter Fifteen

"So," said Jennifer, "I guess I can chalk that one up to experience."

Jennifer and Suzanne sat at Suzanne's kitchen table. Mugs of tea, Jennifer's mostly untouched, were in front of them, along with a plate of vanilla wafers. From the living room came the sounds of play, the Joplin twins busy with a Mousetrap game. Jennifer had gone for a walk along the shops on Commercial Row yesterday, after picking her stuff up from work, and had bought the game.

She hadn't gone into lurid details of the New Year's Eve fiasco, nor had she told Suzanne how when she'd gone in to retrieve her potted cyclamen, her desk calendar, and the framed picture of herself and Cindy on Splash Mountain, the office girls had all ignored her and Alex hadn't appeared at all. Not that she wanted to see him. But Suzanne only said. "You'll find something else sooner or later. I mean, you're OK for a while, money-wise?"

"Sure." She was OK for more than a while, but Suzanne didn't need to know that.

"Then it's all for the best. To be honest, I didn't think that was a great place for you. It's no secret that Alex Salto sometimes expects a lot from his employees." She put the slightest bit of emphasis on the word *lot,* gave Jennifer a level look. "Especially if they're young and pretty."

Jennifer felt a wave of crimson wash over her face and recede quickly. It was not so much embarrassment, oddly, but guilt for underestimating Suzanne, writing her off as a lightweight. One more thing to make amends for.

Before she could apologize, Suzanne clapped her hands together dismissively. "Look at it this way, the year can only get better."

"I heard that," Jennifer said, smiling in spite of everything. "Spilled milk under the bridge, as my kid sister says. And on a totally different subject, do you know how to get to the big linen store in Vancouver?"

"Of course. You need towels?"

"I need more than that." It was true. The white box of her bedroom was working on her nerves. White walls, milk-glass globe light overhead, her bed with its tarnished brass headboard, the duvet she'd had since college, once a pretty peach but now faded to beige. It was like sleeping in a refrigerator — worse because at least a refrigerator has something on its shelves. "Are you free tomorrow?"

"Yes."

"Care to do a little shopping with me?"

The next evening Suzanne lay on Jennifer's living room sofa. The weather was damp and Suzanne's red-brown hair was frizzy, fanned out around her head. "Call Bill, tell him I can't summon the energy to walk home."

Jennifer, sprawled on the floor, replied, "I can't, I'm too tired to get to the phone."

"You're a liar."

"I *am* tired."

"No, about the shopping. You said 'a little shopping.' Little. I can prove it. The house is bugged, I've got it on tape."

Shopping bags lay strewn across the floor, their contents spilling out. Sheets and throw pillows. Towels for kitchen and bath. A down comforter. Blankets. Drapes. Rolls of wallpaper. Little odds and ends, candles and knickknacks. It had taken them half an hour to cram all this into Jennifer's car, and that was after they'd realized they couldn't take the drapery rods, not unless they wanted to drive back to Haven Cove with the rods sticking out the windows like jousting poles. The rods, along with the headboard, the clothes hamper, the silk ficus tree, and the vanity set, would be delivered.

"I think you've got some repressed nesting instincts," said Suzanne, propping herself up on one elbow to survey the purchases. "And I think you're that store's favorite customer."

"I regret nothing." Jennifer didn't, though it wasn't something she'd planned.

She and Suzanne had left early, about 8:30, armed with coffee and blueberry muffins. The day was gray and drizzly but still lovely as they drove down the coast, the ocean slate-blue trimmed with white wave foam, the mountains snow-dusted. They arrived at the store still wired from caffeine and Jennifer enthused by the drive. The store was one of those big home linen shops, more or less everything you'd need for every room in the house, and if you couldn't find it, chances were they could order it for you.

Jennifer didn't quite know what took hold of her. Really, all she had gone there for was some sheets and drapes. She had intended to stick to what she knew. The safe things. Pastels that would be mix-and-matchable. What her mother would approve of.

Perhaps she could blame Suzanne, for she'd been standing here, holding a pillow — red velvet with heavy gold fringe. "This sort of stuff always cracks me up," Suzanne said. "I call this style 'San Francisco cathouse'. Not that I've been to a San Francisco cathouse, but you get the drift."

Jennifer took the pillow from Suzanne, held it for a moment. Lurking deep in her was a secret yearning for over-the-top home decoration. She thought of that Edgar Allan Poe story, "Masque of the Red Death," Prince Prospero's castle with each room in a different color including all the decorations and windows. Like her house, now that she thought of it, with the rose marble living room, country kitchen, aquarium-hued bathroom. Each room with its own personality, except for her bedroom.

Abruptly she put the pillow into the cart, snatched up the pastel blue sheets and put them back on the shelves. "Where'd you find the pillow?" she asked Suzanne.

"Over there," Suzanne said, pointing at a display piled high with velvet and fringe and beads. Suzanne had a cautious but excited look in her eyes, as if she was watching a dangerous circus act. Not sure where this was heading but not wanting to miss a moment.

Four hours, two shopping carts, and a considerable amount of money later, Jennifer and Suzanne drove in the laden-down VW to get some lunch. Over cheesecake — by now, they needed the sugar badly — Jennifer said, "I think it's either going to look great or awful. But either way it won't be boring."

"Here's to an end to the drab." Suzanne raised her water glass in a toast.

Several days later Jennifer, in paint-spattered jeans, her hair coming down out of its ponytail, walked out her front door and waved to the Delacroixs, who were pruning their roses. "Is it ready?" Bill asked. "From what Suzanne told me, I can't wait to see it."

"For better or worse, it's ready," Jennifer said.

She'd done the work — even the wallpapering — herself. She didn't know why, it just seemed right to have this room be hers. Entirely hers. She felt almost shy asking them to come over, fearing that she had bored and inconvenienced poor Suzanne with that marathon shopping. But the Delacroixs immediately dropped their pruning shears and bag of rose food, and were on her doorstep in a matter of seconds. She hung back in the hallway while they walked into the bedroom, then followed them inside.

The white walls were now covered in cream wallpaper, with a pattern of roses in muted red and gold tones, almost a moiré effect. Red velvet drapes, pulled aside by gold braid ropes, bordered the windows; cream-colored sheers let the sunlight into the room while softening the light's harsh edge. The old brass headboard was gone, replaced by a wrought-iron one, and the bed itself was covered by a red velvet duvet and piled high with pillows in red, green, and dark blue velvet, beaded and fringed. By the south window, overlooking the ocean, a wrought-iron table and two chairs sat, waiting for someone — Jennifer, for instance — to enjoy her morning coffee. The old overhead light was gone, replaced by a ceiling fan with a Tiffany-look stained glass shade; another Tiffany lamp, this one with beaded fringe hanging from its shade, rested on the night table. On the wall above the bed, a framed print of Leighton's *Flaming June.*

"I know, I know, San Francisco cathouse," Jennifer found herself babbling. "And the wallpaper's kind of crooked but —"

"Hush," Suzanne said, the way she did to the kids she watched when they started getting rowdy. "It works. I wasn't sure it would, but it really does."

"And how," Bill said. "And it's yours."

Mine, thought Jennifer, and basked in the ruddy glow of her room, and in the Delacroixs' praise. It was the first time in nearly a year that anyone had anything good to say about something she'd done.

They invited her to dinner, and she was too tired to refuse. Over potstickers and beef fried rice Bill said, "Jen, you still looking for a job?"

"I should be. But I've been so busy with the decorating I haven't given the help wanteds a good look yet."

"Well, I happen to know that Mr. Bradbury, who runs the main library — down on Victoria Drive? — is looking for an assistant. Not a whole lot of money, but he's a good sort. Arthritis is really slowing him down, unfortunately, so he's in need of help," Bill said. "Give him a call, if you're interested."

Jennifer had no library experience, other than a semester's worth of work-study back in her community college. Still, what was there to lose? "That sounds nice." Nice would be good, after her last employment experience. "Thanks for the word, Bill."

Bill smiled, the smile of Santa Claus filling a stocking. "My pleasure."

If Bill Delacroix was Santa Claus, Mr. Bradbury was one of his elves. Or a garden gnome. The world's tallest garden gnome, though Mr. Bradbury was not tall, in fact was a half-inch shorter than Jennifer. He had a very round head and almost no neck, his hair and beard were silver. The lenses of his glasses were thick; she thought of the bottoms of wine bottles. Behind the lenses his eyes were bright blue, and the first time his gaze fell on her she felt she was on a stage, the spotlight shining on her. It should have made her uncomfortable but it did not, for he smiled as well, and she felt special rather than singled out.

"Good afternoon, Ms. Thomson," he said when she arrived. His voice was naturally low from years of a library's hushed tones.

"Hello, Mr. Bradbury. It's good to meet you." Jennifer pitched her voice low to match his. They shook hands. His grip was very gentle, no more than a clasp.

"Dawn," Mr. Bradbury said, turning to the girl at the circulation desk. "Would you look after things for a few minutes?"

Mr. Bradbury ushered Jennifer into the back office. It was a small room, with only one window, but the dimness felt cozy rather than cramped. In one corner a small refrigerator, on top of that a hot plate with a teapot resting atop it. The walls were adorned with prints of Victoria Island, Tigertail Beach, Ansel Adams' photos of Yosemite. Mr. Bradbury's desk, an old mahogany rolltop with a laptop that provided a jolting touch of modernity, was awash in papers, but apparently there was a method to his madness; he plucked her resumé from the desk without a moment's searching, from under a granite paperweight. Carved into the paperweight: *If we are willing to attempt the impossible, God is willing to perform the miraculous.*

He offered her tea; it felt like a genuine offer, not like Alex Salto's offer of refreshment, which had felt like a ploy. She accepted the offer. He looked at her through the Darjeeling-scented steam rising from his mug, smiled. "How are you liking it here in Haven Cove, Ms. Thomson? A bit of a change from California, no doubt."

"That's very true," she replied. "But please, call me Jennifer."

The talk turned to her months in Haven Cove, the weather, the people. He knew the Delacroixs well; in fact, seemed to know almost everyone in town. When she mentioned her most recent place of employment, his mouth turned down slightly at Alex Salto's name, and she was relieved, knowing that the shortness of her employment there would not be held against her.

"I see that you worked in the library one semester at your community college," he said. "How did you like that?"

"It was all right," she said. "I didn't really work with the books themselves, I was at the reference desk, mostly looking up things for people."

"What was the strangest thing someone asked you to look up for them?"

She thought it over for a moment. "A lady once called and asked what temperature to bake an angel food cake."

He chuckled. "I had the same thing happen once, only the caller wanted to know how long to bake an apple pie."

Jennifer was expecting a question about her library experience, such as it was, and was trying to remember if she'd dealt with Library of Congress or Dewey Decimal. She didn't even know what system they used here in Canada.

Instead, he asked, "Tell me, do you like to read?"

"Some. Not as much as I probably should." She immediately regretted her answer. Of course she should have said she was a complete bookworm. But there was something about Mr. Bradbury's gaze, keen and patient, that made a lie in his presence difficult.

He must have seen some of this on her face. "Don't worry, that's all right. The inveterate readers are usually the worst people to work in a library. They spend all their time reading and none of the books get put away. I can't lie to you, Ms. Thomson. This isn't a very high-paying job. And it isn't very exciting. I can take care of the administrative end of things, answer the reference questions. Even the ones about the angel food cake. What I need..." He sighed, held up his hands. Even her inexpert eyes could see the slightly swollen joints of his fingers. "Arthritis. My hands simply aren't what they used to be. I need someone who can take care of the books and the day-to-day hands-on tasks of the library. And I need someone who's here more than one school quarter at a time. I love the high school students, of course, but these days they're more interested in the Internet than in musty old books. Do you see what I mean?"

"You need someone to be your hands," she said.

His face lit up. More than ever he looked like a garden gnome. "Yes, that's what I need. Are you interested?"

She was.

The Haven Cove library was well-stocked, and seemed to be rather larger on the inside than its outside dimensions would have permitted. There was the large room with the main stacks, fiction and nonfiction. There was a separate room for reference books, including three coin-operated photocopiers, and not once did Jennifer see all three in working order. "I keep trying to get funds for new copiers," Mr. Bradbury said with a deep sigh, "But that's not easily done." The children's books also had a separate room with bright-colored posters on the walls, the shelves crammed with thin, tall books with colorful spines. That room always seemed to smell like crayons, a waxy, nostalgic scent.

Within a few days she had mastered the classification and shelving. Canada did indeed use a different system from the States, but learning it presented no problem. "If you can count and know the alphabet, you can find any book here. And if you don't, well, perhaps we can find you a literacy program," Mr. Bradbury said with a smile. In those same few days, she got to know the routine. She arrived at nine, half an hour before opening. Mr. Bradbury, who did not drive, was dropped off by the bus a block away and usually walked through the library doors at a quarter past, always with his umbrella in his right hand, a book or magazine or newspaper tucked under his left arm. She found herself looking each morning to see what he was reading, for it changed from day to day. On Monday it might be a collection of Emily Dickinson poems. On Tuesday, a Margaret Atwood novel. Wednesday, a weekly news magazine; Thursday, a biography of the wives of Henry the Eighth; Friday, the *New York Times Book Review*. Saturdays she had off, and Sundays the library was closed.

Jennifer liked the Haven Cove library. Most of all she liked its smell, a slightly musty, cinnamon scent that reminded her of her grandmother's old house in San Francisco. She liked her work: the orderliness of it, the comforting surroundings. And most of all, she was doing something useful rather than serving as a cog in a machine. Perhaps it was only a very small sort of usefulness, nothing important in the great scheme of things, but that did not diminish her pleasure in it.

Most of all she liked Mr. Bradbury. There was something familiar about him that she could not pin down. He did not remind her of her grandfathers; both now dead, one had been obsessed with golf and the other's mind was lost in the fogs of dementia. He did not remind her of any teachers she'd had, though in his way he was a teacher. Not a day went by without Mr. Bradbury quoting some writer or other, or making an allusion to some novel or poem. Yet she never felt he was doing this to show off his knowledge, or even to persuade her into reading something. His head was simply full of things, and they spilled out without him being aware of it.

They were organizing the little office, making room for a small desk she could use. "I've been needing a reason to clean up my desk," he said. "It's all gone to wrack and ruin." He stacked papers, crammed them into the cubbyholes of his desk. She knew that in a matter of days they would be all over his desk again.

Jennifer had noticed the ancient radio he kept in the office. Depending on the time of day it was tuned to the classical station, the jazz station, or the NPR station from the States, reception thin and crackly. "I brought in a boombox," she said. "Not a real big one, but I think it might get better reception. And we can play CDs, if that's all right."

"As long as the volume is low, it's fine. Here, I'll go get it."

He left the room to get the boombox. After he left, she walked over to his desk, where she'd seen the picture, earlier that day. She did not mean to pry but could not help it, needed to look up close and see if it was what she thought it was.

A younger Mr. Bradbury. Some forty years younger, she could see that even if the date hadn't been written on the matte bordering the photo. A Mr. Bradbury in a black robe, a soutane they called it, she'd read that somewhere, with a white collar. Beside him a man and a woman, older than he. He had the man's round head and nonexistent neck, the woman's bright keen eyes and her smile. *Holy orders,* said the writing on the mat, and a date forty years ago.

It did not answer all her questions about Mr. Bradbury — who he was, why she felt calmed in his presence. In fact, raised even more questions. But she understood now why she had not been able to lie to him.

Chapter Sixteen

A new year, and nothing was different at Du Lac's Grace Methodist Church save that the Christmas decorations had been taken down, leaving the church hall looking bereft and, though the meeting was well-attended, rather empty.

Sean sat a bit more toward the front than he usually did, the better to put himself in Doug MacReady's field of view and demonstrate that yes, he was interested in meeting with those who had sent MacReady. He waited, engaged in small talk about the weather with those seated nearby. Without craning his head around he looked about for MacReady, and finally saw him off to one side.

MacReady was talking to another man. He had only seen this other man once before, and through binoculars, so it took Sean a second to recognize him. Tall, bearded, a certain air about him. Almost kingly, you could say. Richard Blaine.

MacReady and Blaine had their heads together, talking. Sean curbed his desire to watch them, only gave quick glances their way, as if he was just interested in saying hello to MacReady. Out of the corner of his eye he saw MacReady nod, tilt his head slightly, and then both of them were looking directly at him. Their scrutiny lasted for no more than two seconds, but he felt it keenly, like a floodlight appearing out of darkness, making him visible for a moment, and then sliding away. He felt nothing in their gaze beyond assessment; whether it was positive or negative he would have to find out later.

Then Blaine clapped MacReady on the shoulder. They parted, and Sean kept his face carefully still and his expression slightly bored, trying to watch the two men out of his peripheral vision. Blaine was heading to the edge of the small lecture platform; as he neared it a red-haired woman approached him, spoke, and pointed toward the back of the hall, to the refreshment table. Blaine nodded, smiled, said something and then leaned toward the woman, perhaps for a kiss. Sean did not see this, for MacReady was approaching, easing his way down the aisle.

"Doug," Sean said, "How are you doing?"

"Very good, very good," MacReady replied. He looked as if he'd spent much of the holidays outdoors. There was a stripe of sunburn across his nose. "How was your New Year's?"

It seemed something ran an icy hand down his spine. Nothing showed in his face or voice. "Uneventful," he replied. "Yours?"

"Interesting. I'm sorry you missed out."

"I am too." Meant it more than he would have imagined.

"Well, I've got good news. One of the people I really wanted you to meet is here tonight. He'll be the speaker. Maybe you could come up and introduce yourself, afterwards," MacReady said with the shrug that was his trademark.

"I'll do that."

"Great. I have to go, see you later, Sam."

"Later."

A few minutes later the minister of Grace Methodist, a thin, reedy little man named Svenson, went to the podium, tapped the microphone, blew into it once or twice. "Ah, hello, ladies and gentlemen." He waited for them to quiet, then said, "Our speaker tonight is, I believe, well-known to many of you. He and his lovely wife have done a great deal for our community here in Du Lac, and I'm very pleased to have him here tonight. Ladies and gentlemen, Richard Blaine."

Sean applauded along with the rest of them, wondering what Blaine would say. Certainly not a call to arms or a recruiting speech. That would arouse too much suspicion. Blaine was adept at deflecting attention away from himself. A Web search of antigovernment group monitors found no mention of his name. Sean had scoured the local papers and found no mention of Blaine beyond the annual human interest fluff piece about Blaine's Christmas tree farm, some charity event news, and, from nine years ago, an announcement of his marriage to Anna Cleary of Fairview, Minnesota. There was nothing to indicate that Richard Blaine was anything other than an upright, honest citizen who was active in his community.

Had Henry Connolly lied? Sean didn't think so. He hoped not, for then he'd be sorely tempted to dredge Connolly up from the bottom of the quarry where he was currently moldering and spit in the little rat bastard's face. No, Sean felt certain that he had the right man.

Blaine took the stage, stood at the podium. He did not bother tapping the microphone or asking *Is this thing on?* He did not fumble for notes or give those half-defiant, half-apologetic looks that mark someone with no skill for public speaking. Watching as Blaine looked out over the audience, Sean had the feeling that if he asked every member of the audience, no matter where they sat, they would say that Blaine was looking directly at them.

"Hello, my friends and neighbors," Blaine said. His voice was deep and rich; he could have had a broadcasting career with no trouble at all. "It's a new year for all of us. And I also find myself looking back on last year. Looking back on the last few years, in fact. And as I do this, I want to be happy. But I find, often, that I cannot.

"I look back and I see many things that trouble me. I see families lose their farms because of the economy, and stand by watching their property, even their dishes and their children's toys, be sold at auction to the highest bidder. I see people surrender land that has been in their families for generations, to the environmental agencies. To people who care more for owls and squirrels than for their own countrymen. Understand me," Blaine said with a slight smile. "I like animals. Ask my wife, she'll tell you. But I know the pride that comes with owning land. It is not merely a possession, it is part of you. And to be asked — no, forced to give that up. To give up your inheritance, your birthright. And for what?" Blaine spread his hands wide in a gesture of emptiness.

"I see parents taking their children out of the public schools, not wanting to subject their children to a place where profanity is smiled upon but please, don't mention the name of Jesus Christ. Where atheists and homosexuals are free to recruit, but our children are not allowed to hold Bible study after school.

"And most of all, I see fear. I see good Americans afraid of what their country has become. It is not bad enough that even last year, in Los Angeles, foreign militants have attacked our way of life. But in our own country, we feel afraid. Threatened. At times, under attack. Our birthright to this country, our rights as citizens, our ability to live our lives in the way we know is right — all these things are under threat. And not from the Islamic jihad or any other foreign power. But from within our own country.

"You would think that as I thought about all this, I was not happy." A faint ripple of laughter in the audience. Blaine gave them a quick smile. "I was. But not downhearted. There is a difference. Unhappiness is temporary. To be downhearted is to let a poison into your soul. And I am not downhearted. Because I see past these things I've mentioned. I see the people of Du Lac and other towns joining together to help their friends and neighbors who are in need. I see parents who have taken their children out of our so-called public schools, who have sacrificed their time and money in order to teach their children not just reading and math, but the values that they cherish. I see people who are willing to take action—"

Sean felt a jolt all through his nerve endings. *Knew* Blaine was his man.

"—to defend their way of life. And when I see all these things, how can I possibly be downhearted?" Blaine smiled.

Sean could have sworn that Blaine's eyes were misty. Never mind a career in broadcasting, this guy could have an Academy Award handed to him.

"I am here tonight to ask for your help. As you know, late last year there was a fire at the textile mill over in Green Falls, and many people here in Du Lac have lost work. The mill owners had hoped to have things up and running by Christmas, but unfortunately, they are having some disputes with the state government.

"There are many men and women who are struggling to provide for their families until the mill is reopened. And I know that things are tight, and that money is always hard to come by after the holidays. But I am asking you to give what you can to help. And we need more than money. Donations of clothing, canned goods, anything that will help. These families will appreciate it. And so do I, from the bottom of my heart. Thank you."

The room broke out into thunderous applause as Blaine left the stage. Sean joined in, sincerely enough, for he knew the value of a good performance, and was able to appreciate one that was not simply good, but remarkable. Even if the performer was the enemy.

After the meeting Sean began to make his way through the crowd toward Blaine, to introduce himself and to congratulate Blaine on his speech. It was only as he drew near, waiting his turn while Blaine spoke with others, that Sean began to wonder just how much of it was a performance. He wondered how much of it was real.

If it was a performance, it was a hell of a good one, and it hadn't stopped when Blaine left the stage. Sean noticed that when Blaine spoke to someone, he never took his eyes away from that person. It was as if, when talking to Blaine, you were the only person in the room. Sean watched the expression in peoples' eyes when they talked to Blaine, saw that they were surprised to find that he was listening to them, instead of merely waiting for his turn to speak, as most people did. It was a rare skill, to make people feel that way. Robert had that talent. So had Edwards, Sean's first boss, the one who had recruited him.

Then he was standing in front of Blaine. *Play it right.* "Mr. Blaine, I'm Sam Lewis. I have to tell you, I very much liked what you had to say tonight."

Blaine's eyes seemed to light up when he saw Sean. "I'm glad we could finally meet. Doug MacReady told me about you. And please, call me Richard."

They shook hands. Blaine's grip was firm and confident; his own grip matched Blaine's. The time for shirking the spotlight was over, he needed to get into Blaine's confidence. Needed Blaine to see him as someone useful. Someone necessary.

"I'm sorry you couldn't make it at New Year's, Sam. From what Doug's told me, I think you'd have found things interesting."

"I know, I wish I could have been there. Maybe next time? Sooner rather than later, I hope."

Blaine's eyes were gray, not a pale, washed-out gray, but closer to the color of steel. "Yes, very soon. You like venison?" Blaine asked.

"Haven't had it in years and miss it more than I ever thought I would."

Blaine chuckled. "There's going to be a little excursion next Saturday. Six in the morning, at the Deer's Head Lodge. Know where that is?"

"No, but I've heard of it."

"It's easy to get to. Doug can give you directions. Make sure your license is up-to-date. We play by the rules." For the first time there was a flicker of something else behind Blaine's steel-colored eyes. "When it suits our needs, that is."

"I'll be there," Sean said. They shook hands again, their eyes met. Sean knew what he'd met tonight, and the realization both shook and fascinated him.

In his own way, Blaine was an equal.

Midnight at the Lakeview Terrace. Darkness in apartment 233. Silence in 233 as well, though the room was occupied. Sean was a silent sleeper, a listener would have been hard-pressed to hear the sound of his breathing. This had always annoyed Monique. "You're so quiet," she'd said once. "You don't snore or mumble anything. Half the time I can't hear you *breathe*. It's like sleeping with a dead person sometimes."

"And how would you know, Moni?" he'd replied. "You're a necrophile? I didn't know you were so kinky."

She'd hit him with the pillow and laughed. "But it's creepy!"

He didn't know what Monique was complaining about. Hell, he'd seen Robert sleep with his eyes open; now *that* was creepy. But for all his silence he was a light sleeper. When the banging on his door started he was awake almost instantly; the gun snatched out from under the pillow next to him. He was braced and ready to shoot in a few seconds.

Who was it? One of Blaine's friends? An emissary from his old employers, sent to do the job Beatty had failed at?

That icy hand caressed his spine again. Was it Beatty himself?

He tried to dismiss the idea and failed. The hammering on his door was too much like the hammering on the ice. He heard feet shuffle outside the door and it was all too easy to imagine Beatty standing there like some ghoul from the old horror comics. Raising his water-bloated fist to pound on the door. *Can't you hear me knocking, Irish? Come on, let me in.*

Another flurry of pounding on the door. Should he stay silent, pretend not to be here? Or ask *Who goes there?*

A slurred voice called out, "Stacy? Yo, Stacy, you there? It's Jay."

"Jesus Christ," Sean muttered, lowering the gun. He called out, "No Stacy here, my friend."

"What the — " A pause. The voice became contrite, if no less tipsy. "Oh shit, wrong floor. Sorry, man, my bad." The sound of footsteps going down the hall, and then silence reigned again.

Sean sighed, put the gun back under the pillow. For some time he lay awake, staring into darkness. His eyes did not want to close; troubled thoughts darted around the edges of his mind. Thoughts of Blaine and his cronies, and what he was up against. Thoughts of Robert, wondering if he was well, wishing he had his counsel. Most unwelcome, thoughts not so much of Beatty himself, but that he had so vividly imagined Beatty on the other side of his door. That sort of thing had never happened before.

Then again, he had never killed a friend before.

With the discipline of years he shoved the thoughts out of his mind. He would attend to the task at hand, get some needed sleep, and as for Beatty, well, Beatty shouldn't have tried to take him out. That was all.

Still, it was quite some time before he was able to sleep again. That had never happened before either.

Chapter Seventeen

"Sorry I'm late," Jennifer said as she struggled out of her raincoat. "Storm must have done something to the power. My alarm clock went all wacky and didn't go off this morning."

"Think nothing of it," Mr. Bradbury shrugged. His book was in front of him. Today it was a collection of Ernest Hemingway short stories. "Half the winter I'm in late because the buses are running behind. You would think that people would remember how to drive in bad weather, seeing as how it happens every year."

"I have to say that sometimes I miss a warm, sunny winter," Jennifer said.

"Care for some tea? The water's all ready."

"I think today's a coffee day. Don't we have the third-graders coming in this afternoon?"

"Oh dear. Let the wild rumpus start." Mr. Bradbury closed his eyes and breathed deep the scent of Darjeeling as if it had restorative powers. Maybe it was his version of aromatherapy, Jennifer thought and repressed a smile. "I'd forgotten that. I wish their regular teacher would come back. Mrs. Kemper seems a bit scattered to me."

"I hear that. Who's the regular teacher?"

"Ellen Riordan. Lovely woman. She took maternity leave six months ago."

"She should be back soon, then."

Mr. Bradbury shook his head. "She and the baby both had a lot of complications. Things are better than they were, but no one's sure when she'll be back. Or if she'll be back."

"That's too bad. For her and for the third-graders." Jennifer went into the back room to make coffee, taking the plate she'd brought in with her. While she waited for the java to brew she took the foil off the plate. The scones, a dozen of them, were on the plate; for a moment she regretted bringing them in. But yesterday had been too rainy to go out, the Delacroixs were out of town, and she was bored. Her predecessors at the house on Douglas had, for reasons unknown, left behind two banker boxes full of cooking magazines. For something to do, she'd been looking at them, and on a whim decided to make lemon-poppyseed scones. Jennifer wasn't sure what scones were, exactly, but the word conjured up afternoon teas and chamber music, both of which she could easily imagine Mr. Bradbury enjoying. So she'd made them, and though she followed the recipe she wasn't really sure they were any good. They looked lumpy and rather unappetizing. She considered throwing them out, then decided the worst he could say was that they were bad.

She must have done something right, because when she went back to the circulation desk, her coffee in one hand and the plate of scones in the other, Mr. Bradbury said, "Something smells good." Then his eyes lit up. "Oh! You made scones."

"I hope they're good, I mean, I never made them before and if you don't like them I'm…"

He held up a finger to his lips. "Shhhhh. Never apologize ahead of time." He plucked a scone from the plate, took a bite.

She was sure she'd screwed up. For a moment he had a strangely pensive look on his face. Probably thinking about how to politely say, *Jennifer, your scones would serve better as doorstops.*

"You've never made these before?"

"No, never. That bad, huh?"

"That good. Like the ones my mother used to make."

"Really?"

"Really. You ought to have a little more faith in yourself, Jennifer."

She let that one slide by. "So when do the third-graders arrive?"

"Two o'clock. That should give us time to eat all these scones. The last thing those children need is more sugar."

Jennifer found the book after the third-graders left, while she was straightening out the juvenile room. They weren't bad kids, just kids, and there was the usual mess of paper wads and pencils scattered over the tables, books lying helter-skelter. She had finished tidying up, shelved the cartful of books she'd brought in, and was getting ready to leave the room when she saw the book, far off in the corner, on the floor.

She walked over, knelt, and picked the book up. A children's book about Canadian wildlife. Must be science report time, she thought, and flipped to a random page.

Someone, some kid, had drawn all over the pages. No, not drawn. Scribbled, big looping scrawls of pencil, in some places so hard the pencil had gone through the paper. Bad enough that she found graffiti in the restrooms, but at least some of that was occasionally amusing. She'd been working at the library long enough to feel protective of the books, and defacing one was just uncalled for. "Creepy little vandal," she said, glancing out the window to see if the school bus was still there. It wasn't.

Jennifer brought the book back with her to the circulation desk, handed it to Mr. Bradbury. "Looks like we've got to replace this one."

He leafed through the book, his eyebrows slightly raised. "It happens. Not often, but it does."

She was a little surprised at how annoyed she felt. "I thought I'd gotten away from all that. But it's like the graffiti taggers in L.A." It was a scratch on the shining surface of Haven Cove. A tiny one, but a scratch nonetheless.

Mr. Bradbury turned to the back of the book. A sheet of paper slipped out; it had a wrinkled look, as if it had been crumpled and then smoothed out, shoved into the back of the book. He gazed at the paper a moment, then handed it to her. "Look at this."

The paper was a school assignment, asking the student to write a theme. A list of half a dozen topics was provided, but what Jennifer noticed was more of those pencil scrawls, and for the first time, words. *Stupid stupid stupid.*

"Someone hates their homework as much as the book."

Mr. Bradbury took the book and the assignment paper back from her. "Well, there's the reason. And then there's the real reason."

"What do you mean?"

"What seems to be the reason someone does something, and what that reason really is, are often very different."

Jennifer was silent. Thinking of the phone calls she'd gotten after she sold her story, the names she'd been called. All she'd wanted to do was tell them why she'd done it, just explain things. So they could know the real reason instead of the reason they wanted to believe.

Mr. Bradbury went on. "This doesn't feel like someone writing dirty words on the wall. It's not even 'Kilroy was here.' Something else is happening."

"I'll keep an eye out next time they're here. See what I can see."

He nodded. "I think that's a good idea."

A week later, the third-graders back again. Mr. Bradbury took charge of the circulation desk while Jennifer patrolled the juvenile room as stealthily as she could, quietly shelving books and calling no attention to herself.

It was toward the end of their hour that she saw him. Off at one end of the room, away from the others. A boy with his blond head bent over the book in front of him, nose nearly touching the page. One hand held a pencil, and he was poking the pages of the book, leaving little black dots. The other hand was clenched in his hair. As she watched he sat up straight, looked at the clock on the far wall, and for a moment she thought the look on his face was one of anger. No, not anger, she realized as she looked at his eyes. Frustration.

She thought of those scrawled words *stupid stupid stupid.* It wasn't the book he was calling names. It was himself.

Jennifer walked over to the table. He had his head bent over the book again and didn't notice her until she spoke. "Hi," she said in her library-quiet voice.

He looked up at her, startled. His eyes were brown, an interesting contrast to the blond hair, brown and wide. His eyes got even wider when he saw her: the adult, the person in charge. But she wasn't angry any more.

"OK if I sit down?" she asked.

"Yes, ma'am," he said in a small voice.

She sat, instinctively put her hands out in front of her so he could see they were empty, nothing in them to hit him with. "My name's Jennifer. What's yours?" She hoped she wasn't talking to him like he was a baby, but she hadn't talked to an eight-year-old since she herself was eight, two decades ago.

"Matthew Tally, ma'am." His eyes were not quite so wide now.

At least he had manners. She began to think Mr. Bradbury was right, this wasn't just vandalism. "I work here at the library. I wanted to talk to you about something."

He looked down at the book, at the little black pencil dots on the page. "I'm sorry. I'll bring in the money and pay for the books."

"We can worry about that later." She thought of telling him that it wasn't right to mess up things that weren't yours, but she could tell he already knew that. But the question remained, and she asked it. "Can you tell me why you did that?"

It took her ten minutes of gentle prodding, and a promise not to tell the teacher. "I didn't mean to mess things up," he finally said in that soft, polite voice. "I just…it makes me...all the books and the stupid words, stupid me, I don't know how…" He didn't finish. He didn't have to.

"You don't know how to read," she said, not sure if it was a question or a statement.

It didn't matter. Matthew Tally looked back down at the desk with a fierce, fixed look, blinking too much. She recognized it. Trying not to cry.

"Matthew," she said as gently as she could. "Hey, Matthew. Look at me."

He finally did. He wasn't crying but his eyes were shiny. "Am I in trouble?"

"No. No, don't worry." What to do, she wondered. Talk to the teacher. She thought of the substitute teacher, harried and disorganized. No. "Is it OK if I talk to your Mom?"

Matthew's eyes got a strange look, sad and yet distant. "My Mom's gone."

Dead, he meant. Poor baby. "How about your Dad? I won't get you in trouble, I promise. I just want to talk to him, OK?"

"OK," he said.

From the other end of the room came the sounds of children gathering their books. "I have to go," he said.

"All right. Can you do one thing for me?"

"Yes, ma'am."

She held up the book. "Don't go scribbling in any more books. Can you do that?"

He nodded, got to his feet and gathered his books and papers.

"Thank you for not getting me in trouble," he said.

"We'll work it out. I promise."

For the first time he smiled at her, a quick, shy smile. Then he joined the other kids, leaving Jennifer sitting there, wondering what she would say to Matthew's father.

Jennifer got up early the next morning and drove down to the harbor. Mr. Bradbury didn't have a home address or number for Matthew Tally's father, but he did have a name and an occupation. "Gene's a fisherman," he said. "And when the fish aren't out, he's usually helping fix up someone's boat. The harbor's your best bet."

She'd only been down here a few times. Once to stroll around, the other times to have some dinner at one of the seafood restaurants; she thought it was worth moving up here just for the salmon, so fresh and melt-in-your-mouth perfect. Jennifer got out of her car, feeling very much a landlubber. And yet she liked it, the bustle of people, men mostly, going to and fro on their boats, even liked the smell — salt water, diesel fuel, and fish all combined, the tarry scent of the docks underneath.

Harbormaster said a sign on a small shack, and she walked over. The man inside was barking into a radio. "I did not say that. If I said that, I would be a liar. I don't lie — I'm a Christian, damn it! Over and out." He hung up the radio and looked at her. His voice was brusque, probably from years of shouting into radios, but his face was kind and he smiled at her. A gold tooth winked at her from the corner of his mouth, making him look like a cheerful pirate. "Can I help you, miss?"

"Ah, yes. I'm looking for Gene Tally."

He pointed to Jennifer's right. "Gene's the trawler with the blue trim."

Jennifer stared blankly. She wouldn't know a trawler from the *Queen Mary*, and more than ever she felt like an idiot.

The harbormaster took pity on her and said, "About ten slips down. His boat's called the *Tally-ho*. Gene's a blond guy, starting to go bald."

"Thanks," she said. She made her way down the docks with no difficulty and found the *Tally-ho*. On the front part of the deck — she wondered what the names of all the parts were, and which was port or starboard — was a man, kneeling and tying some sort of knot. She couldn't make out much of his appearance, but she could hear him humming some tune as he worked.

"Mr. Tally? Sir?" she called out, and he looked up at her. His resemblance to his son was striking, except for the eyes. Gene Tally's eyes were not brown but blue, a strangely pale blue, as if their original hue had been faded by years of looking out at the sea and the sun.

He looked back at her and did not immediately answer. A faint frown line appeared between his brows, as if he was trying to remember something. "Yes, that's me," he said finally.

"My name's Jennifer Thomson, can I talk to you for a minute?"

"OK, sure." He got up, walked over, and nimbly jumped from the boat to the dock. As he stood in front of her that little line appeared between his brows again. "What can I do for you?" His Canadian accent was a bit different from others she'd heard.

"I want to talk to you about Matthew."

The frown line deepened. "Is something wrong? Is he OK?"

"Yes. No. What I mean is that I work in the library, and I found him messing up some of the books. Scribbling in them. But you see —"

"I'll pay for the damage," he said.

"No, it's not that. I talked to him and asked him why and he did it because he's upset. He says he can't read, Mr. Tally."

Gene's thin mouth got thinner; he turned his gaze to his feet, then to the sky, anywhere but toward her. Finally he sighed. "Did you talk to his teacher?"

"I thought I should talk to you first. The teacher's a sub, I don't know if she can handle this. And well, you are his father," Jennifer said.

He sighed again, a sound of disappointment. She hoped he wasn't going to give Matthew grief over this. "I'll talk to him," he said.

"I think you should do more than that."

"Like what?"

She felt something thrumming inside her like a live wire, and she realized that she was getting very annoyed with this man. "Well, maybe you could help tutor him."

For the first time since she told him Matthew couldn't read he looked her in the eyes. "I can't."

"Why not? Are you too busy?"

"It's not what you think." He walked back onto his boat, calling over his shoulder. "Thank you for coming by, Ms. Thomson."

"Look, I'm not going to leave it like this," she said. She kept seeing Matthew Tally with his hand clenched in his hair in frustration. "Your son can't read, doesn't that bother you?"

He turned back to her. "Yes, it bothers me a hell of a lot!"

"Then why don't you do something about it?"

"Because I can't either."

As soon as he said it a look of shock came over his face; she felt the same look on hers. He couldn't believe he'd said it and she couldn't believe she'd heard it. She turned away, trying to think of what to say, and all she could come up with was that old useless standby *I'm sorry*. She started to say it, but before she got the words out he'd fired up the engine of the *Tally-ho* and was steering his way out of the harbor.

As dusk was falling and softening the edges of the world, Jennifer stood waiting at the *Tally-ho's* slip, a cup of coffee in each hand. As she waited she took the occasional sip from her cup. She was beginning to wonder if a warm-up for Gene's coffee might not be a bad idea when his boat pulled into the slip. If he saw her he gave no sign; he was busy unloading salmon into a large wheeled bin. As she waited, a man with a coverall declaring him to be from the local fish processing plant came and took away the catch. As the man left, Gene raised his arms overhead, stretched and sighed, then stepped onto the dock.

Only then did he notice her. "Oh," he said. "Hello."

"Hi." She walked over and handed him his coffee. "The harbormaster said you liked a cup of coffee after you come in. I told them to give you your usual."

"I see. Thanks." As if to make up for his gratitude he said, "And what are you having, Miss California? A soy milk cinnamon half-caff grande latte?"

"French roast with one cream and one sugar. Same as you," Jennifer replied. She didn't stop to wonder why he called her Miss California, but forged ahead. "I wanted to apologize for this morning. I didn't mean to...well, I still think the most important thing is to help Matthew. And I'd like to help."

"Thank you, but I don't think there's much you can do."

"Why not?" He didn't answer, just began walking down the docks toward the gate. "Look, what is your problem?" she asked as she walked beside him. "So I found out something you didn't want me to know, big deal. The important thing is —"

"Is that I know who you are," he said, cutting off her words. He stopped walking, turned to face her. "Yeah, I know who you are and why you're here. You're just visiting until you can get your head together and go back home, Miss California. You don't know anything about me or Matthew or anybody else here. And I am glad that you're concerned, but really, it's not your business, OK? Thanks for the coffee." He turned and walked up the docks, and she watched him go. What cut her most deeply was not anything he'd said but the look she'd read in his eyes. *I found out something* you *didn't want* me *to know. How's it feel, Miss California? How does it feel?*

Jennifer walked along the docks, her gait stiff. She kept her face up to the wind and blinked more often than necessary, telling herself that she would not cry, not until she was in the safety of her car, would not, damn it.

She made it. Just.

Chapter Eighteen

Sean arrived at the lodge a little after six. It was one of those deeply cold, clear mornings when the very air seemed frozen, would sear your throat if you breathed too quickly or too deeply. His van's heater was balky at the best of times, and his breath steamed, his bad knee ached. Most likely his coffee and breakfast sandwich were stone cold by now; he had an instant's longing for Florida in January, for warmth and for pretty girls in sundresses. As he drove into the lodge's parking lot, he put that longing away into a box and locked it. He parked, got out of the van, checked his watch. Five after six. Not too early, not too late.

He needn't have worried about punctuality. When he walked into the lodge — blessed warmth! — the only two there were Richard Blaine and Doug MacReady. They waved to him, he waved back. They were sitting in the lodge's main foyer, by the fireplace. A large, low table in front of them held several thermoses of coffee and a large plate of muffins.

"Hi, Sam," said MacReady. "Oh, I should have told you not to bring that swill." He waved at the coffee table. "Breakfast compliments of Richard's wife."

"And there's a cooler full of sandwiches out in my truck," said Blaine. "Chicken, roast beef and I think egg salad."

Sean tossed his cold coffee and Egg McMuffin into a nearby trashcan. No matter if these muffins were like rocks, he'd eat them. He had a cast-iron stomach, which had come in handy many times over the years. "Glad I didn't pack a lunch."

"With Anna around, you don't have to," MacReady said. "She's the best cook in the county. Right, Richard?"

Blaine simultaneously bowed his head humbly and grinned with pride. "We'll let Sam be the judge of that."

Sean sat down and poured some coffee and took one of the muffins. The coffee was just the way he liked it, hot and strong. He took a bite of the muffin — real blueberries, my God — and realized with a pang that this was the first decent food he'd had since visiting Robert last year. "Doug, you're full of shit."

"Oh?" MacReady seemed to be bristling at the suggestion that Anna's cooking might not be all he said it was, but Blaine gave Sean a sly smile.

"She's the best cook in the *state.*"

"See, Doug, I told you to trust your instincts," Blaine said with a chuckle. "Oh, more arrivals."

The men began arriving and soon were drinking coffee, laughing, and making happy noises over the muffins. They were all men Sean had seen at the New Year's meeting, and he had the impression that this was the most trusted circle. He felt a moment's triumph that he deliberately repressed; he was too new, too unknown to be admitted to the inner circle so easily. Something else was going on.

The last ones finally showed up, two men, both tall and skinny, clearly brothers. "Sorry we're late," said the one who was losing his hair.

"Battery needed a jump," added the one with the mustache and the beady eyes.

"Not a problem," said Blaine. "Boys, we have a new arrival. Sam Lewis, meet the Wickersham brothers. Steve and Eddie."

Eddie (the balding one) reached out and shook his hand, offered a "Pleased to meet you." Steve shook his hand but said nothing, gave a slight nod. Sean noticed that Steve looked at him a beat longer than necessary; he ratcheted up his caution a notch.

Introductions made, pleasantries exchanged, the coffee and muffins consumed, the group made its way outside. Blaine casually said, "Steve and Eddie, you take the north stand. Doug, you and Walt take the south one. I'll take the east one — Sam, why don't you stick with me?"

"Sounds good," he replied.

"Jess and Irwin, you take west unless you want to trade with the others."

The group split up into their assigned directions. Sean and Blaine walked, and for a long time neither said anything. The sounds of the other hunters had died away and it was just the crunch of their boots on snow, the sound of their breathing. Sean let Blaine lead the way, let him set the pace, which was a good one. A few puffy clouds hung in the sky now, and from time to time they hid the sun. After the brilliance of sunlight on snow, the shade seemed darker than it should have, seemed to leach the color out of the world.

There was a clearing in the woods, on the side of a hill, and Blaine stopped. On the other side of the clearing Sean could see a tree stand. "Let's rest for a bit. I don't know about you, but I definitely need to quit smoking," Blaine said. "I'm getting winded." Smoker he might be, but Blaine did not sound the slightest bit winded.

"Works for me," Sean replied.

"Nice rifle, by the way," Blaine said. "Where'd you get it?"

"A friend gave it to me."

There was a large fir tree, its trunk nearly two feet wide, and they both leaned against it, both pretending to rest. It occurred to Sean that if assassination was what he was after, he could do it right now. That was precisely what troubled him. Was it likely for him to get into the inner circle so soon? To be alone with Blaine before he was tested, proven trustworthy? From down the halls of memory, one of his first missions, he heard Robert saying, *If something seems too good to be true, watch out, because it probably is.*

No probably about it. It might look as if he was alone with Blaine, but he wasn't. He would bet his life — *was* betting his life, actually — that a few of the others were nearby. Hell, the stand assignments were probably a ruse. Blaine probably had the whole route they'd taken mapped out, had men stationed along it so he and Blaine were never out of sight. It made perfect sense. Blaine had his most trusted men here, men he could rely on to shoot straight and well should Blaine give the signal. Men who could be trusted to keep their mouths shut.

All it would take was one false move on Sean's part or saying the wrong thing. Or not even that. Maybe just Blaine deciding that this was not a risk worth taking. Somewhere out of sight, men waited with their fingers on triggers, waited for Blaine's signal, and he wouldn't even hear the bullet that took him out. He had no protection: thinking they might frisk him, he'd left the vest and his pistol at his apartment. Apart from the rifle, the most deadly thing on him was his Swiss Army knife. All they had to do was dump him in the woods somewhere, let him be found and written off as a hunting accident, too bad.

Sean felt no fear. That was an emotion for later, when he could safely let his guard down. He'd lost count of the times that he had kept the fear at bay, only to have the shakes begin as soon as he was behind the door of the safe house. He took a cigarette out of his pack; his fingers were steady. "Would you like one?" he asked. Voice calm and steady, the voice of a man offering a friend a smoke.

"No, thanks, not now." Blaine waited until Sean's cigarette was lit, then said, "Doug told me about some of the things you've said at the meetings. He liked them, and so do I. You think the way we do. You can see how things are going in this country. We've gotten so far away from ourselves..." Blaine shook his head sadly. "I sometimes think, if I have children, I wonder if when they're my age, their America will be one we'd even recognize."

"I see what you mean," Sean replied. "And I'm glad you like what I've said. But I think the time for saying things is over. Maybe the time has come for doing things."

He looked Blaine in the eyes. Here, now, was the gamble. Blaine looked back at him, and in his gaze was the warmth of the idealist and the coldness of a man who had ordered the deaths of several hundred people. "Yes, I think that time has come. Because make no mistake, Sam. The battle lines have been drawn. Waco. Ruby Ridge. Oklahoma City. Los Angeles." Blaine paused, waited for a reaction.

Sean gave back nothing but a nod, a pleased gleam in his eye.

Apparently the response was, for now, acceptable. "I have to know if I can count on you to do your work for the cause," Blaine said. "That work may seem very trivial at times. Or it can call for action that seems terrible."

"As in any war," Sean said.

"You understand then," Blaine said. "That this is a war."

"Yes."

"And you are committed to fighting this war?"

"Yes." Sean knew that if he answered otherwise, he would not leave these woods alive.

Blaine nodded, then extended his hand. This was the part that always bothered Sean, the handshake, though it was inevitable. From his earliest years he had been raised to believe a handshake was a powerful thing, an almost sacred promise of trust. Scout's honor and all that. He had broken the trust formed by a handshake thousands of times, yet it never failed to send a faint twinge of remorse through him. But he let none of this show, merely took the offered hand.

"I think I'll take that smoke now, Sam," Blaine said.

As he held the lighter out for Blaine, the sun came out from behind a cloud and lit up the clearing, dazzling light winking back from the snow and ice, making the lighter's small point of flame nearly invisible.

He saw it. In a winter-dead bush, something else reflecting back at him. Light winking off the glass of a rifle scope.

The cigarette lit, Blaine took a step away from him. Sean's experienced eye saw the scope move slightly, tracking not him, but Blaine.

No altruism in his next action. *Oh no you don't, rat bastard. He's mine.*

"So —" Blaine began.

He lunged toward Blaine, pulled him to the ground. They both heard the whiz of the bullet and the thunk as it hit the tree. As they hit the ground, a chunk of wood from the tree landed in front of their noses.

"What the hell —"

"Shhh. Stay down," he hissed at Blaine, who needed no prompting.

From the woods a confusion of noises. A babble of voices, two more shots, a yell of pain. The rattle and rustle of bushes, the crunch of boots on snow. Above the general din, a voice Sean already recognized as Steve Wickersham's yelling, "*Now,* cocksucker!"

They waited. Blaine looked alert; there was fear in his eyes but nothing close to panic.

MacReady's voice: "All clear, guys. We've got him."

They both got to their feet. Blaine paused a moment to brush snow off his jacket; if he was shaken from nearly getting killed, he gave no sign. They walked to the other side of the clearing. There, on his knees with his hands on top of his head, was a man dressed in winter camouflage. His right leg bled from a bullet wound, one side of his face was swollen and discolored, probably from a blow with a rifle butt. MacReady stood in front of the kneeling man, looking at him with a pensive, almost grave expression. Steve Wickersham stood behind the prisoner, the muzzle of his rifle against the camouflaged man's head; Steve had a dancing light in his eyes, and for the first time today he looked happy. Sean wondered if Steve would bother waiting for Blaine's order before pulling the trigger. Eddie Wickersham leaned against a tree nearby, looking pale but steady.

Glancing around the clearing, Sean saw that the rest of the group had come out of the woodwork. Well, they'd caught an assassin today; just not the one they'd been watching.

"Well, isn't this something," Blaine said, a teasing note in his voice. He might have been in a local tavern celebrating a Packers victory instead of in the woods, facing a man who had just tried to kill him. "Didn't expect to find you here, Carl. Small world, as they say. Oh, allow me to make introductions. It's only fair Sam here knows who you are, since you might have killed him as well as me."

"I doubt it," Carl said. "I don't miss."

"Then how come I'm walking and talking? Sam, this is Carl Miller. He's a higher-up with the Wisconsin Patriots, one of our finer militias. Also runs a very profitable black market ring for automatic weapons and such things, don't you, Carl?"

"You should know," Carl replied. "You bought from me often enough."

"And you gypped me often enough, which is why I no longer do business with you." The amusement left Blaine's eyes, replaced by a cold practicality. Sean recognized that look, having seen it very often during his career. Having seen it in his own eyes, in the mirror.

"Walt, Jess, see what else he's got on him. Steve, step back a few. Carl's not going anywhere," Blaine said.

Walt and Jess stepped over and frisked Carl Miller. They found a very good knife and a 10-millimeter automatic that was nothing special. They handed these, along with Miller's rifle, to Blaine, who looked the goods over, nodded. Blaine kept the knife, gave the guns to MacReady, saying, "We'll add those to the general fund."

"Sure thing," MacReady said, nodding.

"Now then," Blaine said, taking a step closer to Carl Miller. "Why?"

"Because ever since last March things have been going in the tank, that's why!" Miller snapped. "After you assholes did that building in Los Angeles —"

"Bullshit, Carl, they blamed the Arabs for that. Suits me fine, those creeps get what they deserve."

"So how come no one wants to buy, huh? How come we got Feds snooping around the shows? We can't even get a frigging church hall to give us space for a meeting, and it's all your fault."

"That's because you and your yahoo friends are more interested in waving flags and having people think you're a big bad man than in real change. You don't know how to do things quietly, Carl. None of you ever learned that. Well, I have." Blaine stood up straight, raised his voice so all the assembled men could hear. "None of my people have been given any grief by the G. Have you, gentlemen?"

There was a general murmur of *No.*

"That's because they're smart," Blaine said, turning his attention back to Miller. "This — " he plucked at Miller's jacket. "This is the only camouflage you know about. And that won't help you." Blaine looked up. "Steve."

"Yeah?" Steve Wickersham seemed to be enjoying having his gun against a person's head just a little too much.

"You and a couple others take Carl out in the woods and shoot him. Make it look like he was mistaken for a deer. And no unnecessaries this time, OK?"

"Sure thing."

Sean had been standing in silence, observing. This was better than anything he could have planned. He had saved Blaine's life, and Blaine was not a man to forget such a thing. He also knew that he had erased any suspicions that he was a Fed. They would not think that a Fed would let a person be murdered in cold blood. *Ah, Richard, but you don't know the type of Fed I was.* As far as Sean was concerned, Miller deserved what he got; was a means to an end, and that end was gaining the full and complete confidence of Richard Blaine.

Now for the finishing touch. "Wait," Sean said. They all turned to look at him, Blaine regarding him with interest, and something like warmth. "Is there an ice fishing shack nearby on the lake?"

"Yeah," Eddie Wickersham said. "Old man Marston's, right nearby."

"Well, instead of leaving our uninvited guest in the woods, why not weigh him down and toss him down the ice fishing hole? They won't find him for months and when they do, time and the elements will worked him over. It'll take a while to figure out he's not a drowning."

"Who asked you, new guy?" snapped Steve.

"Cool it, Steve," Blaine said. "It's a good idea. Every year they fish at least one idiot out of that lake come springtime. Another one won't matter. I'm ashamed I didn't think of that myself." He gave them all a long, cold look that said he was ashamed of them as well. "And how did you let him get this close, anyway?"

"We were watching —" Eddie began, then shut his mouth with a snap.

Sean saw Eddie glance his way and turn red with embarrassment. Sean suppressed a smile.

"Do it," Blaine said. "Goodbye, Carl."

They stood watching as Steve Wickersham and two others dragged Carl away. "Doug. Eddie. Walt. Go on, relax, see if you can't get a deer. Just let me have some steaks. I promised Anna we'd have venison this week. No, Sam, you stay with me."

Only when all the men had left did Sean see any crack in Blaine's composure. Blaine leaned back against a tree, tilted his head back, up to the sky, his eyes closed, and sighed deeply.

Sean took his hip flask out of his pocket, handed it to Blaine.

"Thank you," Blaine said.

"Don't mention it." Sean noticed that Blaine's hands were shaking the tiniest bit as he took a swig. And why not? Sean didn't hold that against Blaine; for a civilian he was doing marvelously well.

"I meant for saving my life."

I have him. "Don't mention it."

Blaine grinned ruefully. "Well, if I can ever return the favor, I will. In the meantime, here's a belated Christmas present." Blaine handed him Carl Miller's hunting knife. "My apologies for the surveillance, by the way."

"You can't be too careful. As recent events just proved."

"True. We've been a bit jumpy lately."

"Feeling the heat?"

Blaine shook his head. "Nothing like that. Most of the heat's gone overseas. No, a couple months ago one of our members disappeared. We sent him down to some shows to do some buying and he never came back."

"They find his car or anything?" His mind offered up a clear image of Henry Connolly's truck, with Connolly in it, taking a slow, almost graceful plunge into a quarry, sending up a storm of bubbles as it sank to the bottom.

"No, and that's the weird thing. Near as we can find out, he left the show OK and then," Blaine snapped his fingers. "Like that. Gone. As you can imagine, we have to take precautions. And even more so now."

A rifle shot rang out. Both knew what it meant. Neither flinched. Both took note of this.

"Why is that?" Sean asked as if they had not been interrupted. And really, they hadn't.

Blaine took one more swig, handed the flask back to Sean. "Los Angeles was just the beginning. We've laid low for a while, and I feel that enough time has passed that we can start on the next phase. That's what the New Year's meeting was about. To find out if the men are ready for that. They are." Blaine smiled, pride evident in his eyes. "Some of them will only have a small role to play. And others will be in from the first steps all the way to the finish. But they're ready."

"And so am I." He even meant it, though not in the way Blaine thought. Because he needed to get inside, win Blaine's confidence, soothe any suspicions of the others. A simple snatch and grab would not do; if he did it now, he wouldn't get past the state line. The men were devoted to Blaine and would come after him.

"Well then, I'm glad to have you," Blaine said, gray eyes locking on Sean in that compelling way. "And I hate to say it, but I'm not really in much of a hunting mood any more. Care to head back to the lodge and talk over sandwiches and a few beers?"

"Are your wife's sandwiches as good as her muffins?"

"Of course."

"Then twist my arm. Please."

They laughed and began the walk back to the lodge.

Chapter Nineteen

The stairwell was dark, with only a flickering fluorescent light for illumination, and even that light was muted by a fog of dust. Jennifer's head throbbed, blood trickled into her hair with sticky warmth, her arm wouldn't move. *Have to get out of here before the whole thing comes down.* But she couldn't get up, couldn't even move. Something was holding her down. She saw what held her, not Lilliputian ropes but hands, hands that came up out of the debris like grotesque plants. Dead hands, cold hands, holding her pinned. She heard the grinding roar of the building coming down, tried to scream for help and one of those hands clamped over her mouth.

She woke with a startled gasp, felt something smothering her and kicked out frantically at the covers, pushing them off. From the foot of the bed came an indignant mewing. "Oh, Pete, I'm sorry," she said. Turning on the lamp, she squinted in the sudden flood of light. The kitten squinted as well. She'd stopped by the shelter yesterday and adopted the kitten, hoping it would help get her out of the funk she'd been in since the conversation with Gene Tally. The kitten was fuzzy and orange, with noticeably crossed eyes and a habit of forgetting to put his tongue all the way back in his mouth when he was done washing himself; she'd christened him Pete Puma after the cartoon character.

"Sorry, Pete," she said again. Pete mewed — Jennifer took this to mean *All is forgiven if you give me some Kitten Chow* — and went back to sleep. Kittens had it easy. Jennifer looked at the clock. 4:37 a.m. She sighed. It had been three weeks since the last nightmare. But she was familiar enough with the dreams to know that sleep was over for the night.

Might as well make herself useful. She put on sweats and slippers, made her way out to the kitchen and turned on the coffee maker. When the brew was ready she poured a cup, sat drinking it while she leafed through some of the recipes she'd started clipping from the magazines her predecessors had left behind. Alex Salto had asked what her New Year's resolutions were, and now she finally had an answer. She would stop drinking (done), try a new recipe once a week (done, and only once had she burned anything), and she would not, of course, sleep with Alex Salto again (easily done).

She thumbed through the recipes, tired but not sleepy, trying not to think about Gene and Matthew. Trying not to think of how Gene had called her Miss California, and trying not to worry that he was right, she didn't belong here.

"I do," she said. "I want to."

Her only reply was a mew from Pete Puma, who had followed her to the kitchen and was now looking up at her with his huge kitten eyes. At least he was one member of the Jennifer Thomson fan club, along with Suzanne Delacroix and Mr. Bradbury. A small group, she thought with a rueful smile. Exclusive. She reached down and scooped up the kitten. "Care to help me make some cookies, Pete?" Had to do something until it was time for work.

"Lovely cookies, Jennifer," said Mr. Bradbury. "Is it all right if I take some home?"

"Sure thing. Got a sweet tooth?"

"Actually, I have a friend who would just adore them."

"Take as many as you want. Who's your friend?"

"Mrs. Holloway. She runs the embroidery store on Elm. She lost her husband just before Christmas and I go to her place once a week to visit with her."

"That's kind of you." Jennifer meant it. But it galled her as well, for reasons she couldn't understand.

She understood it that afternoon, when the third-graders came in. "I thought they weren't here for two more days," she said.

"Oh, they traded. The fifth grade has a field trip today to the aquarium in Vancouver," Mr. Bradbury replied, taking what remained of the cookies into the back room, away from the mass of eight-year-olds.

Jennifer abruptly got up and wheeled her cart to the far side of the main room, to shelve the economics books. As far away from the juvenile room as she could get. She could not help feeling that she had failed Matthew Tally, and did not want to see accusation of her failure in his eyes.

But as she was heading back to the circulation desk, she saw the third-graders filing out. There was Matthew at the back, head slightly down. As he passed, he looked up, saw her, and smiled, that sweet smile that nonetheless hurt her more than any reproach. *Even when I try to do something good I mess it up. Why can't I be like Mr. Bradbury, do the right thing and do it right. What is wrong with me?*

She let the children pass and went to the circulation desk. She started shoving books onto the cart, heedless of the noise. The titles blurred and her eyes stung. She told herself she wouldn't cry, not in front of Mr. Bradbury, not at work, but her eyes wouldn't obey.

From a distance she heard the sound of pen on paper. Mr. Bradbury said, "Here. Let's go in the back and talk." He taped a note to the desk that said *Meeting in the back room. If you need us, ring the bell. If you have a fine, be honest and leave it here.*

He pulled the chairs from behind their respective desks. Jennifer had her own desk now, a tiny one to be sure, but her own. Her cyclamen and her picture of herself and Cindy were here, along with the red lava lamp that Bill and Suzanne had given her for a housewarming present. A print was taped to the wall, *Midsummer's Eve,* the picture of the woman standing in the circle of fairies.

Jennifer sat down, and Mr. Bradbury handed her a mug of tea. Jasmine, her favorite. He handed her a handkerchief as well. When would she stop needing peoples' hankies?

"What's wrong?" he asked.

She swabbed at her eyes with the hankie. She was not crying, really, but her eyes had started a slow leak she couldn't seem to stop. "It's nothing. If I can just have a couple minutes I'll be fine. We should get back to the desk."

He laughed softly. "It's a library, not a hospital. The books can wait a few minutes. Do you want to talk about it?"

"No," she answered, truthfully as she always did to Mr. Bradbury. "But I will anyway if that's all right."

He spread his hands out as if to say, *That's what I'm here for.*

She told him about Matthew and Gene. "It really bothered me, him saying that. Because maybe he was right. I'm just using this place to get over what happened."

"What was that?" he asked. The steam from his tea seemed to hover around him.

"Last year. In Los Angeles, the federal building that got bombed. I was in the building." Except for telling her story to the ghostwriter, Jennifer had never actually said what had happened. There had been no need. It had become part and parcel of who she was, required no explanation. "They say I was the last one out. I don't know, I was just trying not to die. And when I came here, all I wanted was to start over. Just start a new life. I thought I was getting somewhere. Now I don't know."

"Did what he said bother you that much?"

Jennifer mulled it over. "Now that I think about it, it's not so much that. You see, I got out of that building but I didn't help anyone. I just got out. And that's always...bothered me." *Oh yes, Jennifer, bother, that's a good word, that's why you dream about dead hands holding you down in the wreckage.* "I wanted to help Matthew and I feel like I didn't get anywhere with that."

Mr. Bradbury shook his head. "You helped. I know the Tallys, and now that Gene knows there's a problem, he'll do something about it." He poured more tea for them both. "It's hard, I know. Leaving everything you know behind and starting over. Some people say that's running away, am I right?"

"And how." Thinking of things her mother had said.

"Running away is only bad if that's all you ever do. Running is easy. Staying still is hard. And so is leaving behind everything in your old life to find something new."

Jennifer nodded, thinking of that poem again. *I learn by going where I have to go.* "Thank you, Mr. Bradbury." Before she knew it she blurted out, "How come you stopped being a priest? Oh, I can't believe I just asked that."

To her relief he smiled, his garden gnome smile. "I wondered when you were going to yield to curiosity. You lasted longer than I thought."

"I'm sorry."

"Don't be. But I do think it's a tale for another time. I'll tell you this, though, Jennifer." He folded his hands together, looked down at them. When he looked back up at her, his eyes, usually so merry, were grave.

"Sometimes doing what you need to do — doing what's right — means leaving things behind. Even things that you love."

"Go on," Mr. Bradbury said that afternoon. "I'll lock up."

"You sure?"

"Positive. You look exhausted. Go home and get some sleep."

She stopped protesting and walked outside, heading to her car. As she walked down the library steps, she heard a man's voice say, "Ms. Thomson?"

"Yes?" She turned and saw Gene standing there. He had clearly stopped by his home on the way from his boat. Instead of boots and jeans he wore cords, scuffed loafers, and a turtleneck. He was dressed to make a good impression, but not a romantic one; this felt more like a job interview. He wore a navy pea coat that for some reason made her think of the Old Spice TV commercials they showed when she was a kid. She got a quick flash of Gene walking along the street, whistling that stupid Old Spice jingle, and she bit the inside of her cheek to keep from giggling. Gene didn't look in a giggling mood.

"I wanted to apologize for what I said the other day," he said. "You wanted to help and I was rude to you."

"That's OK."

He shook his head. "It's not. You probably think I don't want to help Matthew. I do. I wanted to talk to you about him. Can we?"

She nodded. "Can we go sit down somewhere? It's been a long day."

"Sure, I know a place close by."

Four blocks from the library was a tavern called the Blue Moose. It didn't look terribly appealing, at least from the sidewalk. The logo of the Blue Moose had faded from bright blue to a pastel shade, the door was in need of a paint job, grass grew through the cracks in the sidewalk. She hung back a moment, and Gene turned to look at her. "It's nicer on the inside than the outside," he said. "Trust me."

She did, and was glad. Inside, the Blue Moose was the sort of tavern she knew and liked, comfortable upholstered seats and dark wood accents, lamps with green glass shades. By the cash register were two chalkboards, one with the day's specials, the other with some important admonitions: *No spitting, no cursing, no lying (fish stories excluded), no Newfie jokes.* In one corner was a pool table, where two men, one of whom she recognized as the harbormaster, stood playing. The rest of the place was full of tables, and most of those tables were full of people.

Gene seemed to be a regular here. At least, the waitress knew him. "Hi Gene," she said. "How's life?"

"Not bad, Kristy," he said. "Is there a deuce in the back open? I need to be able to hear myself talk."

"Straight on to the back. I'll be by in a minute."

They settled themselves in the deuce booth and when the waitress came by, ordered coffee. When the waitress left Gene said, "Sure you don't want anything else? I'll buy."

"I'm fine. And no offense, but let's keep it dutch for now."

Their coffee arrived. Gene stirred his meditatively for a moment. "I'm sorry that I got so upset the other day. What I said, about, you know, not being able..." He sighed, ran a hand through his thinning hair. "It's not something I go around telling people. I cover my tracks pretty good. But that's not what I want for Matthew. And I felt so...ashamed."

"Of Matthew?"

"No!" There was a peculiar tension in his voice she thought might be anger. "No. Ashamed of me. For letting him down." His light blue eyes seemed to almost glow. No, that tension was not anger but love. "You have to understand, Matthew's everything to me. We lost his mother and ... there's no one else in my life. I can't let him down. I have to help him. And I need your help to do that."

Jennifer thought of her own father, a ghost during the weekdays, only present at dinnertime. Busy with golf on Saturday, TV sports on Sunday. He left when she was five, and she could honestly say she barely noticed. There had been none of this devotion she saw in Gene's eyes, this almost ferocious love. "What can I do?" she asked.

"It's a lot to ask, but would you tutor him?"

Jennifer felt her jaw drop. "I don't think I can do that. I mean, I don't have any training. I didn't even finish college."

"Like I said, I know it's a lot to ask. But I talked with Matthew and he said it would help a lot if he could learn from you."

"Why me?"

"He said you were really nice. He thought for sure you were going to yell at him when you caught him messing up the book, but you didn't. He really likes you." Gene shrugged, seeming to imply that he wasn't so sure, but was willing to trust his son's judgment. "I can't pay you a whole lot."

"You don't have to pay me."

"I want to. I don't like taking charity, not unless I really have to."

"You could bring me some salmon."

"Whole thing or fillets?"

"Fillets please. I can't eat food that looks back at me."

"So, do we have a deal?"

"I'll do my best. I've never done anything like this before, so I can't make any promises." She thought frantically. Where to begin, where to begin. "Give me a week so I can get some materials and stuff. Mr. Bradbury can probably point me in the right direction. And then we can set something up."

"Maybe he could come to the library after school?"

"Sure. And I could drop him off when I head home. You're not far from the harbor, are you?"

"No, not far at all."

They sat silent, drinking their coffee, for a few moments. She wondered if she should ask. What the hell, why not? "Just tell me one thing first. How did you know who I was?"

"From your picture. The one ... well, you know."

Oh yes, she knew. How long was all that going to hang over her? Coming up on a year now and people still saw her not as Jennifer but as the girl in the picture. Was she going to be stuck with that for the rest of her life, like a scar?

Probably.

"I'm—" he began.

"It's all right." She cut him off. She'd help his son, but Gene himself was another matter. If he had a problem with her for some reason, let him deal with it. "I'll talk to you and we'll set something up, OK?"

"Great. Thank you," he said. He smiled, she was surprised to see that his smile was like Matthew's; fleeting and sweet, like a ray of sun on a gloomy day.

Mr. Bradbury came through, as she'd known he would. She told him the situation, and went to shelve a cartful of fiction. When she came back, there was a list of books waiting for her, as well as information about home schooling and tutoring programs. If only the rest of it would be so easy.

"Tell me," she asked later that morning as she made out the list of people who needed letters tactfully reminding them to return their overdue books. "When did Gene Tally's wife die?"

Mr. Bradbury gave her a quizzical frown. "Gene told you Rebecca was dead?"

"Well, no, not in so many words." At the same time she realized that Gene had not spoken his wife's name. "It kind of sounded that way, from what he said." Jennifer, again, felt like an idiot. Gene seemed to have a knack for making her feel that way.

Mr. Bradbury shook his head. "Gene and Rebecca are divorced. Two, maybe three years now. Gene and Matthew both took it badly."

Jennifer waited for details, but none were forthcoming. She knew that if she had asked, even if she had promised scones and cookies, Mr. Bradbury would say nothing. She wasn't surprised. After all, she thought with a faint smile, you could take Mr. Bradbury out of the priesthood, but you couldn't take the priesthood out of Mr. Bradbury.

Suzanne Delacroix gave her the full story. Jennifer dropped by on Saturday afternoon with a plate of chocolate mint brownies, thinking that Suzanne's day care kids would like them, and that they might help coax the story out of Suzanne.

But Suzanne needed no coaxing. "I'm surprised you haven't heard about Gene and Becca. It's kind of a famous story around here."

"What happened?"

Suzanne looked around instinctively for little pitchers, but it was just her and Jennifer in the kitchen. "Becca is what happened. That woman was a bitch and a half if I ever saw one."

"You're kidding." Jennifer was instantly intrigued; it was the first unpleasant thing she'd heard Suzanne say about anyone.

Suzanne shook her head violently, sending her red-brown curls swinging. "Becca came up here on a vacation, I think. Something like that. Anyway, near as people can tell, she was from a sophisticated family, or at least they had money. But apparently she thought a blue-collar guy would be more exciting. Like the way some women have a thing for firemen or cops. And pretty soon she latched onto Gene. And he fell hard for her." Suzanne shrugged. "Who could blame him? Becca was beautiful. The sort of beautiful you usually see in the movies. She must have looked like a goddess to him. That's the way he treated her, by all accounts. Bill's office is near the harbor and he said that every day Gene would get off his boat and buy flowers for Becca from that florists' shop there.

"I don't know too many details. I don't know Gene all that well and even if I did, God knows he wouldn't talk about it. But the story is that things started getting rocky after Matthew was born."

"Rocky how?"

"I'm guessing money. Gene doesn't make a whole lot, and Becca didn't want to work. Plus they were from such different worlds. Speaking as a married lady, let me assure you that hot jungle lust can only keep things going for so long. After that, you'd better find things about each other you like, if you haven't already. But whatever the reasons, Becca loaded up a truck with everything that wasn't nailed down and took off. And I don't just mean her things. She took stuff Gene inherited from his parents, some of Matthew's toys — anything she thought she could get money for, really. I heard she even took the ice cube trays."

"She wasn't a woman, she was the Grinch."

Suzanne laughed, the laugh of someone who knows things aren't funny, not really. "It gets better. She changed the locks on the doors. So that afternoon, Becca's hightailed it off to God knows where, and the school bus drops Matthew off." Suzanne scowled. "Why that bus driver didn't make sure Matthew got in the house OK....but poor Matthew knocks at the door, thinking his Mom's going to be there. And she's not. Matthew's a smart kid, he finds the spare key. It doesn't work."

Jennifer sat, openmouthed, cold inside. How could anyone do a thing like that? Leaving, she could understand. Taking her own things, no problem. Taking everything, and then leaving your five-year-old child to wait and wonder where his mommy was? "That was absolutely cruel."

"I second that emotion," Suzanne said, clinking her coffee mug against Jennifer's. "So Gene comes home, finds Matthew scared to death and crying. Gene had to break into his own house, and of course found Becca gone. Along with everything else. Mrs. Sanders, who lived next door, said that night she could see Gene, walking back and forth, just holding Matthew in his arms. Said they both looked like ghosts."

They both fell silent. There was nothing to say. Jennifer wondered where it came from, this cruelty people could indulge in. How could someone plant a bomb and snuff out hundreds of lives and justify it in the name of whatever cause they counted dear? How could a woman leave the man she had wed and the child she had borne, in such a cold way, calculated to hurt them? Was there something wrong with these people, or was such evil in every human heart, only waiting for the right circumstances?

No, not in my heart, don't let it be in me. And yet, what would she do if she could confront whoever had blown up the federal building? Would she ask for blood in return for those lost lives? If she saw Rebecca Tally now, would she exact revenge for the damage she'd done to Matthew? *I don't know.*

"Pardon?" Suzanne asked.

"What?"

"You said something."

"Oh." She must have said *I don't know* aloud. Well, there was one thing she wanted to know. "Do you know if Becca was from California?"

Suzanne thought for a moment. "Now that I think of it, she was. San Francisco, I believe. How'd you know?"

"Lucky guess," Jennifer said.

Chapter Twenty

Sean caught the scent of Blaine's Christmas tree farm before he saw it, the clean aroma of pine. About five miles outside Du Lac's city limits, it was bordered by a high chain-link fence, presumably to keep people from helping themselves to a free tree. A sign over the main gate read: *Evergreen Farm Christmas Trees,* with a smaller sign below, *Merry Christmas all year long!* Beside the main gate, a building painted to look like a red barn, Christmas lights around the roof's edge. He parked the van, got out to open the main gate, and took a moment to look over the building. The windows were all shuttered. *Cashier* read a sign over one window; *Refreshments* over another. The menu was still up. Coffee, cocoa, hot apple cider. Brownies and caramel apples. Treats to induce holiday spirits and keep the kids from getting too whiny. He drove through, closed the gate behind him, and drove up the well-maintained dirt road. He might have been on asphalt, the drive was so smooth.

On both sides of the road he saw rows of trees, some young, some that would be draped with lights and tinsel next Christmas. Then the road curved and he was at Richard Blaine's house. Sean suspected that Blaine made good money; his farm seemed to be prosperous enough, and Blaine himself did not have the tenseness of a man living on the edge of his means. But the house was a one-story, simple and unpretentious. It would be beautiful come spring, if the many flowerbeds and rose canes he saw gave any indication. Who would have suspected that the plans for the Los Angeles bombing had been laid in such a pretty place?

A horse's whinny startled him. At the rear of the house Sean could see a small stable and corral. Poking their heads out of the stable windows were two horses; the brown one he'd seen Blaine ride on New Year's Day, and a smaller palomino. As he got out of his van he saw that he was not alone. Doug MacReady was here already, leaning against his truck and looking at the horses.

"Hi, Doug," he said.

MacReady registered no surprise, and Sean knew he had been waiting for him. "Hey, Sam. Good to see you." He strolled over. "I wanted to be sure I caught you before dinner. There's something you need to know."

"What's that?"

"Don't talk shop at the dinner table tonight. We'll go to the den after dinner and talk there."

"That's no problem. But why?"

"It's Anna, Richard's wife. She thinks this is just local business stuff. And Richard aims to keep it that way."

"I understand." Sean didn't believe it for a moment. Because they always knew what was going on — the wives, the mistresses, the girlfriends. He didn't hold it against them: few played any role in their men's misdeeds, and most would have left the men if they could have. Sean felt sorry for most of them. But they knew, despite all their protestations to the contrary. In all his years he'd only found one of the women who truly knew nothing of her husband's deeds. He was a money-man for an Islamic terrorist group who kept his wife literally under lock and key. She didn't know what year it was, let alone what her husband was up to. Since then, whenever he and Robert were bored, they argued about the money-man's reason for imprisoning his wife, whether it was extreme jealousy (Robert's view) or an outright phobia of women (Sean's view).

But he'd play along. "No problem," Sean said, and he and MacReady went inside.

Richard's living room was what Sean expected it to be, oak paneling and a handsome riverstone fireplace, over which a ten-point buck kept eternal watch with glass eyes. As he and MacReady entered the house Sean caught the mingled scents of wood burning on the hearth and dinner wafting in from the kitchen. It reminded him of Robert's house in Maine — could it really be nearly a year since he'd sought Robert's counsel? He felt a sharp pang like a knife thrust into his heart. Robert was the last friend he had, and it was almost a year since he'd heard a friendly voice or spoken to someone without subterfuge. Sean felt the knife twist, for he did not even know if Robert was still alive.

Of course he is. They can do lots of things with surgery and chemo these days. He's fine, he's off in his little castle in Maine and by fall this will all be done. Blaine will be dead, Jennifer will have justice, and I'll go see Robert and tell him everything. Even about Beatty.

Sean let none of his thoughts show, even though Blaine himself reminded him of Robert. It was Blaine's assurance that did it, the confidence that comes with being secure in your own domain, so secure you don't mind greeting guests in your stocking feet, as Blaine was.

"You guys want something to drink?" Blaine asked as they put away their coats.

"Sure," MacReady replied.

"We've got Coke, Sprite, Becks, and Bud," said a female voice. "Oh, and cranberry juice cocktail," she added with a laugh.

Sean turned to see a small woman with red hair. The hair was caught back in a simple ponytail and she looked young, perhaps only a few years out of college. He recognized her from the meeting when he'd first met Blaine.

"Sam, this is my wife, Anna. Anna, this is Sam Lewis," Blaine said.

Sean and Anna Blaine shook hands. Her hand was small in his but not fragile. A hand used to duties of home and hearth; the nails were short and unpainted. "It's good to meet you," he said, surprised to find himself meaning it. But why not? Her muffins and sandwiches were the first decent food he'd had in God knew how long.

"And you. Richard's told me all about you." She smiled, then turned to Richard. "How many will we be having?"

"Just the Wickershams and Walt Sorensen."

"Jess can't make it?"

"Not tonight."

"I'd better go set the table. Good to see you again, Doug. Nice meeting you, Sam. Oh! Drinks!"

"Just a Coke for me," Sean said. He wanted all his wits about him.

"Becks for me, Anna," MacReady said.

"Done and done," Anna said, and disappeared into the kitchen with a swirl of long paisley skirt.

Sean and MacReady sat down to wait for the others and talk small talk with Blaine. In less than a minute Anna had returned with beverages and a bowl of pretzels for them. As she went back into the kitchen he watched her from the corner of his eye, and again felt that stab in his heart. And this time, could not explain why.

Dinner was chicken and dumplings with plenty of gravy. As Sean sat down at the table he had to bite the inside of his cheek to keep from laughing. All of the men save Blaine had such doleful, stray-dog looks in their eyes, as they sat with a home-cooked meal in front of them, waiting those endless seconds for everyone to be seated and for Blaine to say grace.

For that's what they were, Sean thought as he began to dish food onto his plate. Stray dogs. All of them save Blaine were divorced or never-married. Their lives were ones of discontent, lived paycheck to paycheck, taut and with few comforts. The only surprise was that the group did not have more members; how could these men resist the appeal of an intelligent, charismatic leader who articulated what they only felt and gave them a plan, a group of like-minded people who would make them feel a part of things, and some great food to boot. The illusion of family. Of belonging.

He took a bite of chicken and dumpling, knowing what to expect from the muffins and sandwiches, but this dinner left those in the dust. The chicken was tender, the dumplings light and airy, the gravy so thick and rich it was nearly seductive. *Good God, if Robert and Anna could hold a cook-off, let me be the judge. I'll die very fat and very happy.*

"How is everything?" asked Anna.

"Great," replied the Wickersham brothers in unison.

"Terrific," said MacReady.

"Marvelous as always," Blaine said, and smiled.

The other man, Walt Sorensen, could not reply as his mouth was full, but nodded happily.

"Ambrosial," Sean replied. Anna smiled, the other men laughed save for the Wickershams. Eddie was frowning, puzzled. Steve sent a cold glance his way, a look Sean could read with no trouble at all. *You think you're so smart.*

The den was downstairs, fifteen steps in all, a journey made in a matter of seconds. And yet in that short time and distance Sean saw a transformation work over Blaine. Upstairs, he piled dishes in the kitchen and asked his wife if she needed anything, leaning down to her for a kiss. Downstairs, he sat at an octagonal poker table, steepled his fingers together, and sat silently. The warm glow left his eyes and they became not so much cold as resolute. Hard. They all sat at the table and he looked at each one of them in turn, as if gauging their commitment to his cause.

Sean gave back Blaine's look evenly, wondered what Blaine saw in the eyes of the men who sat at this table. He could make a decent enough guess. In Doug MacReady: a loyal lieutenant, forever the second-in-command. In Eddie Wickersham and Walt Sorensen: clay ready to be molded, but not sent into the kiln. Their clay would crack there. Steve Wickersham: a firebrand, someone to set things in motion, who could be thrown aside if he became too volatile.

As for him, what did Blaine see? He wasn't sure of that yet.

"So," Blaine said without preamble. "Los Angeles was a success. I congratulate you." He raised his cup of coffee high, gave them a quick smile. His eyes pulsed briefly with warmth, then they were businesslike again. "Yes, a success, and a failure as well."

The men exchanged quizzical glances. Sean had an idea of what Blaine was driving at, but held back, forcing himself to walk that line between reticence and eagerness, not to overplay his hand.

"What do you mean?" MacReady asked. "We pulled it off. We didn't get caught. Hell, no one even suspected us at all. The Arabs got all the blame."

"Exactly," replied Blaine.

The men again looked baffled. Except for Blaine.

Except for Sean.

Eddie Wickersham said, "But isn't that what we want?"

Sean saw Blaine start to reply, but he spoke first. "If it was just about destruction, that would be fine. But it's more than that." He saw Blaine give a small, approving smile and went on. "It's about sending a message to the G that what they're doing won't fly any more. They need to know who it's coming from. In a general sense, of course."

"Exactly," Blaine said again. "The trick this time will be to make it clear that this comes not from outside, but from within. That our government" — Blaine's voice oozed sarcasm — "has brought this on itself because of what it's done to the country and to us. No blaming it on the Arabs or whatever this time. But at the same time, well, I don't think we're ready for martyrdom."

"Not yet," MacReady said. The others laughed and Blaine gave a small smile.

Sean smiled but also knew that martyrdom was what Blaine longed for, on some level. Probably hadn't admitted it even to himself. But like most fanatics Blaine was a curious blend of the romantic and the practical. He could coldly engineer the deaths of hundreds, yet in his secret heart dreamed of some grand sacrifice that would rally millions to his cause.

The talk went on as they discussed what the next target should be. Sean kept fairly quiet, again walking his fine line. Only towards the end of the evening did he make a contribution beyond general agreement or disagreement. "Here's a suggestion," he said.

"Fire away," said MacReady.

"How about the IRS?"

"Don't be a dumbshit," Steve Wickersham said. "They get threats all the time, they're too hard to get to."

"That's exactly why they're a good target," Sean said, ignoring Steve's insult. "Think about it. Why do they get threats? Because everyone in the country hates them. I'd bet three out of five random people have some tale of woe."

"That's a lot of angry people," said MacReady.

"A lot of people who might start to wake up to what needs to be done," Sean said. As he said it, could practically read the look in Blaine's eyes. Again, it was the contradictions of the idealist, the zealot. To know the world is against you yet secretly believe that if you do or say the right thing, the support of the masses will be yours for the asking. He could see

Blaine's eyes light up at the thought of millions of angry taxpayers gaining sympathy for his cause.

"I like that," Blaine said softly. "I like that a great deal."

"It's going to be a real pain to pull off," said Steve, and Eddie Wickersham nodded emphatically.

"And?" Blaine asked. "No one said this was going to be easy." He shook his head. "Change never is. It's hard, and it's painful. But we know what we're doing now. We need to start thinking, and planning. I want to call it a night soon. Most of you have work tomorrow, right?"

Nods around the table.

"Doug will send the word for the next meeting. And think about this. Remember what we did right in Los Angeles and what we did wrong. That'll go a long way to helping us this time," Blaine said.

Steve Wickersham smirked. Gave him a look that said, *Looks like you're out of the loop, new guy.*

Sean said nothing, but he read Steve's look clearly and so, it seemed, did Blaine.

"And last but certainly not least," Blaine said, raising his coffee cup once again in a toast, "the hardest part of any plan is deciding what the end goal is. But we have that tonight. Thanks, Sam."

"Don't mention it," Sean replied. As the meeting broke up and they began making their way upstairs, he heard Blaine pull Steve aside and say something in a low voice. The word *attitude* was all he caught, but he concealed a smile as he went up the stairs.

As he came upstairs he was greeted by the scent of warm chocolate, and breathed in deeply. Anna Blaine was sitting at the dining room table, reading a book. She looked up as he walked in and put the book aside. "Hi Sam," she said, getting to her feet. "I made something for you. Just a Hi, new friend thing." She was not as young as he'd thought; there were faint lines around the corners of her eyes when she smiled, and the skin on the backs of her hands was slightly rough. Probably in her early thirties.

She handed him a foil-covered plate, and the scent of chocolate was stronger than ever. "Some brownies for you. I wasn't sure if you liked nuts, so I didn't put any in."

The plate was warm. She must have been baking these while the men met. He looked into Anna's eyes and realized that she truly did not know about what her husband was, or what he had done and planned to do. Sean felt an inexplicable urge to give the plate back to her, to flee this house and Du Lac and Wisconsin itself, to leave his quest for justice behind and let it go, all of it.

The impulse lasted only a second. Just a crazy moment, that was all. "Thank you, Anna," he said. "If they taste half as good as they smell, I don't know what I'll do."

"Any time. A friend of Richard's is a friend of mine. And now, if you'll pardon me, I'm off to bed. Busy day tomorrow. 'Night."

"Good night."

He took his leave and stepped outside. The night seemed not warmer, but less cold than usual. Spring was coming. He stood for a moment on the walkway, took a deep whiff of the brownies and smiled. Ambrosial indeed. Maybe one before hitting the road.

Something hit him in the back and the side, hard. Only quick reflexes kept him from dropping the plate; only the need to preserve his cover kept him from obeying his first instinct, which was to pull out his gun and put a round in his assailant. But it was only Steve Wickersham who had pushed him. "Oops," Steve said with a grin. "Gotta watch where I'm going."

A few steps behind Steve, brother Eddie giggled nervously.

Sean said nothing, began walking to his van, knowing that silence would incense Steve more than any words could.

"What's the matter, smart guy?" Steve asked. "No ten-cent words to throw around?"

He stopped and without bothering to turn around said, "Actually, I've plenty of words. But I haven't all evening to help you increase your word power. Try *Reader's Digest,* Steve-O."

Sean started walking to his van again. Steve caught up with him, grabbed him by the arm and jerked back. He faced Steve; a vein pulsed in Steve's forehead.

"Look, asshole," Steve said. "You may be Richard's new best friend, but you're flyshit to me. Understand?"

Sean made no move, stood holding the plate of brownies. But he let the mask slip, just a bit. He looked over the mask's edge, gave Steve Wickersham a steady look. His voice was not loud but careful, measured, and very cold. "Take your hand off me."

"What if I don't?" Steve asked. "What are you gonna do?"

He let the mask slip away entirely and gave Steve a smile that the late and unlamented Henry Connolly would have recognized. *What am I going to do? Oh, try me, Steve. I know in my gut you pulled the trigger in L.A., you killed all those people and hurt Jennifer. Give me an excuse and you'll find out what I can do. Ask your late friend Henry Connolly. Ask that arms dealer in Turkey, the one whose hobby was hooking little girls on smack and putting them to work in his brothel. What was left of him you could fit in a shoe box. Find out, Steve. I really want you to.*

Less than a minute, thirty seconds at the most the mask was down. It was enough. Steve let go of his arm and backed away as much as he could without revealing fear. Steve seemed about to say something; his throat worked but no words came out.

Sean turned and walked to his van, as he did so he heard Eddie's reedy voice. "Holy crap, Steve. Did you see his *eyes?*"

He didn't linger to hear more. He set the plate of brownies down carefully so it would not spill, got in his van and drove away.

Chapter Twenty-one

Monday afternoon. Jennifer drove to pick up Matthew Tally from school; then they'd head back to the library for their first tutoring session. Despite Gene's confidence, Mr. Bradbury's encouragement, and a weekend spent boning up on remedial reading, she was one big jitter. Her knuckles were white on the wheel as she drove, and though she tried to believe it was driving through the rain that set her on edge, she didn't fool herself. She was used to foul-weather driving by now, had adapted very well for a Los Angeles émigré. No, might as well tell the truth. It was the tutoring session that twisted her nerves. And why not? It was easy for Mr. Bradbury to say she'd do fine. *He* was smart, *he* knew how to help people. She was just Jennifer Thomson, nothing special, former receptionist and current assistant librarian, 2.7 GPA from a second-rate community college. Exactly the sort of person to trust your child's literacy to, no question about that.

She threaded her way through the maze of cars, parked, and got out. The rain drummed on her umbrella as she craned her head about, looking for Matthew. She was awash in a sea of children, all of whom seemed to be clad in bright yellow rain slickers and hats with the occasional red or blue coat thrown in. In the end, it was he who found her.

If Matthew was nervous as she, he didn't show it. "I like your car," he said as she maneuvered out of the parking lot. "It looks like something from *Tron.*"

"I haven't seen that in years," she said.

"Dad got me the video for Christmas last year. And the first Harry Potter movie too. I'm gonna ask for the second one for my birthday."

"And when's that?"

"March 20th."

"Not too far away." She let Matthew chatter on about *Tron* for the rest of the drive, only half listening. Partly she was focused on the driving, mostly she was remembering March 20th of last year. A Sunday. She'd been up late the night before, at the movies with some friends who'd all made themselves scarce after the bombing when it was "just too weird to be around you now, Jen, sorry." She'd woken, made coffee and a blueberry-and-banana smoothie. Frittered away the day, doing halfhearted housework. Spent the evening eating cold leftover pizza, watching "ER" reruns and mooning over George Clooney. All the while blissfully ignorant that in less than 24 hours she would have a front-row seat at mass murder, that if not for a broken photocopier she would be ashes now. Last Christmas, the ghostwriter had asked her how it felt to dodge a bullet, or rather, a bomb. "A relief," she'd said, but that was a lie. There was no relief, only a constant wondering why she'd made it. Only the task of earning that grace, or luck, or whatever it was. Only waiting for the other shoe to drop, for fortune to reverse and even out the balance of things.

"Miss Thomson?"

She blinked. Realized that she was parked at the library, just sitting behind the wheel thinking things over. How long has she been doing that?

"Miss Thomson?" Matthew said again. "You OK?"

She smiled. "Fine. Just spaced out there for a minute."

They got out of the car and, as if a switch had been thrown, Matthew's chatter ceased. She knew it for what it was, nervousness. Jennifer resolved to not let her own doubts show; she got hot chocolate for the two of them, and they sat down to the books.

She dropped Matthew off at his house an hour later. The Tally house was close by the harbor, as Gene had said. A small house, not unlike her own. An old pickup truck was in the driveway. The truck had a ladder rack, just beginning to show rust spots here and there, and a boxy thing in the pickup bed that she assumed was a tool chest. Gene had mentioned that when the fish weren't running, he did boat repair, got car engines running again, that sort of thing. He'd offered to do any household fix-it chores if she got tired of salmon as payment for Matthew's tutoring. She was thinking of asking him to look at her bathroom sink, which drained far too slowly and made odd gurgling sounds sometimes.

"Thanks, Miss Thomson," Matthew said as he got his book bag.

"Call me Jen. See you tomorrow," she replied. "Same bat time, same bat station?"

He nodded and gave her a smile, ran through the rain to his front door. She watched for him to make it inside, saw his silhouette against a spill of light from the open door. As she was getting ready to drive away another silhouette, a taller one, appeared in the doorway, then made its way out onto the walk. Gene emerged out of the gloomy drizzle. She rolled down the window.

"Hi," he said. He was bareheaded in the rain but it did not seem to bother him. Most likely he was used to all kinds of weather. She caught the scent of the harbor from him, ocean and rain and diesel smoke.

"Hello."

"How'd it go?"

"OK. We're still finding our way."

"All right. Well. If there's anything I can do."

"I'll let you know."

Jennifer wished that Gene had his son's eyes. She could read Matthew's eyes. Gene's were like the sky, or like the ocean. She saw the surface, but no deeper. Was he happy she was tutoring Matthew? Resentful? Did he still see her as Miss California, an emissary from the same state that had brought him beautiful, hateful Becca? No, most likely not that last, he would not have entrusted Matthew to her if he thought so. But what did he think? And why did she care what he thought?

She didn't know, and decided it didn't matter. Helping Matthew was what mattered.

Friday evening she dropped off Matthew, exchanged hellos and remarks about the weather with Gene. She accepted a plastic grocery bag containing four large salmon fillets, each sealed in a freezer bag with the date written on each bag in permanent marker.

As she pulled into her driveway, Suzanne came outside and waved. "The mailman left some packages for you. I brought them in so they wouldn't get rained on."

"Thanks much. Are they from Land's End?"

"Yeah. More towels?" Suzanne asked as she handed several flat packages over the fence.

Jennifer shook her head. "Clothes. Pants and stuff mostly. I've put on a few pounds lately. Need to run my ass around the block a few times."

Suzanne shrugged. "If it makes you feel better, I think you look great. No offense, but you were starting to look kind of peaky back around Christmas."

Jennifer had never, to her knowledge, been described as "peaky" before but she took Suzanne's meaning clearly. "Gene gave me some salmon, sort of payment for helping tutor Matthew. You and Bill want to come over tomorrow night? I've got a recipe I've been wanting to try."

"We'll be there."

Jennifer went inside, tossed the boxes on the couch. She'd deal with those tomorrow. These last few days of tutoring Matthew she'd been getting an idea, and she needed to spend a night doing some research to see if her hunch was the right one. She made an omelet for herself and a bowl of Friskies for Pete Puma. Pete, no fool, disdained the Friskies and followed her into her office, hoping for some of the omelet. As she fired up the Mac she ate and tried to fend off Pete, eventually giving in to his begging, knowing that she'd most likely be cleaning up cat barf in the morning. Between Pete Puma and Matthew Tally, she was becoming quite the sucker for a pair of big vulnerable eyes.

Online now, her omelet eaten, she began searching. She had come to realize that Matthew *could* read. But not well, and not quickly. And something else was going on. Today she'd asked him to write something, just copy a sentence out of one of the books, and noticed that he used b's instead of d's and vice versa, swapped letters around making strange not-quite palindromes. She thought of an old boyfriend from high school, with a button on his jacket that said *Dyslexics untie!*

She supposed she could have talked to Mr. Bradbury. But she wanted to do this on her own, see if she could not just nail down the problem, but find a solution as well.

After a couple hours online she was heading out to the kitchen for a coffee break when the phone rang. "Hello?"

A familiar whiskey voice: "Jennifer, it's Amber."

"Hi, Amber. How are you?"

"Fine, considering. Did you get my message about the problem with the book?"

"Yes, I did." The book had been delayed. There were two other books about the bombing on the market already, not survivor's stories but "what really happened" exposés, both crackpot affairs as far as Jennifer could tell (one of them blamed the bombing on fanatical Scientologists). But no publishers were willing to take her book yet. "I'm all right with that."

"I'm really sorry. I'm sure we'll be able to get it out before the end of the year. But I wanted to let you know that the movie will be on in March."

"Sounds great," Jennifer said. She didn't bother to tell Amber that she'd never see the movie, she was in another country now. Now that the movie was actually made and no longer just a possibility, Jennifer found the idea creepy and fascinating in equal measure. Against her better judgment she asked, "Who's playing me?"

"A girl who used to be on 'Buffy the Vampire Slayer'."

She tried to envision it, couldn't. "That's fine. Talk to you soon, Amber."

She hung up, made a cup of instant, and went back to her computer. Pete Puma curled up in her lap and went to sleep. She clicked and scrolled and read far into the night, until she could comprehend no more information. By the next morning, she had a plan she thought would work.

Jennifer sat across from Matthew. "I have something you might be interested in." She reached into her tote bag and took out a hardcover edition of *Harry Potter and the Sorcerer's Stone.*

Matthew's eyes got wide, as she'd guessed they would.

"You liked the movie? Well, the book is ten times better, trust me." Jennifer smiled. "And it's yours. Just one thing."

"What's that?"

"You have to read it to me. Out loud. And when we're done, it's yours."

Matthew shifted uncomfortably in his chair, much as she'd known he would. It took a week's tutoring and a weekend of research but she thought she knew what the problem was. Matthew had dyslexia. His problem wasn't that he couldn't read — it was just slow for him, he was left behind in the dust of his classmates. Her weekend research had found that many dyslexics could read, they just needed more time, needed to take it one word at a time. Slow and steady. If she could help give him confidence in his abilities, that would be half the battle.

She told him some of this. "Just take it one word at a time. Don't rush it. Say the word, see if it sounds right the way it looks to you. If not, we'll figure out how it should sound."

Matthew said nothing.

"What do you think?" she asked.

He swallowed, nodded. She saw fear in his eyes: of failure, of disappointment, of being left behind in school. "OK," he said, and reached out for the book.

Brave boy. She felt her heart swell with pride as if he was hers.

There were red construction paper hearts in the school windows when she picked up Matthew. Hearts sprinkled with glitter, bordered with lace, dappled with paint. The fourth graders had possession of the library on Valentine's Day, and she found chalky candy hearts with messages like *Be mine* and *Oh you kid* off in the corners of the stacks for the next few days.

Cindy sent her a small bouquet of white and red carnations. Jennifer was enormously pleased, for it was one more valentine than she'd expected to get, even if it was from her sister. But she did get another. Matthew handed a red glittery paper heart to her, shyly said, "Here," and then ran up the walk to his house.

"So you've got a suitor then?" Cindy asked on the phone that night.

"Not hardly. He's eight years old. This is 'crush on the teacher' time I think."

"Hey, get them while they're young! But seriously, is this the kid you've been tutoring?"

"Yes, that's him."

"Well, you said his dad's single. Who knows?"

Jennifer snorted. She didn't think Gene even *liked* her. "Doubtful, Cin. Our conversations haven't gone beyond how Matthew's doing and how about that weather. As my boss says, 'There is no there there'."

"I think that was Gertrude Stein, actually."

"Well, knowing Mr. Bradbury he probably met Gertrude Stein at some point. Probably played poker with her and Ernest Hemingway in some Parisian café."

Cindy laughed. "Jen, I have to tell you, you sound so different."

"Don't tell me I'm saying *aboot* and *eh*. Am I?"

"No. You sound happy. I haven't heard you sound this way in a long time."

"Really?"

"Really."

Jennifer thought it over. Thought what so many people would say about her life now. Going nowhere. Maybe so. *I live in a small town in British Columbia, where I'm an assistant librarian. I putter around with books and have tea with my boss and we talk about what we're reading. I have a cross-eyed cat and a tiny house with fish painted on the bathroom walls and a bedroom done in early San Francisco Whorehouse. I tutor a fisherman's son. I hang out with my next-door neighbor and bake cookies. I've put on five pounds since New Year's and my only valentines this year were from my sister and an eight-year-old kid. This is my life.*

"You know something, Cin? I think you're right."

Chapter Twenty-two

"...and so the doctor says, 'Are you sexually active?' and I say, 'No, I just sort of lie there and let her do all the work!'"

Groans from around the table. Sean stared at his cards, a pair of kings and three junk cards. Dared not laugh, though the joke was one of Beatty's better ones. Laughter would only encourage him, and they all knew where that would lead.

"Beatty, your jokes are like a bottle of Montrachet I once had," Robert said, not taking his eyes off his own cards.

"Aged like fine wine?"

"Quite the contrary. Turned to vinegar upon decanting."

Sean decided to chance it, hope he got something good to augment the kings. "I'm in."

Junk cards handed in, Robert began to deal. "Here is Belladonna, the Lady of the Rocks, the lady of situations," he said, distributing cards as the players requested. Clockwise around the table. Robert, Halsey, Beatty, himself. "Here is the man with three staves, and here the Wheel. And here is the one-eyed merchant, and this card, which is blank, is something he carries on his back, which I am forbidden to see."

"I do not find The Hanged Man," said Beatty rotely, bored.

"Fear death by water," said Halsey.

Three cards waiting for him. Sean added them to his hand without looking at them.

"Irish? You in?" asked Beatty.

"Yes," he replied. Still not looking at the cards.

"How much?" asked Robert.

"All of it. Everything."

"Oh, Christ almighty," Halsey said, glaring over his cards. "This is exactly the sort of thing I've been talking about. I mean, you honestly can't expect us to excuse this level of risk. If I wanted you to think outside the box I wouldn't have put you in the box to start with."

"It worked for B. F. Skinner," Robert said.

He looked at his cards. All five were blank. *Something he carries on his back, which I am forbidden to see.*

"Who?" asked Halsey.

"Never mind," replied Robert.

I do not find The Hanged Man. "Finish the game without me," he said. "I think I should go."

"No need to rush off. Stick around, I'll tell the one about the Jew, the Frenchman, and the nun." Beatty leaned forward, rested his chin on his fists, grinned. "And besides, go where?"

"Florida." The first thing he could think of.

Halsey snorted. "Florida's *gone.* "

"What do you mean?"

"What I said, *gone.* We went through that in your debriefing. You *were* there, weren't you?" snarled Halsey.

"Don't be mean to Irish. I didn't know, either."

"Beatty, you've been dead for three months. That gives you an excuse to be out of the loop."

"Point taken."

Sean stared at the blank cards. He wanted to raise his eyes from the cards, raise his body from the chair and leave, but could not. "I think I should go," he said again, hoping that by saying it he could make it so. With an effort that brought sweat to his forehead he managed to put the cards down, put his palms flat on the table to push himself up. "I'll see you later," he said.

A hand shot out, caught hold of his left wrist, held it fast. "Not too much later, my friend," said Robert. *"Tempus fugit."* Robert's grip was like iron, but the hand itself was emaciated, skin stretched tight over the bones, a sick man's wasted claw.

Another hand caught hold of his right wrist. This hand was cold, very cold, slimy and gray and bloated. Yet the grip was iron-tight as well. "After all, what are friends for?" Beatty said, voice gurgling and brackish.

Sean stared at his blank cards, at the hands that held him fast. He would not raise his eyes, would not look beyond their hands, would not look at their faces. Felt some force take him gently by the head and tilt it back, slowly and inexorably. *I won't look, I won't, I —*

Opened his eyes. Saw the darkness of two a.m., felt the bed beneath him. A dream. So many years had passed since he had dreamed, he thought he had lost the ability. He let out his breath in a deep sigh, feeling a tremor in his chest.

He thought of a time about six years ago, at Monique's apartment in D.C. She sitting up on the bed, wearing her glasses and one of his dress shirts and nothing else, something he always found tremendously sexy. He lay with his feet by her head, propped up on his elbows, painting her toenails. They enjoyed doing little favors like that for each other; favors that would have grown stale had they seen each other every day, year in and year out. He remembered the color of the nail polish, a dark burgundy called Paris Promenade, and the movie that was on her TV, *Casablanca.* Both of them had seen it so many times they no longer needed to give it their full attention, could recite the dialogue to each other if they were so inclined.

Monique was going to Europe on business; he'd written up a list of handy phrases for her in several languages, and now she read it over. "Not that I don't trust you completely," she'd said, "but when I tell the cab driver *Nehmen Sie mich zum Flughafen,* I'm not really saying 'My hovercraft is full of eels'?"

"Certainly not," he'd replied. "It means 'Why not come back to my place? Bouncy-bouncy!'."

"Yes, well. That puts my mind at ease."

"Moni? Do you dream?"

"You know how to change a subject," she said, taking off her glasses and looking at him. "Subtle, Flint." Flint, as in *Our Man* and *In Like,* the nickname she'd given him when he'd told her, in a general sense, what he did for a living. "Everyone dreams."

"I don't seem to," he said, applying the second coat of Paris Promenade to her right toes.

"You probably don't remember them. Some people don't, that's all."

"Do you?"

She nodded. "In fact, I keep a diary of my dreams. I've got a little book in my table here, and every morning when I wake up I write down what my dreams were. And no, you can't read it."

"You're a tease. So, what was playing at the dream theater last night? At least tell me that."

Monique put her hands back behind her head, leaned back and looked at the ceiling. "I was running up this grassy hill. It was at night, and the moon was out, but I could still see how green the grass was. And I came up over the hill, and I saw this little valley below it. Here's where it gets weird. The valley was, oh, five feet deep in stuffed animals and plushy toys. Over the whole floor of the valley, as far as you could see. And it was like the grass, I could see all the colors even though it was night." She closed her eyes, the better to see through memory's veil. "So I went running down the hill, down into the valley. I was running over all the stuffed animals, bouncing along, doing cartwheels and somersaults and having a great time. And that's it." She looked at him, grinned. "Pretty silly, right?"

"No, it sounds like it was fun." He was thinking that he would like to tell Robert about Monique's dream. Robert had recently mentioned one of his own dreams, a very long and complicated one involving, among other things, Louis Armstrong coming to his door to sing a Christmas carol. *How come I never dream, and if I did I wouldn't dream anything that neat?* he'd wondered, and that was why he'd asked Monique if she dreamed. "It's got a David Lynch feel to it. All you need is a dancing midget."

She made a face. "Ugh. I dreamed about that damned midget once. Don't remind me. And don't feel bad, Flint."

"I don't."

"You do, or you wouldn't have asked me. Dreams are just the garbage disposal of the mind. They don't mean anything."

Six years later, he thought of that conversation and he hoped that she was right.

Sean sat at the kitchen table, a tiny table but fine for his purposes. He'd lain for an hour after the dream, waiting for sleep to return, and when it did not, got up and went into the kitchen. He did not put on the light, though it was still hours before dawn. He knew the apartment as well as a prisoner knows his cell and needed no lights. With a cup of coffee before him, he sat. And waited.

Waiting. He thought of one of his first missions, he and Robert intercepting an arms shipment. The beginning and end of the mission were fine: the beginning with its challenge of gaining trust and establishing the plan, walking the tightrope; the end with its life-and-death fight, a rush of adrenaline that washed away fear. The middle, though. The waiting. That was different. He remembered pacing back and forth in the safe house, not so much fearful as desperate to do *something,* and mentioned this to Robert.

"You are," Robert replied. "You're waiting."

On an intellectual level he knew — as they all did — that waiting was necessary. To move too soon could lose the entire mission, not to mention your life (the latter was an acceptable loss, the former was not). He'd learned to live with it, if not enjoy it. So why did he sit here now in his dark apartment, drinking coffee and feeling something gnaw away at his insides? It was not the usual sense of impatience, wanting to see some action.

No. Not impatience he felt but uncertainty. The uncertainty was not about the mission — that was clear to him. When the time was right, snatch Blaine. Though he felt fairly certain that with the head dead, the body would also perish, he might have to eliminate anyone capable of carrying out the next bombing in Blaine's absence. Take Blaine to Jennifer Thomson. Give her a gun. Beatty's .38 perhaps, the grip was a good size and the kick not bad. After that was done, go to see Robert and find out how he fared, tell him how the mission had gone.

That wasn't the problem.

What would happen after that?

For the first time, he didn't know. No return trip to D.C. No debriefing. No R&R when he could play poker with Robert and Beatty, or take Monique to movies and to restaurants and to bed. No time simply to relax at home, for where was home, now? Florida? No, Florida *was* gone, in all the ways that mattered. He had no desire to return to the place of his exile, and besides, they would be waiting for him.

Never mind where he would go. What would he do?

For the first time since he turned his back on Halsey in the D.C. coffee shop, he realized that there truly was no going back. Especially after

Beatty. Before, there was still a chance that he could have gone back. It would have been on hands and knees, begging, saying his *mea culpas,* but it could have been done. But now, having turned rogue and killed one of his own, that chance was lost. As lost as Beatty.

As lost as himself. For that's what he was. Adrift. No land in sight, and he hated to admit it, but he was tired of squinting for the horizon. His arm ached from holding his hand up to shield his eyes, his head ached from the strain of watching out, everywhere, constantly. There was weight on his shoulders like a heavy stone. The weight of uncertainty, of looking over his shoulder to see who was behind him, of wondering which old compatriot he might have to kill next. The weight of the past, of wondering about other paths that might have been taken, of the growing suspicion that Robert was right and that they had been used. The weight of the future, and where that path might lead. If anywhere.

He took a sip of coffee, surprised to find it was cold. Outside the window, gray dawn was coming, soon to be blue morning sky. Good. The weather was warming, the crocuses were poking their heads up in Anna Blaine's flowerbeds, and he was glad to see the last of the winter's gray chill.

Sean watched the sun come up, felt the weight ease off his shoulders as daylight came. But not entirely. Somehow, somewhere, he had lost that old ability to throw off the weight.

Down in Richard's den, the radio was tuned to a 24-hour news broadcast. The volume was low, but all ears there were sharpened to hear one thing. If, as the one-year anniversary of the Los Angeles bombing neared, there was any hint of the perpetrator being anything other than Middle East crazies. By now all the men present at meetings, the core group and whichever messenger boys and minions might be needed, knew the rhythms of the news station and were attuned to listening for what mattered to them.

Sean sat with them, wondering when the time would be right to make the grab. Whether it was latent mistrust, general precaution, or dumb luck, he had never been alone with Richard. Oh, he supposed he could have whipped out the Mini-14 he'd taken from Henry Connolly's truck, blown away everyone but Richard and made his escape. He could have, but he wouldn't. He wasn't like them.

There was something else, something not purely necessary to the mission but an added incentive. Sauce for the goose, as Robert would say. Sean wanted to enmesh himself in the group and gain Richard's full trust and confidence, so Richard would be repaid the full measure of betrayal. For Richard was a traitor to his country, had betrayed 361 lives. Even the survivors, like Jennifer, would have to live with that betrayal, with the fact that one of their own countrymen had condemned them to death for no greater crime than working a government job.

Yes, Richard was a traitor, and the penalty for treason was well-known. The only difference was instead of judge, jury, and executioner, one person would mete out justice. Wasn't that what every victim longed for? Justice?

Richard had betrayed and Sean would repay. Again he felt weight bearing down on his shoulders. He watched as Richard laid plans and listened to his followers and gave them tasks that made them feel important. And realized that betraying Richard was not going to be the pleasure Sean wanted it to be, because he did admire Richard in many ways. The intelligence, the way of fostering loyalty and camaraderie. Other things as well: the tireless charity work, his obvious love for and devotion to his wife. Scarcely a meeting went by when he did not think at some point, *Christ, Richard, I wish you were on our side. I really do. Even one of you for every ten numbers-men like Halsey, what that could do. If you were on our side.*

But what was his side? Was he not, in his own way, a traitor?

That's different, he told himself. It was different, it had to be, even if he was no longer sure exactly where the distinction lay.

After the meeting he went upstairs. As he walked past the kitchen he saw Anna there, washing dishes. "Something wrong with the dishwasher?" he asked.

"A hose clamp went this morning. While I was out, of course," she said with a rueful smile. "Water all over the floor when I got back."

"Ouch," he said.

"You said it. The part won't be in until tomorrow. Richard said I should just wait but," she shrugged. "I wasn't raised to let dishes sit overnight."

"Need a hand drying?" Sean asked, not entirely sure why he was offering.

"That's sweet of you." She handed him a towel.

They said nothing for a while but the silence was not uncomfortable. For reasons still a mystery to him, Anna's presence soothed him, made the ever-present weight on his shoulders ease a bit. Strange that this should be so, for if there was anyone he needed to hide his true purpose from, it was her.

On the refrigerator was a calendar; next week would be the anniversary of the bombing. The day that had changed so many lives, including Jennifer Thomson's. And his own. He should mark the occasion somehow.

"Anna?" he asked. "Do you know much about flowers? I mean, about what they mean. I know that red roses are for love, but what about other flowers?"

She handed him a bowl to dry. "You're in luck. When I was in high school I worked in a flower shop after school. I don't remember a whole lot, but let's see. For the roses, some people say yellow roses are for jealousy, but others say they're for friendship. Go figure. Pink carnations are for Mother's Day." Anna's eyes lit up, she smiled. "Say, Sam, you don't have a ladyfriend, do you? Is that why you're asking? Don't be shy, I won't tell."

Sean bit his lip to keep from laughing. His last ladyfriend of any consequence had been Monique, and she had never been much on flowers. A good bottle of wine or some pretty jewelry had been more her style. "Ah, no, not a ladyfriend."

"Darn, and here I thought I'd uncovered some good gossip." Anna sighed, flicked soap suds off her hands. "Nobody tells me *anything.*"

He dodged that topic quickly. "Just someone who's had a hard time of it lately, and I want to wish her well."

"Hmm. Let me think." Anna washed and rinsed a few more plates. "There's lily of the valley, for return of happiness."

"I like that."

"There's zinnias, for absent friends. Daisies for innocence. Somewhere people got the idea that white chrysanthemums are just for funerals, but really they stand for truth."

He stood with a plate in his hands, wiping it carefully with the towel. "What would you like to receive from someone?"

"Roses are always sweet. But I think the one with the nicest meaning is sweet alyssum. It means 'worth beyond beauty'." She smiled. "I like that. Beauty doesn't last, but worth does. Or should, anyway."

212

"Yes," he said, "It should."

Chapter Twenty-three

She drove up the coast, thinking that it was strange to be spending a Tuesday morning here, in her car, instead of in the cinnamon-scented sanctuary of the library. Strange that the sun should be so brilliant today, the sky without a single cloud in it. So used had she become to dim library light and overcast skies that this clear weather seemed wrong, as if she'd been transported back to Los Angeles. Ah, but Los Angeles skies were never this pure of a blue. Even the coast of Ventura and Santa Barbara, much as she loved it, did not have Canada's beauty. No softly rolling brown foothills here but gray stone and green pines, and in the distance snow-dusted mountains. It was a rougher beauty but somehow seemed more real.

The park was Suzanne and Bill Delacroix's recommendation, a place popular with fishers, boaters, and day campers. Jennifer drove into the parking lot. There was only one other car there; as the Delacroixs had said, on a weekday at this time of year she'd have the place to herself.

She got out of the car. For all its sunny brilliance the day was chilly, and she put on her sweater. Resting on the passenger seat was a picnic basket, laden with food and some other odds and ends. Jennifer picked up the basket, slung it over her left arm, and began walking toward the beach.

Other than visits to the harbor, she had never been down to the shore during her time in Haven Cove. The beach had meant different things to her in California; it was a place of warmth and sunbathers. A place where the sands were soft under your feet and flags warned you of rip currents. This was different. The shore was rockier, the waves did not fall gently on the beach but beat themselves against granite, sending foam into the air. The sea itself was different, a darker blue, and the strong breeze ruffled the surface with whitecaps. This ocean was not a backdrop, the way it seemed in southern California. It was something not quite tamed. Something to be reckoned with. She thought of the Haven Cove marina, all those men like Gene who made their living out on the sea. What must that be like, to face that huge sea in all weathers every day? Was it brave, foolish, or simply a job to be done? Or all of the above?

She walked along the shore, not beachcombing or even looking for a picnic spot. The wind blew through her clothes, seemed to blow through her skin and bones as well. It was cold, yet comforting. A clean feeling, like letting the air into a musty house, blowing away cobwebs and dust.

Jennifer wore no watch, did not wonder about time. She had all day. She walked until she was tired of walking. She set down her picnic basket in the shade of a boulder, and walked out on the rocks until she was close to the water, enough to feel the spray of a particularly big wave. She sat, gazed out at the ocean. Mr. Bradbury said that soon you would see whales, making their way up the coast from their winter haunts in Mexico. She would like to see whales, and sea otters too. Perhaps Matthew and Suzanne and some of Suzanne's day care kids would like to head down to the aquarium in Vancouver some time.

She sat, turned her face up to the sky, relishing the warmth of the sun on her winter-white skin, the coolness of the breeze and the ocean's spray. Jennifer reached into her pocket and took out the letter she'd received yesterday. She had not opened it yet. The envelope was ivory-colored, with a faint watermark pattern. The address was in black ink; after a moment she recognized the style of ink. A fountain pen. Mr. Bradbury had one, that was how she knew it. She turned the letter over in her hands, looked at the return address on the back of the envelope. Dr. Duncan Levinson of Los Cielos, California.

It was a week ago that she had realized that March 21 was coming, and she had never given Dr. Levinson the one thing he had asked for. *Learn by going where you have to go. And tell me what you find when you get there.* So she'd written, and told what she'd found so far.

Jennifer opened the envelope, took out the letter, and read.

Dear Jennifer:

I was so glad to hear from you, and find out that you're doing well. It seems that you've found a good place for yourself. Haven Cove is aptly named. And it seems that you've surrounded yourself with some nice people as well, never mind those "one or two exceptions" you mentioned.

Ever since our conversation I wondered how you were doing. You said that it had been a year, and that this was a good time for reflection. That's true. And it's not for nothing that tradition speaks of a year of mourning when there's been a loss. I've often thought this year gives us a time to experience a full set of seasons, holidays, anniversaries, those sorts of things. To come full circle, so to speak, and realize that no matter what, life does go on.

If nothing else, I want to answer your question about earning the life you've been given. You asked when you know that you've earned it. And I can't lie to you, Jennifer, I don't think you can know that. It's hard, but I think that the answers we want most are the ones that are the most difficult to find.

All you can do is what you have been doing. Be a good person, and a good friend. And yes, you've made mistakes. That means you're human, that's all. And it seems you've learned from them, so don't worry.

I'm glad we talked last year, and I'd love to talk with you again some time. If you're ever in California again, hop down to Los Cielos. You're always welcome here.

Hoping that you and life treat each other well,
Duncan Levinson

Jennifer read the letter over again, then folded it and put it in her pocket. She didn't know if she would ever feel like she had earned this life she now had, nor if she would ever have what they called closure. She had no desire to ever return to the States, let alone California, for more than a short visit. Bombs had rained down on the Middle East in retaliation, but there was no trial of conspirators, no justice had been meted out. In a way she missed the innocence she'd once had. She had learned many lessons over this past year, and they were not lessons she would have asked for, given the choice.

But who was ever given the choice in these matters? She had not asked for the building to be blown up, not asked for her picture to be splashed across newspapers and computer screens.

Speaking of which.

Jennifer got to her feet, brushed off her behind. Did a little dance as the needles-and-pins sensation went through her feet. She made her way back to her picnic basket and opened it. A sandwich: roast chicken and provolone cheese. The last of the winter's tangerines. A bottle of ginger ale. And another bottle.

She took the bottle out, held it up in front of her. It had an elegant, fluted shape, and it had once contained rosemary-infused olive oil.

Last night she had rinsed the bottle clean, peeled all the labels off it. She had set the bottle aside, and rummaged through a box until she found what she was looking for. A souvenir, of a sort.

A copy of a weekly newsmagazine. A year old, now. She held the magazine, stared at the woman on the cover. Physically little had changed. She was a bit heavier. Her hair had grown out some. Her left arm sometimes ached if she bumped it the wrong way. There was a scar down the instep of her right foot. Very much the same, and yet she felt she barely knew this woman, crying in the arms of firefighter. *Who was he? I never thanked him for saving my life. Where is he, how is he doing a year later?*

She'd torn the cover off the magazine, crumpled the paper with her image on it and put in a glass bowl. Jennifer lit a kitchen match and set fire to the paper, remembering too late that she probably should have turned off the smoke alarm. It didn't go off — so much for technology. Pete Puma, intrigued by the smell of burning, mewed and bumped against her legs. "Later, Pete. Mama's busy."

When the ashes were cold she'd taken a spoon and mashed the burned wad of paper into fine dust. Then, scooped the ashes carefully into the bottle, stuck the wooden stopper in the top. Another match lit, this time a candle set alight. She let wax drip around the stopper until it was sealed completely.

Now she stood on the beach with the bottle and its ashes inside it. She smiled. A strange message to be sending in a bottle. If anyone found it, what on earth would they make of it? No matter. She strode back toward the beach, walked out onto the rocks to get as far out as she could. With all her strength, she threw the bottle as far and as high as she could into the sea. A brilliant flash of pale green as it caught sunlight, then plunged into the water, sending up a splash like that of a fish leaping. A few seconds later the bottle surfaced, and she watched as it caught the ebb tide and floated out to sea, out of her sight, and then was gone forever.

She wanted to say something to mark the occasion. Could not think of a thing. She turned, walked back to the shade of the boulder, and ate her lunch. She spent the rest of the day at the beach, until the sun was sinking and it was time to go home, and drove back to Haven Cove with a sunburn and a light heart and her pockets full of pretty stones and sea glass.

Chapter Twenty-four

Spring came early to Wisconsin that year, and not a moment too soon, as far as Sean was concerned. If nothing else, it meant he could start running outdoors again. He'd been forced to go to the YMCA two towns over, which had a circular indoor track. Something to run on, to be sure, better than outside where he would most likely go flying on a patch of ice and crack his head open. But God, it bored him until he thought his brain might implode.

As soon as the weather warmed enough for the ice to melt away he found places to run. His favorite was a path in the woods, across the lake from the Deer's Head Lodge, on the national forest land. So good to run with earth underneath his feet instead of asphalt or warping parquet wood. What a pleasure, one of the few he had, to feel the warmth of sun and the coolness of wind, to breathe in the scent of the forest. Even the scent of Richard's Christmas tree farm could hold nothing to it, for the woods scent was natural, not cultivated. The only thing that pleased his senses more than the scent of the Wisconsin woods in spring was the Blaine kitchen, pleasantly warm on cool spring evenings, sometimes smelling like fresh-baked bread, sometimes like apples and cinnamon, sometimes like fresh rosemary.

The woods and the kitchen. Fine things to look forward to, one for every morning, the other for meetings. He was a bit surprised that the meetings were not held more often, but then Richard was cautious, reluctant to do anything to cause suspicion. All it would take was someone to notice all-too-frequent gatherings, perhaps connect that to a body (or two) fished out of Deer's Head Lake, and the game would be up. Sean wanted to avoid suspicion as much as any of the group, for above all, he did not want the law to catch Richard. If the law got Richard he'd no doubt get the needle, but only after years of hearings and appeals, all the while getting his three hots and a cot — though prison cooking would be a big step down from Anna's fare. But Richard would be better off than those 361 others who would never eat a nice dinner again. Better off than Jennifer when he'd last seen her picture, poor thing, so thin. No, his way — and Jennifer's way — would be much better for everyone.

They sat in a circle, seven men. Sean, Richard, MacReady, the Wickersham brothers, two others. Richard toyed with a ball-point pen, as was his habit, but he wrote nothing down, never did. Richard's eyes went to the person he wanted to address before he spoke to them. Now he looked at MacReady, and after a second he asked, "Doug, what do you have for us?"

MacReady smiled quickly, then got down to business. What he had was a list of IRS buildings that might make good targets. Reciting from memory, he offered up the proximity of other government buildings and of the local and federal law enforcement. The next logical step would be to send people to scout out the areas. "Look things over, so to speak. Get the lay of the land," MacReady said.

Sean had to admit he rather liked MacReady. He was the sort of person that was often overlooked and yet so essential, the born second-in-command. Reliable and capable, but not able to make that leap toward leadership. It was a rare breed — most were too hungry for power to play the role, and others were too incompetent.

Speaking of which.

"What was that last one, Doug?" asked Eddie, jotting away in the looping scrawl of the high school dropout.

Sean reached across the table, across Steve Wickersham — who, as always, sat next to him — and took the notepad from Eddie. "Hey," said Eddie, "Hey!" as he ripped the page Eddie had been writing on, plus the two beneath it, out of the notepad. Without a word he crumpled the papers into a tight ball, and tossed the notepad back at Eddie.

"What are you —" Eddie began.

"Throw that in the fireplace on your way out tonight, Sam? Thanks." Richard turned his steel-colored eyes toward Eddie. "I'm not going to remind you about that again."

"But —"

"If you can't follow the rules, I need you to leave," Richard said in a voice that would allow no argument. "There's a lot at stake here and no room for goofups. Understand?"

Eddie nodded, turned crimson.

Richard's voice and eyes softened a bit. "You're a good man. But that's not enough. I need good soldiers. If you can't do that, then leave. I won't think less of you, nor will any man here. But if you stay, no more slip-ups. Got it?"

Eddie said nothing.

Brother Steve said, "We got it. We're in."

Sean could feel Steve's eyes on him, ignored the subdued malice in them. Steve had said no more than ten words to him since their confrontation — if you could call it that — the first time he'd come to dinner. But if Steve's words had lessened, his animosity had grown. Sean knew whenever Steve's eyes fell on him; a prickling sensation ran along his nerve endings, as if dislike and distrust had a physical touch. He knew that Steve always sat next to him at the meetings because he was waiting. For a slip. A giveaway. Some reason — or excuse — to denounce him.

Perhaps Steve was one of those people, rare but out there, who had a sixth sense about the wolf in the midst of the sheep. *Spook radar,* Beatty had called it. (God, when would he be able to think about Beatty again without feeling that cold stab in his heart?) Let that wolf look and smell and act and sound like a sheep, but these sorts could always sense the wolf. Perhaps Steve was one of those.

Or perhaps Steve Wickersham was just an asshole.

Sean was inclined toward this latter view. He felt sure that Steve's dislike had not escaped the notice of Richard or MacReady — one would have to be a far bigger fool than those two were not to notice. But if they thought anything of it, he'd had no sign of it. He would just have to watch himself around Steve, and trust in his instincts. The usual routine.

March.

The group kept a low profile, tiptoed around the anniversary of their handiwork like cautious cats. The Saturday just before the 21st, he and Richard sat in the living room, talking their camouflaging small talk. On the television, a "One year later" show was about to begin; he watched Richard out of the corner of his eye. Richard's expression was that of mild boredom, the look of a man who is wondering what is on the other channel. Nothing more. No triumph, no guilt, not even a glance toward his wife, who had just brought in a plate of cheese and crackers. Anna stood holding her mug of tea, looked at the TV screen with wide eyes, said, "Oh, those poor people. That poor girl." Sean dared not look up at that last because he knew who she was talking about and if he looked up it would be all too tempting to tell Anna who her husband was and what he had done and what he was planning to do again. So he said nothing, helped himself to Havarti on whole-wheat crackers, and later, in the safety of the downstairs lair, Richard said, "One hell of a poker face you've got, Sam. My hat's off to you." And gave him a grin both conspiratorial and charming.

How would it feel to empty the gun into that grin, to watch the spray of bone and blood and teeth? *More of a poker face than you know, Richard,* he thought. But only said, "Thanks much," and tipped an imaginary hat back at Richard.

He was at a meeting the night the TV movie they made of Jennifer's story was on. Just as well. He didn't want to see it, even though he'd always had a thing for the lead actress; the commercials made it look like a hack job. His only worry was that Anna would be watching it, but when he came upstairs after the meeting she was watching *Some Like It Hot*, eating popcorn and giggling as Jack Lemmon lay on the bed waving maracas in the air. *Good taste, Anna.*

April, and the plans became firmer. Richard narrowed their targets down to a possible eight sites scattered throughout the Midwest. That was what Richard wanted, to strike the heartland, for that was where the country's discontent came from. "We'll split up and survey the sites. Four in May and four in June. Each take two. Then we'll pick the target and get going."

"Any idea of a date yet?" Steve asked. Eddie automatically reached for a pen and quickly pulled his hand back, clearly hoping that no one had noticed.

"When we're ready," Richard replied. "The date itself doesn't matter."

"But wouldn't the anniversary of something be better? Like, I don't know, Ruby Ridge or tax day?" asked MacReady.

Before Richard could say it, Sean did. "No," he said. "It always has more impact when it's not expected. Besides, my guess is they tighten up security around likely anniversaries."

Richard grinned. "My thoughts exactly, Sam."

"Kiss-ass," muttered Steve, low enough so they could all pretend not to have heard him.

He couldn't care less what Steve thought or said. Before too long, Steve would cease to matter, because as soon as they left for their scouting runs, he would go not to his target but after Richard, catch him, and take him west to Jennifer. It was the perfect opportunity, and no alarm would be raised for days. Weeks, possibly.

That night he checked his gear. Cracked his knuckles in anticipation. Next month, it would begin.

May, and everything went to hell.

One Friday night he was heading out the door to the movies when his phone rang. Richard was on the line. Richard had never called him at home.

"Sam, I need to meet you. Know where the Hot Plate is?" Richard's voice was casual enough, but Sean could detect a note of tension underneath it.

"Of course." The Hot Plate was a diner on the south side of town. He knew it well; it was one of the only places other than Richard's house where he could get a decent cup of coffee.

"Meet me there in twenty minutes." A command, not a request. It felt very familiar. "Look for me at one of the inside booths."

Richard sat by the kitchen, where the noise of clanking dishes and calls of "Fries are up!" would cover their conversation. Once again Sean was surprised, admiring, and a bit uneasy at how well Richard knew what to do, the way he kept his body language and facial expression one of casual, pleasant discussion. You would have had to look deep into his eyes to see what this was really all about.

It was the same look he'd seen during the hunting trip, when they'd had to dispatch Carl Miller, Richard's would-be assassin. Anger, fear, cold practicality. He wondered if this look was directed at him.

Not likely. If Richard had found out something, they would not be in conversation. He would likely be dead by now.

"The shit has hit the fan, Sam," Richard said. "Remember our old friends the Wisconsin Patriots?"

He nodded. "The uninvited guest back in January."

"Yes. We used to buy things from them. Turns out people were buying other things from them. Meth, to be precise." Richard's lip curled down in disdain. "And today they got busted, big time."

"Oh, Christ," Sean said, and his trepidation was genuine. All this work and effort to capture Richard, and it might be for naught thanks to a bunch of dope-dealing, pickup-driving yahoos.

"Nothing's happened to any of us yet, as far as I know. But I don't know how far the Patriots are going to go to save their own necks. They could rat out everyone who's ever bought from them, they could keep their mouths shut to avoid other charges. And I don't know how much they know, or if Carl put two and two together on his own. You see how it is."

"I do." He did. "You want us to lie low."

"Yes. And I mean low. Don't go anywhere near the places we talked about. Meetings are off until further notice. Don't contact the others, don't even go out for a beer or anything."

"Keep the volume down."

"Put it on mute. I'm very serious on this," Richard said. That air of command was heavy on him, even sitting he seemed taller than he was. "If it was just our own necks I wouldn't mind taking chances. But I have Anna to think about. The Wickershams have their parents. Jess, some of the others, they've got families. Brotherhood is what this is about, Sam. Petty shit like you and Steve rubbing each other the wrong way aside, we're in this together. There's no room for a loose cannon who could jeopardize everything. Do we understand each other?"

Through it all Sean never took his eyes off Richard's. No, he understood, very well. It was the sort of spiel he'd heard a hundred times before, from all his bosses from Edwards on down to Halsey. He responded in kind, with all the conviction that was in him. Because he wanted Richard for himself and Jennifer. "We do."

For the first time, Richard smiled. "I knew I could count on you, Sam. I just wish we'd met sooner. I mean, the others are good men, reliable. Get the job done. But you understand. You know what the situation is."

"Thank you." He also wished that they had met sooner, that he could have brought Richard into his world, that he could have had respect and admiration untainted by hate. He wished this not because it would have spared 361 lives, but because he would not be dreading the moment of betrayal.

Sean did not hear from Richard again until Labor Day weekend. The rest of the summer he waited. At times he had to remind himself, when he woke, that he was not in Florida but in Wisconsin. It got harder as the summer wore on, because there were so many similarities and none of them were good. The summer heat, not as humid as Florida but not exactly a dry heat either, just as many mosquitoes and even an early morning run left him drenched with sweat. The waiting for a phone call. For something to happen. Anything. He almost began to wish for the law to bring its hammer down, if only because then he would have something concrete to work against.

There was loneliness to be reckoned with as well. Hateful though the group's goals were, detestable as their actions had been, over the months he'd enjoyed not so much the company but the challenge of matching his wits against someone like Richard. And of course there was Anna; he missed her cooking, but was surprised to find that he missed her, badly. He hadn't realized just how much her presence soothed him, eased the weight of doubt and lies and suspicion.

As the summer went on he worried. About Robert, who for all he knew was in remission or fighting the sickness of chemotherapy or perhaps even dying (he did not allow himself to think Robert might be dead). About Jennifer, who had now gone over a year without the justice that was her due; he wondered what she was doing, if she had fashioned a new life out of the ashes of the old, or if she was still sifting through debris. About Anna, who he saw in the grocery store just before Labor Day. She was in the freezer section, looking over the ice cream and frozen yogurt (trying to decide on a flavor, it seemed). He kept out of sight, thinking it best for her not to see him and ask questions about where he'd been all summer. But though he only saw her for a few seconds, he was struck by how pale and tired she looked; her eyes had dark circles under them and all the curl seemed to have gone out of her hair. It took a surprising amount of will not to ask her if she was all right. He told himself it was just the summer heat and humidity working on her. He hoped it wasn't Richard's situation working on her. Or Richard himself, which seemed highly unlikely, but you never knew. He almost hoped that someone *was* giving Anna grief; someone like (to pick a name totally at random) Steve Wickersham, someone he could then beat the living shit out of. That would cheer him up immensely.

Thankfully, just a few days later he was finishing his morning run, was heading back to his van when he heard the thud of hoofbeats on one of the trails. Even as he registered the sound, Richard rode into the lot, on the palomino this time instead of the brown horse. The worried tension had left Richard's eyes, and Sean knew instantly that things were back on track.

"Anna said you were a runner," Richard said, "And Doug said I might find you here." He smiled. "Me, I let the horse do the running." He patted the palomino's neck.

"How has your summer been?" Sean walked over and stroked the horse's velvety nose, though to be honest he'd always been a bit afraid of horses.

"Quiet."

"Too quiet?"

"No, just quiet."

"Good." After a moment he asked, "How's Anna?"

"She's fine. Care to sample some of her barbecue on Saturday? We're having a big get-together. Lots of stuff going on," Richard said and gave him a wink.

"I'll be there. Name the time."

"Any time after noon. See you then." Richard turned the horse about, then cantered off down the trail into the woods.

Labor Day weekend. Sunny skies and a cool breeze to take the edge off the summer heat. Tall glasses of iced tea and lemonade. Barbecued chicken with two kinds of sauce, sweet and spicy. Slices of watermelon for dessert, the kids spitting the seeds at each other. The women showed each other vacation photos, pictures of trips to the Dells and Disney World, lamented the high price of school supplies. A late summer weekend get-together like any other. Save for one thing. The moment when the party's host gathered a group of the male guests and informed them that plans to take action against the country that had given them this life, plans that would result in the deaths of hundreds of innocents, were back under way.

Sean's assignment was an IRS building two states over, and he went to the state and the town but did not bother to go to the building. He'd been to that building some fifteen years ago, ironically enough, when they'd received threats from the Posse Comitatus. Since then, security had been drum-tight. No hope of the group getting in there. He lingered for a week and a half, enough time to pretend he was looking things over.

He arrived back in Du Lac late on a Friday. The night was heavy with warmth and alive with the sound of crickets. He could not bear to go back to his cheerless apartment. What he wanted was to go to the Blaine house, drink iced coffees with Anna, and watch fireflies. That was impossible; instead he stopped at a roadhouse just outside the city limits. He ordered Scotch and took that outside, sat out on the patio with its splintery floor and its strings of light bulbs overhead. Sat and drank that Scotch and then another, gazing out at the lake. He thought of how very tired he was of waiting, wondered why it bothered him so. It never used to bother him that much. Out on the lake something splashed, a loon sent up its lonely cry. Despite the night's warmth he shivered. Had Beatty been found yet? And wondered why he wondered, for it was no surprise when an agent was never found; Beatty had, after all, been killed in the line of duty. Yet it troubled him to think that Beatty's bones would lie forever at the bottom of this lake. Might even be —

Stop it. This was a different lake, not Deer's Head, and it didn't matter anyway. He went inside to the bar, got another Scotch, and when he went back outside found that he was not alone on the patio. Doug MacReady was there.

"Sam!" MacReady's eyes lit up. "You just got back?"

He nodded. "And you, I take it."

"Yes. Been a long couple weeks, thought I'd get a beer on the way in."

"I'll buy." All the waitresses had gone home, he had to go inside to the bar to get the beer.

"We're closing in a few," the bartender said without looking at him.

"One drink and we're gone, don't worry." He went back to the patio, where MacReady sat, staring pensively at the lake. "How'd it go?" he asked as he handed MacReady the beer.

"Thanks. Went well. I think this is the one. You?"

Sean shook his head. "Looks like a dead end."

"Too bad. But one is all we need." MacReady sighed, took several deep swallows of beer. Again he gazed out at the lake. "It was a hard job, Sam. Very hard."

Sean was intrigued, for he had never seen this sort of mood in MacReady, the ever-loyal and competent assistant. Who probably equated doubt with disloyalty, and had probably never expressed such a thing to Richard. Sean said nothing, thinking that perhaps silence was the way to encourage MacReady to speak.

He was right, for after a moment MacReady sighed again. "It's hard. I mean, I know we're doing the right thing but still, to watch all the people go into the building. Because they're the ones that are going to die, if we're successful. That was the worst part of Los Angeles, you know. I actually worked there, as a maintenance guy, got stuff set up and everything, and it really bothered me sometimes to see all the people."

MacReady was the one. All this time he'd thought it was Steve, and he felt annoyance with himself for thinking that Richard would have trusted such an important job to a hothead like Steve. But mostly he could feel anger, like a match touched to a piece of dry kindling, the flame small and slow, but growing hotter.

No, not hotter. Colder.

"You?" Sean said. His tone one of mild interest, even as he felt cold burn its way up from his heart to his brain and his hands.

MacReady smiled, a self-effacing grin. "I thought you knew."

"No, I didn't." Mild wonder, mostly at himself. For being a fool. For thinking MacReady was different from any of the assorted rogues he'd fought and tracked over the years.

"I thought Richard would have told you. You know, I never did much great shakes in high school. Never made the team. Football *or* baseball." MacReady chuckled. "When Richard asked me to join, you know, it was like being picked for the team."

Sean's fingers itched, longed to squeeze a trigger, pull a garrote tight.

MacReady stood, walked over to the patio rail. Inside the roadhouse the lights had gone out, the bartender had apparently locked up and left the last two customers to find their own way home. "You know how Richard's got a way about him. Makes you feel special. When he asked me to make Los Angeles happen, boy." He smiled. Shook his head as if in disbelief at his own good fortune. "It was like getting picked for the All Stars."

Sean went to stand beside MacReady. Cold anger burning along his spine, through muscle and nerve, heading toward his brain like a lit fuse. He could feel the weight of his gun in its holster, reassuring.

"I didn't want to say so, but for a while I wasn't sure I could do it. I mean, looking at a picture is one thing, saying 'Yeah, I can do this.' But when you're there, seeing the place every day, and the people, get to know the cafeteria workers and the secretaries. That's different."

No, not the pistol. Someone might hear.

"I thought Richard was gonna be pissed when I told him this, you know, that I wasn't sure if I could do it. But he told me that I had to think of the way things were in this country like cancer, and what we were doing was like chemo. That you have to take out some of the good if you want to get rid of the bad, do you see?"

"Yes. Yes, I do." *I'll give you cancer, you rat bastard.*

"I knew you would. You know, Sam, I really wish you'd been with us then."

His hand went to his belt, to the hunting knife in its leather sheath. Shouldn't do it, he knew. Too soon.

"It would have been great to have you on that job."

Fuck it. He clapped MacReady on the shoulder, a gesture of commiseration that went vise-tight in a second, held MacReady fast while his other hand brought the knife out of its sheath. Shoved the blade into MacReady's chest, up under the sternum and into the heart in one swift motion.

MacReady blinked, looked down at the knife handle protruding from his chest, then up at Sean. He wore a look not of pain or even fear, but of surprise, as if he couldn't quite figure out how that knife had gotten there. A look that said *That wasn't supposed to happen.*

Sean leaned close to MacReady, and as he gave the knife handle a twist, whispered in his ear, "Jennifer sends her regards."

MacReady managed one word.

"...who..."

MacReady fell to the floor, eyes empty and staring at the moon, that look of surprise fixed forever on his face.

Chapter Twenty-five

The plan was for Jennifer and Suzanne to take Matthew Tally and the Reisman kids to the aquarium. But Hannah Reisman went home early on Friday from kindergarten with an upset stomach, and by the next morning the whole family had been laid low.

So it was just Suzanne and Jennifer, in Jennifer's car, who pulled up to the Tally house. Matthew was waiting for them, his anticipatory grin almost as bright as the sun shining on his blond head. "Dad, they're here!" he yelled, and Gene came outside. He carried a toolbox in one hand; Jennifer saw wrenches and screwdrivers and less identifiable things, all with a band of white paint on their handles and the letters GT marked in permanent ink.

This day was a celebration of several things, Jennifer mused. Matthew's birthday, for one. His successful completion, and acquisition, of the Harry Potter book this week. And three days ago, when the third-graders came to the library, a woman came up to Jennifer. She was a little older than Jennifer, and looked rather tired. "Are you Jennifer Thomson?" she asked.

"Yes, that's me," said Jennifer, wondering what this was about.

"I'm Ellen Riordan." The name rang a far-off bell in Jennifer's mind, and then the woman said, "I'm the regular third grade teacher, just got back this week."

"Oh, yes. It's good to meet you," said Jennifer. "How is everything?"

Ellen Riordan smiled, a bit wearily, but a smile nonetheless. "Better than it was. I was on maternity leave, and things were rough. But the baby and I made it through. Hailie's at Suzanne Delacroix's today."

"I live next door to Suzanne."

"So she said. The reason I came by is to talk to you about Matthew Tally. He tells me you've been tutoring him these last couple months."

"Yes, I have." She waited for Ellen Riordan to ask what her training was, what her credentials were, and what made her think she should be tutoring anyway. And after replying with *zilch, Jack Shit,* and *damned if I know,* what else could she say?

"Well, I wanted to thank you. I'm not sure what you've been doing, but I know that it's working."

Jennifer let out a sigh. She'd been holding her breath and hadn't even known it. "That's good to know. And I think you should know, he probably should be tested or something but I think Matthew has dyslexia."

Ellen Riordan nodded. "No, it makes perfect sense. I should have put things together before, but..." She sighed, spread her hands. "At any rate, thank you. And keep up your tutoring."

The teacher turned to go, shepherding her charges toward the bus. Jennifer stood, watching them go, and when they were gone, she heard the sound of gentle applause. She turned to see Mr. Bradbury behind the circulation desk, wearing his garden gnome grin and clapping as enthusiastically as his arthritic hands would allow. "Bravo, my dear," he said. "Bravo."

When Matthew came for his lesson that day, she asked if he wanted to go to the Vancouver Aquarium to celebrate. He was all for it, especially when she told him that they had a tank full of piranhas there (why there was an Amazon exhibit at a Canadian aquarium she could not even begin to guess). And here they were, and Gene waved to them. "Hi, ladies."

"Hi, Gene," they replied in chorus. Jennifer said, "You want to come along? There's room in the car."

"Yeah, Dad, they have piranha fish, Miss Jen told me. They can eat a whole cow in, like, a minute."

234

"I know, I know, you only told me a thousand times in the last three days." But it was said with a smile.

"Come on, Gene, tag along," Suzanne said. Her eyes went from Jennifer to Gene and back again; Jennifer saw this but could not fathom what Suzanne was looking for.

"I can't. I promised John Proulx out on the Point that I'd get his skiff running again," Gene said. "Besides, I see fish every day."

"Well, how about meeting us for dinner tonight?" asked Jennifer. "Six o'clock at the Blue Moose work for you?"

"Oh. Yeah. That sounds good." He turned to his son. "Be good, and don't stick your hand in the piranha tank."

"It's official," said Suzanne. "If there's such a thing as reincarnation, I want to come back as a sea otter."

"I could go for that," said Jennifer. They watched the sea otters gyre and gimble in the water; a group of schoolgirls were also watching, private school kids in plaid skirts. Every five minutes or so the girls sent up a chorus of squeals, and shrill cries of "They're so *cute!*"

"I've been meaning to ask you, Jen, who's your secret admirer?"

"What? Oh, the flowers." They were waiting for her when she got back from the park last Tuesday. White chrysanthemums, lilies of the valley, and something that she did not recognize at first, but after consulting an encyclopedia at the library determined to be sweet alyssum. "I have no idea who sent those."

"No note or anything?"

Jennifer shook her head. "Not a thing. I asked my sister, my mom, Mr. Bradbury. Denials all across the board."

Suzanne shrugged. "Well, at least they're pretty."

"Yes, they are." She didn't tell Suzanne that pretty as the flowers were, there was something disquieting about them. Who sent them, and why anonymously? Perhaps it was just that they arrived on the anniversary of the bombing, but there was something else that bothered her. Maybe it was the choice of flowers, the whiteness of them. They looked like something from a funeral.

"Can we go back to the piranhas?" asked Matthew, who'd been sorely disappointed that no cows were going to be tossed into the tank to be devoured in, like, a minute. He'd been mollified by the sight of a caiman and an anaconda, though.

"As long as we stay out of the butterfly exhibit."

"Oh, come on, Jen, that butterfly looked cute on top of your head. Like a bow."

"Yeah, but he wouldn't *leave.*"

They got back to Haven Cove a little after five, stopping to drop off Suzanne. "Bill should be back from his conference any minute now. We'll meet you guys at the Blue Moose, OK?"

The Blue Moose was almost full up. She and Matthew had to wait twenty minutes for a booth, and when they did get one it was situated right next to one of the big TVs. She had to strain to hear the waitress. "We've got three more coming," said Jennifer. "Any way we can turn down the TV?"

The waitress shook her head. "Not a chance. Big game tonight." She gestured around the room, and Jennifer noticed all the men in sports jerseys. "If I touch that TV we'll have a riot on our hands."

"No problem, we'll deal." She ordered a plate of onion rings, a Coke for Matthew and a glass of white zinfandel for herself. The first drink she'd had since New Year's but she felt it was safe. It had been a good week, a great week, and why not celebrate?

236

Gene arrived at the same time their drinks and onion rings did. The waitress turned and was gone before he could order; he shrugged and sat down. "How was the Aquarium?"

For the next ten minutes Matthew dominated the conversation. Piranhas and sea otters, beluga whales and orcas. He opened his bag of treasure for his father to see. Two books about marine life, a key chain shaped like a shark, a plastic mobile of prehistoric ocean creatures that would glow in the dark.

"Very nice," Gene said with a smile. Looking up at Jennifer, he said, "He didn't drive you crazy, did he?"

"Not at all. We all had a great time. Bill and Suzanne should be here any minute."

The waitress arrived. Gene asked her for a beer and an order of potato skins. He'd had no lunch, he said, and besides, Matthew had already put a very sizable dent in the onion rings.

As the waitress jotted down the order, one of those peculiar silences fell — the sort that always strike a room at the worst possible time. On the television a beer commercial faded out, and there it was.

The screen in blackness, and a portentous voice-over. She recognized the narrator from movie previews. He said, "A story torn from the headlines" and she didn't hear the rest of it because there it was, on screen, for all the patrons of the Blue Moose, everyone in Haven Cove, hell, probably everyone in British Columbia to see, *that* picture, *her* picture. After a few seconds it did a digital fade from her and the firefighter to the actors playing them, but what did that matter? She had thought she was safe from it, had forgotten that Canada was more or less the fifty-first state and that there were such things as foreign rights to broadcast. She looked away from the screen, only to see the eyes of the waitress widen slightly in recognition. Through the music of the commercial — Mozart's *Requiem,*

237

Mr. Bradbury played it a lot — and the narrator's booming voice she heard the waitress say softly, "Oh...*wow*."

She didn't feel herself get up. There was a tinkling and a dripping sound, and she was standing, her glass of wine knocked over. Its fumes rose to her nostrils and made her think of New Year's Day. "Miss Jen?" Matthew's voice was soft and worried. "You OK?"

"Fine. Be right back." Without reaching for her coat or purse she began making her way through the tavern to the front door, needing to get out of this crowd. Too many people, too much noise, too many pairs of eyes looking at her or getting ready to look. There didn't seem to be enough air in the place. She made it to the tavern's door — free! — and opened it to find Bill and Suzanne. Suzanne said, "Hey, Jen. Is...my God, are you all right? What's wrong?"

She babbled something about not feeling well, needing air, prayed they wouldn't follow her. She walked through the parking lot at a fast clip, not quite a run, walked down the block until she found a park bench, looking down a slope toward the harbor. Jennifer sat down, heedless of the cold coastal breeze. Her stomach roiled and she actually longed for the release of vomiting, but nothing happened.

She had made her bargain with Amber LaSalle all those months ago because it wasn't really her, not her story, and she had thought she could ignore whatever movie or book came to light. She'd made the bargain but hadn't counted on the real cost; what shamed her now was not who she was and what she had survived, but that she had traded on that, bought her happiness with blood money. Gene and Mr. Bradbury hadn't known that. Now they all would know. Everyone. Once again she would no longer be Jennifer, whoever that was. She would be the girl who turned tragedy into profit, like Rumpelstiltskin turning straw into gold. Yet what else could she expect? She had made the deal, even if she hadn't realized all the terms of it, and now it was time to pay. *And I'm tired of paying for this, so —*

Footsteps coming toward her. She did not look up to see who it was, kept her face turned toward the ocean. Suzanne most likely, bringing her coat and purse. There would be a cold look in Suzanne's eyes, she would hand Jennifer her things and say, "Here."

"Jennifer?" Gene's voice.

Ah, Gene. Come to tell her that Matthew would be tutored by someone else now, come to ask Miss California what was wrong, didn't she like being famous? She didn't answer him.

"Anything I can do?" His voice was softer than usual, and she looked up at him. He stood with his hands behind him, like a child called on to recite something in school.

"I don't think so." It was her own bed she'd made, she'd have to lie in it herself. "Maybe you should go."

Instead of going, he sat down beside her. "You want to talk about it?"

She shook her head, then blurted out, "What's to say? I mean, I'm the one who sold my story, why am I so surprised when I see me on TV?"

"Because that's not why you did it."

It was the last thing she expected him to say. She turned to look at Gene. His eyes looked paler than ever in the streetlight's glow but for the first time she thought she could read behind those eyes, and found no accusation there.

"I had to get away from Los Angeles," she said. "I couldn't go to work in any of the office buildings without thinking they'd blow up. I wanted to go someplace I could start over and just be me. That's all I wanted."

"And that's what you got." He patted her shoulder gingerly, as if he thought she might break. Or bite.

"No, damn it, not just that. Did you see the look on that waitress' face? Now everyone will know who I am and what I did to get here. Suzanne and Bill and Mr. Bradbury and everyone else I know." She took in a deep breath. "I can't stand to see how they'll look at me."

"They'll look at you the way they always have. Like you're their friend. Nothing's going to change that. They know you. They like you." He paused, looked away from her, out at the ocean. "I like you."

"I thought I was Miss California."

Gene blushed. "I'm sorry for that. I really am. I was upset. What you said about Matthew, I mean, in one afternoon you figured out what I hadn't. It was just one more way I've let him down. That's all I've done, it seems."

How could he say that? If her father had shown a tenth of the devotion Gene showed Matthew, she might actually miss him.

Before she could protest, Gene said, "I guess by now you heard about me and Becca."

She nodded.

He took out his wallet. Buried deep, not in the plastic photo insert but back behind his driver's license was a small wedding photo. Gene in a rented tux, smiling broadly at his good fortune. If there was any doubt in his eyes the camera did not see it. Beside him a beautiful woman: black hair, white teeth, red lips, like in the old fairy tales. And even in the puffs and ruffles of a wedding dress a body that, as the saying goes, wouldn't quit. Large brown eyes, Matthew's eyes.

"I always knew it would never last with me and Becca. It was only a matter of time."

"Why'd you marry her?" she asked.

"Because for the first time in ages I was happy, or something like it. I thought, well, it won't last but I'll take as much of it as I can get. I thought I would be the only one to get hurt." He put the photo away.

"You were willing to make that bargain," she said. *Oh Gene, that's the problem with bargains, they're never as simple as they seem. I know.*

"Yeah. I did. But you see." He dropped his voice to a near-whisper, leaned close to her. She leaned toward him. "We didn't plan for Matthew. Becca hit the roof when she got pregnant. She didn't want to have him. I talked her into it. Once I got over the surprise, I really wanted a kid. I'm the last of my family. My folks are dead, I don't have any brothers and sisters. So we had Matthew, and right away I loved him. That's where it all went downhill for Becca and me."

"Because she didn't want him?"

"That. And I knew then what it is to care for someone. Whatever it was between Becca and me, caring wasn't part of it. We started fighting. I tried not to fight with her in front of Matthew but Becca didn't care. She'd say things." He paused, searching for the right word. "Hateful things."

Jennifer tried to imagine what Becca had said, and decided she didn't want to know. The look in Gene's eyes was enough.

"That night when Becca left, I knew I'd screwed it all up. My son was five and not a week had gone by where he hadn't seen his parents fight. His mom ran out on us and took everything. From day one I let him down. and when you came to see me at the docks, I just felt that all over again. I let my son down."

"I thought, the way you called me Miss California, I reminded you of Becca," she said, hoping it wasn't so.

He shook his head. "It wasn't that. I don't know how to say it. It was partly just feeling, you know, ashamed. But the way you looked when I came back. You weren't going to let it go. You were going to bat for

Matthew, doing more for him than I could, and it made me feel worse, but I admired it too. The look on your face ... I don't know how to say it. Like a lion. Brave."

"Don't make fun of me, Gene, I'm the chickenshit of the century."

"Stop it, OK. You are brave. You started over, got your life back on track. You're helping Matthew, and God knows you didn't have to. Mr. Bradbury wants to adopt you, you're the best thing that's happened to him and the library in years. If you want to talk about chickenshits, talk about me. I got married to someone I didn't love because I didn't want to lose her, I'm a stupid Newfie who can't read and I work the same job that killed my father because that's all I know. So stop beating yourself up."

"I will if you will," she said. Then, asked softly, "Your father?"

Gene looked down at his hands, hard and callused from years of work. "He was a fisherman, back in Newfoundland. He drowned."

Something of Matthew's look in Gene's face, vulnerability kept well-concealed. "How old were you?" she asked.

"Ten," he replied.

"I'm sorry." She reached out and put her hand on Gene's shoulder. "I'm sorry," she said again, not just for Gene's loss but for so many things.

"Thanks."

They said nothing for a while. Suddenly she realized how long they'd been out here. "Where's Matthew?"

"Back at the Blue Moose with the Delacroixs. They're probably on dessert by now. You ready to go back?"

"Yes," she said. "I think so." As they walked back, she kept her hand on Gene's shoulder. It was good to have someone to hold on to.

Chapter Twenty-six

He sat in the Blaines' den, watched Richard pace, and betrayed none of the anxiety he felt. Because what he'd done to MacReady was a mistake, something that could cost the entire mission. Sooner or later, Sean was sure, someone would put things together. Henry Connolly, Doug MacReady. One in a quarry, one locked into the trunk of his car and deposited at a long-term parking lot at Green Bay airport. And Sean the common denominator.

It was an error, and a big one. He had only himself to blame for letting emotion carry him away. That was usually how it happened. You pulled the trigger not out of fear or inexperience but out of anger. It had happened to everyone in his old crowd at least once. They even had a code for it, among themselves, based on the tired explanation their superiors always trotted out. *An MWM,* they said. *Mistakes were made.*

Richard paced, Sean sat. Above them in the kitchen, the sound of Anna loading the dishwasher, singing a Beatles song — "I've Just Seen A Face" — as she worked. "You haven't heard anything from him?" asked Richard, who stopped pacing and looked at him.

"Not a thing," Sean replied.

Richard nodded, began pacing again.

"It's probably taking longer than he thought and he wants to give you the full report," Sean said. "You know how Doug is."

"Probably," Richard said. "He was two weeks longer than we thought he'd be when we were planning Los Angeles." He shook his head. "It's been a hard summer, that's all. The business with the Wisconsin Patriots, having to worry about that. And speaking of the WPs, today I was riding out by the lake to think things over, and saw the local coroner's van. Seems someone reeled up an unexpected catch."

"Our unexpected guest?" he asked.

Richard shrugged. "Who can say? Unless he had ID on him they may never know. Nine months at the bottom of a lake, you don't look too pretty."

"I can imagine." He certainly could. "What's next, then, do we wait for Doug?"

"Of course. His is the place I've always thought was the best target. I'm sorry yours turned out to be a dead end."

"It happens."

Richard began to pace again, then looked up at the ceiling, listening to the sound of his wife walking in the kitchen. "Sam, I need you to do something for me. A favor."

"What's that?"

"I'm going out of town this weekend. There's an old contact of ours who helped get the supplies together for Los Angeles. I want to see if he's still around and amenable."

Sean's nerve endings tingled. This might be the opportunity. Keeping any betraying note of eagerness out of his voice, he asked, "You need a backup? I'm free."

Richard hesitated, looked at him with keen intensity. No suspicion there, yet. But how long would that last? How long before the trust he had earned was outbalanced by the loss of Connolly and MacReady? Not too much longer. If nothing else, he had to move soon for his own sake. He could not risk another MacReady. And he could not bear the weight of this charade much longer without paying some price.

Sean let none of this show, merely waited for Richard to reply. "No," said Richard. "I've got history with this fellow, and it's the sort of history that should just be me and him. But if you could...I feel silly asking you this."

Sean smiled. So strange and oddly endearing to see Richard hesitant. "Spit it out, come on."

"OK. This summer's been rough on Anna. Could you keep her company while I'm away? Maybe take her to a movie or something? There's that new one with Tom Hanks in it, she'd like that."

Sean did not quite know what to say. It was the last thing he'd expected. Who knew that the man responsible for the second most deadly terrorist attack on U.S. soil was currently fretting about his wife? And asking Sean, of all people, to take her to the movies. God, life could be weird sometimes. He couldn't wait to tell Robert this; it was the sort of thing that amused him.

"I'd be happy to."

He had thought it would be strange, going to the Blaines' on a Saturday night not for a meeting but to pick up Anna and take her to the movies. But as they drove to the theater and made small talk, that familiar feeling of ease came over him. Sean was relieved to see that Anna was in excellent spirits. She still looked a bit unwell, though. "Anna, are you OK? I mean, you just look a little tired lately."

She smiled. In the late summer twilight she looked more fatigued than before, but her eyes were warm. "I'm fine. Just been laying off the coffee. Was turning into a caffeine maniac and thought I should give it up for a bit."

He saw no lie in her eyes. "I did that once," he said. "Swearing off the coffee."

"How'd it go?"

"Worst three hours of my life."

Their laughter mingled as they drove through the warm Wisconsin twilight.

He sat next to Anna in the theater. Watched the movie, but thought about Monique. That was no surprise, really. He'd been telling Anna jokes while they waited in line. He liked hearing her laugh, had been ransacking his brain to recall Beatty's jokes (not the dirty ones, definitely *not* the one about the Jew, the Frenchman, and the nun). Anna's laughter was unrestrained, carefree. Like Monique's.

Monique was about ten years his junior, tall, with a long, fast stride and a way of walking with her upper body thrust slightly forward. She had long black hair and dark eyes and her good looks were old-fashioned somehow, like a film noir actress transported to the present day. But her voice was the first thing he noticed about her. He did not know if there was such a thing as bittersweet honey, but that was how he thought of her voice. She was a lawyer with a big corporation that did a lot of work with the government, hence her presence in D.C. He never saw her in court — they kept the business sides of themselves out of their relationship — but liked to imagine it, Monique using that voice to work her will on judges and juries.

Sean met Monique at the bar in a hotel where he was staying; having just finished a mission and the debriefing, he had time on his hands and was eager for some company of the female variety. It was February; the TV in the bar was on, and that year's Oscar nominations were being announced.

"The Academy strikes again," said a woman's voice, entrancingly sweet and husky, a little way down the bar. "Nominates a bunch of art-house pretentiousness where nothing happens for two hours."

He turned to look at her. "Nothing happens, but you feel bad at the end anyway," he said.

"You saw that one, too?" She turned to him and smiled, he smiled back. He knew he was average-looking at best, but he also knew how to make what he had work for him. At least he wasn't as bad off as Halsey, who'd just had his third wife walk out on him and couldn't get laid in a brothel, according to agency gossip. Sean was charming when he wanted to be, and right then he wanted to be; he agreed with her opinion, liked her looks, and oh, that voice. He longed to hear her say his name in the dark.

They had a couple of drinks, discussed the nominations. It turned out that she liked the movies as much and as indiscriminately as he did. They ended up at a little art-house theater and saw a David Lynch film. Afterward a spirited argument about the film, a late dinner, and he invited and she accepted. Once in the room neither said anything at first; they circled each other like cats, eyes always meeting. Like cats, they both pounced at the same time.

It was supposed to be merely a fling, a night's enjoyment. That was what he had intended, and Sean felt fairly certain that was what she had intended. Yet in the morning, neither was eager for the other to leave. In fact, each caught the other dawdling, prolonging the inevitable parting. But the moment came when he was accustomed to saying *Nice seeing you* or *I'll call you some time*; instead, he heard a note of mild surprise in his voice as he asked, "Would you like to have breakfast with me?"

He'd heard the same surprise in her voice. "I'd like that very much."

Sean didn't think it was love. But if not love, it was something both of them were very pleased with. They went to good restaurants and saw many films and the occasional play, whiled away hours in bed at his hotel or her apartment. He bought her presents on his travels, scarves and jewelry, bottles of odd wines and liqueurs. She poked around the corners of D.C. and found unusual restaurants for them, good sushi bars or Moroccan places where they ate with their hands, sitting on the floor. They sometimes drove up to New York for the theater. Sometimes they took a walk through Central Park at night. "I've never done this before," she confided the first time they did that, her honey voice holding an excited thrill at venturing into forbidden territory. This was after he had told her, in general terms, what he did for a living. She never asked him anything about his work after that — she knew better — but understood that he could handle anything Central Park might throw at them.

It lasted for four years, and he marveled that he had a person's company to look forward to rather than just time off. He cherished his time with Monique more and more as the years went on and his old friends were lost to retirement or death. As the world that had once been in black and white became a dull gray. As he watched missions get canceled or end up bungled because those in charge did not want to give them time or equipment or funds. Once, long ago, he had stepped into quicksand, had felt the ground shudder treacherously beneath his feet before he threw himself back onto solid earth. During those last few years, he felt that way much of the time, that the earth was weak beneath him, waiting to pull him down. Only when he saw Monique again, saw her smile at him, heard her bittersweet honey voice, felt her body against his, did that sense of standing on shaky ground leave him. No, not love, but the closest he was able to get to it, and he was thankful for it.

Coming up on five years ago now, the day that Halsey summoned him. Sean walked down the hall, knowing why he was being summoned, feeling the knowledge seep into his heart like icy water. It was not unexpected. Quite the contrary. He was the last of his old crowd. Robert,

Beatty, Hamilton, Harris, Goodman. All of them retired now. At first those who were left placed bets on who would be next, but it stopped being funny when Goodman shot himself six months after they sent him away. His note said, *If I have to tell you why, you'll never understand.*

As he walked down the hall to Halsey's office he saw people glance his way from hallways and cubicles. So many faces he did not recognize. So young, most of these people, and what did they know besides computers and satellites? How many of them could go in undercover with nothing but their wits and a gun, and survive?

He sat, politely refused Halsey's offers of water or coffee. Long and distinguished career, Halsey said, a comfortable retirement for his valuable service. A stipend, enough to live quite comfortably on. Only thing to do for such a distinguished agent.

"Where?" he asked.

Florida. Sean wished he was like Robert, who knew where enough bodies were buried (so to speak) for them to *ask* him where he wanted to go. Or like Juliette, the agency's top assassin — everyone was too afraid of her to send her anywhere she didn't want to go.

"Is there any chance of this retirement being...temporary?" he'd asked.

Oh, of course, of course. They would let him know, call him if he was needed. He noticed the *if.* Not a *when.*

Halsey asked him if that was all right, not really asking, and Sean said yes it was, for what other choice did he have? Halsey said that he knew they hadn't always seen eye to eye, but it had been good working with him over the years, and Sean lied and said, oh yes, likewise. Thinking that he might respect Halsey if the man had come out and said what Sean knew he was thinking: *I never liked you and I'm glad I'm rid of you.* Halsey handed him a gold watch, and Sean smiled and said thank you, thought, *You've got to be fucking kidding.*

When he left Halsey's office, Halsey's secretary was there waiting for him with papers to sign. He signed and thanked her and walked down the halls, nodding at people but not bothering to say goodbye, for although there were people he knew, there was no one he would miss. All those people were already gone.

Only when he was outside, standing in the sun and the cool breeze, did it all come home to him. Only now did he understand what Robert had said when Sean had asked, "So how are you enjoying retirement?"

"This isn't retirement," Robert said. "This is exile."

With an effort Sean got moving. Only two things would dull the pain for a little while. The first was motion, the second was Monique.

He walked back to his hotel, quite a long walk, but he'd had far worse in his days. About a block away from his hotel he spotted a street musician he knew by sight, playing an alto saxophone. Over the years he'd often thrown money into the musician's hat, often enough that, while they had never spoken, they always gave each other a nod.

Now he stopped, stood listening while the musician played some old blues riff he vaguely recognized. Sean had never stopped to listen before. The musician finished, looked his way. "How goes it, my friend?" the musician asked.

"I've been better."

"Something to cheer you up? Maybe a little Bird?"

"How about 'Take Five'?"

The musician grinned, put the horn to his lips, and began to play. For a few minutes, there might have been nothing else in the world, just he and the cool spring day and Paul Desmond's sweet melody. When the musician was done, Sean thanked him and gave him the gold watch. God knew this man would need it more than he would.

Once in his room, he made two phone calls. One to a better hotel, to book a suite, and the other to Monique. "Flint!" she exclaimed. "Hello, stranger. When did you blow back into town?"

"Yesterday."

"Your timing is impeccable. I just got out of deposition hell and could use the pleasure of your company."

"Imagine that. I was thinking the same thing. Can you make it over here tonight?"

"I'll be there with my jingle bells on."

It had been two months since they had seen each other. They would have been famished for each other under normal circumstances, but the day's events had put an extra edge on his hunger, and he pounced almost as soon as the door was shut behind her. She didn't seem to mind; in fact, she was the one who said, "No, on the floor, we've never done it on the floor before."

Later, she strolled out of the bathroom, her hair wet from the shower, wearing one of the hotel robes. Wandered over to the table, where the remains of a room service feast were strewn about, the empty champagne bottle upside-down in its cooler. "Well, you haven't forgotten how to show a lady a good — oh, cheesecake!" She picked up the plate of chocolate-chip cheesecake and a fork, sat down next to him on the bed. Sean lay on his stomach, chin on his folded arms, trying to keep the feeling of defeat away, not wanting to taint this evening with it. "How much did you order from room service, anyway?" she asked.

"All of it."

"I'll say." She rubbed his right shoulder. "So, when are you going to tell me what's wrong?"

"Nothing's wrong."

"Objection. We've had two rolls in the hay, a calorie bomb, a fifth of bubbly, and a shower, and your shoulders still feel like they're carved out of wood. So come on." She set the cheesecake aside, knelt astride him and began massaging his shoulders. "Tell me about it."

For a few moments he was silent. Then he said, "I'm retired."

Monique's hands stopped in mid-massage. "I see." Her voice was unusually quiet. "Did you jump or were you pushed?"

"Pushed."

She said nothing, ran her fingertips over a scar on his right shoulder blade. It was one of his more recent acquisitions, the nerves tingled under her touch. "Where? I mean, what happens next?"

Sean rolled over to face her. "They're sending me to Florida. Guess I'll be a snowbird," he said, trying to make light of it.

She held her thumbs and index fingers together to form a camera lens. "You've just been retired. Now what are you going to do?" she asked in a broadcaster's phony voice.

"I'm going to Disney World!" They both laughed, but it wasn't funny, and they knew it.

She slid off, lay beside him, head on his shoulder. "What are you going to do?"

"I don't know."

The unspoken question was, what was going to happen to them. Because he couldn't stay, and she couldn't leave. The silence stretched out. He had the feeling she was waiting for him to make the decision, but when he tried to see her expression, her face was hidden by her hair.

Finally he said, "It's been good, hasn't it? Us, I mean." Sean hated himself for using the past tense. But what else could he do?

"Yes, it has been." He heard no reproach in her voice. But what did he hear? Regret? Relief? Both? Yes, both.

Neither said anything for a while. Then she asked, "When do you go?"

"Day after tomorrow."

"Well then," she said, propping herself up on one elbow and smiling at him. "We'd better make tonight memorable."

They kissed, and made love one more time. The last time.

The next morning they stood on the sidewalk. "I'm going to miss you," he said, reaching out to stroke her dark hair. A few strands of gray in it now.

"I'll miss you, too." They embraced, held each other tightly. Then stood gazing at each other; he felt her looking into his eyes for something.

"Be careful," Monique said. It was not until later Sean realized it was the first time she had ever said that to him. Strange that she should say it when he was going not to some danger zone halfway across the globe but to Florida.

"I'm always careful," he said.

They said goodbye, and he turned and walked away. He did not look back, much as he wanted to.

Sean hadn't seen Monique since, though they had exchanged letters and postcards over the years, and the occasional phone call. The last time he'd spoken to her was the New Year's Eve before the Los Angeles bombing. There were thunderstorms in Florida, and he was alone, and bored, and a bit tipsy. He called, and on the other end he heard Monique's voice, along with the babble of voices and music in the background. Sounds of a party. A small one, by the sound. A get-together with friends.

"Here, let me get you in the other room," she said. A clunk, the party noise was gone, and it was just the two of them, an hour or so until midnight. They talked, asked after each other's health and welfare, feeling well, staying busy. Then she said, "I'm glad you called, Flint. I have some news I think you might like to hear."

Sean knew what she was going to say. It was in her voice, a special note that could only mean one thing. It hurt him for some reason but he let her say it because it made her happy. "I met someone last year. His name's Michael. He's a wonderful guy, and on Christmas he proposed. We're getting married."

He meant it when he told her he was happy for her. Because Monique deserved that sort of love. "Be happy, Moni," he told her before he hung up. He watched the New Year come in while thunderstorms lit up the sky with lightning, and thought, *Yes, be happy, Monique. One of us should be.*

The movie over, he and Anna sat at the Hot Plate, decaf and pie in front of them. Sean was happy to see that, tired or not, Anna's appetite was fine. She put away a slice of blueberry pie and two scoops of vanilla ice cream with no problem. He asked about the tree farm, how one went about raising a Christmas tree. Although he was interested, and listened to her, part of him was realizing why he had been thinking of Monique this evening. It was not the laughter, nor being at the movies. It was that feeling of ease he had in the presence of these women.

Strange that this should be so, for his feelings toward Monique and Anna were entirely different. If he'd had a sister, he supposed he would have felt toward her the way he felt about Anna. And more — he saw in her eyes a simplicity and honesty that he had thought long gone from this world. She was what she was, a nice young woman from a small town in Minnesota, who'd been crowned the town's Shamrock Queen in high school, who was content with her husband and her life, who kept her house and kitchen and who led half the charity committees at her church. Who knew such a person existed any more? The only thing that puzzled him was why she and Richard did not have children; he would have expected Anna to have half-a-dozen at least. But then, she was mother to all the stray dogs Richard brought home. Maybe that was enough.

"Did you like the movie, Sam?" she asked him as he drove her home. "You were kind of quiet during it."

"Oh yeah. What do you think, another Oscar for Tom Hanks this year?"

"If I were a betting woman, I'd put up a dollar."

Sean walked her to the door, and she said, "Just a minute." Came back with an apple pie. "Here you are. Thank you for a nice evening."

Why did she do this to him? She treated him like a friend, gave him pies and lasagna; at the Labor Day party she'd even asked if he would like to meet her newly single cousin Deirdre. But he was no friend to her. How could he be?

He felt like breaking something. Because he wanted to be Anna's friend and never would be. Just as he had wanted to be more than a lover to Monique and never would be. Whatever he needed, that bit of humanity he had never missed until now, had been destroyed years ago. Taken from him by all the deception, the lies, the killings, all the years and deeds that had done things to his soul. No, not taken — he'd given it away freely.

"Anna." Sean found it hard to speak. "I have to tell you something."

He wanted to say, *Anna, you have to understand that people aren't what you think they are. They seem nice, may even* be *nice, and yet they can do terrible things. They kill people in the name of a cause, say that it's justified. They lie, they deceive, and they say it's all right if it serves their cause.*

But was it Richard he was talking about, or himself?

He looked into Anna's eyes, and saw innocence. Not stupidity, not naiveté. Innocence.

I won't say it. Let there be something innocent left in this world.

"Sam?" she asked. "You were going to tell me something?"

"I'm sorry," he said. "It slipped my mind."

"Well, you know what it means when you forget something you were about to say. It must have been a lie."

"Must have been," Sean said.

Chapter Twenty-seven

Jennifer felt a kind of peace fall on her after the talk with Gene. After the TV movie aired, as far as she could tell no one noticed or cared, no one made the connection between her and the girl on TV. Once, at the grocery store, she felt eyes trained on her. But when she got home she realized it was for a very different reason. There had been a small party at the library that day, one of the high school assistants had made the honors list, and Jennifer had gone to the store still wearing her party hat, her hair speckled with confetti.

As if to give its blessing to her newfound peace, the weather began to warm and sometimes there was an entire week without rain. Imagine that. She took her coffee outside in the mornings, gazing out at the sea. Sometimes she took a pair of binoculars, scouted the horizon, and her vigilance was rewarded one May morning when she saw a pod of whales, huge and yet graceful, sending plumes of spray into the air with their exhalation. She let out a delighted cry, hoisted her coffee cup aloft in a toast, as if congratulating the cetaceans on their performance. Her last glimpse of the whales was a tail fin that seemed to wave at her. *Hi Jen,* the whale seemed to say. *Good to see you.*

She told Gene about seeing the whales the next evening. After their talk on the park bench they'd been passing more and more time in conversation when she dropped off Matthew, and one night he invited her to stay for dinner. She found herself more curious than she would have thought to see the inside of the Tally house. Having shared dwellings with men — her brother Jim, several college roommates, a failed attempt at cohabitation with her last boyfriend — Jennifer had an idea of what to expect. There would be shoes and socks under the coffee table. The fridge would be full of heat-and-eat food and carry-out leftovers, perhaps an empty pizza box on the dining room table, which would be a card table surrounded by folding chairs.

She had seldom been so pleased to be wrong. Instead of dour bachelor adequacy, there was a ramshackle charm to the place. The sofa and chairs were all clearly secondhand, a hodgepodge of different colors and styles. But what should have been a disordered jumble was more like a patchwork quilt, almost festive. The shelves were the planks-and-bricks design favored by broke college students, but Gene had stained the planks a dark cherry color and used red brick instead of homely gray cinderblock; the result was striking. Likewise, the end tables in the living room were cable reels, any paint sanded off, then stained and varnished to a deep glowing gloss. She felt some of the pride she'd taken in her own decorating fall away; she'd bought hers, Gene had made his.

Matthew, giving her the tour while Gene was busy in the kitchen, did not share her interest in the living room. It was old news to him. "Here, look at these," he said, pointing at the framed photos in the hallway. "Dad took these."

The photos were black-and-white, which had always bored her before. Black-and-white was for distant relatives whose names she could not remember, snapshots of old houses long sold off. Once, when she and Cindy were looking through a photo album of their grandmother's, they'd found the black-and-white photo of a five-year-old girl laid out in a coffin, her lacy dress and the photo's sepia tone giving her the appearance of a mummified angel. Cindy had nightmares for weeks.

But these pictures were different. There was a faint silvery quality that made them look like a glimpse into some other, better world, and yet the clarity showed every detail. Every wrinkle in clothes, every strand of hair, every ripple of water. The glass and frame were not to protect the photo but to protect her, to keep what was in the photo from reaching out and pulling her into its reality.

She saw a boat deck piled with fish and a cat sitting above the pile, looking smug, as if he thought the catch was his doing. The harbormaster, dozing in his chair with his head back, a cigarette burned down to ash in one hand and the handset of his radio in the other. The main commercial row of Haven Cove, washed by rain and empty of people, above it a single shaft of sunlight peeking out through a hole in the clouds.

Jennifer walked into the kitchen as Gene was sliding a tray of breaded fish fillets into the oven. There was a pot of macaroni on the stove, and as he said "Hi, Jennifer. Matthew give you the tour?" he began mixing cheese (the real stuff, not the fake orange powder) into the macaroni.

"Indeed he did. I love what you've done with the living room, and I still can't find words for your photos. And dinner smells great, too."

He gave her his quick smile, shrugged. "I can make about five meals, and this is one of them. It's good, or at least Matthew says so."

"How long have you been into photography?"

"Becca bought me a camera, our first Christmas. I wanted to try developing them myself, so I talked to the kid who does the photos for the high school yearbook, learned from him. Built the darkroom," he pointed. "It's just past the pantry there."

"You've got a lot of photos. I mean, as busy as you are, it must be hard to find the time."

"Most of those are from the last few years. Becca said the smell of the photo chemicals gave her a headache. Got so I could only work on photos if she was out of town." He said this without rancor, the calm tone of a man who'd accepted a past mistake. She envied that calmness, wondered when she would be able to feel that way about her own mistakes.

"When I look at the pictures, I don't know, it's like you're looking at things not the way they are. But the way they should be." This wasn't coming out right at all. "Sorry, I'm babbling."

He gave her a long look, stood there with salad tongs in his hands. "No, that's exactly how I feel about it."

"Really?"

"Really. Here, can you take this in to the table?" he asked, handing her the bowl of macaroni.

"Sure. Have you ever tried selling any photos to the local paper or anything? Hell, I bet some galleries down in Vancouver would pay for them. That would be neat."

"No, haven't done that," he replied.

"Why not?"

He looked up at her. "Not interested." She could tell that he *was* interested, but he didn't want to hear them say no. She started to protest, then thought better of it. Gene had enough rejection in his life already, let him be ready to risk it again when he wanted to. God knew she couldn't blame him.

Over dinner she told him about seeing the whales, and he and Matthew looked at each other and grinned. "What's with you two?" she asked.

"Dad takes people out whale watching when the gray whales come up here."

"It's a nice supplement to the income," Gene said. "But I'll do a special trip for you. No other tourists, and at friend prices."

"What might that be?"

"Some of those chocolate mint brownies Matthew's always going on about."

"Done."

The first weekend in June she found herself on the *Tally-ho* with Matthew and Gene. She had never been on the *Tally-ho* before, and was unsurprised to find it much like Gene's house, neat and cozy with more than a few of Gene's photographs on the wall. "Matthew, put on some tunes," Gene called out as he began to guide the boat out to the harbor. Matthew obliged, and soon Steely Dan began declaring that Guadalajara wouldn't do. Curious, Jennifer went into the cabin, where she found a boombox and a drawer full of tapes; more Steely Dan, the Pogues, the Chieftains, the soundtrack to *The Commitments*.

She was worried that she might get seasick once they left the harbor, but her stomach was fine, and by the time they were out on the open sea she was enjoying it tremendously. It was a clear, calm day, the sunshine warm but the breeze cool, and the boat sped along the water's surface like slow flight. Behind them the green slopes of British Columbia and the kite that Matthew had sent aloft, dipping and soaring, waving its long red tail. Above them the blue of the sky and below them the deeper, cobalt hue of the ocean. She had that same feeling she did when she paid her visit to the ocean in March, that the wind was cleansing. Only now it did not seem to blow through her but to lift her up. She thought if she fell off the boat it would not matter, the wind would carry her aloft.

She went to stand by Gene, at the wheel of the boat. He was singing along to the music, in a remarkably good tenor voice. Hearing her, he stopped singing and turned to look at her. "How you like it so far?"

"I love it."

"Not feeling sick, are you?"

"No, never better."

"That's good, you never know who's going to get seasick. Though it's real calm now, if there was a gale there'd be — oh, hello there." He brought the boat to a slow crawl, then cut the motor. "Come on."

They went out onto the boat, Matthew joining them, bringing in his kite. Gene pointed out to the water. "Look there."

"I don't—" and then she did, great gray backs and plumes of water, fins waving. About a dozen whales, big ones mostly, but she managed to spot what looked like a young one in the crowd. She watched, wished she could have a closer look, and then realized she was going to get her wish. "They're coming this way."

"Yeah. Here, come back to the stern."

"Dad, can I touch one?"

"If they come close enough."

Jennifer felt herself a total landlubber, but had to ask. "They won't, you know, hit the boat or anything?"

"You've seen too many movies," Gene said. What could have been scornful was amused, it was clear from his smile and his eyes. "Come on."

It was different seeing the whales close up. They seemed to move both faster and slower, and she realized the great size of them. Despite Gene's assurances she felt nervous; one of these things could smash the boat to pieces if it felt so inclined. But they were not inclined that way, in fact she would have sworn that the whales seemed to be friendly. One broke the surface right next to the boat, got them wet with the spray, seemed to linger alongside the boat, and they all reached out, Gene holding Matthew out and down so he could reach. She stroked the whale's back, dark gray, smooth and rubbery-feeling in some areas, like an inner tube; grayish-white, rough with barnacles in others.

"Pretty neat, eh?" asked Gene after the whales had passed and were heading out of sight.

"You could say that," she replied, and that night lay in bed, looking up at the ceiling in the dark, smiling to herself. This time last year she was listening to her answer machine and its messages of hate, picking up the phone only for her sister or for Amber LaSalle, wanting only to get away. And she had gone away. Gone home.

That summer never did get very warm, but beyond a mild feeling of regret, Jennifer scarcely noticed. She bought a small gas grill for her backyard, had the Tallys and the Delacroixs to her house for barbecued chicken and shish kabob. Weary of spending so much time in her car, shielded from the elements, she bought a pair of roller skates and on sunny days skated to the library or the shops or the harbor. By summer's end she had strong legs and a fine collection of scrapes and bruises, and had ended up on Gene's wall of photos: ponytail flying in the wind as she skated along with Pete Puma, lanky and orange and no less cross-eyed, clinging to her shoulder, his tail like a banner, skating past Mr. Bradbury who stood with his inevitable umbrella and book, wearing a look of amusement as she went by.

"You are a crazy woman, you know that?" Gene said one day that summer. It was the day she wasn't looking where she was going and hit a bump in the sidewalk, landed fortunately not on the sidewalk but in a flowerbed. Jennifer was none the worse for wear after this, but she couldn't say the same for the tulips.

"True, very dreadfully nervous I have been, but will you say that I am mad?" she asked, grinning, brushing dirt off her knees.

"If you're trying to change my opinion, it's not working," Gene replied. "I don't know if I want an insane person teaching my son."

"Why do you think I came up here? To corrupt impressionable minds."

"Sometimes I think you're corrupting my mind. But that's OK." He smiled and walked away before Jennifer could think of what exactly he meant or how she should reply.

July, and Jennifer knelt by her flowerbeds one Saturday, looking over the basil she'd planted and wondering if it was supposed to be yellow, limp, and stunted. Her first guess was no. So far she'd been able to maintain what was growing here when she'd moved in — the roses and lawn were in fine shape — but had no success with anything she'd planted, except for the Venus flytrap, which so terrified Pete Puma that she'd ended up giving the plant to Matthew.

Still, at least her track record was better than Mr. Bradbury's. Over the last six months she'd watched a steady parade of plants wither and die on his desk. Now he was trying his luck with an air fern. Jennifer didn't hold out high hopes for it. Pulling up the basil, she saw the van pull up out of the corner of her eye but didn't look up. Not until a voice said, "What's a girl have to do to get a hello around here?"

"Cindy!" Jennifer jumped to her feet and ran to her sister. Cindy stood there with a suitcase in one hand and a carry-bag in the other. She dropped both and ran to Jennifer, the sisters embraced. "You wench!" Jennifer said. "Why didn't you tell me you were coming?"

"I meant to, but the day after I made the reservations the airline went on strike. And I would have changed but the only other airline with a good fare went belly-up. It was looking like the trip could get canceled any minute and I didn't want to disappoint you. Besides, thought you'd like a surprise," Cindy said with a grin.

"Hey, as long as the surprises are good, I'm always game," Jennifer replied.

Cindy stayed a week. Jennifer felt bad, leaving Cindy at home during the days — she was saving her vacation time for Christmas — but Cindy said she didn't mind. She prowled around the town while Jennifer was at work, did shopping, went out to lunch with Suzanne. In the evenings,

Jennifer came home and they oohed and ahhed over what Cindy had bought, then some nights they went out, some nights Jennifer made dinner. Cindy's last night they went to the Blue Moose, met up with Suzanne and Bill, and Gene and Matthew, and Mr. Bradbury.

Afterward, Jennifer and Cindy took a walk down by the harbor. It was quiet, save for the lapping of the water and the creak of boats. "I have to tell you, Jen, if it weren't for pesky things like a husband and kids and a mortgage, I might kiss the States goodbye and come out here."

"Well, it's not as warm as California. But so far that's the only problem I've been able to find."

"You think you'll ever come back to the old US of A?"

Jennifer was silent, looking out at the ocean for a bit. "I don't know. I mean, I do miss some things. Little things, mostly. Disneyland. Mexican food. But I think about going back, and I just don't know if I could do that. The way life is so fast down in California. I used to like that. Now I think about it and it just seems busy and frantic. Too crowded and noisy. Like things are always coming at you. I want a place where I can see what's coming at me before it gets there."

"Things will always sneak up on you, Jen. I mean, no matter where ... well, you never would have seen that bombing come up on you." Cindy shut her mouth with a snap. "I'm sorry, I shouldn't have brought it up."

Jennifer shook her head. "It's OK." She didn't talk about it, unless circumstance forced her to it, but it was different with Cindy. She had nothing to hide from Cindy. "No, you're right. I guess it just feels that way here. And if that's all I can get, that's what I'll take."

"Amen to that," said Cindy. "So what's going on with you and this Gene fellow?"

"Nice way to change the subject! We're friends. I'm tutoring his kid."

"Still on the Harry Potter books?"

"We're alternating them with the Narnia ones. Mr. Bradbury's recommendation."

"He's good-looking."

"Mr. Bradbury?"

Cindy poked her in the ribs. "I meant Gene."

"I guess. Don't look at me like that. He's just a friend. That's all."

"Why? He's nice as well. And his kid's cool. Not a brat like most of them are nowadays, except for my own of course. Don't tell me you think a fisherman's not good enough for you?"

"Nothing like that, Cin. Trust me." *Yes, trust me, because if one of us isn't good enough for the other, it's the other way around.*

"OK, whatever makes you happy. But I think you're missing out."

Jennifer shrugged. "None of us are going anywhere. Time will tell, I guess."

August, and she sat with Suzanne one evening in Suzanne's backyard. August, and she in a dress and a cardigan sweater. It was rather funny, in a way, to see the locals grousing about the heat when in her opinion it was still too cold for shorts. Jennifer said as much to Suzanne, who snorted. "Jen, this our island in the sun right now."

"I know, I know. Great white north." They were outside, watching Hannah Reisman and Matthew Tally in a hot game of tetherball while the Joplin twins played on the swing set. The twins had apparently just gone through that time-honored school ritual, learning the song about the place called France, and were singing it repeatedly as they swung.

"That's not the version I heard when I was their age," Jennifer said.

"I went to a girl's school, I think that's why my version had 'where the naked boys dance' instead of 'the naked ladies'. I really should shut them up, Ruth will kill me if Hannah starts singing that," said Suzanne.

"Well, if Gene catches Matthew singing that and finds out where he learned it, he'll probably kill me, so we'll end up in heaven or hell together."

Suzanne poured them another round of iced tea. Jennifer cherished what warmth there was. She'd heard tales from Gene of Newfoundland, of snow appearing at any time of year, even the middle of summer, of watching icebergs cruise by on the horizon and the bay becoming a sheet of ice. She tried to imagine it, did not want to. Too much cold. Too hard to find comfort.

Hannah lost the game of tetherball, looked downcast. Matthew said, "Come on, two out of three." Hannah agreed, and in the ensuing game, it was clear to Suzanne and Jennifer, if not to Hannah, that Matthew was letting Hannah win.

"What a kid," Jennifer said. "Gene should be really proud."

"God knows I would be, if he was mine," Suzanne replied. There was a look in her eyes Jennifer had seen before, but now it was more intense than usual. Longing, and resigned melancholy. The look of someone who wants what they will most likely never have.

"Ask me," Suzanne said. "It's all right. I know you've wanted to."

"How come you and Bill..." Jennifer trailed off.

Suzanne took a sip of iced tea. "Back in high school, I was kind of wild. Not very wild, but wild enough. The usual story, you know, you've heard it so many times before. Parents split up, shuffle you back and forth every month. I started looking for someone who would pay me attention of some kind. You get the idea. And somewhere along the line, I ended up getting attention from the wrong person, and I also got one of those unpleasant things that are like the greatest joke on women. You know, no symptoms and for years you're none the wiser. And then, you meet the right guy, and get married, and you find out that the joke's on you, and you're most likely not ever going to..."

She didn't finish. She didn't have to.

Jennifer's hand hovered over Suzanne, looking for some place to lay comfort. Touched the red-brown curls, then took Suzanne's hand in hers. Thought about secrets, about the way the past shapes the future. For Suzanne, the wrong boyfriend. For Gene, the price of a marriage made without love. For herself, the knowledge that her life was saved by a broken photocopier and a brave fireman. She almost told Suzanne her own tale, not the abridged version she'd given Mr. Bradbury or Gene, but the whole thing, entire, from the morning when she'd thought the worst that could happen was a dressing-down from her boss, to the moment of nauseated clarity in Alex Salto's back field.

But in the end, only said, "I'm sorry."

Suzanne turned her gaze away from her charges, looked at Jennifer. Smiled sadly. "Thanks. So am I."

Jennifer said nothing else, only thought of what Cindy had said. That you really couldn't see what was coming next, or where it was coming from. Much as she wanted to think she could see further up here in Haven Cove, she couldn't. Nor was she sure she wanted to. For surely if she could have avoided the bombing she would have. But then, she would not be here. Had what she gained made up for what she'd been through?

"Cold? You're shivering."

She looked down at her forearms. She was. "Nothing. Goose walked over my grave. That's all."

Chapter Twenty-eight

Sean had just come back from dropping off half of the apple pie with Tess Perkins the landlady — no insult to Anna's cooking, the pie was fabulous but he was afraid that he wouldn't be able to eat it all before it went off — when the phone rang. Richard's voice on the other end, and he felt his sense of alertness quicken.

"Sam," said Richard. "I know it's short notice, but can you meet today?"

"Not a problem. How did your trip go?"

"Hold on a minute." The sound muffled as Richard put his hand over the receiver. He could hear Richard saying *No, I don't think so* and *By the way, we're out of eggs.* Sean repressed a smile, lest Richard hear it in his voice. "Sorry. Some interesting news has come my way."

"Interesting in a good way or a bad way?" He wondered if someone had gotten curious about that sedan with its unpleasantness locked in the trunk, at Green Bay airport.

"Best if you hear about it in person. Can you make it?"

"Sure."

They hung up. Sean slipped keys into his pocket, felt the weight of the gun in its holster, reassuring. Trotted down the steps to the parking lot, and as he headed toward his van, Steve Wickersham appeared from behind it, grinning like an evil jack-in-the-box. "Hey there," Steve said. "I was in the neighborhood. Thought I'd catch a ride with you to Richard's."

"I don't think so," he replied. There was an unhealthy glow in Steve's eyes that Sean didn't like. The same glow Steve had back in January, holding his rifle to Carl Miller's head.

"I do. See over there, by the front?"

Sean looked and saw the Wickershams' pickup truck. Saw a figure behind the wheel, in a stance he recognized.

"Eddie's got his sights on that fat landlady of yours. Any funny business on your part and she's history."

Tess Perkins was sitting at her desk, unaware, eating a piece of apple pie and going over the books. "He won't do it. Your brother's a weak sister, Steve, even you know that."

To his dismay, Steve didn't show so much as a flicker of anger at that. "Oh, I know what Eddie is. But he's also an excellent shot. And he does what I tell him to do. He always does. He'll waste her, believe me."

Sean looked at the pickup truck. Eddie was a silhouette, but a steady one, and Sean remembered on that January hunting trip, Eddie was the only one to bring home a deer. It had been a good clean kill, too.

He could let them do it. After all, what was Tess Perkins to him?

But he couldn't and he knew it. He'd kept his hands free of innocent blood all his life, not an easy thing to do. He could not let a nice woman whose only crime had been to lease him an apartment be killed. Not while there was the chance of another way out.

Sean could see no way now. Just had to trust that he would.

"All right then," he said. "What do you want?"

Steve's grin broadened, revealing a tooth gone dead and gray. "Get in. We're going for a ride."

He climbed into the van. Steve sat in the passenger seat. "Where to?"

"I'll tell you."

He began to drive, felt something poke him in the flesh under his ribs. Looked down and saw a .22 in Steve's hand. "No funny stuff, asshole," Steve said. "I've got long rifle rounds in here, and they will fuck you up big time, you know."

Sean knew. Long rifle rounds zipped around the inside of the body like a ping-pong ball, for lots of damage and a painful death. Lots of agents favored them for close-quarters assassination. "Funny, you don't look like Claudine Longet," he said.

"What the hell are you talking about?" They were heading toward a two-lane highway that was not used much since the building of the interstate extension.

"Nothing." He could feel the muzzle of the .22 digging into his skin. "Is this Richard's idea?" That was all he wanted to know.

Steve snorted. "Nah. Richard's gone soft. He likes you, fuck if I know why. You think you're so smart, don't you?"

"No, I don't *think* so."

It was lost on Steve. "I don't like you, I never did. There's something hinky about you. You and your smart remarks and your big ten-cent words. Always sucking up to Richard. Helping that ball-and-chain of his dry the dishes." Steve sing-songed, "'Let me hold the door for you, Anna. Let me carry those groceries for you, Anna.'" He spat contemptuously. "Make a right there."

The road went into the woods, first paved, then dirt. Deeper and deeper into the woods. He let Steve rave on, waiting for a break in Steve's concentration. Even a second would do it.

"Well, you're not as smart as you thought you were. And now I'm gonna let you bleed your guts out. I just wish I could stay to watch." Steve's grin softened to a sweet, contemplative smile. "I've been waiting for this since we met. But I've got to get to Richard's."

"Guess that's my bad luck, then." *Come on, Steve, look away for just one second.*

"Fuckin-A. Now, then ... " Steve kept the gun on him, but turned to look for something, some turnoff or sign.

Now.

Sean stomped on the brake as hard as he could, heard the pop of the .22 and felt the passage of the bullet as it droned past his face. Steve was thrown forward and then snapped back by the seat belt. As Steve landed back against the seat, started to bring the .22 up to fire again, Sean brought his hand around in a flat, whistling arc, slammed the edge of his hand into Steve's throat. There was the wet crunch of breaking cartilage and Steve's eyes went huge with pain he couldn't scream about. He dropped the .22 and his hands went instinctively to his throat, fingers groping at his crushed trachea as if he could free himself from an invisible strangler.

Sean sat watching Steve for a moment. Considered going for his gun, or for the .38 that was under his seat, but he didn't want to risk a mess in the van. Instead, he reached down, casually plucked the .22 from the floor and shoved the muzzle into Steve's mouth. A brittle chipping sound as one of Steve's teeth broke. Steve's eyes rolled, looked at him, mute terror in his stare.

"Guess what, Steve," he said with a smile. "I never liked you either."

Eddie Wickersham waited until the van pulled out of the parking lot. He knew he should follow right away, but he had to put the gun down and rest for just a moment. How he'd let Steve talk him into this he'd never know. Well, nothing to worry about. Sam had gone quietly and now he just had to meet Steve at the old cabin out off Deerpath Road. "Just get him into the car with me," Steve said. "I'll take care of the rest of it."

"Ah, Steve, I don't know if I can..."

"Look, I'll take care of it, OK? Help me bury him out at the cabin, that's all I'm asking."

"But what if he doesn't go along? I don't want to shoot his landlady."

272

"He will. He's not like you and me. We know what needs to be done and we do it." He put his hands on Eddie's shoulders. "I'm counting on you, little brother."

He'd agreed. But as he sat here, letting himself calm down, he felt a different kind of disquiet. He'd asked Steve if he thought he could handle it, and even now he could hear Steve's snort of contempt. "Are you kidding? Of course I can."

"I don't know, there's something..."

"There's nothing he can dish out that I can't handle. I mean, look at him. He looks like a God damn insurance salesman. He's shorter than me. And he's old. Over fifty, I'll bet. You think I can't handle some guy who's old enough to be my father?"

"Well, no, but..."

"Then it's settled."

Maybe for Steve it was settled, but Eddie wouldn't be able to stop worrying until this whole mess was over with. It was at times like these he wished he'd never gotten involved in Richard's group, wished he was heading out to the woods for game or fish instead of burying a man who he had nothing against. Sam had never been anything but polite to him. Steve thought Sam had something to do with Doug MacReady being so late, but Eddie knew that couldn't possibly be true. Yes, he would agree that there was something different about Sam, he'd seen it in Sam's eyes when he gave Steve that look. But other than that...

Eddie snapped out of his reverie. He needed to catch up with them. Hopefully by the time he got there it would all be over. He began to drive, worrying the whole time about getting caught, about what they would say to Richard, if this would bugger up the plans for the next bombing, all sorts of things.

The van was there when he pulled up. He saw no one in the driver's or passenger's seats. Eddie hopped out of his truck, peered around cautiously. In the dirt by the passenger's side he saw footprints, and the twin trails of something — a man's heels, most likely — being dragged to the back of the cabin.

It was done, then. Eddie sighed, felt some of the worry ease. He headed for the back of the cabin, heard the rapid approach of footsteps coming toward him. "Steve," he called out. "Steve, did you — oh shit!"

Eddie turned to run, remembering too late that he'd left his gun in the truck. Two pistol shots broke the quiet of the woods, and Eddie didn't have to worry about anything, ever again.

Sean held his breath as he rounded the turn to Richard's house. For all he knew the entire group could be here, waiting for him. But the only vehicle was Richard's truck. Even Anna's station wagon was gone.

His relief quickly faded, though. Perhaps Richard wanted it that way. Perhaps he was the only one Richard had called, so Richard could personally mete out justice for MacReady. That didn't feel right to him — Richard wasn't one to do the dirty work himself — but then, who was left to do the dirty work?

Sean stepped out of his van, to all appearances looking like a man here to meet with a friend. No sign of what had happened in the last hour, no indication that he had nearly been gut-shot or that two bodies were dumped in the cabin out on Deerpath Road. He stood on the doormat for what he knew to be the last time ever. Ready as he would ever be. Rang the doorbell.

"Who is it?" came Richard's voice over the intercom.

"Sam." The name felt strange in his mouth.

"Door's open, come in."

Richard sat at the coffee table, writing something down. He glanced over his shoulder, gave a quick smile. "Just let me get this. Make yourself at home, Sam," Richard said as he turned back to what he was writing. "Everybody's running late today."

Best news I've had all day. "Anna around?"

"You just missed her. Went to the grocery store."

"I see." *Even better news.* Richard bent over what he was writing, and Sean walked toward Richard. Not even a whisper of sound as he walked, nor as he took his gun from its holster. He placed the muzzle against Richard's head. "You're coming with me."

He'd always found it interesting to see how people reacted when confronted by the gun. In the movies, people were full of witty remarks and cool bravado. It was enough to make you forget what a gun could do, that one simple movement and your brains would be turned to pulp, your life snuffed out before you knew what had happened.

Richard knew. He froze, went pale beneath his tan. Richard took in a breath, said in a slightly unsteady voice, "Joke's over, Sam."

"No joke," he replied.

"Steve and Eddie will be here soon."

"No they won't."

Richard swallowed. "Look, I—"

"Put your hands on top of your head. Slowly. Then stand up. Let's get this over with before Anna comes home."

Richard's eyes closed. "She's nothing to do with this, don't hurt her."

"Don't make me." His voice icy. Sean had no intention of killing Richard unless it was to save his own skin, and would not hurt Anna for the world. But Richard didn't need to know this. "Go on, get up."

Richard sighed, slowly got to his feet, his hands on top of his head. A shiver ran through him, for a moment he was unsteady on his feet. Then he straightened his spine, stood tall and unwavering. Ready for martyrdom.

Once again Sean felt that unwilling admiration. "Nice and steady, Blaine." He kept the gun against Richard's head with his right hand, with his left reached into his pocket for a set of handcuffs, their chain shortened so a limber man could not slip his feet through his arms, bring his hands to the front.

They were focused on each other, on the gun. He was opening the cuffs, ready to snap them around Richard's wrists when the door opened. Sean dropped the cuffs, locked his left arm around Richard's throat, and stood, the gun to Richard's head.

Anna stepped inside. "Would you believe I forgot my—" She stopped, stared at them with eyes wide, like a startled kitten's. "What's going on?"

Chapter Twenty-nine

"Everything OK, Jen? You look a bit down," said Mr. Bradbury.

Jennifer shook her head. "It's nothing. Too chilly to skate in today and that just made me realize that I've gone the whole summer without wearing my bikini once."

"I take it you've found that Vancouver isn't the place for working on one's tan. Which reminds me, you're coming up on a year here in Haven Cove, aren't you?"

She nodded. It was actually a year and a week ago that she'd picked up the key from Katie Granville and begun unpacking. So long ago that seemed. When she thought about last year, there were some blank spots. It wasn't the bombing she had trouble remembering. It was the time afterward, that fog she'd stumbled through, like the dust cloud of the building's collapse, wandering and unable to find her way. Even after she moved up here, those blank and directionless few months of working at Alex Salto's. Hard to believe that she'd done that, hidden behind her locked bathroom door drinking too much wine, sat bored at her receptionist's desk filing papers and ignoring Alex's suggestions they go out some time. Well, it was a while ago now, and time healed all wounds. And wounded all heels, if you were lucky.

"Something funny?" asked Mr. Bradbury, with that mock-stern expression that fooled no one over the age of five.

"Nothing funny." Her curiosity finally got the better of her. "How long have you been here?"

"Fifteen years now. Moved out from Ontario after I left the priesthood." He settled back in his chair, took a sip of tea. "That's the way a lot of people end up in British Columbia, you know. Leave somewhere else, head west until they run out of land."

"Kind of like Los Angeles," Jennifer said. Heading for orange groves and Disneyland, a chance at getting into Hollywood.

He nodded. "Why do we never go east, I wonder? Something to think about." He sat, silent, his gnomish face calm and his gaze turned inward, contemplating something. The past, the future? Something as mundane as the cup of tea in his hand, perhaps.

She began sorting books onto a cart. She would not ask, though she had wanted to know for months. If he wanted to, he would tell her.

"It's strange. I have a brother and a sister, and all three of us knew when we were young what we wanted to be when we grew up. My sister wanted to be an archeologist. Spent her childhood digging holes in our backyard, hoping for dinosaur bones. Never found anything but scrap metal and some petrified cow patties, but was happy enough with those. She's in Montana on a dig right now, will probably be dusting off *T. rex* teeth when she breathes her last, and will die happier than most people. My brother, God rest him, wanted to be a painter. He was, though never a very good one. Married a lovely woman who left him alone on Sunday afternoons to paint. Didn't matter that his paintings came out looking like Jackson Pollock crossed with Thomas Kinkade, as long as he had that on weekends, he was happy.

"I suppose you've guessed what I wanted to be. It's one of those things that are so hard to explain, feeling the call. Though I suppose many people feel something like it when they meet the person who is their true love, or find the thing in life that is what they were meant to do. If you've felt any of those things, you know how it is." He turned, rummaged in his CDs and brought out one, loaded it into the player. After a moment the music poured out, sweet and yet melancholy, slow.

Jennifer looked at the CD case. Barber's *Adagio for Strings.*

"This is what it's like. Doesn't matter if you're saying Mass for five hundred people or if there's no one but you in the church. You feel God's presence, like a hand held over you, ready to touch you if you need comforting or help you up if you fall." He closed his eyes. "And not a day goes by that I don't remember what that was like."

Jennifer sat, listening to the music, watched Mr. Bradbury. She felt tears sting her eyes, for he had been happy then, she could tell. A rare sort of happiness that she could only guess at. And he had left it behind.

"A year before I left, I was transferred to a parish in Toronto. The other priest there had recently been transferred as well. It was an older parish, the other priests were retiring. It was busy there, quite a lot going on. I was working with the older churchgoers, running the administrative end of things. The other priest was interested in youth work. Very interested. Particularly with the grade-school children." He shook his head, gave her a grim smile. "You can probably see where this is heading."

She nodded.

"I was busy, but not so busy that I didn't put things together eventually. And when I did, I went to see the bishop, told him what I knew. It turned out that he already knew. In fact, this priest had been transferred twice after similar knowledge had come to light. And they simply moved him along. Out of sight, out of mind.

"I remember feeling so angry. For a man who is God's servant to do that. It destroys so many things. How can a child love God when..." He shook his head. "I said as much to the archbishop, who reminded me that this priest's family was very wealthy. Very powerful contributors to the Church, and if I didn't want to end up in some parish on an iceberg off the coast of Newfoundland, I'd do well to remember that."

"What did you do?" she asked.

"I went through the other priest's things. I found some...well, let's just say it was pictorial material of a certain sort, and I don't mean *Playboy* magazine. I made two phone calls. One to the police and another to the archbishop. You see, I could have stayed, if this had been that priest's first time caught at this. But I couldn't be part of a system that would deliberately put children at risk, just to cover up scandal and keep a rich family's contributions rolling in. And so I left, with not much money other than what I borrowed from my family, and the clothes on my back."

"Vow of poverty?"

He nodded. "Caught a train heading west and ended up in Vancouver. Made my way up here and the former librarian, a lovely woman by the name of Louisa Rose King, took pity on me and hired me despite having no qualifications whatsoever other than a love of books."

"Sounds familiar," Jennifer said, feeling her mouth twist as it tried to decide whether to be sorry for Mr. Bradbury or amused by the way fate had worked for them.

He smiled, surprised. "Why yes, doesn't it? I never realized that before."

Her mouth decided, turned down.

"What's wrong?" he asked gently.

"It's..." She reached over and turned off the CD player, unable to bear the ecstatic, melancholy crescendo she knew was coming. "I don't know. I'm not really much on God or religion, but I can tell that it must have hurt you so much, leaving all that behind."

He shook his head. "No, no dear. All I left was the building. The bureaucracy. And that's not to say I don't miss it terribly, being able to say Mass. But that feeling of God watching over me? Nothing can take that away from me."

Jennifer looked at him, envied his surety. His belief. How could he still hold on to that, when the ministry he'd devoted his life to had turned out to be corrupt? *Oh, I would love to believe as he does, to feel that hand ready to hold you up. But I can't, not when I know I'm alive because a photocopier was broken, and that all those people who died just happened to be in the wrong place at the wrong time. Where was God's hand in that? If it was there, why me and not Carrie? Or Mr. Danvers? Carlos? Those little kids in the day care on the first floor? If I were to ask Mr. Bradbury I'm sure he'd say it's all for a reason, but right now I don't see what that reason could be. I don't know if I ever will.*

"It must have been hard," she said. "Deciding to leave what you'd wanted your whole life."

"It was. But you know, I still have what I've always wanted. To do my best to be a good man and a good servant of God, in my own way. And now that you've heard my tale, let me ask you this, Ms. Jennifer Thomson. What do *you* want?"

What indeed? "I guess...just to be me. Whoever that is." She blushed, looked down at her hands. "Pretty low aspiration, right?"

"Not as much as you might think. Do you know who you are?"

"I'm getting there."

"Good," he said, with a smile like benediction. "That's more than most people know."

The afternoon went by uncommonly fast, she thought. Surely it couldn't be tea-time, and yet the light in the library was dim. Had the clocks been set back? she wondered as she put psychology books back on the shelves. Spring forward, fall back, every year it seemed to sneak up on her.

Then she heard Mr. Bradbury say, "Oh, holy Christ."

Startled, she dropped her books. Mr. Bradbury's swears were all words like *balderdash* and *fiddlesticks,* and made her giggle every time. Only once had she heard him say *shit,* and that was when he'd slammed his thumb in a file drawer. She'd never heard him take God's name in vain. Jennifer peered around the stacks, saw him standing by the window with a peculiar, fixed stance. It was a heart attack or something, she was sure, and ran to his side. "Mr. Bradbury? Are you all right?"

His gaze didn't leave the window. "I'm fine, Jennifer. But I think Haven Cove is in for some trouble."

So focused had she been on Mr. Bradbury that she hadn't spared a glance outside. And now when she did, her heart gave a great leap and then began hammering away. The news had said there might be rain, but nothing like this. This morning had been chilly but clear; now the blue sky was being quickly swallowed up by a great bank of cloud, so dark and heavy with rain it was almost black. She knew it was a storm, a hell of a storm but just that, only weather, but she could not help but think of another cloud, this one made of dust, reeking of destruction, seizing her in its hungry embrace and choking the life out of her.

"What is it?" she managed to ask. Weather, only weather.

"Which way is the wind blowing?" He craned his head around, looked out the window at the flagpole, where the maple leaf was blowing in the wind, straight out as if it was strung with wires. "From the south. Come on, Jennifer, we're closing up the library."

"Why? What is it? I thought Haven Cove was a safe place in storms."

"It is, most of the time," Mr. Bradbury said, walking to the desk and gathering his things, a determination in his stride that she would not have expected. "But every ten years or so we get a very bad storm out of the south. Angus, the harbormaster, told me they call it the Southern Hammer. The last one was twelve years ago, and it took out half a dozen businesses and homes by the water. The boats all have to be taken out of harbor, back around the point to where they can get shelter. They lost three fishing boats as well, were able to rescue all the men except Denny Gunderson and his son, they were swept off the *Maiden Fair* and never found. Denny Junior had just graduated from high school, too."

Gene. Oh God, she hoped nothing would happen to Gene. "What can we do?" As if in answer to her question she heard a sound she had never heard in real life but still recognized. A siren, like in the old war movies.

"We can't do anything here. I was going to go to the hospital, if you could drop me there?"

"Not a problem."

"I've done some volunteer work in my day, they may need some help."

"What should I do?" she asked, feeling helpless and stupid.

He smiled, patted her on the shoulder. "Go home. Keep your neighbor and any of those kids she watches company. It's a storm and there's nothing we can do but wait it out and clean things up in the morning."

She would never forget that drive home after dropping Mr. Bradbury at the hospital. The sky black overhead, the wind coming strong and cold from its unaccustomed direction. No rain yet, that was the strange thing. Lightning flashed and thunder groaned, but no rain fell. As if the storm was biding its time, waiting. Teasing.

A few fat drops were falling when she got home. She got out of her car and ran, not to her house but to Suzanne's. The door opened and Suzanne stood there, her smile tight around the edges. "Jen, I'm glad you're here."

Jennifer stepped inside and saw Matthew Tally there, going through Suzanne's DVDs. She pulled Suzanne aside. "Where's Gene?"

"You just missed him. He was looking for you, wanted to leave Matthew with you but you weren't home. Then he took off for the harbor. Poor Gene, most of the others managed to get a head start on the storm but he was stuck out on the point for most of —"

"You mean he hasn't gone out yet? My God, Suze, he'll be heading out in the thick of it!"

"Shhhh!" Suzanne glanced back at Matthew. He seemed to be occupied with the DVDs but Jennifer knew better. He hadn't made one "Oh cool!" exclamation, not even for the special edition of *Tron*. "I know. Gene knows, too. He said that if anything—"

Jennifer didn't stay to hear the rest of it. She ran outside and next door to her own house. The rain was beginning to fall now but she barely felt the drops. She ran inside and quickly changed. Hiking boots, wool socks, jeans, two sweaters, her raincoat. In less than a minute she was back outside, heading for her car.

Suzanne stood, braced against the wind and the steadily increasing rain. "Jen, you don't know what you're getting into. Don't do anything dumb."

"I'm not going to let him go out there alone," she said. "Take care of Matthew. I'll see you later."

Suzanne looked into her eyes for a long moment. If she had a question, it was answered. She nodded, then put her arms around Jennifer. "Come back safe, Jen."

"I will."

She felt sure of it at the time. But when she got to the harbor and stood in the rain — she'd forgotten a hat, how dumb could you get? — looking up into the sky, so dark though it was still only afternoon, her heart quailed within her. So huge the storm, bigger than any federal building, the power of it greater than any bomb. So big, and she so small. What could she really do here? Nothing at all.

She stepped outside herself and saw a woman sneaking up on thirty, dishwater blonde hair already soaked. Whose greatest accomplishments to date were escaping and surviving. She could do that now. Go back home. No one would hold it against her. Tell Suzanne that she'd missed Gene. Wait with Suzanne for the storm to end, wait with Matthew for news of his father. Wait in warmth and safety, and shelter the life she'd been awarded.

Shelter it. Or earn it.

Stepped back inside herself, stepped forward. She ran to the harbormaster's shack, where old Angus was bellowing something into the radio. "The *Tally-ho!*" she yelled over the storm. "Is it still here?"

"Gene's just heading out now and — hey! Come back here!"

Angus yelled something more but she didn't stay to hear it. She ran down the docks as fast as she could, feeling the pier vibrate under her feet. Ran down to the *Tally-ho's* slip, remembering when she'd come to talk to Gene about Matthew not being able to read. And the day he'd taken her to see the whales.

The boat was pulling out of the slip as she got there. Jennifer yelled Gene's name but the storm and the boat were too loud. She ran, trying to catch up with the boat. It was out of the slip just as she neared the end, and with a recklessness she would never be able to understand later, she leaped.

She caught hold of the back cleats and hung on, then with a shoulder-straining effort managed to pull herself up onto the boat. Her first impulse was to run into the cabin where Gene was, but she knew he'd just turn around, dump her back on the dock, and be that much later getting around the point. Jennifer waited, crouched by the boat's stern, hanging on to whatever she could find. She didn't dare look back at the harbor because if she saw the safety of land she'd regret her choice, and it was too late to go back.

She waited until the boat was in open water and then ran into the cabin; she didn't know if it was too late for Gene to turn around and bring her back, but the storm frightened her too much to stay out there any longer. Gene's back was to her, his hands tight on the wheel, and on the cabin wall was a new picture — she and Matthew sitting at the dining room table, reading *The Lion, The Witch, And The Wardrobe*. "Gene," she called out.

He jumped, the boat pitched queasily. He turned and stared at her, white-faced. "Jesus God almighty damn," he whispered, and before she could answer he roared: "You...you..." He groped for the right word. Found it. "You nutbar! Bad enough I'm this late, now I gotta turn around and put you back."

"Bullshit. I'm going with you."

He turned back to the controls for a moment, muttering something she couldn't understand – probably some horrible Newfoundland swear words. Then he looked back at her. "Like hell you are. Do you know how dangerous this is?"

"I've got an idea."

"What? There's a very good chance we could wreck out here. You know what that means?"

She clenched her hands into fists, trying to find something to hold on to, but there was nothing, of course. Just her. "I know. And I'm not letting you go out there alone."

"Jen, no—"

"God damn it!" She slammed her fist into the wall, making pictures rattle. "I am done leaving people behind! I won't do it any more. You understand?"

He turned to look back at her. "Jen, I understand. But there's nothing you can do. You don't even know port from starboard."

"Port is this way and starboard is that way," she said, pointing, knowing she had a fifty percent chance of being right.

Apparently she was right, but from Gene's cool, assessing look she guessed he wasn't fooled. She grinned, and while he didn't grin back, he did finally sigh. "You are the most insane woman ever. I just want to get that off my chest."

"I know."

He muttered that oath again, then said, "Here." He grabbed a life jacket and handed it to her. "Put that on. God, I can't believe I'm doing this."

She struggled to put on the jacket. "To be honest, neither can I."

She did start to believe it, though, as the waves buffeted the boat, and what had seemed like such a solid vessel on calm seas now seemed very fragile. She had a moment when she wanted to scream, run away, go back to her house and hide under the warm covers until the bad storm went away. She sat in the cabin's little chair, arms crossed over her torso, hands clutching her elbows.

He looked over at her. "You feeling sick?"

"Sick? No. Scared? Yes." She felt ashamed to admit it. Waited for Gene to say it was her own fault, she shouldn't have come out here in the first place.

But instead he said, "I know." Took his hand off the wheel for a moment, reached out to her. She took his hand in hers, for a moment their fingers twined together, like knots in a ship's rigging. "I am too."

Chapter Thirty

"What's going on?" Anna looked at them, at the gun. Eyes wide, the look of a woman who has just found her world turned to some terribly wrong angle, as in a horror movie when hallways stretch and stairwells disappear.

"Anna, get out." Richard's voice had that air of command in it, only the slightest edge of fear. Impossible to tell if it was fear for himself or Anna. "Get out, take the car, go to the Henderson's. Stay there."

She didn't seem to hear him. "Richard? Sam? What are you doing?"

Sean began walking slowly toward the door, left arm around Richard's neck, gun held to Richard's head. It was slightly awkward, for Richard was taller than he. "This doesn't involve you, Anna. Do as he says. Get out."

"Tell me what's going on!"

"He's crazy, he might kill you, now do as I say and get out of here!" Richard said.

Sean said nothing, continued making his way toward the door. Let Richard say what he wanted; the important thing was getting him out of here. And yet... Sean stopped for a moment, looked at poor Anna standing there, frightened and bewildered. "Your husband's a murderer, Anna," he said. "I'm taking him out of here. I'm sorry." And he was. For her.

She backed away from them a step or two. Sean was relieved, knew that Richard was too by the way the tension in his muscles eased a bit. He saw something in Anna's eyes, something he had never seen there before. Like a spark from a campfire flying up into the night sky.

Before he could even wonder what that spark was, she flew at them, grabbed at his right arm and pushed the gun away from her husband's head, digging her nails into his arm. At the same time Richard broke free, began pulling Anna away toward the door, but she wouldn't let go of Sean's arm, kept pushing it up, the gun pointed to the ceiling. "Anna, stop it, get out of here!" Sean said, trying to free his arm without hurting her.

Anna yelled over her shoulder, "Richard, run!" Richard did turn and go, not towards the door but to the phone.

Oh Christ, if he dials 911 everything's screwed. Sean yanked his arm free from Anna's grip, her nails scoring bloody tracks in his skin that he didn't feel. He sidestepped around her and shot Richard in the back of the right thigh, just above the knee. Richard fell to the floor, several yards away from the phone. He started to crawl to the phone, dragging his leg after him.

Sean took a step toward Richard, and then Anna was at him again. "Leave him alone!" she screamed, trying to grab the gun from him.

"Let go!"

"Don't hurt him!"

Richard almost at the phone now. *God damn it, no, can't let this happen.*

"I said let go!" He shoved Anna away from him. Shoved hard.

Too hard.

Sean watched as Anna stumbled away from him, tripped over the hearth rug and fell. Heard a crack as her head struck the riverstone fireplace. Stared in stunned disbelief as she fell to the hearth, convulsed briefly, and lay there looking small and very, very still.

He was frozen. Couldn't move, couldn't even breathe. His hand stretched out to call back the irrevocable, his skin burning where it had touched her. *Take it back, oh please I'll do anything, just take it back.*

Sean could breathe again but he still couldn't move. Stood watching as Richard crawled over to his wife, the phone forgotten. "Anna? Anna, sweetie?" At the sound of that endearment something inside Sean seemed to die. *Say she's all right, Richard. Tell me we can get her to a hospital, I'll let you go, it's over now, just say she's not...*

Richard looked up, stared at him. Said nothing but demanded an answer.

He tried to say something. Finally managed it. "I didn't —"

Richard was on his feet with the strength and speed of the bereaved, his wounded leg forgotten. Still frozen, Sean couldn't move and Richard was on him, he was on his back on the floor with Richard pinning him down, he'd lost the gun and Richard's hands locked around his throat. Sean managed a quick, instinctive gasp and then the hands tightened and cut off his breath.

His left arm was pinned under Richard's knee. With his right hand he clawed at Richard's hands, but the grip was tight with fury and grief; he could not loosen it. He reached up, going for the throat or eyes, but Richard was taller than he, and long in the arms; he could not reach a vulnerable spot.

The gun. Somewhere on the floor. He groped over the floorboards, searching for the gun and not finding it. A crushing pain in his throat, his lungs air-starved and he thought if he could get a breath in, just one, he might have the strength to throw Richard off him.

But he couldn't get a breath, his lungs burned, his fingertips brushed the gun but his hand shook uncontrollably and he couldn't grasp it. Though he could still feel the floorboards beneath him at the same time he seemed to be sinking into a void. The pain in his throat was still there but it was distant, as if it was happening to someone else. Darkness creeping in around the edges of his vision as he went deeper into the void, not sinking anymore but falling, and he knew he'd go on falling forever.

No. Not this. Terror gave him one last burst of energy and he groped wildly for something to hold on to, to pull himself up out of the void. Reached out and found the gun, clutched it tightly.

Even now he remembered that he could not kill Richard. Dared not risk a shot. He focused his dimming sight as best he could and saw that Richard was within his reach now; had brought himself closer, the better to see his enemy die. Sean gripped the gun by the barrel and swung it at Richard with all of his waning strength.

He did not see the blow fall, only felt the shock of vibration travel down his arm. Felt Richard's body fall away from his, off to the side, felt the hands release his throat. Light and pain rushed back into the world as air filled his lungs. He could not seem to get enough air, greedily gasped in oxygen until he was dizzy. But alive.

When his limbs stopped shaking, Sean got to his hands and knees. His throat burned with every breath, swallowing was agony, he did not dare try to speak. He knelt there, staring at his hands, not wanting to look up and see Richard. And Anna. Finally he forced himself to it. Looked at Richard first.

Richard lay on his side, unconscious, but breathing. His leg was bleeding, but it was a flesh wound. It would need a dressing but was nothing major. A bump on his head from where he'd been struck with the gun, but hopefully not a concussion. If so, there was nothing to do about it anyway.

He wanted to take Richard and go. Just go. *No you don't, you rat bastard. You can't get off that easy. Drag your carcass over there. Look at her. Look at what you've done.*

Sean made himself crawl over to the hearth, hoping that his eyes, which had seen death often enough to recognize it at once, had lied to him. They had not. Anna lay crumpled on the hearth. Her eyes were open, the right pupil huge and blown. Blood had trickled from her right ear. He laid his fingers against her wrist, praying for a pulse. Nothing.

"I'm sorry." His throat would not let him make a sound, but it didn't matter. He could have howled the words at the top of his voice and they would have changed nothing. He got to his feet, picked Anna up — gently, carefully, as if he could hurt her any more — and laid her down on the sofa, covered her with an afghan. An afghan he had seen her crocheting all these months, he realized, and went to his knees again on the floor. He knew he should get moving, but he waited. Waited to feel something.

Sean knew what he should feel. Remorse for Anna, pity for Blaine. Terror of the void that had nearly claimed him, relief at having escaped it. Triumph at catching his quarry, plans for the work still to be done. He knelt, waiting.

But felt nothing at all.

Chapter Thirty-one

"How long, do you think?"

It was the first thing she'd said in a long time, and saying it was difficult. Every muscle in her body, it seemed, was wire-tight as she braced herself against the rise and fall, pitch and yaw, the sudden jolts as the boat caught a rogue wave or gust of wind. Her feet seemed bolted to the floor, her hands gripped the armrests so tightly her knuckles were white and her wrists cramped painfully. She dared not release her grip long enough to look at her watch; they could have been out here for minutes or hours, for all she knew.

"Hard to say," Gene replied. "The wind and the current's at our back, but you get this cross-current around the point, pushing us toward shore."

"Isn't that a good thing, to be close to shore?"

He shook his head. "The waves get rougher. And there's rocks. We hit those and..." He glanced back at her. "Well, let's just hope we don't."

The old Jennifer would have been content to leave it at that. But the one who had lived through the L.A. federal building knew better. "What if we do?" she asked. "Tell me, Gene."

He glanced back at her again, as if gauging her ability to stand the truth of the situation. "If the *Tally-ho* hits the rocks, she'll most likely break up, at the least get a hole punched in her hull. She'll sink. We'll have to take our chances in the dinghy."

The dinghy? Not that rubber thing with the little propeller motor on the back? If the *Tally-ho* didn't have a chance in this weather, what would happen to that dinghy? Of course, she and Gene both had life jackets on, but how much good would those do? Jennifer looked over her shoulder, out the window. Nothing but black out there, but then a flash of lightning lit the world. For an instant she could see, and she was glad when the lightning was gone because she didn't want to see it longer than she had to. It was as if the ocean had gone mad, been sent to a roiling boil, but a cold one. She was a fair enough swimmer, but what was that against those waves? And life jacket or no, how long before the cold sucked the life out of you?

If the *Tally-ho* hit the rocks or capsized, they would almost certainly die. It was that simple.

She clutched the armrests harder. She would have cried out but her jaw was locked tight. In her mind was nothing so coherent as a prayer; it was more like a bargain. *I don't want to die, but if I have to, please don't let it hurt too much. If it's both of us, please don't separate us, I don't want to die alone.*

She swallowed hard. Silently voiced the next part of it. The hardest part. *And if one of us has to go, let it be me. Gene has Matthew to think of.*

But once she thought it, it seemed it was the easiest part. She'd known since the federal building was bombed that no one was special, your number could be up at any time. A bomb, a car accident, a cancer undetected and lying in wait, a fall down a flight of stairs. A thousand more. Nothing made her exempt, she had known it then, knew it better now. What mattered was how you met it.

"Jen?"

She thought she would not be able to turn her head, her muscles were so tight. But her fear had eased. It was still there, but she had mastered it. It no longer mastered her. "Yes?"

"It's going to be OK. We're almost around the point and then we'll be through the worst of it," Gene said. His eyes were clear and she could read them. Fear there, but he had mastered it as well.

"Thank God for that." And it did seem that the ocean had calmed a bit; she felt a lull in the waves.

Gene touched her hair, smiled. "I'm glad you're here. It would have—" Abruptly he stopped, peered out the front window, then peered around to the left. Port, or was it starboard? "Oh shit! Hang on!"

"What—" she began but before she could finish something hit the boat on the left side like a car slamming into a brick wall. Jennifer screamed as she was flung back against the wall, bounced and then was on the floor. Dimly she heard the sound of breaking glass. Cold water poured over her.

Curled up into a ball, she wiped water out of her eyes and looked for Gene. He wasn't at the controls. "Gene? Gene!" she called out. There was a rattling sound from the far end of the cabin; several of the cabinets had burst open, their contents spilled out, and on the floor, under a pile of tools and dishes, was Gene.

Jennifer didn't feel herself get up and run to him; next thing she knew, she was there, pulling away a toolbox. As she did, before she could say anything, Gene groaned and sat up, pushing debris aside. He had a cut on his head — like Mr. Danvers back in the federal building, she noticed with a feeling of déjà vu — but otherwise seemed unhurt.

"I'm OK," he said. He lurched to his feet and ran for the controls, seized the wheel with one hand and with the other grabbed the radio handset. Although she stood beside him, she could barely hear him over the sound of the storm, only caught the word *Mayday* repeated over and over. There was a most peculiar feeling, as if the boat was being lifted up slowly, gently. Nothing like it had happened during this voyage; Gene noticed it too. He left off yelling into the radio and looked around in bewilderment.

Up, up, a gentle pause. A downward rush like a roller coaster, but no length of steel track safety here. The boat was falling, and Jennifer dropped to the floor, felt Gene do the same; they clutched each other and anything else they could grab hold of, waiting. A heart-stopping moment of freefall, and then a crashing roar and a jolt and more water spraying in the window. It was the roar that did it; Jennifer screamed as loud as she could. She was back in Los Angeles, the building coming down around her, the air stank of smoke and death and what were the chances she'd get out this time? Because you only got lucky like that once.

Hands on her. Not a gloved firefighter's hands. Bare hands, strong and callused. Gene's hands. A voice, not calling out to her through a dust cloud, but much closer, Gene's voice in her ear. "Jennifer! Jen! Are you OK? Look at me."

She raised her head, saw that she was not in Los Angeles but on the *Tally-ho.* Saw Gene crouching by her, eyes wide with fear and concern and a strange sort of hope. "Are you OK? Answer me. I have to check on the boat but I need to know you're OK."

"I'm all right. I am. Just scared."

"Hang on, I'll be right back." He got up, grabbed a flashlight and ran out of the cabin.

"Gene, wait!" She ran after him, realizing only now that all the roll and yaw and pitch and heave had stopped, and the boat was perfectly still. She ran outside, into the storm. The wind was still howled, the rain lashed, and the waves tossed. But they were still, somehow.

Gene was on the right-hand side of the boat, peering down, shining a flashlight down at the bottom of the boat. As she approached he leaned down, almost as if he were seasick, leaned so far down she thought he might fall, and she clutched at his rain slicker. "Gene!"

He popped back up, turned off the flashlight. There was a peculiar expression on his face, a sort of dismayed amusement. At least he didn't seem afraid. "Holy Hannah," he said finally.

"What's happening? Why aren't we moving?"

"Take a look."

He turned the flashlight on again and aimed the beam below. Jennifer peered down and saw rocks, and shards of wood, some drifting out into the waves. And the sea, churning below but barely touching the hull of the boat. "What's happened?"

Gene turned off the flashlight. "A chance in a million. Looks like that last wave just sort of picked us up and set us down on that rock, nice as you please. The hull's shattered but as long as something doesn't sweep us off, we won't sink."

"You sure?"

He nodded. His mouth twisted as if he weren't sure whether to frown or smile. "We just have to wait it out, and hope another one like that doesn't come along."

She wasn't conscious of reaching for him, or him reaching for her, but next thing she knew they were holding each other tightly. He seemed so steady, and yet she could feel him trembling. She must have been as well, for he said, "You're shaking like a leaf. Come on, let's go in. There's nothing we can do out here."

The cabin was a mess. Broken glass from the windows littered the floor, the carpet was soaked. Pictures had come down off the walls, lay with frames in splinters and glass in shards. Something must have happened to the generator; the lights were out. Gene sighed, then got down to business. "Sit down, Jen," he said, and began sweeping the destruction aside. From one of the cupboards he pulled out an oil lamp and matches, wool blankets and a plastic tarp. He laid the tarp down on the wet floor, arranged the blankets over it. Lit the oil lamp, and its gentle glow filled the cabin. "Here," he said, handing her one of the blankets. "You're still shaking. Wrap up and get warm, I'll get us something to eat."

"I'm not hungry." She sat on the floor, wrapping the blanket around herself. It was itchy and smelled musty, but soon she was warm, and that was what mattered.

"You will be. Besides," he said with a rueful smile. "The generator's toast. If we don't eat what's in the fridge it'll go bad."

He set the oil lamp down, began rummaging in cupboards and the refrigerator. Soon there was a fair pile of food. Three cans of Coke, two bottles of ginger ale. Crackers, wedges of Laughing Cow cheese, cans of sardines. A bag of trail mix, another of dried apples. Gene sat down, started to eat. Jennifer still didn't have an appetite, the tension of the storm and the shock of their strange deliverance left her too shaken. What she really wanted was coffee or tea, something warm, but that couldn't be had. She sat, wrapped in her blanket, listening to the storm rage. And began to cry.

"Are you all right?" Gene sat down next to her, put an arm across her shoulders.

"I don't know," she said. "I guess I'm just scared. I thought for sure I was going to die. Maybe I wouldn't mind so much, but it seems like just a little while ago I thought I was going to die down in L.A. I'm really tired of it. I'm tired of feeling like I'm going to die. It makes it that much harder to live."

She hated saying this to Gene, all this whining about being scared to die when she'd been lucky to live twice over. Yet how could you live, really, when you could still feel the passage of the bullet that you'd dodged? How could you decide what to do on any given day without wondering if it was the right way to spend what could be the last day of your life, or how the person who had caught the bullet would have spent that day?

Gene said, "I know what you mean. And not just this storm either. I told you, didn't I, that my father was a fisherman. Died when I was ten."

"Yes, you told me," she said. "Was it during a storm? Like this?"

He shook his head. "No. It was the end of summer. Warm, that day. Warm for Newfoundland, at least. Dad had good timing when it came to dinner. Always managed to be at the table just before the food was ready. He'd sit down and smile at Mom and me. That smile Matthew has? That's my Dad's."

Gene sighed, rubbed his temples with his fingertips. "One day, he didn't come home for dinner. Mom and I sat there, just watching the food get cold and watching each other get more scared. Mom said later that she knew before five minutes had gone. Things can go wrong and make you late, but Mom said she knew. Sun was going down when we got the call from the harbormaster. Said they found the boat. The nets were out. He'd fallen overboard somehow, got caught in the nets."

She drew in a breath. Her mind was conjuring images she didn't want to see, of a young Gene sitting at a dinner table and waiting, of a man trapped underwater in a prison of fishing net. Jennifer reached out and took Gene's hand, felt the strength in it, the calluses from years of work. Her own hand felt soft in his. "I'm sorry, Gene," she said. "So sorry."

"The *Tally-ho* was his boat, you know. We had to sell it after he died. We didn't have a lot of money and Mom wasn't well. She couldn't work much, so I did. That's why I have a problem with the reading. I was never much good at it, and then I was working so much. Helping out on people's boats, learning how to do mechanic stuff. Things like that. Had to let school slide.

"I saved up as much as I could. The man who bought it moved to Vancouver, and after my Mom died I called him up, made him an offer. It wasn't enough to just buy it, so we did a trade. I did a lot of repair and upkeep on a sailboat he had. It took me two years of that, but I got the *Tally-ho*. And moved up here."

"That's brave of you," she said.

"What is?"

"To do that work. Even after what happened to your Dad."

He shrugged. "Maybe it's brave. I don't know. For a while I enjoyed it. It was a way to kind of hang on to my Dad and those old days. It's what I know. But I haven't liked it for years now. Ever since Matthew was born, it used to be that at least once a month I'd be taking the boat out and wonder if I was going to come back that day. And ever since Becca left, I wonder that about once a week."

Jennifer thought of asking him why he did it, still. Then did not ask. Because she knew how hard it was to start over, even when the break was clean.

"That's why I wanted to leave Matthew with you tonight," Gene said. "I was afraid that...I thought that if I didn't make it back, you could take care of him."

She sat, openmouthed. Jennifer, the girl no one asked to come and water their plants while they were away on vacation. And Gene was entrusting his child, the only thing in the world he cared about, to her.

Before she could ask, he answered. "Because I know you care about him. I know you'd look out for him."

She began to protest. Then was done with it. No, it was true, she could and would look after Matthew. If she'd stayed. "You probably wish I hadn't come, then."

"No," he said after a moment. "I'm glad you're here."

300

"Suzanne would take care of Matthew."

"It's not that. I was pissed as all hell, but part of me was glad that I wouldn't be out here by myself. I mean, I know we all have to go one day, but I don't want to be all alone like my Dad. Thank you."

"No," she said. "Thank you." They sat in peaceful silence as the storm blew around them.

It was not quite dawn when Jennifer woke. Hard to say what woke her. Perhaps the floor, hard under the inadequate cushioning of blankets. Perhaps her body, which ached from being tossed about. Perhaps Gene, who lay a foot or two away from her, snoring. She climbed to her feet, wincing and wondering just how bruised up she was. At least nothing was broken.

Jennifer stood, listening for the storm, and realized what had woken her. Stillness. No sound of rain, no motion of the sea. A faint whistle of wind. Nothing more.

She made her way onto the deck, looked around her. Jagged rocks poked up out of the water, in the predawn light she could see the white foam as waves broke over them. Beyond the rocks, to the east, the shore of Canada, the Point they had been trying to get around. To the north, the south, the west, a wide expanse of sea, calm now, untroubled. She thought of Pete Puma's first day at her house, when he ran frantic about the rooms in play for two hours solid, then collapsed in an exhausted heap. That was how the sea was, at rest now.

Jennifer walked to the bow of the ship. A chair was there, bolted to the deck, and she sat down, looked around her. The sky as peaceful as the sea, some feathery clouds on the eastern horizon but otherwise clear. Waiting for the sun, a pure blue that she could not ever recall seeing before, anywhere. If white was the color of heaven, and black that of hell, then what might this blue be?

A gentle breeze caressed her, lifted her hair. Silence save for the white noise of the ocean breakers to the east. Not even the cry of a gull shattered the silence. She breathed deep of the breeze; it was chilly but she did not notice the temperature. Only the taste of it, the clean ocean tang. She listened to the sound of her breathing as the air went into her lungs, filled them, then out again, the air warmed by her body, joining the rest of the breeze. A part of it. Part of everything.

I know that color of blue. It's the color of life. I'm alive.

The moment the thought was complete, she looked to the east. The blue beginning to change, and for a moment she felt sad, that she had lost that blue forever, would only see it in her dreams. But sadness was lost in wonder as the eastern horizon began to lighten. The feathery clouds kept the sun itself from view but let themselves be painted with her light. Deepest lavender, delicate cotton-candy pink, red and gold edging the clouds like a Christmas ribbon. With every second that passed the palette of the eastern sky grew in beauty, and with every second Jennifer felt sure that it could not become more lovely, was joyful to be proven wrong.

Such beauty. Such life. And I'm a part of it.

She did not know much. She was simply Jennifer Thomson, no more, no less. She did not have Mr. Bradbury's faith, did not feel that hand over her, ready to catch or comfort. But she knew that no matter whether it was fate, or chance, or God's will, she was here, and glad to be here.

And grateful.

"Thank you," she whispered. Tears ran down her face, cooled by the morning breeze, glowing in the dawn's light. "Thank you for my life."

No sooner had she said it than the glow began to fade from the sunrise, began dulling to ordinary daylight. *No, stay that way. Just a minute longer. Please stay.*

But it wouldn't stay. Of course it wouldn't. She had to remember this moment always, for it might never come again.

"Thank you," she said one more time.

The glory fading out of the sunrise, but the silence was hers. For a few moments, at least, and then she began to hear a buzzing sound. Annoying as hell. Like some great insect, how dare it intrude. No, not a buzz, a choppy sound, that of...

A helicopter. In the distance, heading their way.

"Gene!" She jumped to her feet, ran back to the cabin door. "Gene! Come here!"

"What? Where?" Gene, startled, sat up and his head hit the table. "Ow! Jesus!"

"Oh, sorry. I'm sorry. There's a helicopter coming."

In an instant Gene was on the deck beside her, rubbing his head. He stood blinking, wincing as she had earlier. Put his arm around her and grinned. "Well, what do you know, Jen. I think we're rescued."

In less than a minute the helicopter was there, circling overhead. "Ahoy!" yelled a voice over the bullhorn. "You two OK down there? Anybody hurt?"

"We're fine!" Jennifer yelled.

Gene, knowing they probably couldn't hear over the sound of the rotors, gave a thumbs-up with his right hand and an OK with his left. In a few seconds a rope ladder was lowered down to them, and Jennifer went up first. The ladder was not too steady, and the rush of wind from the helicopter was strong. But she was not afraid. How could she be?

She was going home.

Chapter Thirty-two

A number of years ago Sean was on a mission in Afghanistan when the transport hit a mine. He was somehow thrown clear, came to and found everyone else dead, the transport and all supplies in smoking ruins, and himself a hundred miles from nowhere with half a canteen of water, and shrapnel in his right leg. There was nothing else for it, so he pulled out the shrapnel, bandaged the leg as best he could, and set off across the desert, back to the ops base over the border. By the end of the second day the water was gone, his leg wound was infected and sent jolts of pain through him with every step, he would have given anything for an hour's shelter from the merciless sun. Some time after noon on the third day his legs gave out but he kept going, crawling. Sean remembered being faintly surprised by his own determination, his refusal to yield to the inevitable and lie down. He kept on, scarcely aware of which direction he was heading in, crawled until his limbs gave up and let him fall. He remembered lying there in the desert, how after a while the earth seemed not so harsh and stony, the sun's heat seemed to be fading. He'd been glad, because maybe he could get some sleep and forget about his thirst and the heat and the pain in his leg and the fever that made him shiver and burn. He had done his best, been defeated by the elements, that was all.

There was no desert heat on the drive from Wisconsin to British Columbia. He was driving, not walking, and there was food, water, and shelter in abundance. No enemy in pursuit. And yet it was worse than the lonely trek across the Afghan desert or any other journey of the old days. Back then he'd known where he was going, and why, and that it was for some purpose. Back then he didn't have innocent blood on his hands.

That time in Afghanistan, he'd lost consciousness in the desert, and woke up in the medical tent of the ops base. Opened his eyes and saw Robert sitting in a chair nearby. Robert put down the book he was reading, smiled, and said, "Welcome back to the land of the living. How's the weather in Hell? Hot, I gather."

"Yeah, but at least it was a dry heat," he'd replied and they both laughed.

Sean had no anticipation of such a pleasant end to this journey.

Behind him, Richard Blaine was bound hand-and-foot. Lying on the van's floor, still unconscious. As far as he could tell Richard's vital signs were strong. From time to time Sean glanced back as he drove, to see if Richard was awake yet. Hoping he was, so he could be sure Richard was physically fine. Praying he was still out, so he did not have to see the look that would be in Richard's eyes or hear what he would have to say.

He drove, and first it was all right. While he negotiated surface streets and smaller highways, had to keep an eye out for turnoffs, he could stop thinking about Anna, dead by his hand and lying under a blanket, could stop hearing that awful crack as her head hit the stone fireplace. But once he hit the interstate and had nothing but those hundreds of miles west, a straight shot through Wisconsin and Minnesota and on to the coast, it all started coming at him in quick little flashes, making his hands white-knuckle tight on the wheel so it was hard to uncurl his fingers, sent adrenaline through his system until his muscles trembled with it.

A little past nightfall, he parked at a highway rest stop just over the Minnesota border. He could go no further tonight. Sean got up and made his way to the back of the van. Richard was awake. He did not struggle against his bonds nor did he speak, only stared at his captor with a look that was familiar.

Sean knelt in front of Richard. "I'm sorry," he said, his voice barely more than a whisper. It hurt to talk, but he thought it would hurt in a worse way if he didn't speak. "I'm so sorry about—"

"Why Anna?" Richard snarled. "I was the one you came for, why not just me?"

"It was an—"

"Why her and…she didn't have anything to do with this."

"I know."

"Then why?"

Sean felt something then, thank God. Anger, like a flame, warm and comforting. "Ask *me* why. Ask yourself. You killed three hundred people and they were just as innocent as Anna. At least I didn't mean for it to happen." *No, but then why can't I stop hearing her head hit the fireplace, stop seeing her lying there so small under that afghan?* "You're getting what their families got. I hope you enjoy it."

Sean turned and went to the front of the van, sat down in the driver's seat. It was a small flame, the anger inside him; there was too much cold and emptiness for the flame to last long, but he cherished the warmth it gave him for a little while.

He moved the seat back as far as it would go, closed his eyes. Listened to the sound of crickets, the drone of the highway. Felt the weight of his limbs, heavy with exhaustion and spent adrenaline, longed to let the weight pull him down into sleep. He would feel better, and the escape would be more than welcome. But sleep did not claim him until the moon had risen and made its way along the sky, out of his field of vision. Escape lasted for a few hours, until a nightmare woke him and he sat, breathing hard, looking out at the dark Minnesota countryside. Not a sign of dawn yet, but he knew that there would be no more sleep for him tonight. He was just thankful that his protective instincts kept him from remembering the details of the nightmare — all he was left with was a sensation of cold and the distant echo of a scream, he was not sure whose. Sean could have stayed, and rested, but instead he started up the van and started west again, spurred by a sense of urgency. *Go on,* the voice of instinct that had helped keep him alive all these years said, *Go on, keep going. Get Richard to Jennifer before it's too late.*

Too late for what? he wondered, but the voice had nothing to add on that subject.

He hoped to see the sun rise over the woods and farms of Minnesota, see it sparkling on the lakes he saw occasionally. But before dawn a storm rolled in, and he drove through the rain all that day. The rain slowed his progress, the straightness of the highway gave him the sensation that he was on some kind of treadmill; time was passing but distance was not. He breathed a sigh of relief when he crossed the border into North Dakota. He was getting somewhere, after all.

Richard had been silent all day. He was not catatonic; he took the food and water that were provided for him, often seemed to be lost in some reverie. Sometimes his lips moved silently, as if in prayer. But Richard did not speak until that night. "You killed Doug MacReady, didn't you? Along with the Wickershams."

Sean nodded.

"Anyone else?"

"Henry Connolly. He told me about you."

"You made him tell you."

"Yes."

"This is personal, isn't it?" Richard asked.

"What makes you say that?" Sean's voice was a little stronger now, it did not hurt so much to speak.

"Whoever you used to work for, you're not working for them now. You've got no backup. If you wanted an arrest you'd never get it through court. And if you wanted to just take me out, you could have done that months ago." Richard shook his head. "No, this is revenge. I can practically smell it."

Sean said nothing.

"Look, Sam, or whatever your real name is. Might as well tell me. What's the point in lying to each other any more?"

None that Sean could see.

"So who did you lose in Los Angeles?" Richard asked. "A child? Your wife?"

"No one," Sean said. "I don't have anyone to lose."

"Why, then?"

"I'm doing this for one of the survivors. Jennifer Thomson."

"Which one was she?"

"The last one to get out. The one who was in all the pictures."

"Ah," Richard said. "How much did she pay you? Or was this just a favor?"

"She didn't pay me. She doesn't even know." Might as well say the rest. "I saw her on TV. I felt sorry for her, wanted to help her. And so I'm bringing you to her. So you're right, this is revenge. But not mine."

Richard stared at him. For the first time there was fear in his eyes. "You mean...she doesn't know?"

Sean nodded.

"So you're just going to show up on her doorstep and say 'Hi there, look what I brought you'? My God, it's been over a year, and you're going to barge into whatever her life is now and then what?"

"Justice. I'll let her do the honors, and give you what you deserve."

"You're insane."

"You're a traitor and a murderer. And she's going to give you what's coming to you."

"Oh, I've always known that's the price I might pay. I made my peace with that long ago. But to go through all this for someone you don't even know? And how do you even know she wants this?"

The same question Robert had asked, so long ago back in Maine. "Who wouldn't?"

"Anna wouldn't."

Sean said nothing, for he knew Richard was right.

"Maybe this Jennifer girl will, maybe she won't. But go on, drop into her life. Tell her how many people you killed to catch me. Tell her how you killed my wife and my…"

Sean lashed out and hit Richard in the jaw, cutting off his words. He watched as Richard spat out blood and a tooth, then he turned and went back to the front of the van to try and rest. Behind him, Richard was silent now, sinking back into that state that might have been meditation or lethargy. Sean stared out at the night, his throat burning and throbbing. He had painkillers in his kit but did not take one. In a way, he craved the pain. It was part of the pound of flesh he had to pay for Anna.

He got as far as Montana before he had to go to ground.

Sean told himself it was mostly exhaustion. Too much driving with too little sleep, what slumber he did have troubled by dreams. But mostly it was the road that did it, that straight shot west, the sky huge and uniform gray above him. No rain to liven things up, just a lowering gray wall of cloud above him and an endless succession of farms and small towns and fast food restaurants and highway rest areas, never the same and never changing. So locked into this straight-arrow journey west that he wondered if he'd recognize the end when he reached it, or simply drive through a guardrail on the Washington coast and take the van, Richard, and himself down to the water and rocks below.

Sleep, that was what he needed. In a bed, not slumped in the seat of his van. Sean found a motel on the outskirts of some small town. Modest but clean, not unlike the Lakeview Terrace apartments back in Du Lac. He got a room on the ground floor, easy to get in and out of, at the back, out of sight. It was a chance, but not much of one. He'd be out of here by dawn, and he had some stuff in his bag that would make Richard sleep tight the entire night. Something for himself as well, a bottle of Johnnie Walker he'd picked up back in North Dakota.

Once they were in the room he poured two inches of Scotch into a motel glass. "Want some?" he asked Richard.

Richard, tied up and sitting in a chair, replied, "No thanks. Never got a taste for it."

Sean drank in silence, waited for the alcohol to help him relax. He had the feeling it was going to take more than one glass.

After a while Richard asked, "Where exactly are we going?"

"Canada. British Columbia. A little ways north of Vancouver." Through some judicious research and a phone call to Jennifer Thomson's agent in Los Angeles he'd found that Jennifer lived in a small town called Haven Cove. He'd looked it up on the map and was relieved. Haven Cove was only ten miles north of an old safe house on the coast. It was more of a vacation house than a safe house in the strictest sense of the word. Missions seldom took them to the geopolitical hot spot that was British Columbia. That safe house was where he'd gone once for R&R. After that time in Europe, the mission where Beatty saved his life.

He poured another drink. The safe house, that's where all this would end.

"You know, Richard, I wish we'd met under other circumstances. I mean, earlier on. I would have liked to have had you on our side. You would have been good," he found himself saying. Perhaps the alcohol was working already.

Richard didn't smile. A resigned, reproachful look was in his eyes. It was very familiar. "Do you think that's a compliment?"

"Yes."

"It's almost funny. Look at you. You're on a crazy mission for this woman you don't even know, thinking you're going to charge into her life like some Dudley Do-Right and hand over the bad man. Your side? You don't have a side. You just have yourself."

You're wrong. Once I had a side. Once I believed I was doing right. But now I think Robert was right, we were used, all of us. "I could say the same for you."

"Say what you want. I had a cause I believed in. I wanted to make a difference in this country. You're just out for blood."

"Don't talk to me about blood," Sean said, anger twisting inside him. "You've got three hundred innocent lives on your hands. I have one."

"Two," Richard said. "Anna was pregnant."

Once again he felt frozen and couldn't breathe, as if he was back on Deer's Head Lake and it was he, not Beatty, who had fallen through the ice and was drowning. *Don't believe him. He's lying.* But Richard wasn't lying, and Sean knew it.

"No," he whispered.

"She was." No taunting, no rancor in Richard's voice. Just the truth. "Almost four months along."

Now Sean knew where he'd seen that reproachful look before. It had been in Beatty's eyes as his breath gave out and he sank.

He got to his feet, almost falling, his knees were shaking so. Went into the bathroom, ran water in the sink, ran water over his left hand. The hand that had pushed Anna, that had not stopped itching and burning since then. Red and chafed now from rubbing it to quell the burn. Sean stared down at his hand to keep from looking at himself in the mirror, and over the sound of water running in the sink listened as Richard spoke.

"We'd been trying to have a baby for years now. This was our fourth try. We lost all the others before three months had gone. I told her, maybe we shouldn't try any more, but she said…she wanted so much to…She wanted to wait another month before telling anyone, until she was far enough along that…"

The water wasn't helping. Sean turned off the faucet and dried his hands with a motel towel, white and rough.

"I didn't know," he said. The signs had been there. But he hadn't seen.

"Would it have changed anything if you'd known?"

"I never meant to hurt Anna or the baby. It was an accident."

"I know. But would it have changed anything?"

He could lie. But didn't. "No." Then: "But no matter what, three hundred is still a lot more than two."

"You think that makes you better than me?"

Sean walked over, grabbed Richard by the shirt and hauled him up so he could speak into his face, look into his eyes. "I know it does."

But Richard only smiled. It was a smile made frightening by the bitterness in it. Sean thought of a poem Robert had quoted to him long ago, about a desert creature eating its own heart, because it was bitter, and because it was his heart.

Richard wore the smile of a man eating his own heart and said, "No, you're not better. You're just not as bad."

Richard was safely doped up for the night. Wouldn't wake, wouldn't yell, probably wouldn't notice if the Four Riders of the Apocalypse flew through the room.

Sean shut the door behind him, locked it. Pocketed the key and took a long pull from the bottle, no point in bothering with a glass any more. Stood looking up at the sky. It was overcast, no moon, no stars. Just a black pool overhead. Sean would have liked to see stars. There had been stars wheeling overhead, more than he could ever count, that time in Afghanistan. Even through the pain and fever and thirst and the sure knowledge that he would die and his bones would be picked clean by the desert scavengers, he'd taken comfort in the beauty of the stars.

That patrol should never had found him. Yes, he would have died, but he would have died with his faith in the cause and people he served intact, before time and events shook and finally destroyed his faith. Would not have seen his former masters betray and reject, watched his old colleagues fall away. He would have died without the blood of friends and innocents on his hands.

No stars to give him comfort. He walked toward the motel office, to the pay phone on the wall. No stars, but he could find comfort of a different sort, through miles of wires and cables. Sean had no idea what time it was but Monique had always been a night owl. Chances were good she'd be awake. He dialed the number from memory. He wouldn't tell her any of it. Just needed to hear her voice. *Talk to me, Monique. Say you're all right. Let me know that there's one good thing in my life I haven't destroyed. Say that you cared for me once. Hell, tell me you loved me, even if you didn't, because God knows I'll never hear that from anyone, ever.*

The phone rang three times and then Monique's bittersweet honey voice said, "Hello?" In the background Sean could hear a movie.

Casablanca. Renault saying he was shocked, shocked that gambling was going on here. "Hello?" she said again.

Monique, it's me. But the words wouldn't come out. *I need you.*

He heard a male voice ask something, heard Monique say, "I don't know" to the man. "Anyone there?" into the receiver.

Sean said nothing, didn't make a sound. He was sure of it. But Monique's voice became softer, concerned. "Flint? Is that you?"

He hung up. He could not talk to Monique, and his bruised throat and hoarse voice had nothing to do with it. No, he had forfeited any right to seek comfort from Monique when he killed Anna. Only two women in the world he cared about, and he could not seek one's help when the other was dead at his hand. *I'm sorry, Monique. Forget you knew me. Have the happiness you deserve. You never would have found it with me.*

For a while he stood by the phone, fingertips idly running over the buttons. Then he picked up the receiver, began to dial again. Area code 207 this time. Maine. Robert's number. Robert was the one he really should talk to. Because Monique could only give him comfort. Robert would understand. He could tell Robert everything. It would be like when he was a child back at Saint Stephen's, only confessing into a phone instead of a cloth screen. Instead of a priest on the other side of the screen Robert would be in his castle on the rocky coast of Maine, surrounded by his books, with a glass of brandy in one hand, a fire roaring in the fireplace, and classical music on the CD player. He would say *Robert, you were right, the whole mission went wrong, so very wrong.*

Dialed 1, then the area code, the first three digits...and then stopped, finger hovering over the keypad. Torn, for hand-in-hand with his longing to talk to Robert was the fear — almost but not quite a certainty — that Robert was no longer there to talk to. That the cancer had done what the dangers of countless missions could not. Killed him. Sean told himself it was not true, but what if it was? What if he got a rote voice saying the number was disconnected? Or some stranger's voice telling him that the man who used to live there isn't with us anymore, so sad? If he heard that, what then?

If he didn't have the hope of talking with Robert, could he even go on?

He hung up. Once, his own will had been enough to sustain him. A year and a half ago, the plight of Jennifer Thomson had put him in motion. But too much had happened, and now his will was nearly spent and he had trouble remembering the image of Jennifer that had once haunted him. No home to go back to, no more missions for him. No more Monique. There was only the hope that he could talk to the one person who would understand, and maybe find absolution. Or something like it.

Sean walked away from the phone, away from the motel, down the highway, occasionally taking swallows of Scotch, never mind how it burned his throat. Walked away from the lights of the motel, found a fence and climbed it into a cattle pasture. In the distance a few Holsteins stood, asleep on their feet, paying him no mind. He walked without looking, until he stumbled and fell, rolled and lay on his back, looking up at the sky. Put the bottle to his lips and was surprised to find it empty.

He let the bottle fall to the ground, looked up at the sky. Still no moon or stars, just an infinite expanse of black as far as he could see. Like the void he'd nearly fallen into, and now he wondered why he had been afraid. If he was falling forever in darkness he wouldn't have to keep hearing Anna's head hit the fireplace, or Beatty's desperate pounding on the ice. He could stop seeing Anna dead along with the child inside her, stop seeing the look in Robert's eyes as he said that nothing could wash the blood away from their hands.

Sean looked up at the sky in appeal and said, "I wanted to help Jennifer. That was all I wanted. To do my job again."

And now? He looked up into darkness and knew that he could have what he wanted. It would be very easy. He knew how. Eight rounds in the gun's magazine, and all he needed were two. One for Richard, one for himself. It would be doing Richard a favor, really. Himself as well. And whether he liked what he'd wanted wouldn't matter any longer.

Sean had just about made up his mind when he heard Robert's voice. Not echoing down the halls of memory but as if Robert was here, standing among the cows in this Montana pasture. *Giving up?* Robert asked. *That's most unlike you.*

"I can't help it," he said in his new hoarse voice. "You tried to warn me and it's gone wrong. I should have listened. I'm sorry."

What's done is done, my friend. But after all this, to leave it unfinished? Then it really will have been all for nothing.

"I don't care."

You do. At least keep your promise to come see me when it's done. Can you finish the job, and do that?

Sean wanted to say no. But Robert was right. He had never left a job unfinished before. He should see it through, otherwise it was all for nothing. And when it was done, he would drive back across the country, from one land's end to the other, and see his friend. If he was still there.

"All right then," he said. "Be seeing you."

No answer to that. He hadn't expected one. Nor did he know what he would do when he got back to Maine. If Robert was there, they would talk, but what then? And if he wasn't there, what then?

He'd figure it out when he got there. Improvise. He was good at that.

316

The gray van hit the road again just a little after dawn. Sean drove with a dry mouth and a dull ache behind his eyes, sipping Gatorade to rehydrate himself. Richard was still a bit doped up, but had recovered himself enough by noon to say the last words he would utter for the rest of the drive. "What if she won't do it?"

"She will."

"But what if she won't?"

"Then I will."

Richard did not seem surprised. "That's what I thought. I just wanted to know for sure."

Sean stood for a moment, looking into Richard's face. Saw that something was different. It wasn't exhaustion, or fear, or the dope from last night. No, something essential, the thing that had sent Richard on his crusade to reshape the country in the way he saw fit, the thing that had made him command men and inspire admiration — that thing was gone. Wounded by betrayal and killed by grief. Gone. The Richard he was bringing to Jennifer was not the one who had ordered the bombing. That Richard was gone forever, with no way to exact justice. This was not the same man.

But he would have to do.

Chapter Thirty-three

Haven Cove and its inhabitants weathered the storm well. No lives were lost, though there were several people in the hospital. The Coast Guard had to rescue a fishing crew caught out in the storm, and several of the crew were suffering from exposure. Angus, the harbormaster, had a mild heart attack but was already well enough to complain loudly and often about the hospital food, leading Mr. Bradbury to remark that Angus was the only man he'd met contrary enough to be feistier after a coronary than before one.

Four fishing boats had been lost, including the *Tally-ho*. The harbor was damaged, though not as much as everyone had feared it would be. A bait-and-tackle shop was wiped out completely, and several other harbor businesses were going to need a good clean-up. But the town considered itself lucky, and everyone was pitching in to help.

The sight of the *Tally-ho* on its lucky and unlikely perch brought the news media to Haven Cove. Jennifer managed to elude the reporters and photographers but Gene, having no compunctions, appeared more than once on TV describing what had happened, wearing that same look of dismayed amusement he'd had when the boat wrecked. When Jennifer asked him what was going to happen to the *Tally-ho,* Gene seemed remarkably calm. "There's no way they can get it off the rock," he said. "And even if they did, no way to tow it back without it sinking. I guess she'll stay there. Might become a tourist attraction."

"Maybe you could sell tickets," she said, and he laughed.

It was a Thursday night, a few days after the storm. The Delacroixs were helping to coordinate a food drive their church was putting on for the people whose boats and businesses had been damaged, and now Jennifer and Suzanne sat, having some pizza while they took a break from loading canned goods and other nonperishables into boxes.

"I can't wait until the men get here, to help us lift all this," Suzanne said, reaching for another slice of pepperoni with extra cheese.

"Gene's at Bill's office, right?" asked Jennifer.

Suzanne nodded. "Gene's insurance company tried to tell him they wouldn't pay for the boat because technically it hadn't sunk. So Bill's giving them an earful. Gene'll get his money, sooner or later."

"Believe me, if I was in Gene's situation I'd want Bill on my side. And speaking of storm damage, I ran into a blast from my past today."

"Do tell," said Suzanne.

"Drove past Salto Mining. What a mess. That big tree outside the office fell over and knocked out half their windows. Alex was out there bitching at the crew cutting down the tree."

Jennifer had been on her way back from a lunch errand when she saw Alex standing in front of his office. He was yelling and wincing with every bit of glass that fell to the sidewalk. She was at a stoplight; he turned and saw her. It was the first time she'd seen him since the New Year's debacle, but the sight of him didn't bother her. That was so long ago. He gave her a rueful shrug as she saw the damage, then a grin and a wink. She couldn't help it; she flipped him the bird, laughed, and drove on her way.

"Well, I'm not taking up a collection for him. Unless you want to throw some of these cans at him." Suzanne held up a can of Campbell's tomato soup.

"Nah, one of the Chunky soups. Can's bigger," Jennifer replied with a giggle.

At the door a knock, and Gene's voice calling out, "Hello, hello."

"Come on in!" Suzanne said.

The door opened and Gene and Matthew came in. Matthew ran over to Jennifer and gave her a big hug. Since the storm he did that every time he saw her, and she didn't mind at all.

Gene followed, making his way through the boxes of food. He had a bucket of take-out chicken in one hand and a bag of sides and drinks in the other. "Hey, I brought — oh, you've got pizza."

"Fear not, Gene, I'm sure it'll get eaten," Suzanne replied.

Gene plunked the food down on the table. He seemed remarkably chipper for someone whose means of livelihood were gone for good. "I didn't just bring food. Check this out." He dug in the bag of sides and brought out a stack of newspaper supplements. On the cover was the headline *The Hammer Falls,* and a picture of the *Tally-ho* on its perch. "Take a look."

"I'm sorry, Gene," said Suzanne.

But Jennifer, leaning forward to look at the photo, saw what Gene really wanted her to see. The credit for the photograph. *Photo by Gene Tally.* "That's your picture!"

He nodded happily. "Got John Proulx to take me out there the other day, get my pictures and tapes and things. And I took a few shots, gave them to one of those reporters that was around. And last but not least," he took a slip of pale blue paper out of his pocket. "Here's my first paycheck for something that didn't involve fish."

Jennifer, Suzanne, and Matthew applauded.

"Best of all, I go down to Vancouver on Monday to show them my other pictures. Seems they're looking for photographers."

"So you'd probably get some freelance out of it?" asked Jennifer.

"Maybe even full time," Gene said with a grin.

"Gene, that's wonderful!" said Suzanne. "We need to celebrate."

"I think I can help with that matter," said Bill, who walked in and held up two six-packs of beer.

Four bottles were opened (and a Sprite for Matthew), and clinked together in a toast. "To us," Bill said.

"Amen to that," Jennifer said and they all drank. She'd never had much of a taste for beer but this one tasted finer than anything she'd had in a long time.

The five of them laid waste to the pizza and the chicken. When the food was consumed, Gene let out a sigh. "I suppose we should load those boxes into the truck. No, stay there, you've done the hard work," he said to Suzanne and Jennifer. "Come on big guy." He ruffled his son's hair. "Little help here?"

"In a minute?" Matthew asked, and when his father nodded and got up from the table, Matthew turned to Jennifer. "Miss Jen, can I ask you something?"

"Fire away."

"Was it scary out there?" Matthew's eyes were wide.

"You bet it was," Jennifer said. "Just ask your Dad."

Matthew rolled his eyes. "Dad's never scared."

"Really?" asked Jennifer. Gene gave her an apologetic shrug.

"Were you more scared than you've ever been in your life?" asked Matthew with the sort of curiosity only a nine-year-old can have.

"No," she said after a moment. "I was scared worse before. Now, go on and help your Dad. Scoot!"

Matthew gave her a grin and ran off to help Gene and Bill. Suzanne and Jennifer sat amid the debris of dinner. Jennifer felt sleepy from the food and the beer, and was startled when Suzanne spoke.

"I can't imagine what it must be like. To dodge a bullet like that must be... overwhelming."

"It is, sometimes," Jennifer said.

"And twice in, what was it, a year and a half?" Suzanne shook her head. "I can't imagine it. You're a hell of a girl, Jen."

Suzanne knew. Ever since the TV movie, she'd guessed that Suzanne probably knew. "When did you find out?"

"About two weeks after you moved here. Mrs. Reisman left a copy of *People* and your picture was in it."

And to think, all that time she'd worried what would happen when Suzanne found out, that her friend would regard her differently. "You never said anything."

Suzanne shrugged. "I figured you'd been through enough. You'd talk about it when you were ready."

Jennifer gave her a hug. "Thanks."

"Don't mention it."

She rode in Gene's truck as they dropped off the boxes of food at the church. "That's such great news about the thing on Monday, with the newspaper," she said as they neared her house.

"Well, wish me luck. Oh, they gave me some application paperwork. Could you help out with that?" Gene asked.

"No problem. Why don't you come over for dinner Saturday?"

"Name the time, we'll be there."

She looked at Gene, at his hands, so capable on the wheel, the blue eyes no longer unreadable, at least not to her. "How about just you?"

"Just..." He frowned for a second, then his eyes lit up with understanding, and he smiled. "I'd love it."

She smiled back at him, and her only regret was that she hadn't asked him sooner.

Jennifer got home a bit late the next night, having stopped at the grocery store after work. She'd spent most of the day trying to come up with ideas for a nice meal for her and Gene. She figured they were both weary of seafood, wrote off chicken as too boring and game hens as too pretentious, finally settled on filet mignon with béarnaise sauce. She drove through the streets toward her home, singing a song she'd heard on one of Gene's tapes. The leaves were turning and the air was cool. Fall was here already. She found herself looking forward to it, to the rain and chill, for it made the warmth inside all the sweeter.

She parked in her driveway, hoisted bags into her arms. As she slammed the car door, Suzanne came trotting out with a grin on her face and a hand behind her back. "Someone's got a date tomorrow," she sing-songed.

"Is this published somewhere?"

"Hey, not a lot happens here. We take our gossip where we can get it." Suzanne's smile softened. "Besides, Jen, people have been hoping for this for a while now. We were wondering when you two would finally get together."

"It's dinner, Suze. Not like we're engaged or anything."

"Whatever. Anyway, I brought you a little something for the big night tomorrow." Suzanne produced two tapered candles and handed them to Jennifer.

Jennifer set down her grocery bags and looked at the candles. They were lovely, a pale blue at the tips, shading gradually to a dark cobalt at the base. A faint honey scent of beeswax. "They're beautiful. Thank you. Where did you get them?"

"My friend Eskimo Sally sent them to me. She runs this New Age hippie shit store down in California, around Santa Cruz."

"Well, they're just — wait. Her name's *Eskimo Sally?*"

Suzanne rolled her eyes. "Long story. Oh shoot, phone's ringing." She ran back to the house. "Later, Jen!"

"Bye!" Jennifer tucked the candles into one of the bags, then carried the bags into the house. Once inside she headed straight for the kitchen and set down her bags. "Oh Pete Puma-kitten, Mama got you some yummy—"

Behind her, a *thunk* as the front door closed.

Jennifer turned around, eyes wide in the dim kitchen. The front door didn't close on its own. If you didn't do it yourself it would sit there wide open until Judgment Day. "Suzanne?" No answer.

She listened hard, and heard Pete Puma mewing. But the sound was muffled, and there was a scratching. Pete scratching at her closed bedroom door.

She never left Pete locked in her bedroom, where there was no food or water or litterbox for him. And no way could he shut the door himself. Even as she realized it she heard a creak on the living room floorboards.

Someone is in the house with me.

For a moment her heartbeat drowned out any other sound. Instinctively she reached for the light switch, then snatched her hand away. If it was dark, she would have the advantage, knowing the house as she did. If it was light, she and whoever else was here would be on the same footing. *Unless he's got those creepy* Silence of the Lambs *night-vision goggles.*

But she wouldn't let herself think of it. Instead, she reached out to the phone, realizing she had no idea who to call. Did 911 work in Canada? Should she call the police? The Mounties? Or just dial zero, like in old movies? *Operator, give me the police.*

She grabbed hold of the phone, and realized before she even got it to her ear that it didn't matter. The line was dead.

For a moment she wanted to panic, to scream for help. But that would lead whoever it was right to her. No, after all she'd been through, she had to be smart. She set down the phone and reached for the knife block, pulled out the first one her hand touched. The carver. Good. Jennifer took a deep breath, psyching herself up. She knew the house, she was familiar with it. She would run out of the kitchen, act like she was going straight into the living room and then buttonhook around the hallway. Hopefully get to the door before Mystery Man knew what was up. And if she didn't, well, maybe this knife would give him something to think about.

One, two, three. Jennifer ran for the door, then switched and ran down the hall. She heard no footsteps behind her, and for a relieved moment thought that it had just been a gust of wind and her mind playing tricks on her.

Then hands seized her, one clamped over her mouth and muffled her scream. She flailed with the knife but her assailant's other hand caught hold of her wrist, gave it a sharp but painless squeeze and she dropped the knife. She screamed again behind the gag of his hand, lashed and kicked with all her strength but his arms were too strong, they held her tightly. Dimly she realized that he did not seem to be trying to hurt her, though he held her fast. But that thought was swallowed up in her terror and a wild sort of rage. *This will not happen, I will not let it happen. I did not live through the L.A. bombing and the Southern Hammer just to get murdered by some catburglar.*

She pried at the arm across her neck and shoulder, dug in with her nails. A low hiss of pain from the man but no loosening of his hold. Jennifer twisted again, and then his left arm shifted, brought something up toward her face. She had time to register a wad of white cloth, an acrid chemical stink, and a hoarse voice saying, "I'm sorry about this."

And then knew nothing.

She woke, feeling slightly queasy. Heard the sound of the sea; breakers, not the gentle lapping of the Haven Cove harbor. Blinking, she looked at her surroundings. She lay on a leather couch. The room was unfamiliar, spartan. No pictures on the walls. Most of the furniture draped with sheets. Under one sheet, a shape she couldn't recognize. The room seemed spacious enough but the air felt stale, as if it had been a long time since a window was opened. The only light came from a single torchiere lamp, off in the far corner.

Jennifer tried to sit up, and found that her wrists and ankles were tied. But not tightly. The bonds were secure but did not pinch or hurt her. She maneuvered herself to a sitting position and looked around, wondering where she was, who had brought her here, what they wanted with her. Not murder or rape, perhaps; physically she seemed to be all right. But then why?

She licked her lips, took a deep breath and felt the last of the fuzzy feeling leave her brain. She was about to ask what was going on when a hoarse male voice said, "Hello, Jennifer."

She turned and saw a man sitting in a chair, off to one side. He was so still, she hadn't seen him at first in the dim light. She shrank back, recognizing his voice, knowing this was her captor. But he made no move toward her, threatening or otherwise. Merely sat there, looking at her.

Jennifer looked back at him. He was older than her, probably in his middle fifties or so. His hair was dark brown or black, impossible to tell for certain in the dim light; a receding hairline, a few streaks of gray showing. His eyes were brown, dark-shadowed with weariness. A face of no particular distinction, neither ugly nor handsome, anonymous and unmemorable. She had never seen him before, she was sure, although with a lab coat and safety goggles he would have looked a bit like Mr. Burnham, her high school chemistry teacher.

He sat looking at her, and there was something strange about that, something that sent an odd chill through her. Maybe it wasn't his look, but the way he sat, poised, relaxed but tense. Or maybe it was the bruises she now saw, all up and down his throat. Finger marks, as if someone had tried to choke the life out of him not too long ago, and nearly succeeded.

If her scrutiny bothered him he did not show it. After a moment he spoke again. "You let your hair get longer," he said. "It looks nice."

Jennifer took a deep breath. "Who are you?" she asked.

Chapter Thirty-four

The man didn't reply at first. "Who are you?" Jennifer asked again.

"My name's Sean Kincaid," he said. "I used to work for the government. Covert work, infiltration."

Jennifer took a breath, trying to keep her fear at bay. It was easier than she'd thought; if he was going to hurt her, he'd had time and opportunity by now. Curiosity began to get the better of her. "You mean the CIA?"

Kincaid shook his head. "Not exactly. It was...well, you wouldn't know the name. It's a classified group, what they call black ops."

Oh great, I've stumbled into a Tom Clancy novel. Jennifer tried to work out what was going on; she hadn't felt so confused since the bomb ripped the federal building apart and she was staring out a hole where the hallway had been. What was she doing here? How did this man know who she was, and why had he captured her? Why did he just sit there, looking at her in that strange way, as if she was the answer to some question? "What do you want with me? Where am I?" she asked. "How do you know my name?"

Kincaid smiled, and she thought of those mysterious flowers she'd received back in March. Pleasant yet somehow disquieting. On the surface there was nothing wrong with the smile. It was gentle, made him almost handsome. Yet she didn't see the smile reflected in his eyes. That was what bothered her, more than the choker of bruises he wore, or the wiry strength she could see in his hands and wrists, or the slight bulge under the left side of his jacket. *Jesus, he has a gun.* No, it was his eyes, hard and blank as glass.

She couldn't read his eyes, had no idea what lay behind his face. She'd have to take her chances.

She tried to keep her face expressionless, but some of her apprehension must have shown. "You don't have to be afraid of me," he said. "I would never hurt you."

From somewhere in the room a sound like a muffled laugh. She had no idea where it had come from.

Got to get out of here. "Prove it," Jennifer said. "Untie me."

She expected him to protest, but he only said, "All right." Kincaid stood, walked over to her, knelt in front of her. Now that he was close to her she could see how tired he looked, as if he hadn't slept in a week. But his hands did not shake, they untied the bonds easily and quickly.

The knots undone, he stepped away from her. She sat for a moment, massaging her wrists and ankles, then jumped off the couch and looked for the front door. She saw it — saw *a* door, anyway — and ran for it, expecting any moment to feel his hands on her or to hear a gunshot. But there was nothing. She was at the door, yanking on the knob. It was locked.

"You can't get out that way," Kincaid said. He had returned to his chair, sat there watching her calmly. "The windows are bulletproof glass. It's a safe house, you see. And there's ten miles of dirt road to the highway and another fifteen miles to Haven Cove. I know this must all seem strange. But please," he said, gesturing to the sofa. "Sit down."

What choice did she have? Jennifer walked back to the couch and sat. "What do you want with me? You said you were with the government, is this some kind of interrogation or something?" *I haven't done anything,* she started to say, then stopped. Better to volunteer as little information as possible.

"I'm sorry," he said. "If there was another way to do this, I would. It's strange for me, too. I've waited for this for a year and half now. Same as you."

Jennifer felt herself go cold. A year and a half. Nothing else it could mean. The bombing, something to do with the bombing.

"I saw you on TV," Kincaid said. "When the fireman carried you away. I still don't know why, but ever since, the only thing I wanted was to help you." He smiled again. "I've brought you something."

She felt cold, sick, afraid. And angry. The picture, the damn picture. He didn't want to help her, he wanted to help that girl in the picture. Why couldn't anyone understand? "That's not me."

He blinked, looked confused.

"I'm not that girl any more. I came up here to get away from her and Los Angeles, and that damn picture has followed me everywhere I go. If you want to help me, take me back home, right now. And whatever you've brought, I don't want it."

"You do."

"I don't." And yet... "What is it?"

Kincaid got to his feet and walked over to the odd-shaped object draped with a sheet. Something familiar about the way he walked, and she realized that he reminded her of Gene. Like Gene he was only medium-built, but carried himself with the assurance of a taller man. "It was the way you were crying. How lost and afraid you were. I wanted to help you, and I knew there was only one way to do that. And that was to bring those who had hurt you to justice."

With that he pulled the sheet away, and she flinched, not knowing what horror might be under it. Kincaid might mean her no harm, but that didn't mean he wasn't a danger to others.

The sheet was off, and before her was a man, gagged, bound to a chair, strapped with duct tape so that only his head was free to move. He was tall and bearded, eyes the color of steel, and he looked even more weary than Kincaid did. The man took in his surroundings, and then looked at her. She saw recognition and dismissal; his gaze went off into the middle distance.

"Who is he?" she asked.

"His name is Richard Blaine. He's the head of an antigovernment group based out of Wisconsin. Last year one of his toadies posed as a janitor and put explosives around the support columns in the garage of the L.A. federal building. And boom," he said softly, holding up a fist and then uncurling and spreading out his fingers. "That's all she wrote. He's the man behind it all."

Jennifer could not believe what she was hearing. She made it a point to avoid the news, but of course she knew that no perpetrator had been caught, though bombs aplenty had rained down on the Middle East. "No," she said, trying to make sense of it. "No, it was the Arabs who did it, everyone said so."

"That's what they said." Kincaid's smile twisted bitterly. She looked away from it, looked back at the bound man. "But they lied. That's what they do best. I know. You see, it was better politically to blame the ragheads and lob some air strikes their way than to admit there was trouble at home," Kincaid said. "Isn't that right, Richard?"

Blaine aimed a look of weary hatred at Kincaid.

Kincaid seemed unruffled, but Jennifer caught a flicker of something behind those dark blank eyes, as if he understood that look of hate, knew that it was deserved. Curious, but it was the least of Jennifer's concerns right now. "Is it true? I mean, did he really do that?"

"Answer the lady, Richard."

Blaine nodded. He looked as if he wanted very much to say something, but he could not speak around the gag and Kincaid made no move to remove it.

Jennifer stood, staring at this man. This ordinary man. This American, just like her. No foreign face of hate staring out from a magazine cover. Right in front of her. She groped for something to say and found the one question that had been asked after the bombing by everyone and was satisfactorily answered by no one. "Why? Why would you do that?"

"Because he hates the government. And thought the best way to get his point across would be to blow up a federal building," Kincaid said, then spread his hands out as if to say *I don't get it either.*

Jennifer took a breath. Too much going on. Being kidnapped, trapped here in the safe house, Kincaid and his unreadable eyes, Mr. All-American in front of her. Too much, too much, she needed to think about it all. Tried and she kept seeing the boardroom full of people cut to ribbons. The man who caught the cable and fried right in front of her. Carrie walking down the hall, waving at her, never to be seen alive again. Carlos with his neck broken at the bottom of the stairs. Mrs. Danvers asking her *How does it feel?*

Can't take this. "Why is he here? Shouldn't he be in jail? Why am I here?"

Kincaid let out a deep breath, as if some moment had arrived he'd been waiting for. Something about it sent a chill through her. "You're here to give this man what he deserves."

"And what's that?"

He reached into his pocket and took out a revolver. Laid it on the table in front of her, and for a moment all three of them stared at it. Then Kincaid looked up at her.

"Justice."

She stared at the gun. The prisoner. Kincaid. Felt as she had in those weeks after the bombing when she could not escape from her own image. When she could not walk past tall buildings without cringing, waiting for them to fall, or go into offices without feeling nausea and panic rise up in her throat. When strangers came up to her to tell her how brave she was, unintentionally twisting the knife of guilt deeper into her heart. When she read the list of the names of the dead every day in the paper and knew somehow that they were dead only because she was alive. She remembered it all, remembered how she'd had to flee — not just Los Angeles, but her home, her country. Her life.

Jennifer felt some sound rising up out of her. She wondered what it would be — a scream, a wail, a demand for revenge. It was laughter. She giggled and the harder she tried to make herself stop, the louder the laughter became. *So this is what it's like to go off your nut. I always wondered.*

She was still laughing when she looked back at Kincaid. He was smiling. He thought she was happy, that he was doing her a favor. She took a breath and once again did not know what she was going to say until it was out of her mouth. "You son of a bitch!"

Kincaid's smile lasted a second longer. The second it took for him to realize she was not saying it to Richard Blaine but to him. The smile vanished as abruptly as if she had slapped it away, and he took a step back from her.

"How can you ask me to do this? What gives you the right?" she asked. "After all this time? Do you think I've been sitting around waiting for this? I've been putting my life back together after bastard here," she pointed at Blaine, "ripped it apart. And now that's what you want to do, rip my life apart. I won't have it, do you hear me? Take your present and give it to someone else."

Kincaid seemed stunned. What had he expected? That she would be happy? Yes, that was exactly what he had expected. "I wanted to help you," he said. "That's all."

"This isn't help. And even if it is, I don't want it."

She turned and began heading for the door again. Locked or not, bulletproof glass be damned, she felt wired enough to smash it all down if she felt like it, and walk all the way back to Haven Cove. A hand seized her arm, and she was whirled around. Found herself staring into Sean Kincaid's face.

Now she could see behind his eyes. They were burning with some emotion she did not recognize. He held her by the upper arms, and his grip was tight, almost painful. "I did this for you," he said, his voice low but so intense he seemed to be shouting. "I turned my back on everything I cared about to help you."

"I don't—"

Kincaid's eyes blazed, his fingers bit deep into the flesh of her arms. "Do you have any idea what I've gone through? Do you want to know the things I've done?"

Only a gut feeling that he wouldn't deliberately harm her gave her the courage to speak. It was not his hands or his voice that frightened her but his eyes, rage and despair and something she couldn't name, something she had never seen before and never wanted to see again. "You're hurting me," she said.

He looked down at her arms, saw that his fingers would leave bruises. Let her go quickly, as if the touch burned him. "I'm sorry," he said. "I just—"

Laughter from behind them. Hearty laughter, as if at a joke well-told. Jennifer and Kincaid turned around, and she saw that Richard Blaine had managed to work the gag out of his mouth. He smiled at them. "Go on, Sean," he said with a chuckle. "Tell her."

Kincaid started walking back to Blaine. "Shut the hell up, you—"

"No."

Jennifer's voice made the two men stop and look at her. "No," she said again. "I want to talk to him."

"I don't think that's a good idea," said Kincaid.

"You did this for me, right?" she asked. "Right?"

Kincaid nodded.

"Well, I want to talk to him."

She walked over and stood in front of Blaine. The gun was on the table, within reach of her hand, but she didn't think of that. She wanted to know why. She wanted to ask him something.

"It's true, isn't it." Not a question. "You did it."

"Yes, I did. It's hard to explain, and I don't expect you to understand." Blaine's voice was low and rich. Even now, sitting here tied to a chair with certain death facing him, he sounded calm. Persuasive. A man who knows he is right, and is willing to die for what he believes in. "But it wasn't personal. I never meant anything against you, or any of your friends. The machine was what we were striking out against. You and the rest were just the cogs in that machine."

Jennifer stood there, feeling sick. Maybe he did have some sort of legitimate grievance. She wouldn't know. But what did she or any of the other people have to do with that? Mr. Danvers and Carrie and Carlos, the hundreds of others she had never known other than as faces in the crowd. But all lives, all special to someone in some way. All gone now. Because of this man.

"They weren't cogs," she said. "They were people. They had lives and families just like you."

"They were working for a government that betrays its own people."

"All they wanted was to work and raise their families! What sort of crime is that?"

"They should have found another way. I don't hold that against them, or you. It's too bad, but really you were just...what's the term you and your friends like to use, Sean? 'Acceptable losses'?"

Kincaid said nothing.

Jennifer stood, shaking. She swallowed hard and asked the one thing she wanted to know. "Are you sorry for what you did?"

Kincaid took a step closer, as if anxious to hear the answer himself.

Blaine looked directly at Jennifer. Looking into his eyes, she saw determination and pride. And something she had not expected. The look of a man who had sustained some blow, and was half-welcoming the ease that death would bring. But even without that, she was sure his answer would have been the same. "No. I'm not."

She had expected it, but was still surprised at the anger that blazed up in her. For months she had borne the weight of guilt for simply surviving. Would still carry that weight, in some way, for the rest of her days.

And this man, who had actually done the deed, could not even say he was sorry.

She slapped him as hard as she could. The impact stung her palm fiercely, made that anger blaze warm inside her. His head rocked back but he made no cry. She wanted to hear him make some noise, protest. Wanted to hear him ask for mercy. Say he was sorry. She hit him again, and again.

Jennifer stood there panting, her palm feeling as if it were burned. A gentle hand took hers, placed something heavy and cool in her hand. The coolness was soothing against her skin. She looked down. She held the gun.

She had never so much as touched a gun before, and was surprised by its weight. Heavy, for not a very large gun. The gun's metal slightly oily. She held it by the grip, which was rubber, and well-used. She could feel the grooves that a hand had worn into it. A man's hand, larger than hers. But the handle fitted snugly into her palm, almost as if it belonged there.

Jennifer stood, looking at the gun, at Blaine. Kincaid left her side, began to walk slowly around the two of them in a circle, round and round, and she thought of a snake going up a tree, winding its way up and up.

"That's a Ruger .38 you have there," Kincaid said. His voice was quiet, but it carried well. She heard him quite clearly. "You don't even have to pull the hammer back. Just pull the trigger and it's done. It's over."

Jennifer held the gun. Felt its weight, and the knowledge that this was serious business. Once the trigger was pulled, there would be no undoing it. And it was tempting, of course, but was it what she wanted? What she needed? What was right? "I don't want to go to jail," she said, trying to buy time and think.

"No one's going to jail. I told you, we're at a safe house. There's no one around for miles. I'll take care of everything for you. You can go home and sleep tight knowing that you rid the world of a murderer."

She stood, hesitant. He must have seen it, for his voice became softer, cajoling.

"We could send him to jail but the appeals will last for years. He'll get three hot meals a day courtesy of the taxes. The same government that inspired his crime will pay for the punishment. If you can call it that."

Jennifer said, "I don't know. I mean...I don't think I have the right to do this."

She meant that she had not lost enough in the bombing. *Give this chance to Carlos's widow, to Mr. Danvers' widow, to the mothers who had lost their babies in the day care center.*

"Why not, Jennifer?" asked Kincaid. "So much guilt you felt just for living that you had to leave the country? Why should you have been punished for something you didn't do? Look at this man. He ruined your life and he's not even sorry for it. And this isn't some sort of brave last stand. I've sat at his dinner table for a year now and if he'd said he was sorry just once I might have let it go. But he didn't. He was even planning to do it again."

Kincaid now stood next to her. "Let it end here."

She wanted to. Very much. She was angry, and grieving, and most of all she was tired. Let this be closure. Not the sort the psychologists talked about, but maybe the best she could find. Jennifer stood, looking at Blaine, not raising the gun, but not putting it aside either.

Blaine's nose was bleeding from the blows she had dealt him. He snuffled back blood and looked at her. One side of his face bright red, as if from sunburn. "It helps, doesn't it? Hurting the people who've hurt you." Blaine asked. "Believe me, I know." He glanced over at Kincaid, who had been observing, smiling.

Now Kincaid's smile vanished and he went pale. "Don't."

"Don't what?" asked Jennifer.

"Something you should know before you decide, Jennifer. You want to know what your friend Sean had to do to bring me to you? Want to know how he got those bruises on his neck?"

She didn't want to know, but found herself nodding anyway.

Blaine's eyes were cold, his voice colder. "I gave them to him. After he killed my wife."

Jennifer stared at Kincaid. He stood, looking back at her. His eyes blazing with that peculiar look again. "Is it true?"

But knew it was, for now she understood what lay behind his eyes. A damned soul looking out at her. "It was an accident," he said. "I didn't mean for it to happen."

"But it's true."

He closed his eyes, softly said, "Yes."

She turned away from the both of them. She was cold, wanted one of those wool blankets from Gene's boat to warm her. Even a chance for justice was bought with blood. When was it going to end?

"All I wanted was to live my life, same as any other person," she said. "To have a job and friends. That's not too much to ask for, is it?" Jennifer turned back to face them. "Why won't you let me do that? What is wrong with you that you have to kill people to get what you want?"

Silence for a few moments. Then Kincaid said, "I thought you would want this."

"No," she said. "*I* didn't want this." She didn't want it. But she had it. And what was she going to do with it? Jennifer put the gun down on the table. "I need to think about things. How much time do we have?"

"As much as you need," Kincaid said.

She sat in a chair by the window. Behind her silence as Kincaid sat and smoked one cigarette after another, and Blaine merely sat. She looked out the window at the coast. During the day it would have been a lovely view, but now she could see nothing but varying shades of darkness. If not for the steady sigh of the breakers, she might have been at world's end instead of just land's end.

A safe house, Kincaid called it, but she did not feel safe here. She wanted to go home, to her warm house and her friends and her cat. She wanted to feel Gene's strong arms around her, his steady presence.

But first a decision to be made.

He ruined your life, Kincaid said, and she supposed that was true. *But I have another life now, and it's a better one.* That was true also, and yet she could not forget those hours of terror and months of rebuilding her life. *What falls away is always. And is near.* Surely payback was owed for that.

And not just for herself. For all 361 of those lost lives, and the hundreds more those losses had touched in ways great and small. For Carlos and Nancy and their child who would never know his or her father. For Carrie and Mr. Danvers. For the others who were just nameless faces in the hall or whom she'd never laid eyes on.

What made it easy was that Blaine was not even sorry.

How could he not be? He knew about loss now, if he hadn't before. Surely he understood the pain; clearly he had sought to punish Kincaid for that crime. *How does it feel?* she wanted to ask him. *How does it feel?*

A simple decision to make. And yet. Did she have the right?

No long arm of the law throwing a switch, no grainy CNN footage of targeted air strikes. Just things at their most simple and elemental. Could she pick up the gun, place it against Blaine's head, and pull the trigger?

More importantly, could she live with it afterwards?

And what about the other way the coin could fall? If she let him go, could she live with that? Setting free a man who had brought so much hurt and was unrepentant?

Either way, she had blood on her hands. No escaping that. And could she live with that? No answer yet.

Jennifer's head ached with the weight of decision. She slammed her fist into the wall in frustration; behind her a startled breath from Kincaid but she paid it no mind. *I can't make this choice. I never asked for any of this. Why has this come to me?*

She had lost no one. She had not even been badly injured. She might even be a better person now than she had been. Yet she was haunted, would always be haunted, by the knowledge that chance had kept her alive. Providence and a broken photocopier. A random act of chance.

Jennifer's eyes widened. She put her hand against the window as if she could reach out to something, touch the night. Her hand flat against the glass, but in her mind she reached toward something, found it. Perhaps not the best choice, but one she had the right to make.

One she was strong enough to live with, no matter what the outcome might be.

She stood, turned toward the men. Wearily she wondered what time it was. They looked up at her; Kincaid stubbed out the cigarette he'd been smoking. She walked over, picked up the gun from the table, and stood in front of Kincaid, who looked up at her expectantly.

"I need your help." She pointed at the cylinder.

"It's fully loaded," he said.

"I know. I need this part to come out. You have to show me, I've never used a gun before."

She expected him to refuse, but he took the gun from her. Did not even ask why she wanted him to do this. He pushed a small button on the side of the gun and the cylinder popped out. Kincaid handed the gun back to her and she looked at it. Six bullets. Six holes. No, not holes, chambers. It was what they said on TV.

Jennifer stepped in front of Blaine, to where both of them could see her. Looked Blaine in the eyes. "I'm going to give you something," she said. "What you didn't give the people in that building. What he didn't give your wife."

"And what is that?" asked Blaine.

"A chance." Jennifer took three bullets out of the cylinder. The chambers were alternated. Empty, full, empty, full, empty, full.

Carefully, holding the gun so neither she nor they could see the final outcome, she spun the cylinder. Once, twice. A third time, to break the tie if there was one. Then she snapped the cylinder back into place.

She stood looking at the two men. Calm resignation in Blaine's eyes, and something that looked like respect. In Kincaid's eyes, more than respect. Admiration.

Jennifer walked over to Kincaid. She wanted to say something but couldn't think of what it might be. What he had given her was not something she wanted or needed. Yet she looked into his eyes and saw that no matter what else had happened, no matter what he had done, he had truly wanted to help her. And this was the only way he knew.

"Thank you for wanting to help me," she said.

He looked back at her with all defenses and disguises put aside. She felt a wave of pity wash over her, for the fire in his eyes had nearly gone out, leaving only ashes, and emptiness, the prospect of a long road leading into darkness. What was going to sustain him on that road?

Jennifer knew that whatever happened, empty chamber or full, she could live with it. Bear it as she had borne many things. She wondered if Kincaid could bear it, anymore.

"So strong and brave," he said softly. "I never expected to find that." He raised a hand, touched her hair for just a second, as if reassuring himself that she was real. Or that he was. For a moment his eyes shone with tears, and she could see the man he might once have been looking out at her. A blink and the tears were gone. "I'm sorry I scared you," he said.

Jennifer nodded. She walked over to Blaine. He sat with his head bowed, his lips moving silently. She wondered if he was praying. Perhaps he would find some mercy, somewhere, no matter how things ended. But mercy was not hers to give. Only the chance of it.

She placed the gun against the back of his head. She pulled the trigger.

And let God sort it out.

The story continues in *Reckoning (Ashes #2)*

The story continues in *Reckoning*

Read a chapter from *Reckoning* now!

Deirdre Monahan tossed her purse and a bag full of dirty laundry onto the passenger seat of her truck, then sat down in the driver's seat. She'd had the truck since high school and it still ran well. The trick was getting it to run. You had to push the clutch in *just so*, give it precisely *this much* gas, and then — success.

"Good girl." Deirdre patted the dashboard. She was fond of the truck, faulty starter and all, and even more fond of it since the divorce had gone through. Her mother couldn't understand why she had let Randy have the Mustang; couldn't understand why Deirdre took as little of the things she and Randy had bought together as she could live without.

It was simple, really. She wanted to start over, on her own. Once her anger at Randy for putting them into a debt sinkhole and losing his job and cheating on her with that all-tits-and-no-brains floozy had subsided to a dull roar, once she was faced with legal papers and signatures to end the marriage, she'd found herself wondering what to do with her life. She'd said as much to her cousin Anna, who put things in perspective.

"You know what they say, Dee," Anna had said. "But everything happens for a reason. And when life closes a door, it opens a window as well. Did I miss any of the other clichés?"

"Every cloud has a silver lining."

"That too. Take your pick."

Deirdre liked the one about the door and the window best. So she had slammed the door (hoping to catch Randy's fingers in the jamb), and jumped out the window. She jumped out by herself, and that was why she'd kept the truck — she wanted to do this on her own, and she'd never been on her own before. After high school she'd lived with her folks, then with

Randy, and now she was twenty-eight and had never had a life she could call hers alone.

So far it was working out all right. The job wasn't the best — she was a clerk at the new Wal-Mart over in Lakeside, but it paid the bills until she could find something she liked better. Likewise the apartment. It was threadbare and she was still living out of boxes, but she liked the freedom of eating whatever she wanted, cleaning up the house when or if she felt like it, and not having to share the TV remote with anyone.

Anna had offered her a room at their house. Deirdre hadn't known how to refuse without hurting Anna's feelings; Richard had come to her rescue. He'd seen her distress and said, "You need to sort things out and stand on your own feet for a while, don't you?"

Relieved, she'd replied that was true. They understood, but told her she was welcome at any time to stop by for a hot dinner, or use their washer and dryer, or go for a ride on one of the horses. It all sounded wonderful to Deirdre.

Deirdre had last talked to Anna on Sunday, nearly a week ago. Anna was glad to hear she was settling in. "Now that life's not too crazy you'll need to come by for dinner more often. Should we make it a standing date for Sunday?" Anna asked.

"That's not too much trouble, is it?"

"Of course not. Richard's always bringing his friends over, but they're all men. It'll be nice to have some female company for a change. Which reminds me, Dee. There's one of Richard's friends I think you should meet."

"I don't know if I'm up for meeting anyone new just yet."

"Just see if there's any sparks."

In spite of herself she was intrigued. Deirdre always felt weird going to restaurants or the movies by herself, and a date would be welcome. "Wait, it's not that Steve guy you told me about? He sounded like kind of a yo-yo."

"Have a little faith in me? His name's Sam, he's a very nice guy. A real gentleman."

"What's he look like?"

"Well, he's older than you, I'm not sure how much. Not too tall, not too short. Losing his hair."

"Sounds dreamy."

Anna never talked trash about people, and she didn't now, but she did say, "Handsome is as handsome does, Dee." Meaning that good-looking as Randy had been, as a husband he hadn't amounted to much.

"Touché."

"Not that I'm matchmaking or anything, but you need a steady guy. And he needs a nice girlfriend, not some slutbunny."

Deirdre laughed. "Nan! Do you kiss your mother with that mouth?"

Richard's voice boomed in the background. "Who's a slutbunny? Where can I meet her?"

"Oh stop!" giggled Anna. "Just think about it, that's all I'm asking. You'll see him at Thanksgiving, I'm sure, if not sooner. See how you feel about it then. You *will* be here for Thanksgiving?"

"Wouldn't miss it for anything."

"Good." Anna's voice dropped a bit. She sounded both shy and happy. "I may have some good news for you then."

Deirdre's heart had done a flip at these words. Anna wouldn't say what the news was, but Deirdre could make a good guess. Anna was expecting. Deirdre knew that Anna had wanted a child badly ever since she'd married Richard, but they'd had no luck yet. There had been two miscarriages that

Deirdre knew of — she suspected there had been at least one more, judging by how unusually moody and silent Anna had been two Christmases ago. Deirdre was happier than ever that she'd moved close to Anna and Richard. If Anna was indeed pregnant, she'd need to get her rest, and what better way than for Deirdre to come by every Sunday to help with the housecleaning and errands, and whip up a batch of her famous Eggs McMonahan.

Now, thinking about all this, Deirdre put her truck into gear and began driving to Anna's house. It was a gloomy day, threatening to rain, but she didn't mind. It would be warm and cozy at Anna's house. It always was.

She opened the gate that led to Richard and Anna's Christmas tree farm, pausing to take a deep breath of the pine-scented air. Christmas was only a few months away; Deirdre had never been to the farm at the holidays. Anna said it was chaotic but fun, and another set of hands were always welcome. If cutting trees and tying them onto car roofs didn't suit her, there was always ringing up orders or running the snack stand.

After closing the gate behind her, she drove down the smooth dirt road to the house. Not for the first time, she felt an unwelcome twinge of envy. There was no resentment in it, no ill will. She just wondered why she couldn't have a life like Anna's — the farm, the pretty house. The husband who was not just handsome and charming but who clearly loved Anna more than anything else.

She was in luck. Richard's truck and Anna's station wagon were both in the driveway. She hated surprising them like this, but every time she'd called this week she'd gotten the answering machine. They hadn't called her cell; they must have been busy. She grabbed her purse and walked up to the front door.

The door had an intercom; a good safety precaution, Richard had told her, considering how many visitors they got with the tree farm. She pressed the intercom button. No answer. She pressed again; although she knew her voice wouldn't carry, she called out anyway. "Anna? Richard? It's Deirdre."

No answer.

Deirdre was positive Anna had said they'd be home Sunday. Anna had even told her Richard might be able to look at the truck and see if he could fix the starter. Deirdre stepped off the porch and began to walk down the driveway, toward the back of the house. As she passed the stables a shrill whinny made her jump. Both horses were looking out of the stable windows at her. The palomino looked tired, almost ill, and the bay was tossing his head in agitation. Deirdre walked over to the stables, murmuring soothing noises to the horses. "Hey boys, hey pretty ponies," she sang as she got close to the horses. The bay whinnied again, and Deirdre looked inside the stables. She was shocked to see the feed bins empty, and the stable floor in need of a good cleaning. Still crooning to the horses, she found a basket of carrots outside the stables and put a half dozen in the feed bins; they were devoured in no time, and the horses looked at her expectantly. "Wait, guys, let me find Anna."

She headed back to the driveway, not quite running. Her spine felt crawly and she wiped her sweaty palms on her jeans. She stood indecisive in the driveway for a moment, then went to the back of the house, to the kitchen door. She banged on the door, called out Anna's name, and when there was no answer, tried the door. It was unlocked. Deirdre opened the door and stepped inside.

The smell hit her with the force of a slap. She stepped back, bumped into the door, and caught hold of the doorknob to steady herself. Deirdre pinched her nostrils shut and breathed through her mouth, but that didn't banish the smell — it was just lying in wait, pressing against her skin, waiting for her to relax her vigilance and breathe through her nose again. "Anna?" she called. Her voice seemed unnaturally loud. For the house was not just quiet. It was silent.

She blinked, her eyes adjusting to the dim light of the kitchen. After a moment she found the source of the smell: a whole chicken, taken out to thaw and left forgotten on the counter.

Her relief was short-lived. What was a rotten chicken doing left out in Anna's immaculate kitchen? Why were the horses unfed and their stables dirty? Where the hell were Anna and Richard?

Deirdre walked quickly out of the kitchen, into the hallway. The silence had a sound now, ringing in her ears. "Anna? Richard? Are you here? Please say something."

She went into the living room and stopped, staring. As she tried to make sense of what she was seeing, she forgot to plug her nose and the smell hit her harder than ever. She gagged and bit down on her arm to kill a scream. Plugging her nostrils, she looked around the room.

There wasn't much wrong with it at first glance. It was only if you knew Anna and what a good housekeeper she was that you'd know something had happened. Anna wouldn't leave dirty scuff marks on the floor, wouldn't leave the hearth rug bunched up and the fireplace pokers in a heap.

Then there was the afghan on the sofa, covering something. Covering someone.

Yes, someone, because there was a person-size shape under it. The afghan mercifully hid whatever lay under it, save for a pair of pink sneakers protruding from one end.

Deirdre swallowed hard, trying not to recall that she'd seen those sneakers on Anna's feet two weeks ago. She felt herself walking over to the sofa, saw her hand reaching out to that afghan. She didn't know why at first, and then understood. Because once she pulled it back and saw that it wasn't Anna after all, then the world would be OK again. There'd be an explanation somehow. Because it wasn't Anna here, it couldn't be. She just had to see for herself.

"Please," whispered Deirdre, and pulled back the afghan.

PRAISE FOR KELLY COZY'S DEBUT NOVEL
THE DAY AFTER YESTERDAY

The events of a single night can change a life forever, as musician Daniel Whitman discovers when he loses his family and home. Overwhelmed by grief, unable to find solace in his music or accept comfort from his friends, he flees up the California coast. Daniel thinks he's leaving everything behind, but his journey will take him to the places and people that will help him find his way back. *The Day After Yesterday* is a story of hope, friendship, and the redemptive power of music.

"Ms. Cozy has a definite gift for writing that allows the reader to intimately know her characters...There is so much going on, throughout, that it could have been a bit overwhelming, but instead, it drew you even more into the lives of the characters. I fell in love with them. A beautiful story by a talented writer." - *Literary R&R*

"This novel captured both my attention and my heart. The characters are realistic, multi-faceted, and endearing. I shared in both their laughter and their tears, and was saddened to reach the end of their tale. Ms. Cozy's masterful look into the human condition provides a message of hope and understanding for anyone that has experienced a loss, or knows someone who has. I highly recommend this book and look forward to reading any future ones." -Mary Smith-Fuller, *Flurries of Words*

Available in print and ebook

For more information, contact smitepublications@gmail.com

ABOUT THE AUTHOR

Photo © Loa Allebach

Kelly Cozy is the author of *The Day After Yesterday* and the *Ashes* suspense series, available in print and ebook. She is currently at work on her next novel.

Her first nonfiction work, *A Nerd Girl's Guide to Cinema*, will be available in 2014 from Smite Publications.

She lives in California with her husband, son, and cats. Visit her online at:
Blog: kellycozy.blogspot.com
Twitter: @Kelly_Cozy
Facebook: Kelly Cozy, Author

www.ingramcontent.com/pod-product-compliance
Lightning Source LLC
Chambersburg PA
CBHW070637180626
46817CB00006B/2156